Run to You

Georgia Beers

Run to You

© 2016 BY GEORGIA BEERS

THIS TRADE PAPERBACK ORIGINAL IS PUBLISHED BY BRISK PRESS, BRIELLE NEW JERSEY, 08730

EDITED BY LYNDA SANDOVAL
COPY EDITED BY HEATHER FLOURNOY
COVER DESIGN BY STEFF OBKIRCHNER
FIRST PRINTING: JULY 2016

ISBN-13: 978-099667745-5

By Georgia Beers

Novels

Finding Home

Mine

Fresh Tracks

Too Close to Touch

Thy Neighbor's Wife

Turning the Page

Starting From Scratch

96 Hours

Slices of Life

Snow Globe

Olive Oil and White Bread

Zero Visibility

A Little Bit of Spice

Rescued Heart

Run to You

Anthologies

Outsiders

www.georgiabeers.com

ACKNOWLEDGEMENTS

When you've been doing this for as long as I have, writing acknowledgments feels kind of like I'm saying the same thing over and over again. And I suppose that's at least a little bit true, but the people I thank each and every time deserve my thanks each and every time, and so much more. So let's do this.

Thank you to Carrie and Susan at Brisk Press. They make a process that could (and often does) become difficult and tedious easy and painless instead. I realize what a lucky author that makes me, and I couldn't be happier to work with them.

Thank you to my editing staff, Lynda Sandoval and Heather Flournoy. They make me look good. And when I don't look good, not only do they correct me (gently) (most of the time), but they explain to me *why* so that I learn and maybe get it right next time (or not). Their expertise is an invaluable tool for my career.

Thank you to my friends, Nikki, Melissa, and Rachel, for their love and support. They are with me in some form every single day and a day when one of them is missing seems weirdly unbalanced to me. They encourage me, keep me sane, help me stay positive, and make me laugh when I need it. And sometimes when I don't..

Thank you to Steff Obkirchner, not only for the strength of her friendship, but for her amazing cover-creating talent. Nobody has the eye she does and I am never disappointed with a cover. Ever. She blows me away every time.

Thank you to all the pets who've come in and out of my life, mine or those belonging to my loved ones. Each of them has touched me with their unconditional love in some way, shape or form, and I am eternally grateful for that, especially my Finley. I know he won't be with me forever physically, but he will be in my heart always, and that's a pretty amazing gift.

Thank you to my wife Bonnie for getting me like no other person, for putting up with my crazy mood swings and weird obsessions, for throwing countless ideas and suggestions at me, even when I'm wearing my No Girl hat, and for supporting me, always, no matter what. I'm so lucky to have her in my corner..

Last but never least, thank you to you, my readers. It is because of you—your support, your messages, your emails—that I can keep doing this weird, wonderful, crazy, awesome job of mine. You keep reading, I'll keep writing, deal?

CHAPTER ONE

SATURDAY NIGHTS AT JOPLIN'S almost always boasted a full house. That's the way Catherine Gardner liked it. A full house meant more tables to wait on. More tables meant more tips, and more tips were the point of working a second job in the first place, weren't they? Instead of getting irritated at the gentleman at table sixteen (who had ordered his Porterhouse well-done—a tragedy in and of itself as far as Catherine was concerned—then turned around and sent it back because it was dry), she simply conjured up an image of the Michael Kors Sedgwick Embossed-Heel Black Leather boots she'd seen online that morning. They'd been marked down from $275 to $206 and Catherine was sure there was a pair in her size just waiting for her to rescue them from the lonely shelf in the big, scary boot warehouse.

Tips, tips, tips. Tips will get me boots. She hummed a little tune, but kept the words in her head.

As she pushed her way into the kitchen, Bobby King, resident chef, saw the plate in her hand and rolled his brown eyes.

"Let me guess. Too dry?" he asked, heavy on the sarcasm.

"Ding, ding, ding!" Catherine said with a half-grin.

With a loud sigh, he pulled out another steak and tossed it on the grill where three others sizzled away. "I'll never understand why well-done is even a thing," he said, shaking his head. "Don't they know it ruins everything good about beef?"

"And don't *you* know the customer is always right?" Catherine teased him.

"Yeah, that's crap and we both know it."

While Bobby prepared a new steak for Mr. Doesn't Understand Beef, Catherine headed back out to the dining room to wait on the new couple at table thirteen. She took them in quickly as she approached. Two women, one somewhere around thirty, one a bit older. Nicely dressed, both of them. The older one had blonde hair, cut in one of those expensive angular styles only certain people can pull off (she could). The younger one had dark hair that hung loose around her shoulders, and when she turned toward Catherine, her soft brown eyes were smiling and a dimple appeared on her left cheek. Catherine's stomach did a tiny little flip at the sight.

She smiled as she clasped her hands behind her back and greeted them. "Good evening, ladies. Welcome to Joplin's." She went through the specials for the night, flawlessly rattling off every detail of each dish. That had been the hardest part when she'd started working there…the memorization. None of the servers had pads or paper of any kind. Each day, they were given a description of the specials and they committed them to memory, the restaurant before opening looking a lot like the wings of a theatre, actors mumbling the lines they're trying to remember. Each order placed was memorized and punched into the touchscreen on a nearby computer. Luckily, Catherine's head for numbers somehow seemed to make it easier for her to remember each thing. "Can I start you two off with a cocktail?"

The blonde rattled off a year and vintage of wine that was obviously meant to impress the woman across the table, and Catherine immediately concluded the two were on a date, which was kind of cute. However, the blonde never looked at Catherine once, so points were immediately deducted from the cuteness department. The brunette, on the other hand, seemed to be trying to make up for the rudeness of her date by looking directly at Catherine with an intensity that bordered on sensual. Catherine cleared her throat and headed off to retrieve the wine.

"They on a date, you think?" Bradley Snyder whispered to Catherine as she emerged from the wine room. He was her fellow server, had shown her the ropes when she'd been hired, and was as gay as an interior designer. At a Broadway musical. Drinking a Cosmo.

"I think so. The blonde is working hard to be impressive," Catherine said. "But I'm not sure if they've been together for a while or not."

"Nope. Blind."

"You think so?"

"They arrived in separate cars and shook hands in the parking lot." At Catherine's raised eyebrow, he went on with a shrug. "I was out back having a smoke. Wasn't sure if it was a business meeting or not."

Filing away that information, Catherine approached their table, set down two wine glasses, and showed the label of the bottle to the blonde. At her nod, Catherine set about opening it, noticing how any conversation between the two women (had there been any?) ceased as she used the manual corkscrew.

"Is that a pain for you?" the brunette asked, her brown eyes fixed on Catherine. "I mean, there are so many newfangled, automatic openers. I wondered if using the manual kind is a pain for you."

Catherine smiled, noting the blonde still not looking at her. *Rude.* "Actually, I'm partial to the old-fashioned wine key. I like the feel of opening the bottle myself. Makes me think I've accomplished something." As if on cue, the cork popped out and Catherine poured a small amount of wine into one glass. The blonde made a show of swirling the Pinot Noir, sipping it, rolling the wine around in her mouth. Catherine already leaned toward not liking her, but this display sealed the deal.

"Oh, that's good. That's very good." The blonde nodded at the brunette. "We'll take that."

Catherine almost said, "Are you talking to me?" but managed to hold her tongue. It amused her that the blonde went through the whole tasting routine as if that's why restaurants gave that first sip. In actuality, it wasn't for the customer to decide if the wine *tasted good*. Taste didn't matter, as once the cork popped, you'd bought the wine. It was to make sure the wine hadn't *gone bad* due to a faulty cork or exposure to light or whatever. *That* was the purpose of the initial taste. For all her obvious refinement, the blonde apparently didn't know this tidbit of information. And while it was true that, in fact, most people didn't know it, Catherine still took delight in the blonde showing off knowledge she didn't really have.

The wine was very beautiful. Catherine loved that. As with footwear, she had a fondness for good wine and she actually really enjoyed pouring a nice red. You could almost anticipate the taste just by looking at it in a nice crystal glass. She used a white cloth to wipe the drip from the edge of the bottle, then set it down on the table. "Enjoy."

She took care of a couple other tables before heading for the kitchen. A glance back at the two women saw the brunette looking Catherine's way, one corner of her mouth quirked up in a half-grin.

Bradley was making two salads at the salad counter and looked up as she entered. "How goes the blind date?"

"Not sure," Catherine replied, waiting on two entrees for table twelve. "The blonde is still trying to show off, and she hasn't looked at me once."

"Ugh. I hate that. So freaking rude."

"The brunette has, however."

Her tone made Bradley look back up at her and laugh with delight. "Go, you."

"You don't think *that's* rude?"

"What? Her looking at you?"

"Her looking at me when she's on a date."

"A blind date," Bradley corrected her. "One she is obviously not enjoying." He swooped up his salads and opened the double doors with his backside as he winked at her.

"Well, *I* think it's rude," Catherine muttered, grabbing the two plates that Bobby's sous chef slid her way.

After delivering the entrees, she stopped by the women's table to take their orders.

"I'll have the filet," the blonde said. "Well, please. And I'd like steamed rice instead of potatoes. What's the vegetable?" Unsurprisingly, she said every word to the woman across the table rather than to her waitress.

"It's a mixed vegetable medley tonight consisting of peas, carrots, and green beans sautéed in a lemon butter sauce."

"Well, I suppose that'll have to do."

Catherine gave a nod, working hard not to roll her eyes at the blonde's tone. When she turned to the brunette, she caught a split second of her finishing up a quick eye roll and Catherine had to smother a grin.

"Why even order the filet?" the brunette asked, and it took Catherine a minute to realize she was speaking to her date.

The blonde looked confused.

"If you're going to cook all the flavor out of it, why bother?" At the blonde's sheepish shrug, the brunette turned to Catherine and the spark of her brown eyes made Catherine's stomach squinch a little. In a good way. "I am also going to have the filet, but I'd like it still mooing, please." At Catherine's polite chuckle, she amended, "Well, almost. I'd like a baked potato and those veggies that sound awesome." Much as Catherine wanted to glance at the blonde to see what expression she was making now, she couldn't. Something about the brunette's eyes…

Mentally shaking herself, Catherine took their menus, asked for their salad dressing preferences, and hurried back to the kitchen, feeling strangely out of sorts.

As was typical for a Saturday night in an upscale restaurant with a good reputation, things had picked up steadily for the past half hour and the kitchen had gone from busy to super-bustling. Kitchen staff scurried around like worker ants, grabbing pots, pans, food, ran in and out of the walk-in freezer, listened to orders barked from the other end of the room. Pans bubbled on the enormous industrial stove and meat sizzled on the grill adjacent to the burners. Bobby called out for his Hollandaise sauce like he would die without it. The whole place was loud and chaotic, but Catherine's full-time job was in an animal shelter, so she was actually used to such cacophony. She heard Bradley's voice in her ear and jumped, not having heard his approach in all the noise.

"You were totally right about that couple. I just watched that entire exchange. The blonde didn't look at you once, and the brunette barely looked at anything *but* you."

Catherine grinned, shrugged, and shook her head. People were so weird.

Once she'd delivered their entrees and refilled their wine glasses, Catherine was able to focus on other customers beside the couple. Even so, she'd glance occasionally at them and, more than once, she found the brunette looking her way. She even threw Catherine a flirty little wink, which Catherine was ashamed to admit made her blush like a schoolgirl, and she literally shook her head at her own reaction.

When they were finished, Catherine took their plates and asked about dessert.

The brunette looked to the blonde, then Catherine, then the blonde again. "I could do dessert. I mean, if you want to."

"Oh, no," the blonde said. "I never eat dessert. I'm not a sweet person."

Obviously, Catherine thought.

The brunette was clearly disappointed, but said, "All right. I don't want to eat it alone. I guess we're done then."

"I'll be right back with your check."

At the computer, she finalized the bill. She smiled at other members of the wait staff as they hurried by, few of whose names she knew. It may have seemed cold, but this wasn't her main job. She only worked one or two nights a week and she was here to make money, not friends. Bradley was an exception, only because he was relentless in his attempts at conversation. In the end, it was easier to talk to him than try to remain aloof. Plus, he was kind of hilarious.

Tucking the bill into a black leatherette folder, Catherine returned to table thirteen. She didn't know what came over her at that moment, but she suddenly felt a little streak of rebellion. *I'm channeling Bradley here.* The thought flashed through her mind as she recalled the superhero Bradley had invented. Snarky Gay Man (*righting fashion wrongs with the wave of a judgmental finger and criticizing homophobic straights with a single sarcastic word...).* Knowing full well that the blonde was running the show and most likely paying the bill, Catherine slid the black folder down in front of the brunette instead. "I can take that up whenever you're ready," she said, then turned on a heel and walked away, feeling smugly satisfied.

A few moments later, she returned to the table to pick up the credit card. The blonde, not surprisingly, didn't look at her, but radiated irritation. The brunette, however, openly grinned at her. Catherine rang up the sale, also unsurprised by the 12% tip, and for that slight, again left the folder in front of the brunette. "Thank you so much. Enjoy your night."

And in a move utterly and completely out of the scope of what would be considered Typical Catherine Behavior, she winked at the brunette before again turning on a heel and walking away.

What did it matter? She'd never seen these two women before and she would most likely never see them again. Plus, it felt good. She felt like she was walking on air, which was not at all a feeling she was used to. Snarky Gay Man was going to be so proud of her...

CHAPTER TWO

"HEY, HOW DID IT GO Saturday?" Clark Breckenridge hit the gas as the light changed to green.

Emily Breckenridge snorted loudly from the passenger seat. "You, Big Brother, are never ever allowed to set me up again. Ever. Did I say never, ever? Because I meant never, ever. Ever."

"What?" Clark glanced at her in shock before putting his eyes back on the road. "Tiffany is a catch. She's sexy. She's rich. She runs a business."

"She's conceited. She's self-absorbed. She's rude."

"You are impossible." Clark turned the wheel and slid the black Mercedes coupe smoothly into a parking space in front of the main building of Junebug Farms Animal Shelter.

"Dude, this is a handicap spot." Emily blinked at him as he shrugged. "Seriously, Clark, just move over two spots, for Christ's sake." She motioned at the empty space literally twenty yards to their left. "What is the matter with you?"

With a great, put-upon sigh, Clark shifted the car into reverse and did as his sister asked. "God, you're a pain in the ass."

"Yes, I'm a horrible sister for not wanting you to take a parking space away from somebody *in a wheelchair*. I'll probably go to hell for that." Emily rolled her eyes.

"Oh, you'll go for other reasons first, my little lesbian sibling."

Emily swatted at him. "Shut up. This is business."

He snickered. "Know what's kind of bizarre about this place?"

"I mean it, Clark. This is professional. Act like it. Don't talk to me like I'm twelve in front of these people."

He feigned hurt, widening his eyes and pressing a hand to his broad chest. Then, like he waved a wand, the expression slipped away and it was as if none of the conversation had happened. "You didn't answer my question."

Emily looked at her big brother. People said he was ridiculously handsome, it was true, but she couldn't see it. Maybe she was too close to him. Women everywhere swooned when he walked into a room. Six feet, three inches tall with a lean, muscular build, thick, dark hair, and startlingly blue eyes, they said he was a gorgeous specimen of man. Problem was, he knew it. And he used it. She muffled her sigh. "What question?"

"I asked you if you knew what's kind of bizarre about this place."

"Tell me."

"There are some hot women here. I mean *hot*." He licked his thumb, then shifted so he could press it to his own ass and make a sizzling sound. Like a fourteen-year-old.

"Do you even get why we're here?" Emily asked, exasperated. "We're here because of your sexual harassment habits. Complaints have been lodged. Mom was involved. You're turning the reins over to me so the women here don't have to worry about you coming on to them again. They don't know that, but I do. And you do. Or you should. Has any of that sunk in?"

"*Hot* women," he corrected her. "So the *hot* women here don't have to worry."

Emily stared at him in disbelief for a full five seconds before muttering, "Oh, my God." She yanked the door handle and threw herself out of the car, overtaken with the need to get the hell out of such a small space where she was trapped with a man she alternately loved and wanted to punch in the scrotum.

Taking in a deep lungful of fresh autumn air, Emily looked around at the grounds. She'd spent all day yesterday, a Sunday, doing research and learning all she could about Junebug Farms. It was the largest no-kill animal shelter in upstate New York, run by owner and CEO Jessica Barstow. Ms. Barstow had inherited the facility from her grandmother several years ago and had used her business savvy to grow the place into one of the most well-known nonprofits in the state. Emily and Clark's mother was a huge animal lover—as was Emily—and Junebug was always first on her list to receive donations. Anytime Junebug ran a fundraiser or drive of any kind—and there were several a year—Cheryl Breckenridge was right there with her checkbook. Emily loved her for that.

The place was expansive, that was for sure. The main building was one story and sprawling. Emily suspected there was much of it she couldn't see from the parking lot. The muffled sound of barking reached her ears and mixed with the bleats coming from her right. A glance in the direction revealed a large structure with ramps and barrels all fenced in to make what looked almost like a playground of sorts. Several goats leaped and climbed and Emily couldn't help but grin at their antics. Off to the left, about two or three hundred yards away from the main building, stood a large red barn. Four horses shuffled around in the corral. She suspected there were more inside.

"You ready?" Clark was at her side.

"This place is impressive."

"It is." With a nod, he held out his arm toward the door and followed his sister up the walk.

Inside, the noise grew exponentially. Barking, howling, and whining combined with ringing phones and the hum of several conversations going at once, and Emily had to take a moment to acclimate herself. "Wow," she breathed.

"I know, right? It's crazy loud in here. All the time." Clark led the way across the faux-marble floor to the front desk. Leaning against the horseshoe-shaped counter, he turned up the wattage on his smile and gave all his attention to the woman sitting near the phone. Her nametag said she was "Regina – Volunteer." Emily watched her brother work. "Well, hello there, Regina. How are you doing on this fine Monday?"

If Regina could have swooned from her seat, she probably would have. Emily suppressed the urge to roll her eyes.

"I'm just fine, Mr. Breckenridge," Regina said with an enormous smile. She wasn't unattractive. Her light hair was caught in a clip at the nape of her neck. She wore jeans and a green V-neck sweater. She was slightly chunky, but it looked good on her. The rounds of her cheeks tinted pink as Clark focused all his considerable charm on her. "You have a meeting this morning, right?" She glanced down at her computer screen.

"I do. With Ms. Barstow," Clark said.

"And Ms. Gardner."

Clark gave a nod. "Hey, did you get your hair cut?"

Regina's blush deepened and she ran her fingers self-consciously through her bangs. "I did."

"Well, it looks great. Really brings out your eyes." Clark winked at her then, and Emily fully expected Regina – Volunteer to melt into a puddle on the floor.

"Thank you. Why don't you two head right into the conference room and I'll let Ms. Barstow know you're here?" She waved in the direction of the far wall where Emily saw an open door with a small window in it.

"We'll do that," Clark said with a rakish grin.

"Can I get either of you coffee or something?" Regina asked, her expression telling Emily she wanted to hold onto this moment with Clark for as long as she could.

Clark looked at Emily, then back at Regina. "You know what? Coffee would be great."

Emily gave a nod and smile, then held out her hand to Regina. "Hi. I'm Emily Breckenridge. My brother has obviously forgotten his manners."

Regina shook her hand, and the wet fish method immediately dropped her a few more pegs in Emily's eyes. "It's very nice to meet you," Regina said, but her gaze barely left Clark.

Story of my life, Emily thought.

She followed Clark across the lobby to the open door. He hit the lights and a surprisingly large conference room was illuminated. Nothing inside was new or even very modern, except for the massive cherry table, but it was neat and clean. Significant in size, the table gleamed, surrounded by twelve unremarkable but functional chairs. The walls held several pictures of animals —everything from cats and dogs to horses and llamas—and Emily assumed they were success stories from Junebug over the years.

Clark took a seat and Emily followed suit just as Regina came in carrying two mugs of coffee. She set them down, then reached into her pocket for packets of sugar and a handful of little creamers. "I wasn't sure how you took your coffee," she said to Clark, never once glancing at Emily.

"Oh, this is perfect. Thank you so much, Regina." Clark smiled at her and Emily half-expected her to cover her mouth with her fingers and titter like a schoolgirl from the 1800s.

"Ms. Barstow and Ms. Gardner will be right with you."

The second Regina closed the conference room door on her way out, Emily turned to Clark and said, "You are ridiculous."

Clark laughed, a big booming sound he'd had since he was about twelve. "Hey, I can't help it if I have that effect on women."

"Unbelievable," Emily muttered, half-annoyed and half-amused. She stirred two packets of sugar into her coffee and asked, "Who's Ms. Gardner? I thought we were just meeting with the CEO."

"She's the numbers chick," Clark said, pouring a creamer into his mug.

"Woman, Clark. Don't say chick. Say woman."

"Whatever."

The door opened before Emily could say more and a gorgeously tall auburn-haired woman dressed in black slacks and a fitted sweater with funky black and white stripes entered the room. Her hair was pulled back in a simple ponytail and she managed to look casual and elegant at the same time.

"Hi there," she said, holding out her hand to Clark. "Good to see you." They shook and then she shifted her blue eyes to Emily. "And you must be Ms. Breckenridge. I'm Jessica Barstow. It's so nice to meet you."

"Emily. Please." Emily stood and shook Jessica's hand, the handshake far surpassing that of Regina – Volunteer. "It's nice to meet you as well. I've heard a lot about Junebug Farms, but this is my first visit in a very long time, I'm ashamed to say."

"Well, the Breckenridge Foundation takes really good care of the animals here. We can't thank you enough." She gave a soft smile and it was suddenly clear to Emily, even though she'd never met Jessica Barstow before, that she was worried. Had Clark told her nothing about this meeting? She probably thought they were going to pull funding or something horrendous like that.

Emily opened her mouth to set the woman at ease when a second woman walked in. "Sorry I'm late," she said quietly as she closed the door behind her, sealing out the noise of the animals…or at least muffling it some. When she looked up, she locked eyes with Emily and stopped dead in her tracks.

The hair was down this time, its unique shade of light brown glimmering with gentle, almost red highlights. The beautiful blue eyes were now veiled behind a pair of black-rimmed glasses that sat a bit too low on her nose. And the clothes had changed from black pants, white shirt, and black waist apron to a slick navy blue pantsuit, a white blouse with silver stripes underneath the jacket. Emily couldn't see the shoes, but it didn't matter. She knew this woman. They'd met on Saturday. Ms. Gardner had waited on Emily's table during her disastrous blind date. The weirdest part was that Emily was stupidly happy to see her.

"Catherine? You okay?" Jessica's voice seemed to jumpstart activity in the room again. Catherine Gardner literally shook herself, then pasted on a smile.

"Yes. Yes. Fine. Sorry. Zoned out for a moment there." She held out a hand to Clark. "Good to see you, Clark."

"Likewise," he replied.

"And this is Clark's sister, Emily Breckenridge," Jessica said, by way of invitation. "Emily, this is Catherine Gardner, our accountant and resident queen of all things number related."

Catherine reached across the table as Emily stood from her chair and leaned forward to grasp her hand. Soft, warm, strong. Her grip was everything Emily hoped and they shook firmly.

Emily had to force herself to let go. Once they were all seated, Clark surprised Emily by taking the reins and actually acting almost professional.

"So, I'm sure you're wondering why we called this meeting. Rest assured, everything is just fine between the Breckenridge Foundation and Junebug Farms. No worries there."

The relief on Jessica's face was so apparent, Emily almost laughed out loud.

"That being said, we are making some changes, doing a little…restructuring, if you will. We're shifting people around a bit, trying a few new things." With a small flourish, he gestured to Emily. "That's where my baby sister comes in. She's taking over the management of the Breckenridge Foundation and therefore, she will be your liaison from here on out."

Catherine's eyebrows rose up toward her hairline, her surprise clear. Then it seemed to sink in and she gave an almost imperceptible nod. Emily wondered if she understood exactly why this change was being made.

"Well," Jessica said, her face hard to read. "We'll miss having you around, Clark."

"Oh, I'm not disappearing," Clark said with a grin. "I'm sure I'll pop in every now and then. Make sure my little sister's doing a good job." It sounded almost threat-like and Emily arched an eyebrow at him. He caught the look and winked at her, which irritated her even more.

Emily turned her gaze to the other two women in the room, gave them a reassuring smile, and used her most professional business voice. "I may be new to this position, but I'm not new to my family's business. This organization holds a very special place in my mother's heart—and mine—and I have promised her I will do the very best job I can working hand in hand with Junebug

Farms. To be honest, I look forward to it." Actually impressed with herself for being able to look both women in the eye rather than focusing only on the gorgeous face of Catherine Gardner—which was really what she wanted to do—Emily picked up her mug and took a sip of her coffee.

Clark took over. "This was really just an introductory meeting so you could meet Emily. I'm sure she'll want to go over some things in detail down the line, but we know you're not necessarily prepared for that at this moment. Right, Em?"

Emily nodded, watched as Catherine shuffled through some papers in the portfolio she'd brought in with her. "Exactly. In fact…" She pulled her phone out of her bag and called up the calendar. "Why don't we set something up now?" She looked up, snagged by Catherine's blue eyes.

Next to her, Jessica nodded. "That'll work. You'll be dealing mostly with Catherine, as she's our bookkeeper." She turned to her. "You have time this week, I assume?"

"Yes." Catherine flipped pages in a small planner, which Emily found endlessly amusing. And kind of endearing.

"Old school, huh?" she asked. When Catherine looked up, puzzled, Emily gestured at the planner.

"Oh." And then the first ghost of a smile appeared and Emily was reminded of why she hadn't been able to take her eyes off Catherine Saturday night. "I like pen and paper," she said with a half-shrug.

"I get that."

For a very short beat of time, it felt to Emily as if they were the only two people in the room. She watched Catherine run a finger down a list—the woman had gorgeous hands, feminine, with long fingers and neatly filed nails. The glasses were ridiculously sexy, but at the same time, Emily wanted to slip them off Catherine's face, get a good, clear look at those eyes that were the color of an August sky. Emily watched as Catherine turned the page in her planner, then absently reached up and tucked her hair behind her ear, giving Emily an unobstructed, sensual view of her neck and throat.

"How about Wednesday?"

Emily flinched and hoped nobody noticed. Blinking rapidly and working to get her mind out of the gutter, she wet her suddenly dry lips and nodded. "Wednesday is good." Realizing she'd better actually check, she glanced down at the phone in her hand, relieved to see that Wednesday was indeed good. *Oh, thank God.*

"Eleven?" Catherine asked.

"Eleven it is." Emily smiled at her and felt the sudden urge to lose herself in those blue eyes when Clark's voice—though at its usual volume—seemed to boom through the conference room like a basketball bouncing in an empty gym.

"Great. Well, I think that's all we needed." His chair made a loud screech as he pushed back from the table and stood. "Just wanted to get you guys acquainted with my baby sister." He held out his hand to Jessica, who stood and grasped it. Catherine did the same thing, then Jessica reached to Emily.

"I'm really looking forward to working with you. Thank you so much for all you do for Junebug Farms. It means the world to us, and more so to the animals you help."

"Well, it means a lot to us as well," Emily said, touched by Jessica's words. She turned to Catherine and when she had her hand held firmly in her own, she gave a gentle squeeze as she said, "I look forward to Wednesday."

Those blue eyes seemed to look right into her for a moment before Catherine gave a subtle nod, and Emily felt an inexplicable sense of disappointment when Catherine let go of her hand.

Clark's charm switch clicked back on as they exited the conference room and parted ways with Jessica and Catherine. He detoured by the front desk again. Regina – Volunteer was not there this time, but Judith – Volunteer was. It was all Emily could do to keep from rolling her eyes so hard they rolled right out of her skull to bounce along the lobby floor as her brother complimented everything about Judith – Volunteer, from her fun sweatshirt with the chickadees on it to her horn-rimmed glasses. She got just as pink as Regina did. Maybe more so, and Clark flirted mercilessly with her for a good five minutes before rapping the desk with his knuckles and waving a farewell to her. He tossed in a wink for good measure. *Because of course he did*, Emily thought.

Out at the car, she looked at him over the roof.

"What?" he asked, opening his door.

She got in and when both doors had been slammed shut she said, "You are a piece of work."

Clark chuckled as if he completely understood what she meant, but said, "What do you mean?" anyway.

"Seriously? With the flirting?" She scoffed as he keyed the engine.

"What's wrong with making a woman feel nice?" he asked, backing out of the spot and steering through the parking lot.

"That's not the issue, Clark, it's that there are times and places for that kind of thing and when you're in a professional capacity, it's not then."

"Speaking of pieces of work," he said, turning onto the road and talking as if he hadn't heard her at all. "How about that

Catherine Gardner? Is she hot or what? God. I've known her for a while and she never gets any less sexy."

Emily stared at him in disbelief while trying to ignore the snarl of possessive anger that was building in the pit of her stomach.

"I mean, she's kind of cold, doesn't smile much. She's always so serious. But, man." Clark glanced at her, then laughed. "Please. Don't try to tell me you didn't notice because I know you did."

She made a "that's ridiculous" expression at him and was immediately aware that she may have overdone it.

"Please," he said again. "I know the face you make when you find a girl hot."

"You do not," she retorted, but it lacked conviction because she knew he was right.

"Yeah, okay," he said with a snort. "Hey, wanna race?"

Emily turned a confused face on him. "What? To where?"

"To a bed, of course. Let's see which one of us can tap the lovely Ms. Gardner first. Wanna?"

"Seriously, Clark, you sound twelve. And like a pig."

"You're just afraid I'll win."

Emily thought back to Saturday, to the smiles and the eye contact and the conversation she'd received from Catherine. She felt a corner of her mouth tug up in a tiny grin. No, Clark wouldn't win. She was reasonably sure of that.

"I haven't really made a serious effort to ask her out," Clark said, interrupting her train of thought. "But now that I'm not her contact for the Foundation, it would probably be okay."

Emily shook her head, unable to believe the depth of her disbelief. "You're an idiot." It was all she could think of to say. "You're my brother and I love you. But you're a freaking idiot."

"You say that now. Let's see what you say when I win. What do you say? A hundred bucks?"

"I am not taking your ridiculous, unprofessional, *sexist* bet, Clark, and this is not a romantic comedy. Forget it."

"Chicken. You know you'll lose."

He gave a chuckle, and for a moment, Emily was ten years old again, wanting to hang out with her big brother and his friends, only to have them call her names and pick on her, as thirteen-year-old boys tend to do to their little sisters. She shook her head in a combination of frustration, disgust, and disbelief. Gazing out the window as they headed away from Junebug Farms, Emily allowed her thoughts to turn to Wednesday—when she would be alone with Catherine Gardner. It was business, she knew. The last thing she wanted to do was act like her brother.

That being said, she'd be lying to herself if she said she wasn't looking forward to seeing her again.

CHAPTER THREE

JESSICA BARSTOW RAPPED HER knuckles gently against the doorjamb of Catherine's small office.

Catherine looked up from her desk, over the top of her glasses. "Hey. Come on in." She pulled the glasses off and focused on Jessica. "What's up?"

Jessica stepped toward the two chairs positioned in front of the desk. The room was small, but neat and tidy, tasteful despite the unglamorous cinder block walls and public school-like furniture. Catherine knew how to make just about anything look good, and her office was no exception. Three thick, green houseplants flourished in different corners and added a lushness to the atmosphere. An abstract painting in warm, earthy tones of sage green and rust orange hung on one wall. A soft, oval area rug in burgundies and greens tempered the coldness of the linoleum floor. Jessica, amazed as always by Catherine's ability to look like the most put-together thing in any room, no matter how nice the room was, took a seat.

"What did you think?" Jessica asked. She and Catherine had known each other long enough that she didn't need to clarify.

Catherine set her glasses on the desk and sat back in her chair. "I think the Breckenridge Foundation finally got enough complaints about Clark that they decided they needed to do something about it."

"That's what I thought, too." Jessica crossed her legs, made herself comfortable. "I noticed they never said that. I wonder what other organizations have become part of the 'restructuring.'" She made air quotes.

"I guess it depends on how many complaints they got. Honestly, the man makes my skin crawl."

Jessica didn't hide her surprise. "He does? I mean, I feel the same way, but you always seem so comfortable and friendly around him. I'd never know you didn't like him."

"He disgusts me." Catherine wrinkled her nose. "Frankly, I'm surprised he hasn't openly hit on me yet. He's stayed pretty subtle about it up to this point, complimenting my skirt or telling me I smell good. That's fine for a friend. Not for a business colleague." She gave a visible shudder.

"And what did you think of the sister?"

Catherine gave a shrug.

"Have you two met?"

"Yeah." Catherine blew out an annoyed breath. "I waited on her and her date Saturday night."

"Ah, that explains it." At Catherine's raised eyebrows, she went on. "The stutter step at the door. You recognized her. She obviously recognized you as well. And seemed happy about it." Jessica winked, taking some of the seriousness out of the exchange. It wasn't a secret that Catherine worked a second job, but she was sometimes self-conscious about it.

With a chuckle, Catherine said, "Well, I give good service. What can I say?"

"She pings my gaydar."

Catherine grinned. "Her date Saturday *was* a woman, so…"

"Yeah? Well, she's cute."

"I wonder if she knows exactly why the family is pulling Clark." Catherine neatly avoided Jessica's comment, which Jessica noticed, but let slide.

"I would think it'd be hard for her not to know, but…" Jessica let the sentence dangle.

"She may not be any better than he is."

"What do you mean?"

"When she was at dinner on Saturday, all she did was ogle me. She barely paid any attention to her date. I mean, she didn't openly flirt with me, but…" Catherine shrugged. "Maybe being a letch runs in the family?"

"I suppose it's possible. Let's hope not." Jessica sat forward in her chair, elbows on her knees. "What was her date like?"

Catherine shook her head with a grin. "No idea. She never looked at me once."

Jessica made a face, because in her book, anybody who didn't look at Catherine was an idiot. "Really?"

"Really. Not once."

Before they could delve into the subject further, there was a racket outside the door. A shout. Two. Something crashed to the floor. Jessica turned around in her chair just in time to see something on four legs fly through the door, across the floor, and around Catherine's desk to stop underneath. All she could honestly say was that it was brown and white, and considering where they were, she'd guess it was probably a dog. With a squeak of wet shoes on the linoleum, a body burst into the room and stopped short just inside the door.

Ashley Stiles was a volunteer at Junebug Farms, one of their best. Jessica liked her very much. She stood still, her chest heaving as she sucked in air. Dropping her hands to her knees, she said, "I am so sorry!"

Catherine bent over the arm of her chair to peek under her desk. Jessica watched the soft smile play at the corners of her mouth as she spoke to the animal. "Well, hello there. Whatcha doin' under there? Hmm?" Catherine bent further, then came back up with the end of a red leash in her hand.

"I'm so sorry," Ashley said again, obviously embarrassed as she crossed the room and took the leash from Catherine. "He's so fast. And smart. He lulls me into a false sense of security, and when I loosen my grip, bam! He's gone like a shot." She shook her head. "He's gotten me twice now. He needs an escape artist name. Houdini or something." She gave a gentle tug and the dog came out from under the desk, giving Jessica and Catherine their first good look at him.

His fur was mostly white and wiry, with brown spots on his rump, the middle of his back, over one eye like a patch, and on the tip of one perky ear. Jessica knew dog breeds well, and this one was obviously part terrier of some kind: Jack Russell (but bigger)? Fox terrier (but squattier)? Something along those lines. He was smallish—maybe twenty to twenty-five pounds, but scrawny and definitely in need of some nourishment. His white legs were brown with mud up to his little dog knees and something occurred to Jessica.

"Were you outside when he got away from you?"

Ashley grimaced. "Yeah."

"And he ran….into the building?"

Ashley gave a nod. "Somebody was coming in the front door, and the little stinker timed it just right, scooted through right between the poor woman's feet."

A slight exhale of a laugh escaped Jessica's lips. "Interesting that he didn't run toward the woods or the road or the goat pen or something."

"He likes this office, I think," Ashley said, her eyes catching Catherine's. "Last time he got away from me we were inside and he ran here, too."

"You got some bacon hidden in your desk?" Jessica asked Catherine.

"Sadly, no," was her reply. She held the dog's gaze.

Jessica watched, amused.

"Come on, you," Ashley said, giving another tug on the leash. The dog followed, but his eyes stayed on Catherine as long as possible. "I'm really sorry," Ashley repeated.

Catherine shrugged and smiled softly. "It's no problem." She watched them go.

Jessica smiled and stood. "Okay. I've got work to do. Just wanted to get your take on the Breckenridge siblings."

"If nothing else," Catherine said, sliding her glasses back onto her face, "it'll be interesting." She lifted her shoulders in a long shrug.

"It will." Jessica left the office and headed down the hall. She waved to David Peters, head of fundraising, who sat in his own office and spoke into his phone as he lifted a hand to her. The hallway spilled her out into the open lobby, and she took a moment to just stand there and gaze.

It was busy. And loud. As it always was. The barking was pretty much nonstop. Combine that with whining, howling, meowing, the hum of conversation, and ringing telephone lines, it made for a fairly hectic environment until you got used to it.

To her left was the information desk, three volunteers working feverishly behind it, answering phones, filing papers, tapping the computer keyboards, directing visitors to the right places. To her right was the Wall of Cats, a giant Brady Bunch-like checkerboard of windows that showed most of the cats Junebug Farms had for adoption, and a few people stood in front of it, cooing and making faces at the various felines. Next to that wall was a set of double doors that led to the dog wing, a long,

long aisle with kennels on each side, an adoptable dog in almost every one of them. That was too many, and Jessica knew it. They were going to have to step up their efforts. Good thing there was a big fundraiser this weekend.

Jessica let herself lean back against the wall and just take it all in. Her grandmother had loved this place, had dumped her heart and soul into it, and Jessica was pretty sure she'd be proud of the things her granddaughter had done to keep it running. It wasn't easy. In fact, it was downright stressful the majority of the time. But Jessica loved animals, she loved Junebug Farms, and she loved that she was in a position to help.

As she grinned and nodded to herself, Regina from behind the desk called her name.

"Ms. Barstow?" She pointed at the receiver. "You have a call?"

Pushing herself off the wall, Jessica smiled. "Give me two minutes, then send it to my desk."

Heading to her own office, she couldn't help the surge of pride the puffed up her chest. Junebug Farms wasn't easy to run, but she managed, and she managed well.

I've done good, Grandma. I wish you were here to see it.

━◆━

Catherine sat in her office, nibbling on the earpiece of her glasses, and gazing out the window at the gray fall day. It had started slightly sunny, but thick clouds had moved in and now it was overcast and just…depressing. Like her mood suddenly.

It was because of Pablo. She did okay when she wasn't thinking about him, but having that little dog run to her the way he had only served to remind her how lost she was without Pablo. The wound was healing, had scabbed over, but that little dog made her think of him, which was like picking at it and now it was bleeding again.

She'd known immediately upon meeting Pablo, who was a three-year-old German shepherd mix of some sort, that they were destined for each other. Catherine had heard stories more times than she could count about people "just knowing." She always thought it was bullshit.

Then she'd met Pablo.

His brown eyes were astonishingly soulful, and when he looked into hers that first time, she would swear on any God you named that she saw something almost human there. His owners had a new baby and no time for him, so they'd surrendered him to Junebug. Catherine had gone to Jessica immediately and staked her claim. There'd never been a question, and they'd spent ten beautiful years together until old age had taken him almost three months ago. She was with him for his last breath, and though it just about wrecked her, sent her to bed for nearly a week, she wouldn't trade her time with him for anything.

Maybe it's time...

The thought scratched at her brain. Catherine blew out a breath as she watched the birds in the feeder outside her window scrabbling for seed. "I don't know..." she whispered.

"What don't you know?"

Startled, she looked up to see Anna St. John standing in her doorway, and did her best to stifle the groan of irritation she felt build in her chest. "Nothing," she said, forcing a smile. "What's up?"

At five foot one, Anna was a petite woman. People often referred to her as "cute"—which she despised—and it was an apt description. Her blond hair was pulled back into a haphazard ponytail more often than not, her wispy bangs brushing her forehead. Her brown eyes were slightly too big for her head, giving her a bit of a doll-like appearance. She had a kind heart, a smart intellect, and a wicked temper, the receiving end of which Catherine had been on for the better part of the past four months.

That's what I get for hooking up with somebody at work.

"Your floor's all muddy," Anna said as her eyes moved from the doorway and along the path to the chair where Jessica had sat not long ago.

"Oh. Right. I need to call Bill." Catherine picked up the handset on her phone and dialed the number of the front desk. Much to her dismay, Anna took a seat. "Hi, Regina. Next time you see Bill, could you ask him to come to my office with a mop? I've got a muddy floor." She thanked the woman and hung up. Turning back to Anna, she folded her hands on her desk, pasted on a soft smile, and waited, steeling herself for whatever was to come. Because lately, it was always something she needed to brace for.

Today was not the exception.

"How are you?" Anna asked in the small voice she used when she was trying to soften Catherine up.

"I'm fine." A beat of silence passed, one during which Anna was waiting for Catherine to ask her the same question. Which Catherine would not do because that was engaging, and engaging meant the beginning of what would inevitably be an emotional, uncomfortable conversation. It seemed over the past weeks, Catherine spent the majority of her time trying to avoid those types of connections with Anna. Her success, sadly, was hit or miss.

"I talked to my mom last night."

Shit. Anna was no dummy. Playing the mom card was low because she knew how much Catherine liked her mother and she knew Catherine couldn't *not* ask about her. Swallowing a sigh, she did just that. "How is she?"

"She's okay. Getting excited for the upcoming holidays. You know how she is."

Catherine nodded.

"She invited you to come for Thanksgiving."

And there it was. Catherine knew there was going to be a hook and she briefly congratulated herself for pegging that fact. Now, however, she was walking in a minefield and it didn't matter how carefully she stepped. There would be an explosion.

"Anna." Catherine breathed in slowly, then let it out at the same speed. "You know I can't go to your mother's for Thanksgiving."

A current of anger flashed across Anna's brown eyes. "Why not?" The question was short, the words clipped.

"You know why not," Catherine said, her frustration growing despite her attempts to keep it tamped down. "We're not together anymore. We haven't been for nearly four months."

"Yes, I know exactly how long it's been, thank you very much. I don't need you to tell me."

Catherine pressed her lips together, carefully searching for words. The right words. Problem was, none of them were right. They never would be to Anna. "I appreciate the invitation, but I have to decline."

"I have to decline," Anna sneered, mocking her. "You don't have to get all snob on me."

"I'm not being a snob," Catherine said quietly.

"Fine. It's fine." Anna stood. "I'll just tell my mother that you're too good to come to Thanksgiving dinner at her place.

That won't crush her. No problem. I got this." With that, she turned on her heel and stormed out of the office, almost running into Bill Tracey as he pushed a bucket and mop down the hallway.

"Whoa," he said, flattening himself against the wall as the little blonde whirlwind blew past him. He stood there, shaking his head slowly back and forth as he watched Anna exit down the hall. Turning to Catherine, he said from just outside the doorway, "That woman has a heck of a temper. Remind me never to get on her bad side."

"Please," Catherine said with a scoff, sliding her glasses back onto her face. "I live on her bad side. I run the place." Refocusing her attention on the screen of numbers in front of her, she absently hoped the conversation with Anna meant she wouldn't have to have another one for a while.

CHAPTER FOUR

EMILY STOPPED IN HER tracks just inside the front door of Junebug Farms and took a second to absorb the difference in sound from outside to inside.

"Wow," she breathed quietly, taking it all in. It wasn't unpleasant, the soundtrack of the shelter. It was simply... constant. Never-ending. She wondered how long a person had to work here before they were able to tune it all out and focus on whatever their job was. A day? A week? A month? She honestly wasn't sure how long it would take her.

Getting her bearings, she headed to the front desk where Clark had flirted so mercilessly with Regina – Volunteer on Monday. Today, the desk was manned by Julie – Volunteer, and her smile was open and friendly as she asked Emily if she could help.

"I have an appointment with Catherine Gardner," Emily said with a friendly smile of her own.

"Of course. Can I tell her who's here?"

"Emily Breckenridge."

If she was being honest, Emily had to admit that she didn't always dislike the change in demeanor the mention of her last name tended to cause. Oh, there were sporadic occasions when it was a little embarrassing. And she did her best not to take advantage. But her family was well known in this city. Very well known. Very wealthy and very well known. Luckily, they were also well respected and spent a lot of money on good causes, so most people leaned toward liking her. When she gave somebody her name, they sat up straighter, took notice, and switched into Best Behavior Mode as Julie – Volunteer did now. Something about that made Emily feel she should do the same. Mutual respect was a good thing. She smiled and stood a little taller as Julie picked up the handset of her phone and announced Emily's arrival, then hung up.

"She'll be right with you."

"Thanks." Emily turned her back to the desk and wandered across the large lobby, stopping to peruse the various photos and plaques on the wall that she hadn't had time to look at when she was here with Clark. There were framed letters of thanks from people who'd found their soulmates in the animals they'd rescued. There were plaques depicting various sports teams sponsored by Junebug Farms. There were before and after photos of animals who'd come into the shelter in horrific shape, only to be nursed tenderly back to health and adopted out into loving families. It really was an uplifting array and, not for the first time, Emily understood why her mother had begun donating to Junebug Farms so many years ago.

"Ms. Breckenridge?"

She turned to find the source of the voice and was once again taken aback by the appearance of Catherine Gardner. Absently wondering if this was going to be a regular thing, she did her best not to give her a once-over, much as she wanted to. Instead, she took in as much as possible in a glance as Catherine approached. Her black pantsuit was impeccably pressed, the sleeves of the jacket pushed up to the middle of her forearms, the silver watch on her left wrist glimmering in the overhead lights. She wore a silk shell of powder blue underneath and the softness of the color made the blue of her eyes pop, especially since her glasses were missing. Her hair was down today, just past her shoulders, a mass of gentle chestnut brown waves, swept to the side. Her heels made a click-click-click as she walked toward Emily, hand held out in a businesslike greeting.

"Ms. Gardner," Emily said, with a wide smile, as she grasped Catherine's hand and tried not to focus on its warm smoothness. "Please. Call me Emily. Ms. Breckenridge is my mother."

With a nod, Catherine smiled pleasantly and said, "And I'm Catherine."

"Look at us. We're on a first-name basis already."

Catherine's reaction was less than exuberant, but she did manage to hold the smile.

Okay. I'll take that. "I'm looking forward to this tour," Emily said, keeping her voice light and friendly. "I have always loved this place. I love animals and I love what you do for them here. My mother has sung the praises of Junebug Farms since I was a kid, but I never really paid close attention until recently."

"Well, Junebug Farms has been operational for more than twenty years, but we've really grown over the past few, since Jessica Barstow took over running things when her grandmother died." As Catherine spoke, she began strolling through the lobby to the cat wall. She told Emily the number of cats that came in on average each year, as well as how many were adopted out. Then they moved into the dog wing, where the noise was so abundant, Emily hardly heard a word.

Which didn't matter at all because she was barely listening. All she did was watch Catherine's mouth while she talked. She couldn't help it. She caught herself several times and purposefully shifted her gaze up to Catherine's large blue eyes, but eventually she'd focus right back on those full, glossy lips. Emily hoped there wasn't a quiz after all this information because she'd fail miserably.

When the tour took them outside, Emily started to feel better, less trapped and claustrophobic. The fresh air hit her in the face, and it was the equivalent of a cup of cold water. She felt like she'd been jerked awake. *Thank God.*

"We take in much more than dogs and cats," Catherine was saying. Her voice was very matter-of-fact, almost rehearsed, as if she'd given this speech, this tour, a hundred times. *She probably has,* Emily thought. Still, she wanted this to be a more personal conversation. For some reason, she wanted Catherine to look at her differently than she looked at every other donor to Junebug.

"I see the goats," Emily said, pointing toward the goat pen. "They're adorable."

The first genuine smile broke across Catherine's face then, and Emily took note. "Aren't they? They're really very sweet animals. They love people and visitors give them lots of attention." She turned in the other direction and walked toward the barn. "We also take in horses, burros, even cows at times."

"Seriously?"

The asphalt gave way to a gravel path, which Catherine navigated expertly somehow, given her heels. "Seriously. We take in a lot of abuse cases. Horses that are neglected, malnourished, that kind of thing."

Emily shook her head. "That makes me sick."

"It can be difficult."

They went on like this for the next half hour, Catherine talking fondly, but also very businesslike, about the shelter, Emily nodding, asking occasional questions to pull Catherine into a more casual tone, all the while trying not to stare at that lovely mouth.

Once back inside, Catherine led Emily into Paws & Whiskers, the adorable little gift shop located just inside the front door.

"How did I miss this the other day?" Emily asked softly as she took in the walls and racks of toys, collars, and bowls. The space was small, but used brilliantly, the collars and leashes displayed in a rainbow of colors, in the correct order. Emily ran her fingertips along them, smiling like a little kid.

"We don't carry as much as we'd like," Catherine explained. "But we try to keep a good selection in stock so people who adopt feel like they go home with everything they need." She stopped at the counter, behind which stood a small, smiling woman of about sixty. "This is Maggie Simon. She runs the shop. Maggie, this is Emily Breckenridge."

Like most other people's, Maggie's face lit up at the mention of her name and Emily crossed the small space to shake her hand. "Nice to meet you, Maggie. This store is adorable. I want to buy all the things."

"Do you have pets?" Maggie asked.

"I have a dog. Dave. He's a rescue and he's my love."

Catherine's expression showed surprise, which Emily found amusing, then it shifted to something Emily was fairly certain was approval.

"He was a birthday gift from my mother, who adopted him from here a few years ago."

"Dave," Maggie said with a grin. "I love it."

Emily chuckled. "It fits him. I have no idea why. He's just...a Dave."

"Totally understandable. Sometimes, you just know."

"In fact..." Emily wandered over to the wall of toys and picked up a stuffed lobster. "He would love this." She set it on the counter and pulled her wallet from the bag she had slung over a shoulder. She saw Maggie glance at Catherine as if asking a silent question. "No, no. I am paying for this."

Catherine studied her for a beat and Emily fought the urge to squirm under her gaze. Finally, relenting, Catherine gave one nod to Maggie, who picked up the lobster and rang it into the small cash register.

"Dave loves stuffed animals. He's this barrel-chested, kind of fierce-looking pit bull mix. People are hesitant around him at first because he looks kind of intimidating. But they don't know. He will carry this thing around so carefully, like he's the mama and this is his baby."

"That's adorable," Maggie said, putting the lobster into a bag and then accepting Emily's money.

"He is never what anybody expects of him." Emily took the change and scooped up the bag. "Thank you, Maggie. I'm sure I'll see you again." Turning to Catherine, she said, "Lead on, my queen."

Catherine quirked an eyebrow at her, but Emily was sure she saw the ghost of a smile tug up one corner of her gorgeous mouth as she turned and headed out of the shop and back into the lobby. When they reached the horseshoe-shaped front desk, they stopped and Catherine turned to her. A whiff of her musky perfume hit Emily's nose and she quietly inhaled, taking in the unique scent.

"That's it," Catherine said, leaning against the counter. "You've seen it all."

"Well, I love it." Emily looked around the expansive lobby, sad to have her tour—and by extension, her time with Catherine —come to an end. The double doors to the dog wing opened as somebody exited, then turned and held it open for a person who was following. Through the doors and down the hall, Emily could see a tall woman with short hair and a forest green shirt holding a leash in her hand, but looking over her shoulder behind her. The dog at the end of the leash was smallish, white with brown spots, and was looking determinedly at the open double doors.

It all happened so fast, Emily wasn't quite sure the order of things.

The dog was off like he was sprung from a slingshot and the short-haired woman had zero time to react, the leash snapped out of her hand before she even realized it. The big eyes of the dog were focused intently on the door and he was through in a split second, his short legs deceiving because he ran like a jackrabbit. The short-haired woman gave a cry as the dog ran right for Emily and Catherine, and before anybody even realized what happened, he'd run right around them and tucked himself between Catherine's legs and the front desk, the red leash acting like an indicator to where he was, wrapped around Catherine's heels and leading behind her.

The most surprising thing to Emily was Catherine's reaction. As in, she barely had one. People had turned to look, a few cries of surprise came from behind the desk as the short-haired woman's feet smacked against the floor in her efforts to catch the dog. But he hadn't startled Catherine at all. In fact, she hadn't even moved. She simply looked down at him, an unreadable expression on her face. The dog, conversely, looked up at her with such devotion in his warm, brown eyes that Emily almost laughed out loud.

"Your dog?" she asked Catherine, quirking an eyebrow at her.

The short-haired woman got to them, and her expression was one of irritation. "I'm really sorry, Catherine." She turned to

Emily, her green eyes so startlingly beautiful that Emily nearly caught her breath. "Hi. I'm Lisa Drakemore. I apologize for this guy." She held out a hand.

Emily shook it. "Emily Breckenridge."

Lisa's eyes widened at Emily's name, and she looked over at Catherine, slight panic obvious on her face.

"And it's no problem. That was entertaining." Emily did her best to alleviate any concern by squatting down to peer at the dog, who studied her carefully. "You're kind of a nut, huh?" He continued to gaze at her from between Catherine's shins. Lisa and Catherine were talking in hushed tones, so Emily took the opportunity to whisper, "You've got good taste, buddy. I'd have run here, too." Standing back up, she said, "He's a little daredevil, isn't he?"

Lisa shook her head, clearly embarrassed. "I don't know how he does it. He just…goes. This is the third time I'm aware of."

"Geronimo," Emily said with a laugh. "That should be his name because he just…leaps. He obviously likes you," she said to Catherine, who shrugged, but still held onto that not-quite-readable expression even as she gazed down at the dog, who hadn't budged.

Lisa bent to scoop up the end of the leash and gave it a gentle tug. "Come on, Geronimo. Let's go."

He didn't fight her. He went. But he glanced over his shoulder at Catherine more than once the whole way back to the double doors. When they closed behind him, Emily felt a profound sense of sadness.

"That dog is in love with you," she said to Catherine, whose gaze was also on the doors.

Catherine smiled softly, but said nothing.

"Do you have a dog?" Emily asked, suddenly wanting to know more personal things about this woman.

A shadow crossed over her face as she glanced down at her feet. "No."

"Well, maybe you should." Emily pointed in the direction of the dog wing. "That one."

With a gentle shrug, Catherine smoothly changed the subject. "So. That's Junebug Farms in a nutshell. What else would you like to know?"

In all honestly, Emily didn't want the tour to end. She really liked being around Catherine. Which was a little silly because it wasn't like she was warm and fuzzy. Rather, she was cool and businesslike, aloof though not unfriendly. She obviously loved the place; that came through in the way she talked about it, the things she'd explained or pointed out.

"I'd like to be more involved," Emily said before she could stop the words. What did that even mean?

Catherine cocked her head slightly. "You would?"

"I would." Straightening up, Emily asked, "What can I do besides write checks? I mean, I know those help a lot—"

"A lot," Catherine echoed with a half-grin.

"But what more can I do?"

"Hmm. Well, we're having a fundraiser on Saturday," Catherine said. "We're trying something new. A fashion show." At Emily's furrowed brows, Catherine laughed. It was the first time Emily had heard the sound, and its slightly musical, very feminine tone made Emily's face split into a smile. "I have no idea. Like I said, it's something new. But you're welcome to come. I'm sure we can find something for you to do."

"Terrific. I'll be here." There was a quick beat of awkward, as Emily didn't want to leave, but knew she had no reason to stay further. "Well. This has been great." She held out her hand and grasped Catherine's firmly. "I really appreciate you taking the time to spend with me."

"Of course." Catherine was back to cool and professional, but her smile seemed slightly more genuine than it had been at the beginning.

I'll take that. "I'll see you on Saturday." With one last grin and a quick nod, Emily turned and headed out of the building.

Once the car door was slammed tightly and she was safely ensconced in the driver's seat, Emily released a huge breath. That visit had been a bevy of opposites. It was comfortable and uncomfortable. It was relaxing but nerve-wracking. She enjoyed being around Catherine, yet Catherine made her jittery.

"Ugh. Get your shit together, Em," she said to the quiet of the car. "This is business, not the place to develop a crush." She pulled her iPhone out of her bag and plugged it into the car. Immediately, three texts popped up as well as a calendar reminder that she had drinks scheduled that night with her good friends, Michelle and Sandy.

Thank God. She could use the distraction.

CHAPTER FIVE

EMILY WATCHED IN AWE as the Junebug Farms Fundraising Fashion Show took place in the main lobby. From what she understood after chatting with one of the volunteers, this was an experiment of a new idea for raising money for the shelter. If it worked, it would be done on a larger scale some time in the future. She stood quietly behind Jessica Barstow and took it all in. Jessica hadn't seen her and Emily preferred to just absorb everything without bothering the woman. From her peripheral vision, she saw Lisa Drakemore heading in Jessica's direction.

"Not bad, huh?" Lisa asked, as she sidled up next to Jessica and bumped her lightly with a shoulder.

"Not bad at all," Jessica replied and Emily saw her wink at Lisa. "Your girl has good ideas."

"She does." Lisa's skin flushed and Emily grinned as Jessica leaned close to Lisa's ear and whispered, "Pink is a good color on you."

"Shut up," Lisa whispered, but Emily could hear the grin in her voice.

"Speak of the devil."

Emily followed their gazes to a young, pretty blond woman as she stepped onto the stage. With her face turned in that direction, Emily could see the tender smile on Lisa Drakemore's face. *I know that look*, she thought fondly, though it had been a long time since she'd smiled like that herself. She continued to watch as, leash in hand, the young woman smiled widely, her blond hair cascading in waves just past her shoulders as she paraded down the catwalk. A voice sounded from the small speakers set up on either side.

"And here's our volunteer Ashley again, with this adorable dog who is a true terrier in every sense of the word. We think he's got some Jack Russell, maybe some fox terrier, and possibly some schnauzer in him, but there might be more. He was found as a stray and brought to Junebug Farms two weeks ago in pretty bad shape. But we've nursed him back to terrific health and he's ready to find his forever home. He's energetic, loving, knows basic commands and is housebroken, and—uh oh—" The voice was interrupted by Ashley's surprised cry and suddenly the dog was bounding off the catwalk and running through the crowd at an impressively fast speed, his leash flowing behind him like a feather boa.

"Oh, shit," Jessica said, and Lisa followed with a worse swear word, and before either could move an inch, the dog had zipped completely around the crowd, past Emily—who smiled as Jessica met her eyes—and right past them. His little paws skidded on the smooth floor, but he stayed upright, circled back around to the stage, and disappeared underneath it. As a collective chuckle rumbled through the onlookers, Jessica seemed to shake herself into action, Lisa close on her heels, Emily right behind them, even though she wasn't sure they realized yet that she'd followed them.

Ever the professional, apparently, Jessica nodded at familiar faces and made a show of smiling and rolling her eyes good-naturedly as if saying, "There's no reason to panic. It's just a dog and dogs get loose at a shelter. No big deal." Emily wondered about the animal's case, though; it had to be hard to adopt out a dog that was such an obvious escape artist. She watched as Jessica peeked under the stage, evidently found nothing but empty space, and continued to smile. Next, she scooted behind the stage and down the hall, Lisa following her, Emily following Lisa. Emily had a pretty good idea where the dog had headed.

When the voice on the PA continued on with the next "model," she heard Jessica breathe a sigh of relief, probably glad somebody had taken control of the crowd and recaptured their attention.

"Which way did he go?" Lisa asked.

"I think I know," Emily spoke up, and it was obvious by the surprise on both faces that they'd had no idea she'd been following them.

"Yeah?" Jessica glanced at her and Emily smiled with amusement.

"Follow me." Emily took the lead and walked straight down the hall to Catherine's slightly open office door.

The blonde who'd lost the dog finally caught up with them. She was out of breath, her hair disheveled, her cheeks flushed a deep red. "Oh, my God, I'm so sorry, Jessica. Did you find him?" Obviously frazzled, she shot a look to Lisa, who squeezed her shoulder.

Jessica looked at her and smiled her best smile of reassurance. "No worries, Ashley. Not your fault."

Ashley. Emily made a note.

"Ugh," was all Ashley could seem to muster.

Emily knocked lightly on the office door, then pushed it open the rest of the way. Inside, Catherine sat behind her desk. The four of them stopped in the doorway as Catherine looked at them over the top of her black-framed glasses and arched one eyebrow. Emily felt a flutter in her stomach.

"I assume you're looking for this?" With her startlingly blue eyes, Catherine gestured down to her feet.

Jessica squatted enough to see under Catherine's industrial metal desk. "That little dog that's sitting directly on your feet? Yes," Jessica said with a half-shrug and an expression of *what can you do?* "We're looking for that."

Catherine raised her hand, producing the end of the leash—which made Emily chuckle aloud—and held it out. Ashley stepped forward before the other three could, apparently ready to fall on her sword. "I'm so sorry, Ms. Gardner. That was my fault. I didn't hold on to the leash tightly enough and he bolted. Took me by surprise. Again. I am so sorry."

Catherine nodded, glancing up from her computer monitor, then handed over the leash.

Ashley thanked her again, made a *yikes* face at the other three as she passed, and led the dog out the door—even as he kept looking back at Catherine—obviously wanting to get out of there as quickly as possible. Lisa followed, close on her heels.

Jessica stood quietly for a moment when she seemed to realize Emily was still there. Her expression was unreadable as she turned to Catherine and spoke. "Okay. I've gotta get out there. Sorry, Cat." She turned to go, the spun back around. "And stop working, for God's sake. It's Saturday. Come out and have fun. There's an awesome Mexican food truck in the parking lot." She winked and gave Emily an indefinable look before leaving the office completely.

And then she was alone with Catherine.

"Cat?" Emily grinned as Catherine raised an eyebrow at her, then went back to her computer.

"Yeah, nobody calls me that."

"Somebody just did."

"Well, she's my boss. She can get away with it." Catherine poked at a couple keys on her keyboard.

"Can I?" The eyebrow was back and Emily caught her bottom lip between her teeth. *God, that's sexy.*

"No."

"Kate?"

"No."

"Cathy?"

"No."

"Well, okay then." Emily laughed as she glanced around the office, her eyes unsurprisingly pulled back to Catherine. "That dog loves you, by the way."

"So you've told me."

"He's the one obviously trying to tell you something."

Catherine shrugged, but said nothing.

"Things are going really well out there," Emily said, trying again.

Catherine gave a nod. "Good. That's good."

Another beat of silence went by and Emily's amusement only grew. "You don't like me very much, do you?"

That got Catherine's attention, Emily noted. She finally looked up, made eye contact with Emily. Pulling her glasses off, she said, "We're business colleagues. Does it matter whether or not I like you?"

"Which doesn't answer my question." Emily cocked her head. "Or maybe it does." She moved farther into the room and took a seat, uninvited. She crossed her jean-clad legs and studied Catherine's face, pleased when Catherine didn't look away. "Why?"

Catherine raised her eyebrows, silently asking for clarification.

"Why don't you like me? I mean, you don't know me. You know very little about me, in fact." Emily pursed her lips, made a show of thinking. She had to admit that she loved having Catherine's full attention. It gave her a tiny thrill in the pit of her stomach. And a little bit lower. "Maybe it's because of what you do know."

Catherine sat back in her chair, folded her arms, and if Emily didn't know any better, she'd say her expression showed amusement more than discomfort or anger. "Please. By all means, tell me. What do I know?"

"Well, I can think of two things right off the bat." Emily ticked them off on her fingers. "One: I am wealthy. My family has money, which means I have money, which means you probably think I don't have to work very hard to get the things I want. You probably think I'm a spoiled little rich girl." Catherine's only response was to press her lips tighter together and raise one eyebrow. *Okay, that eyebrow thing has to stop. Way too distracting.* "Two, my brother is..." She took a deep breath and just blurted it out. "Kind of a dick." A bark of laughter burst out of Catherine's mouth, and it was so unexpected that Emily flinched before smiling in response. "He can be. I know. That's why he's not here now and I am."

It was very slight, but Emily caught it: the subtle pinkening of Catherine's cheeks. And while Emily was happy to have (subtly) made her point, she felt bad that she'd embarrassed Catherine, even just a little.

"So, in my defense," Emily went on, "I think you should wait until you get to know me a little better before you decide whether or not to like me. Okay?"

Catherine wet her lips and looked down at her hands, then back up. With one nod, she said, "Fair enough."

"Good." Emily rubbed her hands along her thighs and then stood. "I've looked at some of the figures in the reports my mother gave me from the past couple of years and I'd like to go over some of them with you next week, then talk about future numbers. Do you have time?" She watched as Catherine slid her glasses back on and consulted her paper planner.

"Tuesday?"

Emily nodded. "Let's do eleven. We'll go to lunch after that."

To her credit, Catherine only hesitated slightly before giving her assent and writing the appointment into her calendar.

"Excellent," Emily said. "I'll see you then." She turned and headed for the door, but stopped just shy of it. Turning back to Catherine, she said, "And you need to adopt that dog. He was obviously meant to be with you. Stop fighting it. And name him Geronimo. It fits." Then she winked and left the office, shutting the door behind her.

Once in the hall, Emily let herself fall against the wall as she blew out a huge breath of relief. "Oh, my God," she whispered, all the bravado she'd displayed two minutes ago leaving her like the air of a deflated balloon. She wasn't averse to standing up to somebody who deserved to be knocked down a peg or two. In fact, she was good at it. She relished it. This certainly wasn't the first time somebody had made a judgment about her based on the size of her bank account only, and frankly, Emily didn't give a flying fuck if somebody didn't like her. But Catherine? Catherine was different and something about *her* not liking Emily didn't sit well. At all.

Emily literally shook her head free of the thought, not wanting to analyze further.

Luckily, the crowd at the end of the hall burst into applause at that moment, which captured Emily's attention and focus. She was here to volunteer. To work. To help run this place that she was growing to love with every day she visited. Heading down the hall, she forced her mind to look for Jessica Barstow and see what else she could do for the shelter today.

She tucked her confusing jumble of thoughts regarding Catherine Gardner into a little box in her mind and set them on a very, very high shelf. She'd deal with them later. An image of Catherine and her one arched eyebrow suddenly appeared in Emily's mind and she sighed loudly.

Or, you know, now.

━◇━

Catherine did not enjoy being called out by somebody who didn't know her. She didn't enjoy being called out by anybody, of course, because who did? But in this case, the caller-outer was correct. Catherine didn't enjoy that either.

She pulled off her glasses and tossed them onto her desk, then pinched the bridge of her nose. She didn't have to be here. It was Saturday, after all, and the place wouldn't fall down around the fundraiser if she'd stayed home. But Catherine was a hard worker. Not only that, Junebug Farms meant something to her. Pretty much everybody who worked there felt the same way. The shelter was a part of them. In their hearts, in their blood. Each employee as well as each volunteer put in 110% on any given day. The only one who was at Junebug more often than Catherine was Jessica.

Daylight was fading, she noticed, as she glanced out the window. The sky had become the color of a dull nickel, a sure sign of impending precipitation. It still felt too early for snow, but a couple more weeks and they'd be into December. She was one of the few people she knew who didn't mind winter. True, she did not love being cold, but she'd always thought of winter as a way to begin again. New-fallen snow was like a clean slate, fresh and blank. January 1 was her favorite day of the year because she used it to start over, to let go of every bad thing that happened the previous year and begin again, this time hopefully fixing the things that had gone belly-up in the twelve months prior.

The loud rumbling of her stomach reminded Catherine that she hadn't eaten since breakfast and the darkening sky told her it was probably near five o'clock. The fundraiser would be wrapping up—she'd try to grab the receipts and donations before heading home—and she hoped the food truck hadn't left yet. A burrito sounded like heaven right about now, so she tucked a ten-dollar bill in the pocket of her blazer and headed out.

Bill Tracey, resident custodian/handyman/Mr. Fix It, was working with two younger volunteers to take down the makeshift catwalk. People still milled around the lobby, some with animals on leashes already, others peering into the glass of the cat wall, cooing at the various felines looking for homes. A glance in the direction of the double doors that led to the dog wing told her there were a lot of visitors looking at the adoptable dogs. That would make Lisa very happy.

Once in the parking lot, Catherine wished she'd thought to grab her coat; it was colder than she'd expected and she wrapped her arms around herself as she stood in line behind one other person at the La Fiesta food truck, the smells of cilantro and fresh tortillas filling the air and teasing her empty stomach. Cars were on the move as people loaded up and left, headlights being turned on in the growing dusk. The air was crisp and cold, and Catherine shivered a bit as she paid for her bean and cheese burrito and walked quickly back to the main building.

Nodding and smiling at various people who said hello to her, Catherine bit into her burrito, unable to wait until she returned to her office—she was that hungry. A mouthful of beans had never tasted so wonderful. A glance to her left stopped her in her tracks as her eyes fell for the second time on the double doors to the dog wing. Before she had a chance to second-guess herself— or talk herself out of it—she hurried across the lobby and pushed her way in. The chaotic symphony of barks, whines, and howls assaulted her brain like gunfire.

She hadn't been in this section of the shelter in more than three months before she'd given Emily the tour. Not since she lost Pablo. A small grin of memory tugged on one corner of her mouth. He'd been the best dog in the world for nearly ten years. Letting him go had been the hardest decision of her life and she still wasn't over it (as indicated by the tears that suddenly misted her eyes as she thought about him), but she did miss having a dog. She missed that companionship. The unconditional love. The knowledge that there was someone at home, waiting for her.

Before she realized what she was doing, she began to wander the dog wing. She'd avoided it for fear that it would be too hard to see dogs in her fragile state, and she was right. It was horrendously difficult. But she kept walking.

"Hey, Catherine." Lisa was clearly surprised to see her, sitting at her desk halfway down the aisle, poking at her keyboard. Not a lot of people were left—better things to do on a Saturday night than peer at abandoned dogs, Catherine figured, but she nodded at Lisa and continued her slow stroll as she chewed the last of her burrito and watched each dog at the door of its kennel, wagging its tail, barking for her attention.

It was a different sight at Kennel 16.

He was curled up in the back corner on some blankets, seemingly not interested in the people who wandered by, napping or pretending to. Catherine stopped at the door and stood quietly. When he opened his eyes and saw her, his little tail thumped once, twice, and he popped off the blankets like they were covering an ejector seat. He zipped to the kennel door, so obviously happy to see Catherine that her eyes misted over yet again. She squatted down, stuck her fingers through the metal, and allowed him to lick them. He wasn't a big dog and Catherine tended to like big dogs, but there was just something about this guy.

"What is it?" she asked him quietly. "Hmm? What is it about you and me?"

He looked up at her as if he completely understood what she was saying and had the same question. He was barrel-chested, built like a cinder block, his short legs seemingly too small for his body, but Catherine suspected there was a ton of unexpected strength packed into that little package. The brown patch over his eye made him look suspect, like a bandit. He was deceptively soft, and he turned his head to allow her better access to his ear, which she rubbed between her fingers like a piece of felt.

Had Catherine not been dressed for work, she'd have plopped onto the floor and stayed there for a while. The way she seemed to calm the dog, he seemed to do the same for her. She suddenly felt relaxed, content. But she was wearing a suit and her legs had begun to protest her squatting for so long. She stood up and smiled down at the dog, whose tail continued to swing back and forth.

"All right. I've gotta go." She spoke softly, so only he could hear her. "You stay here for now. Okay, Geronimo? All right, Mo? I'll be back." Once again, as if he completely got what she was saying, he turned and went back to his blanket. He turned in a circle. Once, twice, three times, before settling back down. He gave Catherine one last look, then lowered his head and closed his eyes.

Catherine felt something squeeze in her chest. She took a step back, then turned and headed down the hall to the double doors, walking quickly, not looking back. Which meant she didn't see the smile on Lisa's face as she passed, or the "hold" order Lisa entered on Kennel 16.

CHAPTER SIX

"SO? HOW GOES THE new position?" Michelle Edmonds stabbed a tomato with her fork and stuck it in her mouth, her eyes never leaving Emily's face.

Emily nodded, took a sip from the straw in her soda before replying, "Not bad. It's been a lot to absorb, but I'm getting there."

"I can totally see you on your couch at night," Sandy Cooper commented with a knowing grin. "Poring over numbers, doing research, jotting notes."

"Just like college," Michelle agreed. "Study nerd."

"I seem to remember attending several frat parties with you two. I did more than study." Emily grinned—good-naturedly, though. Sandy and Michelle had been her suitemates for three years of college and she never understood how she'd gotten so lucky as to have scored not one, but two friends for life using only the luck of the draw.

"That's because you were the only one of the three of us who could do both: party and get good grades." Michelle took a bite of her turkey club sandwich, then dabbed a blob of mustard from the corner of her mouth.

"Well, we all ended up just fine, didn't we?" Emily looked from one to the other, and her heart warmed, as it always did in their presence. These two women were her saviors, the people who kept her head above water when she felt like she was drowning, the people who kicked her ass when she needed it. Or deserved it. In turn, she did the same for each of them.

"So, what's been the best part of running the Foundation so far?" Sandy popped a French fry into her mouth, her blue eyes sparkling. She was sporting yet another new hairstyle, this time short and light brown, her ends nearly bleached. Anybody who couldn't guess that she worked in a salon wasn't paying attention.

"I really like Junebug Farms."

"The animal shelter?" Sandy asked.

With a nod, Emily explained. "My mom loves the place, has always donated a boatload. I think we're their biggest donor and —of course—they'd like to keep it that way. So Clark took me over and introduced me around..." At the snorts and eye rolls, Emily had to nod. "I know. I'm hoping he's learned his lesson."

"Fat chance," Michelle muttered.

Not wanting to have to defend her brother (mostly because there was no good way to do so), Emily went on. "I had the accountant give me a tour."

"The accountant?" Michelle asked around a bite of her sandwich.

"Yeah. Catherine Gardner. The place is huge. It's not just dogs and cats. They have goats and horses and donkeys and some livestock on occasion. I'm going back tomorrow to sit with Catherine and go over some numbers." She put a forkful of salad into her mouth and looked up as she chewed, only to see her two friends exchange a glance, then look at her with knowing expressions. "What?"

Sandy shook her head. "Oh, nothing. Right, Michelle?"

Michelle nodded with great enthusiasm. "Oh, right. Absolutely right. Nothing at all, except..." One corner of her mouth quirked up and Sandy made the same face.

Emily set her fork down and gave them a look. "Except what?"

With a shrug, Sandy bit into another French fry. "We were just curious what this Catherine might look like."

Emily poked the inside of her cheek with her tongue and tried hard to smother a grin. She was unsuccessful.

"I knew it," Sandy announced, pointing a finger at her. Michelle joined in on the not-so-gentle ribbing with her trademark tinkling laughter, which was totally not what people expected from a tall, solidly built black woman.

"Knew what?"

"She's hot, isn't she?" Michelle asked, her dark eyes glittering with delight.

Emily made a show of being nonchalant as she answered, "I don't know. She might be."

"Yeah," Sandy said, picking up her last two fries and pointing at Emily with them. "We've met you, so…" She let the sentence dangle as she chewed, her eyes holding Emily's in a stare-down until Emily finally let out a cry and looked away. Sandy held both arms up like she'd just scored a goal. "You can't out-stare me, Breckenridge. I don't know why you try."

Emily shook her head as her laughter subsided and she caught her breath. "I don't either," she admitted. When both friends looked expectantly at her, she sighed in defeat. "Okay, okay. Yes, she's hot. She's very hot. She's…I-could-look-at-her-all-day hot. That kind of hot. Stunning. Gorgeous." Both Michelle and Sandy opened their mouths to speak, but Emily silenced them with a held-up finger. "But," she said, before either could speak. "This is business. I'm new to this job. I don't need any distractions. I'm just looking. I promise."

Michelle said, "Mmhmm," which made the other two laugh.

"I *promise*," Emily said again. "Looking but no touching."

Sandy glanced at Michelle, a puzzled expression on her face. "Have we heard that before? Because I think we've heard that before."

"Oh, we have most definitely heard that before," Michelle replied, neither of them looking at Emily.

"All right, Key and Peele. You're hilarious. I get it." Emily shook her head and went back to her salad.

"When are you seeing her again?" Sandy asked. "Oh. Wait. Sorry. I meant, when is your next 'business meeting' with her?" She made air quotes with her fingers.

"We have a business meeting tomorrow."

"A business meeting?" Michelle asked. "Or a 'business meeting?'" She, too, used the air quotes on the second mention.

"I hate both of you right now," Emily muttered, knowing they were just playing but feeling a little picked on.

Sandy pushed at her shoulder. "Oh, you do not. We're just messing with you, babe."

"Well. We are and we're not." Michelle's voice took on a bit of a serious edge and Emily looked up at her. "We're looking out for you. That's what we're doing. You know that." She held Emily's gaze until Emily had to nod in agreement.

"You are. I know." Emily grinned and, to lighten the mood, added, "She hates me anyway, so you have nothing to worry about."

"Well, now I know you're talking crazy," Michelle said. "'Cause hating you is not possible."

"Oh, believe me. It is and she does." Emily forked a bite of salad into her mouth and chewed while her friends shook their heads in tandem.

"Then she's an idiot. Why in the world would she hate you?"

Emily squinted as she searched for words. "I think…" She chewed some more, conjuring up an image of Catherine Gardner in her head. "She seems a little…buttoned-up? Straight-laced?"

"Rigid?" Sandy offered.

Emily tilted her head to one side, then the other. "No. I don't think she's that bad. But who knows? I'm not sure what it is. She's just kind of…cool when I'm around." She pointed a fork at her friends. "I can tell you that I'm pretty sure Clark didn't help matters."

Sandy snorted. "Clark rarely helps matters."

"True statement, right there," Michelle agreed.

"Just be your charming self, Ems." Sandy smiled at her and Emily was instantly grateful—for about the billionth time in her life—to have these two women as friends. With a wink, Sandy added, "You'll wear her down eventually."

"Ha ha." Emily gave a shrug. "I hope you're right, though. We're going to be working together pretty often. I'd like it to be pleasant, you know?"

"Of course," Michelle said. "No problem. You just get things started on Tuesday. Right?"

"What things?" Emily asked.

"Winning her over," Michelle responded with a wide smile and a waggle of her eyebrows.

━◆━

"Ms. Gardner? Your eleven o'clock is here." Amusement tugged up the corner of Catherine's mouth as she listened to her intercom. It was obvious that Beverly, the volunteer working the front desk this morning, had worked in a professional office setting for years before she retired. They were casual at Junebug.

First-name basis, joking and laughing—easygoing. But Beverly always called her Ms. Gardner and acted in a hugely professional capacity at all times. Occasionally, Catherine wanted to tell her it was okay to lighten up. Most of the time, though, she liked the formality of it.

"I'll be right out," she said, grabbing several sheets off the printer on the credenza behind her. The credenza that was actually a rectangular folding table and shook perilously the entire time the printer was printing. Catherine had mentioned to Jessica more than once that she was willing to spend her own money and get some nicer office furniture, but Jessica didn't want that.

"We can't look too well-appointed," she'd explained. "The animals need the money and if we have nice furniture and look too put-together, people will donate less. We're needy and we need to look like we are."

She was right. Catherine knew that. But she also believed in working hard and saving money to get something you wanted. It was a lesson she'd learned from her mother as she grew up as the younger of two girls with a single mom. If you wanted something, you worked hard, you saved up, and you went and got it. It was the reason she had a second job, the reason she'd always had a second job.

Pulling on a drawer, she winced as it made a metal-on-metal shriek. "I swear this desk is older than I am," she muttered, yanking a manila folder from inside, noting that she needed more. She jotted a reminder in her phone to stop at Staples on the way home. There were some things she *would* buy on her own. What Jessica didn't know wouldn't hurt her.

The printouts tucked into the last new manila folder, Catherine stood and headed out toward the lobby. Her path down the hall gave her a full view of the front desk and, in addition, anybody standing at the front desk. In this case, Emily, who was leaning her forearms on the surface and talking to Regina, the volunteer working with Beverly today.

Catherine didn't intend to scrutinize her, but that's exactly what she did, even as she slowed her pace just a bit to accommodate the roaming of her eyes.

Emily seemed to be a pro at blending casual and upper-class attire. Catherine had learned this in their two previous meetings. Today, she wore black boots that stopped just below her knees. They weren't cheap. Catherine's knowledge of shoes told her that. Tucked into the boots were dark jeans, snug, and very complimentary to Emily's behind. Catherine chewed on her bottom lip as she noticed. On top was a tunic-length sweater with purple and black chevron stripes, the sleeves so long that Emily had the ends of them grasped in each hand as she spoke with Regina. Her dark hair was pulled back in a simple ponytail and what Catherine could only assume was a diamond stud glittered in the exposed ear she could see.

In a nutshell, Emily looked fantastic. Classy, casual, sexy.

Catherine chose to pretend she didn't think that last descriptor.

Taking a deep breath, she quickened her pace and entered the lobby just as Emily turned to her and caught her gaze, her face brightening noticeably, her smile widening as she gave Catherine a quick up-and-down. To her horror, Catherine felt her face warm, but tried to cover by holding out her hand.

"Ms. Breckenridge."

Emily rolled her eyes, but continued to grin as she took Catherine's hand in her own firm, warm grip. "Haven't we been through this already? I'm Emily. Remember?" She poked herself in the chest. "Emily." Turning to Regina, she added, "We go way back, me and Cat."

"To last week," Regina supplied, and Emily laughed.

"Exactly. You get me, Regina."

Catherine shook her head and did her best to keep her own amusement at bay as she saw Regina's face turn pink. Probably much like her own had just done. Emily Breckenridge sure knew how to dole out the compliments. "Let's sit in the conference room," she said, holding an arm out toward the proper door.

"Sure." Emily pulled a leather portfolio from the surface of the lobby desk and walked ahead of Catherine, who did her best to keep her gaze at eye level.

Once in the conference room, it was much easier to focus on the task at hand. They sat side by side and Catherine pulled the printed sheets from the manila folder while Emily did the same from her portfolio. Before sharing them with Emily, Catherine set them on the table and laid her palm flat against them.

Pressing her lips together, she took a moment, then said, "You know, this is new. This sharing of information, the meeting, the overview. I've been here for several years and I've never once sat down with Clark to go over figures."

Emily's eyes were a rich, warm brown, like the baking chocolate Catherine's grandma used for cake baked from scratch. Her gaze held Catherine's as Emily nodded. One corner of her mouth lifted in a half-grin as she said simply, "I know. I'm not Clark."

Immediately chagrined, Catherine felt her entire body flush with heat...and not the good kind. What was it with this woman and her ability to make Catherine blush? Before she could analyze it further or make any attempt at a recovery, Emily closed a hand over her forearm.

"Hey. I didn't mean to embarrass you. You were merely making an observation. I'm sorry."

Catherine gave one nod, carefully extricated her arm, and spread the papers out so Emily could see them. She needed to focus on the business of things, not the warmth of Emily's hand or the pull of her eyes or that damn smile. This was ridiculous, and it needed to stop. Right now. "So, I've printed out the figures going back five years…"

Emily watched the shift in Catherine as if she was observing one of those sand art toys. Just a slight tilt and the colors changed, the shapes morphed, and then the entire thing was markedly different than it had just been. Catherine's demeanor did the same thing. She'd gone from almost friendly straight back to cool businesswoman. Why she couldn't be both, Emily wasn't sure, but it was apparently one or the other. *Something to work on…*

They got down to business, literally, comparing figures, discussing dates, going over the history of the Breckenridge Foundation and Junebug Farms. Before they knew it, almost an hour had passed and both of them gave a little start when the door opened. Jessica Barstow poked her auburn head in and grinned. "Hey there, Emily."

"Hi, Jessica," Emily sat back in her chair, happy to have somebody come in and break up the tension in the air. "What's new?"

"Not much. Catherine said you were coming in to go over past figures?"

Emily gave a nod. "I'm sure it will shock you to hear that my brother did not have a lot of information to pass along to me." She said it with a purposeful grin, which Jessica returned, but inside, the fact bugged the crap out of her. Clark had acted like little more than a figurehead and she was baffled as to how her parents had let him represent them and the Foundation for so long without calling him out. He knew next to nothing about what the Foundation gave to Junebug, how often, or anything pertinent. She'd gone in fairly blind. "I thought it made sense to go over some details with Catherine here so we're all on the same page and I can make sure Junebug gets what it needs from us."

Emily didn't know Jessica well, but she knew the face of a pleased woman when she saw it. That was Jessica at that moment. Pleased and…impressed, maybe? Good. At least Emily had accomplished that.

"That's terrific," Jessica said, then glanced up at the clock on the wall. "You guys headed to lunch after?"

"When we finish up here, that was the plan. Would you care to join us?" Emily was surprised to be struck by the realization that she was only being polite. She wanted Catherine all to herself at lunch, which was not good. (Sandy and Michelle were going to kill her.) Silently, she wished for Jessica to say yes.

Jessica looked from Emily to Catherine, then back. Then at Catherine again. A glance at Catherine told Emily she was studying the numbers on the sheet in front of her. When Emily looked back up, Jessica was nodding. "I'd love to. Just let me take care of a couple things. Be right back." With a quick wave, she backed out of the room and shut the door with a click. Emily was confused by her own disappointment.

Silence reigned for several beats before she turned to Catherine and asked, "That was okay, wasn't it? Inviting her? I didn't even think about it." And that was the truth. Maybe Catherine and Jessica didn't get along. Maybe they hated each other. Maybe this would be the most awkward lunch in the history of all lunches.

"Oh, no, it's fine. It's good. No problem." Catherine gave a cool smile and gathered up her papers. "Let me go drop these in my office and get my coat, and we'll go, okay? Meet you at the front desk."

Emily stood in the doorway of the conference room and watched her go, watched the gentle sway of her hips as she crossed the lobby and disappeared down the hall to her office. When she looked up, she locked eyes with Jessica, who was coming from a different direction and had—as far as Emily could tell—totally busted her watching Catherine. Doing her best to shake it off, Emily smiled and said to Jessica, "I was thinking Magnolia's for lunch. Yes?"

━◆━

The best thing about Magnolia's, in Jessica's mind, was that they were fast. While she very much enjoyed the chance to spend some time with Emily Breckenridge—pick her brain, plead her case, feel her out—there was also a ton to do back at the shelter. It didn't take long, though, for her to set aside her time worries and just listen…and also try not to let any surprise show on her face. Emily was kind of brilliant, not to mention creative and seemingly genuine.

"Catherine, what do you think of the fundraisers?" It was the second time Emily had made an attempt to pull Catherine—who had remained fairly silent even while paying attention—into the conversation. Jessica watched Emily as she watched Catherine and wondered if something had happened she didn't know about.

"Well," Catherine said, then picked up her napkin and wiped the corner of her mouth. "Obviously, I think they're necessary.

You almost always bring in more money when you have some kind of hook. Like the fashion show."

"That was amazing," Emily said with a grin, then took a bite of her sandwich. "Different and fun. Was it worth it?"

Catherine nodded. "It was."

Jessica added, "We'll definitely do it on a larger scale in the summer when we can spread it out on the grounds instead of being limited to the lobby."

"And who came up with the idea?" Emily asked, her eyes on Catherine as if she expected it was her.

"One of our volunteers," Jessica said. "Ashley."

Emily pointed with a grin. "The one who keeps losing that adorable little dog that's in love with Catherine?"

Jessica nodded, noting the slight pink flush of Catherine's cheeks, the way she didn't look at Emily. "That's the one. She was mortified."

"She was. But the whole incident added a fun element of unpredictability to the event, so…" Emily lifted one shoulder in a half-shrug. "Chalk it up to comic relief." She glanced at Catherine again as Jessica watched how she seemed to study Catherine's face, looking for…something.

Interesting.

The rest of the lunch didn't last long, as both Jessica and Emily checked their watches at the same time, then laughed at the tandem gestures. After some good-natured arguing over the bill, Jessica won out and they all headed back to Junebug. Emily said her good-byes, and if she hadn't been looking for it, Jessica might have missed the way her eyes lingered on Catherine a bit longer than normal.

She'd say it again: *interesting…*

⊷◆⊶

"That was good, huh?" Jessica posed the question as she held the door open for Catherine.

"Yeah. It was." Catherine stepped in ahead of her and waved to Maggie Simon in the gift shop as they walked past.

"I like Emily. She seems to get it. I think this is going to be good for the shelter."

Catherine nodded her agreement, but said nothing. Emily was much more engaged than Clark had ever been. She asked insightful questions and seemed to really listen when Jessica talked about the ins and outs of running Junebug, what they needed most, the pitfalls—all those details. Catherine had been quiet for much of lunch, tossing in her two cents when asked for it, but was honestly still a little stung by Emily's chastising of her. Again. Still, these were the times when Jessica was in her element and, as always, it had been a pleasure to watch, so Catherine had tried to set her focus there, watched as Jessica's face lit up, her gestures became animated, and her blue eyes sparkled.

"She's a lot smarter than her brother, that's for sure," Jessica added, lowering her voice.

Catherine snorted a laugh. "Doesn't take much. We now know who got the brains in the family."

"And the looks."

Catherine didn't respond as they crossed the lobby.

"Oh, don't tell me you still haven't noticed. Or have you gone blind in the past week?"

A sudden flurry of more-barking-than-usual pierced the air, saving Catherine from having to answer. Both of them looked toward the dog wing to see the double doors had swung open as somebody exited. Lisa stood, holding a leash with both hands, fighting the little brown and white dog at the end of it, who had obviously seen his love. He barked nonstop, his brown eyes fixed on Catherine.

"There's your boyfriend," Jessica said with a laugh. "You'd better go say hi before he ruptures something trying to get to you."

Catherine didn't hesitate. In fact, she was surprised to realize she was happy to see the little terrier. She pushed through the doors and raised her eyebrows at Lisa.

"Sorry," Lisa said with a shrug. "He was fine until he saw you."

Catherine squatted down in front of him. "What's your deal, little guy?" And just like that, the dog was quiet. He sat calmly, his little half-tail sliding back and forth along the floor like a tiny broom, his excitement to see Catherine making his body tremble, but he stayed quiet. His brown eyes looked directly into Catherine's, and something in her shifted with an almost-audible click. She glanced up at Lisa and reached for the leash.

"I'll take him for a bit. If that's okay."

Lisa smiled. "Absolutely." She handed the leash over. "He's all yours."

"Come on, pal," Catherine said and turned to head toward her office. The little dog fell into step next to her, walking like he'd always been right there by her side.

Like he belonged there.

Once in her office, Catherine closed the door, then unclipped the leash. "Don't give me any problems, okay? You find a spot, lie down, and be a good boy. I've got work to do." He sat at her feet and looked up at her as if every word she said was the most important thing he'd ever heard. She couldn't help but smile, and she bent down to fondle his velvety ear between her fingers. In response, he pushed his head against her hand. *Oh, man. I am in trouble here.*

The afternoon melted away like fluffy snow in the spring sunshine. When her phone rang nearly three hours later, Catherine had almost finished answering her e-mail and the dog was napping under her desk, his little chin warmly draped across one of Catherine's high-heeled feet. She picked up the handset just as there was a soft knock on the door.

"Come in," she said to the door. Then, "Catherine Gardner," into the phone. She pulled her glasses off and pushed her fingertips into her right eyelid as Lisa peeked her head into the office. Catherine indicated the empty chairs in front of her desk as she listened to the voice on the phone.

"Hi, sweetie. I tried your cell, but it went straight to voicemail." Catherine suddenly felt warm and safe, as she always did when she heard her mom. "We still on for tonight?"

"Absolutely. I'll pick you up around 6:30?"

"Perfect. Where are you taking me?"

"Well, if I told you that, it wouldn't be a birthday surprise, now, would it?"

"Nothing too expensive. Promise me."

"I promise you nothing but a wonderful dinner with your favorite youngest daughter."

They hung up and Catherine, smile still in place, turned her attention to Lisa.

"It's dinner time," Lisa said by way of explaining her presence. "I came to get the dog."

Catherine's eyes widened as she looked at her watch. "Wow. Where did the afternoon go?" Then she bit her bottom lip and pointed down at her desk.

Lisa furrowed her brow, momentarily confused, then seemed to get it. She slid off her chair and knelt down on the floor to peek under Catherine's desk. Catherine peeked from her own spot.

The dog slept soundly, eyes closed, a gentle snuffling sound emanating with each breath, his chin still draped over Catherine's shoe.

Lisa looked up at her and mouthed, "Oh, my God."

Catherine nodded. "I know," she said quietly. Doubling over from her chair, she gently ran her fingers down the dog's back. "Hey there, pal. It's time for dinner. Are you hungry?" At the H word, his eyes popped open and Catherine couldn't help but laugh. He came out from under the desk, stretched languorously, then shook his entire body awake. Catherine handed the leash to Lisa.

"Come on, buddy," Lisa said, giving the leash a gentle tug. The dog looked up at her, then back at Catherine, and Catherine felt a little squeeze on her heart.

"It's okay. Go ahead." She gave him a smile and he went, albeit reluctantly. Catherine was not happy to realize she had a hard time watching him leave. She pulled in a big lungful of air and let it out slowly, not wanting to admit to herself that she knew exactly where this was going.

CHAPTER SEVEN

DENISE GARDNER WAS TIRED. It had been a long day at the store and she'd been on her feet for most of it. While the average shopper felt that mid- to late-November was the start of the holiday season, this was not so for those in retail. The store Denise managed—a Big Lots just outside the city—had been bringing in and stocking holiday items for the past two months. Which was ridiculous, but typical.

She didn't love her job, but she was good at it and she had a lot of time invested. She had benefits (not easily acquired in retail) and a 401(k) (also hard to come by), so she didn't plan on going anywhere until she decided to retire. Probably another ten years or so, as she was only fifty-five. She snorted aloud at that thought. There were days, like today, when she felt much closer to eighty.

She pulled a turquoise sweater over her head and checked herself in the full-length mirror of her bedroom. *Not bad.* She may be on the far side of middle age, but she could still clean up nice. She leaned in closer to her reflection. Her hair could use a coloring, as it seemed the gray was taking over her part, but she'd have to wait until her next paycheck. Too many bills due this week. She touched up her makeup, added some more mascara and a fresh coat of subtle lipstick, then stood back and looked again. *Not bad,* she thought for the second time. A spritz of the much-too-pricey perfume Catherine had given her for Mother's Day and a pair of gold hoop earrings topped off the outfit. She was ready.

Catherine would take her someplace upscale and too expensive—Denise knew her daughter well—and Denise would protest a little, but for the most part, she'd keep quiet. As her friend, Jen, always said when she complained about Catherine spending too much money on her, "It makes her happy. Let her pamper you. You deserve it." So, Denise would press her lips together, swallow her protests, and enjoy an evening out with her daughter—something she didn't get often enough, if she was being honest.

Outside, she heard a car slowing and Denise ran her hands down her sides, gave her reflection a nod of approval, and headed down the hall of her tiny house to the living room. A glance out the window confirmed that Catherine had arrived, and Denise took a moment just to watch her daughter's approach up the front sidewalk.

She was a stunningly beautiful woman and Denise would think so even if she hadn't given birth to her, but it was her bearing that drew people to her. She was of average height, but the way she carried herself made her seem taller. Regal was the word that always came to mind when Denise saw her from afar. Her posture was poised, confident. Denise wasn't sure where she'd learned it, but if she herself had had anything to do with the aura Catherine projected, she deserved a huge pat on the back. Her youngest daughter commanded instant respect.

Two raps sounded on the door before it opened and Catherine called out, "Mom?"

"Right here, honey. Hi."

"Hi." Catherine smiled and gave her mother a kiss on the cheek. "Wow! You look terrific. That sweater is a great color on you."

Denise smiled and even blushed a bit as she opened the small coat closet. "Thank you. My daughter bought this for me."

"Well, your daughter has impeccable taste, evidently."

"Just ask her. She'll tell you." Denise winked and shrugged on her coat.

Twenty minutes later, Catherine pulled her car into a spot in the parking lot of Jade, a restaurant Denise had heard and read a lot about, but had never been to.

"Oh, honey. We're eating here?" She leaned forward and looked out the windshield at the soft purple neon lighting the outside of the old brick structure.

"We are. Is that okay?" Catherine turned the car off and looked at her, eyebrows raised.

"Absolutely. I've always wanted to try this place."

"Me, too."

Once inside, they were seated quickly at a cozy, reserved table for two in the back, and the waiter had delivered their drink order—a Cosmo for Denise and a glass of Cabernet for Catherine. They held their glasses aloft.

"Happy birthday to my favorite mom of all the moms," Catherine said, and they touched their glasses in a happy little clink.

"So, what's new with you?" Denise asked. "I feel like we haven't caught up in ages."

As Catherine talked about work and updated her on a couple of friends, Denise settled into her happy place. The vodka in the Cosmo slowly warmed her from the inside and she kept her eyes on her daughter. *This is what life is all about*, she thought, and couldn't keep the grin off her face.

When the waiter returned, they placed their orders and returned their attention to one another.

"What's the plan for Thanksgiving?" Catherine asked.

"The usual, I think. Grandma's." Denise looked up. "Why? You have other plans?"

"Nope." Catherine shook her head. "Anna had the crazy idea that I'd go to her mom's."

"Ah." Denise gave a nod, but said nothing more. Anna was a nice girl. She'd met her on several occasions during the short relationship she'd had with Catherine, but she knew after the first five minutes that she wasn't The One. Sadly, it had taken Catherine much longer to come to that conclusion. "Is it getting any easier at work?"

Catherine shrugged, didn't look up from her drink. "It's fine."

"Convincing."

That got a small smile. "She can be a little…relentless."

"You think?" Denise laughed. "She is not the one for you, honey. And that's all I'll say." She remained good-natured about the subject, but inside, she'd been utterly relieved to learn of the breakup. Catherine deserved so much more than the malleable Anna. Denise would never say such a thing, of course, but that's what she thought after only a short visit or two. Catherine needed a challenge, somebody who wouldn't let her get away with calling all the shots. Somebody who would give her a run for her money. Anna worshipped her and that was exactly the problem. "So. Tell me what else is going on."

"Well." Catherine seemed to steel herself before looking Denise in the eyes. "I've been thinking about another dog."

Denise tried to hide her surprise, but knew immediately that she'd failed. Her eyebrows shot up to her hairline and her glass paused halfway to her lips. Catherine looked away, instead continued to focus on her wine, and that's how Denise knew this was serious. "Oh, yeah? Tell me."

Catherine swallowed hard and seemed to need a moment to get her bearings, which was understandably difficult for her mother to watch. Pablo's death had hit her hard. Harder than Denise had expected and certainly harder than Catherine had been prepared for. Her daughter was tough as nails, not a woman who was emotional or easily affected by emotional things. She was cerebral, in her head, and when she needed to deal with something, she did so quietly and alone. She'd always been like that; Denise was one of the few people in the world who understood these facts. But losing Pablo had rocked her more than either of them had expected. Denise had never seen her daughter sob that way, not once. She rarely cried, but this had completely devastated her. She'd reverted into herself, hadn't spoken to anybody for nearly a week, to the point Denise had become worried. She'd called her high school friend who was now a doctor, and asked if there was anything she could do. As a mother, Denise had been simultaneously heartbroken for her child and terrified with worry.

Catherine had pulled through, had come out the other side eventually. Dark circles underlined her eyes and she was several pounds thinner, but she emerged, and gradually regained her strength.

"There's a particular one at the shelter. He's small, which is weird for me, but..." She gazed off into the restaurant before bringing her eyes back and looking at Denise directly. "There's something about him."

"You felt that way about Pablo," Denise pointed out. "And look how great he turned out to be."

Catherine nodded. "I know."

After a beat, Denise supplied, "But?" Her heart squeezed as she watched Catherine's blue eyes, so much like her father's, mist up.

"I'm scared." She said it so quietly, Denise almost didn't hear.

"I know, baby. I know."

"I'm just…not sure."

Denise set her glass down and dipped her head to catch her daughter's eye. "Tell me this: would you trade the time you had with Pablo? Given the option and considering all the pain you went through with his loss, would you change any of it?"

"No," Catherine said without hesitation.

"Well. There you go." Denise let that sink in, watched it take root in Catherine's brain.

Catherine took a sip of her wine and gave a slight nod. "Yeah," was all she said.

"Only you can know if it's right, honey."

"Yeah," she said again.

"How's Jess?" Denise asked after a beat or two, changing the subject.

"She's great." The waiter stopped by with their food. Once their plates were settled in front of them, Catherine went on. "We had an interesting change. Remember Clark Breckenridge?"

"That cad that can't keep his eyes or hands to himself?" Denise asked, recalling the name from several stories Catherine had shared in the past.

Catherine laughed. "I love that you call him a cad. Are we in 1947? But yes. Him. Well, I think our complaints about him were finally taken seriously." Catherine took a bite of her dinner. "I mean, we can't possibly be the only people to say something, can we? How many other organizations do the Breckenridges donate to?"

"Dozens, I'm sure. Maybe more."

"Last week, he scheduled a meeting with Jessica and brought in his sister, Emily. Jess had me sit in. Anyway, he said they'd done some 'restructuring' at the Foundation and that Emily would be taking over his duties there."

Denise blinked at her. "So...no more grab-ass from him?"

Catherine laughed. "I don't think so."

"What's the sister like?"

Something zipped across Catherine's face, but it was too quick for Denise to identify it. "Hard to say. I've only met her a couple of times. She already seems to be much more into her job than Clark ever was, so...I guess we'll see."

"Well, I am happy for all your volunteers and future volunteers who won't be subjected to that creep. And I hope the sister—what's her name?"

"Emily."

"Oh, that's pretty." Denise studied Catherine's face as she spoke. "I hope the sister turns out to be...valuable."

Catherine met Denise's eyes, then looked away. "Me, too."

⚓

Later that night, Catherine was home alone, having dropped her mother off. They'd had a great time, which they always did, and not for the first time, she was thankful to have the kind of relationship they had. Her mom had her quirks, as everybody did, but they rarely butted heads. And her mother was beyond supportive. Catherine was surprised to realize how good it had felt to talk to her about getting another dog.

Plopping onto the couch, she picked up the remote and clicked on the TV. Toeing off her shoes, she stretched out and propped her feet on the coffee table as she absently thumbed through channels. In her peripheral vision, she caught sight of the big, puffy dog bed tucked in the corner of the room. That led her eyes to the large basket of dog toys across in another corner. She hadn't been able to bring herself to pack them away. She'd taken care of the food and water dishes in the kitchen, but the bed? No. And the toys? Uh-uh. It felt too much like erasing Pablo from the house and she couldn't bear that.

Cocking her head to the side a bit, she tried to picture Geronimo (because, damn that Emily Breckenridge, that was his name in her head now) crashed out on the dog bed after a long day of hiking or playing tennis ball in the backyard or walking the neighborhood. It wasn't difficult, and the vision brought a tiny smile to her face. Her phone beeped, pulling her back to the present. A text from her mother.

Thank you so much for a lovely evening. 😊

Catherine grinned and typed back.

You're very welcome. Happy birthday.

Another text came after a moment. *Thank you. I love you, honey.*

Love you, too, Catherine texted back.

She tossed her phone on the table next to her feet and returned to channel surfing. Again, her eyes were drawn to the canine items still strewn around her living room, but this time, she felt the certainty that came with the making of an important decision. She stopped on HGTV, set the remote down, and picked her phone up once again. Opening the Notes app, she began to make a list of things she'd need to get.

Food. Treats. Collar. Sweater.

The last one made her grin like a fool.

CHAPTER EIGHT

THE CONFERENCE ROOMS HOUSED in the Breckenridge Building were kind of pretentious.

Emily had always thought so, at least a little bit, but after being in Junebug Farms's conference room, with its nice table, inexpensive chairs, and pictures of animals on the walls, this one seemed almost haughty. The mahogany table was polished so intensely, Emily could fix her makeup in the reflection it tossed back at her. The chairs not only swiveled, but rocked and were upholstered in a buttery burgundy leather that was so soft and comfortable, nobody wanted to leave their seat. The large windows overlooked an adjacent park, complete with a wooded sanctuary and several birdfeeders that were currently being visited by no less than a dozen birds.

It was actually a gorgeous setting, and Emily wasn't sure why she all of a sudden had decided to hate it. Maybe it was the obvious money that had gone into its décor. Nothing was cheap. In fact, most everything was top-of-the-line, including the lead crystal water glasses and matching pitcher that sat in the center of the table next to the tray of very expensive morning pastries, one of which Clark was happily stuffing into his mouth.

They were part of this world, the expensive things. Emily knew this, had grown up with them. Maybe it was because, as the new head of the Breckenridge Foundation, she'd spent the last week and a half going into the offices of organizations that *needed* their donations. And if you are in *need* of donations, you cannot afford to feed your visitors fresh croissants and artisan coffee each morning. If the fabric on your chair rips, you shrug, or better yet, grab some duct tape. You use the ink in your printer and the toner in your copier until every conceivable drop has been sucked out of the cartridge. As somebody who knew she was privileged, but had never really thought about it, this new job was eye opening.

"Good morning." Emily's mother, Cheryl Breckenridge was impeccably dressed, as usual, in crisp black pants and an elegant royal blue silk blouse. She carried a leather portfolio and took a seat across the table from Emily and Clark. While she projected the refined air of "experienced businesswoman," she visibly softened when her eyes landed on her children. It would have been easy to be the stereotypical wealthy woman, poised, regal, and slightly condescending, but Cheryl Breckenridge, while easily able to pull of poised and regal, never looked down on others. It was the thing Emily admired most about her.

She set the portfolio down on the table in front of her, folded her hands on top of it, and said, "So. How are things? How has the shift in positions been perceived? Tell me how it's going out there."

Out of respect, Emily waited a beat to allow Clark to chime in first, as he was not only older, but the one who'd been "shifted," so to speak. When that beat passed in silence, she spoke up. "For me, it's all been going very well, very smoothly." She listed the seven organizations she'd met with over the past two and a half weeks, along with the six more she had scheduled. She told her mother honestly how she'd been received and whether she'd heard any rumblings about the changes in the Foundation (she'd heard very little). "Everybody has been very welcoming."

"Of course they have," Clark said around a mouthful of chocolate croissant. "We give them money. What are they gonna do, turn you away?"

Emily opened her mouth to give a retort, but her mother beat her to it.

"Excuse me, young man, but a large cause of this entire reorganization has been you and your reprehensibly embarrassing behavior, so if I were you, I'd dispense with the sarcasm." Cheryl didn't raise her voice. She didn't need to; her tone was icy and her eyes flashed fire so very clearly, Clark would've had to be blind not to understand he had ticked her off.

"Yes, ma'am," he said, and Emily flashed to him being eleven again, scolded for playing catch in the house with his buddies and shattering the glass in their mother's favorite picture frame. "Sorry."

Turning back to Emily, she indicated for her to go on.

"I have additional meetings this week with The Carter House and Junebug Farms. I've been to both places already, The Carter House once and Junebug…I think three times. They do a great job there. I love it. I'm interested in seeing if we can increase our donations this year."

Clark snorted at that. Both Emily and her mother looked at him.

"What?" he asked, all wide-eyed innocence. "I'm just laughing because she goes to Junebug for the hot accountant, not the shelter itself."

Emily felt scalding heat flush her face in an instant. "You are unbelievable."

Clark shrugged, his smug smile still in place. "Just telling the truth."

"Not everybody is like you, Clark." Emily was seething now. He could embarrass her all he wanted, but not in front of their mother, and not when it came to something this important. She'd worked hard to show Cheryl she was capable of taking on a bigger role in the family business and she was not about to let Clark wreck her chances of succeeding. "I don't hit on everything that moves."

"No, just the girls."

Emily growled through her teeth, trying hard not to let her anger take over, trying hard not to revert back to their childhood when he would poke her and poke her and poke her until she lashed out with her fists because he made her so mad. She never hurt him; he was too strong, and he'd laugh off her attempts at striking him, which only made her angrier.

"Enough." That one word from Cheryl was all it took. She stared at her children, looking from one to the other and back until they subtly squirmed in their chairs.

"She doesn't even like me anyway," Emily mumbled, her childhood need to get the last word in still accessible somewhere in her brain.

Cheryl merely arched an eyebrow at her.

"Sorry," Emily muttered.

After another beat of silence, where the two Breckenridge kids wilted under the gaze of their mother, the meeting continued. There were no more snide comments and no insults lobbed back and forth. Cheryl nodded her approval of the report and gave the signal that they were finished. Clark exited the conference room like he was being chased. Emily sat quietly, subtly shaking her head at the way she'd let him get under her skin.

"I don't have anything to worry about, do I?" Cheryl's words startled her and she looked up, surprised.

"What do you mean?"

"With the person your brother mentioned. The 'hot accountant?'" Her mother made air quotes around the words at the same time Emily tried to smother a wince. How dare Clark marginalize Catherine that way?

"No, Mom. I promise. Clark's just being a jerk." She shook her head, irritated by the whole thing.

"Good. We managed to keep your brother's…transgressions under wraps for the most part, but it leaked to a small number of people. We don't need a similar situation with you. We have a reputation to uphold and I don't want to have to worry about another black mark on it. Are we clear?"

Emily nodded. "Yes, ma'am."

"Good. Now." Cheryl reached across the table as she stood and grasped Emily's forearm. "Keep up the good work, darling. I've heard nothing but positive things." She smiled, gave Emily a quick wink, scooped up her belongings, and was gone.

Emily sat for a moment in the empty conference room, a mix of emotions swirling around in her head. On the one hand, she was very happy to have gotten the approval of her mother. Oh, she gave it when it was deserved, but it could be hard to come by. Emily had many examples from her childhood of struggling to get a "good work" from her mother and missing it by *that much*. On the other hand, her mother was checking up on her. If she was to think it through—*really* think it through—she'd understand that *of course* her mother was checking up on her. Any employee would be monitored in their first few weeks of a new job. Instead, she allowed herself three minutes to *not* think it through, to just be annoyed…and mildly insulted that her mother didn't trust her.

Emily had a meeting scheduled with Catherine tomorrow to go over the fundraisers scheduled for the New Year celebration. This way, Breckenridge would have the opportunity to get in and sponsor, donate, advertise, and help out in any way and Emily wanted to do that. She'd had so much fun at the fashion show; she planned to participate as often as she could to help get those animals loving homes, Catherine's dislike of her be damned.

Pushing herself to her feet, Emily headed back to her own office and pretended Catherine's unfair assessment of her didn't rankle.

⊷

"What about finding ways to help the public participate more?" Emily posed the question and glanced around the table. The expressions she saw were curious and she liked that. Jessica squinted slightly. Catherine cocked her head to one side as if waiting for Emily to elaborate. David Peters, who was the head of fundraising at Junebug Farms, had the beginnings of a grin forming. She'd heard of him in the past; he'd worked with her father more than once before taking up the mantle here at the shelter. In amazing shape, he was one of those guys that you merely had to glance at to know he spent an inordinate amount of time at the gym, probably with the free weights, and he was knowledgeable and super friendly, with enthusiasm that was contagious.

"How do you mean?" he asked, his deep voice resonating, not unpleasantly, in the pit of her stomach.

"I mean maybe have a contest. Ask them to suggest new ways to raise money." She looked at Jessica. "You said one of your volunteers came up with the idea of the fashion show, right?"

Jessica nodded. Catherine jotted something down on the pad in front of her.

"And you said it made money." Emily focused on Catherine who glanced up and realized the question was directed at her.

"It did," she confirmed. "Quite a bit, considering it was an experiment."

"So, what if we do that? Set up a way for your members, your random visitors, your kids who come on field trips, all of them, to suggest ideas. That, in itself—the contest—will also bring awareness. Advertise it in your mailers. Put it on the website. Send some e-mail blasts. Tweet it. Put it on Tumblr and Instagram. Even go old-school and place a box near the front desk for handwritten entries." Emily watched them absorb the idea, warm to it. "I mean, it's just a suggestion and I'm certainly not as well-versed in the area of nonprofits as you guys are, but... if the idea is to bring in more people, which would bring in more money, it seems like it's worth a try. Maybe?"

She watched the nods go around the table. Even the reserved Ms. Gardner seemed to like her suggestions.

"I'll sit with Anna," David said, talking more to Jessica. "See what she thinks. I like it. I think we can make it work." Turning back to Emily, he smiled widely, his teeth seeming extra bright in contrast to his dark skin, and pointed a finger at her. "I like your fire."

Emily returned the smile, tilted her head in gratitude. "Why, thank you."

Jessica nodded her agreement. "Seriously. This is great, Emily. It's not enough that you're our biggest contributor, but you also want to help us be even more successful. It's amazing. I wish everybody we worked with had your drive."

Cheeks hotly pink, Emily held Jessica's gaze and said softly, "Thank you. I just really like what you guys do." She tapped her chest where her heart was. "I love the animals."

"That's our favorite characteristic in anybody we deal with," Jessica said with a warm smile, and Emily got a quick jolt of realization about how Jessica was able to garner so much love and attention for her shelter. She was kind, charming, and just the tiniest bit manipulative—the perfect combination for somebody who constantly needed money. "So," she said, piling her things up in front of her. "Let me take you to lunch. Do you have time for that, Emily?"

"I do," Emily said, understanding suddenly that she really liked these people. "Can we all go?" She surprised herself by looking directly at Catherine. "Can you come, too?"

Catherine blinked at her, those blue eyes mesmerizing, then gave a nod.

"Excellent. You guys choose the place."

Half an hour later, they grabbed seats in a small café around the corner from the shelter. Emily had never been there before, never even knew it existed, but one spoon of the potato and cheese soup she'd ordered made her very nearly swoon off her chair, and she made a mental note to come back here. Often. Possibly every day.

Once they were all chewing happily, Jessica posed a question to Emily. "I know you're new to this position at your family's foundation. What did you do before that?"

"I was in the marketing department."

"Well, that explains the great advertising ideas," David said before biting into his turkey club.

"I actually have a marketing degree. That's been my thing for a few years. When my mother needed a solution to her..." Emily let her words trail off, paused, but it occurred to her that the reason for the changing of the guards at the Foundation was no secret, she continued. "A solution to her Clark problem, I sort of lobbied hard for the spot."

"You have a marketing degree?" It was the first time Catherine had spoken in a long while. Emily noticed she seemed to be the kind of person who sat along the sidelines and observed, so her voice was a bit of a surprise. Also showing surprise was the expression on her face.

"I do." Emily almost added, *Does that surprise you? That I actually went to college and got a usable degree rather than being handed a position in my rich family's company?* If they'd been alone, she might have actually said it. Lightly, of course. Instead, she just smiled.

"Why did you want out of the marketing department?" Catherine asked, stabbing a slice of cucumber with a fork.

Emily spooned some soup into her mouth and pondered her answer as she chewed. "I think I'd done all I could there. Breckenridge Associates is so different from Junebug when it comes to things like marketing and advertising. Two different animals, no pun intended. My family's company and all the arms of it that are part of the package can be...a little stuffy. So you can only be so creative with PR before you turn your clients off. Which is unfortunate. I had some great, fun ideas, but they just didn't fly with the older—" she cupped a hand around her mouth "—male, white members of the department."

David chuckled at that.

"For you guys," Emily went on, "I think it's important to make sure you skew a little younger. Junebug was your grandmother's, yes?" She looked to Jessica, who nodded even while seemingly startled Emily knew this information. "I do my research," Emily said with a wink. "Regardless, I think it's important that you make sure you're reaching today's young adults. People in their late twenties and early thirties as well as older. Technology is important. The website. Social media. You need to stay current."

David glanced at Jessica, whose grin was so wide it was almost comical. "I think you might be getting a marriage proposal soon," he joked.

"Seriously," Jessica said, still smiling. "You say exactly the things I have in my head, but can't seem to find time to deal with."

"I can sit with her, go over things and compile a list of ideas." Catherine's voice was low and even and Emily was blindsided by wondering what it would sound like excited. *Or aroused.* She clenched her jaw on the thought.

"I'm good with that," Emily said before she could change her mind. "We could brainstorm." She looked to Catherine for confirmation. Catherine nodded and ate more salad. When she glanced back at Jessica, her expression had changed to something more like worry. Emily read it immediately and held up a hand like a traffic cop stopping a car. "Consider it me volunteering."

Jessica grimaced. "Are you sure? It feels a little like I'm taking advantage of you."

"You are." Emily softened the words with a wink. "But I'm giving you my permission to do just that. So, no worries."

The CEO of the animal shelter didn't look sold, but Emily was okay with that.

"You sure you have time?" Jessica asked Catherine.

"Mm-hmm," was all the answer Catherine gave, and she paired it with a nod as she chewed. When she glanced over at Emily, their eyes held for an extra beat and Emily felt her heart beat speed up just the tiniest bit.

Well, this oughta be interesting.

CHAPTER NINE

CATHERINE HAD MORE THAN one reason to be nervous.

For one thing, she was about to step all over Anna's toes. Public relations was her job at the shelter, after all, and she was not going to like that Catherine stepped in to bat around ideas with Emily. Jessica had pulled her aside after lunch yesterday to make sure she'd been thinking clearly when she offered to brainstorm with Emily. Catherine had brushed it off like it was no big deal, but...Anna was not going to be happy about it. Catherine was going to have to be proactive and talk to her, smooth things over. Soon.

Secondly, she really wasn't creative that way, the way that people in advertising were. She was a numbers girl. She was logic and practicality, not a pie-in-the-sky dreamer who wanted to finger paint the world. What could she possibly bring to the table? Also odd that Jessica knew this about her, yet said nothing...

And third, it was Emily.

Emily.

Emily, who she'd insulted last week.

Emily, who had called her on that insult and put her in her place.

Emily, who seemed to hold no grudge, who was apparently over that whole exchange and had moved on.

Emily, who looked the way she did.

What the hell had Catherine been thinking?

"Well, it's too late now," she muttered as she glanced around her office. It was neat—it always was. She was just going to have to fake her way through the next hour or so. She sucked in a huge breath of air, then let it out slowly. Emily would be here any minute.

The beep from her intercom made her jump and she rolled her eyes at herself even as Lisa's voice came over the speaker. "Hey, Catherine? You in?"

"I am."

"Can you come to my desk for a minute?"

"I've got a meeting in five minutes."

"It'll take two. Promise."

Suppressing a sigh, she said, "Okay. Be right there."

Catherine and Lisa had never been close. In fact, Catherine hadn't really cared for Lisa for a long time. She thought Lisa was brusque, standoffish, and a little bossy. Her opinion had solidified a few months ago when Lisa had accused Catherine of being totally unconcerned about Clark Breckenridge's harassment of one of Junebug's volunteers. Lisa was completely wrong in her assumption, but when Catherine thought about it, she was able to understand how Lisa may have jumped to the conclusion she had. Catherine'd had no idea at the time that the object of Clark's unwelcome advances had been the woman Lisa was interested in. They'd since hooked up, and Catherine had found Lisa to be much more pleasant.

Now, it seemed, they almost actually liked one another.

Catherine pushed through the double doors of the dog wing, the barking and howling increasing exponentially, as a handful of visitors were wandering from kennel to kennel, which always excited the dogs. Halfway down the aisle was Lisa's desk.

"What's up?" Catherine asked.

Lisa kept her voice low. "Normally, I'd finesse this a little bit, but there's no time. See that man down there on the left?"

Catherine followed her gaze. "With the black jacket?"

"Yes." Barely whispering—which forced Catherine to bend in close in order to hear her—she went on. "This is the second time he's looked at your dog. I know you want him. I put a hold on him for you after the last time you visited him, but that was days ago. I told the guy there's a hold, but if you don't do something soon, I'm gonna let him have him. That dog deserves a home."

Catherine didn't need any clarification on which was "her dog." She simply blinked at Lisa. "You put a hold on him for me?"

Lisa blushed a little, but smiled. "I've seen you with him. He adores you and you want him. Honestly, though? I thought you'd have made a move by now."

Lisa wasn't scolding her, but Catherine felt like she was. And Lisa was right. Catherine had been dragging her feet. She'd been all set to make it official and then she'd started thinking about Pablo and she missed him so badly, her chest ached. *Was it too soon?* she'd started to think. *Maybe it was. Maybe I should wait.*

But seeing Black Jacket Man was all the push she needed.

"He's mine," she said to Lisa. And she was almost shocked to realize she meant it.

"I thought so," Lisa said with a nod and pushed herself up from her chair. "Go to your meeting. I got this."

━◆━

Not surprisingly, when Catherine returned to her office, Emily was occupying one of the chairs. She looked impressive yet casual, and Catherine absently wondered how she was able to pull that off. She herself had never felt able to. She either dressed up or dressed down, but had trouble with that in-between gray area that Emily seemed to inhabit with so little effort.

Today, Emily wore black jeans and black ankle boots. Her black trench-style coat was on the hat rack in the corner of Catherine's office, a black-and-white scarf draped over it. The black-and-white striped hooded sweater she wore was expensive, Catherine could see, but again looked effortlessly casual, the zipper up only halfway, revealing a black cami underneath. Emily's hair was down today, and it was the first time Catherine realized how long it actually was, trailing down her back in dark waves that reached Emily's shoulder blades. Whatever perfume she wore subtly hung in the air. On the floor next to her chair was a small, leather messenger bag.

"Hi there," Catherine said as she came around the desk. She held out a hand.

Emily stood and shook it. "Good morning." Her smile was wide and made her eyes crinkle, Catherine noticed. It was cute.

"Sorry I'm late. Got distracted." Catherine waved a hand near her head, sat and pulled out a pad containing some notes she'd jotted down the night before at home.

"By something worthwhile, I hope. That's the best kind of distraction."

Catherine couldn't help but smile. "I think...very worthwhile." She held up her crossed fingers.

"Excellent."

Catherine looked down at her notes, then back up at Emily. "So...I need to be honest here."

"Okay."

"This is not really my thing, marketing and advertising. You should probably be sitting with Anna St. John, our public relations person."

Emily took that in with a slow nod. She sat forward in her chair, elbows on her knees, and looked intently at Catherine. "So noted. My turn to be honest."

"Okay." Catherine drew the word out.

"I'd rather deal with you."

Was the air in the room suddenly heavy? Catherine wasn't sure, but she was sure she'd stopped breathing for a full five seconds while Emily Breckenridge held her eyes so firmly. *No. No, no, no. We are not going down this path. Stop it, Catherine. Stop it right now.*

The rest of her internal pep talk was cut short by a rap on her doorjamb, and Catherine thanked the Universe for sending Lisa at that moment.

"Hi," Lisa said with a smile. "I'm sorry to interrupt, but..." She held up her hand. In it was the end of a blue leash. "I thought you might want to have this guy here for the rest of the day."

The sudden clicking sound of dog nails on the hard floor kicked into overdrive, as if he was dancing. And in a way, he was, so obvious was his desire to get to Catherine. She literally felt the smile on her face widen, immediately lighter and happier, as if somebody had reached into her brain and pulled any and all negative emotions right out of her head for the day. She came around the desk and took the leash from Lisa, then squatted down to meet her new dog eye to eye.

"Hey there, little guy. How's life?"

The dog responded by bathing her face with kisses, his tail wagging so furiously it swayed his entire body from side to side until she was sure he'd make himself flop over sideways.

"I've got all your paperwork at my desk," Lisa told her. "Just pop by before you leave, okay?"

Catherine looked up at her and smiled, startled to feel her eyes mist. "Thank you, Lisa," she said very quietly.

"You're welcome," Lisa said back, just as quietly. With a nod at Emily, she turned and left.

"You did it?" Emily asked, the expression on her face radiating joy.

"I did." Catherine stood and returned to her chair behind the desk, the dog trailing her like a child following the Pied Piper. "This is Geronimo. Mo for short."

Emily laughed and Catherine instantly loved the sound of it.

"Thank you for the name suggestion. And the push to adopt him. I was really uncertain, but…you helped."

Emily got up and came around the desk. "Well, I think since I'm partially responsible for the adorable pairing of you two, I should get to share in the love." She stepped in so close, right into Catherine's personal space, that for a split second, Catherine was sure Emily was going to kiss her. But just as quickly, Emily dropped into a squat and began loving all over Mo. Catherine stood there, tried to swallow down her own confusion, and reached a hand out to brace herself against the desk. When that didn't help, she sat.

What the hell is wrong with me?

Emily had devolved into baby talking with Mo, so Catherine took a moment to collect herself, her confusion turning into annoyance, because that little display of hers was ridiculous and could not happen again. After another moment, she felt like she'd regained her equilibrium and finally spoke.

"So, let's talk ideas, shall we?" Her voice was a bit brusque, but that was fine. This was business. Time to get down to it. Damn it.

For the next forty-five minutes, they brainstormed. Well, Emily brainstormed and Catherine took notes, added her two cents when she had it to offer, and was basically awed by Emily's creativity. When she finally started to peter out, Catherine had four pages of notes.

"Why did you leave marketing again?" she asked with a chuckle. "You are full of ideas."

"I'm full of something," Emily said with a half-grin.

"Well, this is kind of amazing." Catherine scanned her notes, moving from page to page. "There's some really good stuff here. Anna and David will be thrilled." With a grimace, she reminded Emily, "You really should be talking with one or both of them."

Emily shrugged. "I trust you to pass it along."

"I will." Catherine tried not to dwell on the wrath of Anna she'd most likely have to deal with. She also tried not to dwell on the fact that she had no intention of making any changes to appease Anna. She stood up and held out her hand to Emily. "Thank you so much for your time today and the terrific ideas. I hope you know how much we appreciate it."

Emily shook her hand, and her grip was warm, soft, and firm. "I'm happy to help. Besides, it was fun." She smiled that smile and held Catherine's gaze for a beat longer than normal.

"Mo and I will walk you out."

Mo was a bit of a hellion on the leash, pulling out in front of Catherine, forcing her to wrap the leash around her hand a couple times for a better grip.

"I see you have a little work to do with your new dog," Emily said teasingly.

"Ya think?"

The hallway spilled them into the lobby where Emily seemed just as surprised to see Clark standing at the front desk as Catherine was. He was doing his best to charm the socks off of the volunteers, and judging by all the blushing going on, he was doing a great job. Catherine suppressed the urge to roll her eyes and instead, put on a happy business face while, out of the corner of her eye, she noticed Emily stiffen just slightly.

"Mr. Breckenridge," Catherine said cheerfully. "What a nice surprise."

He shook her hand, his smile wide. "I told you I wouldn't be totally gone. I was in the neighborhood, so thought I'd drop by and say hello, maybe take you to lunch." He gave her a fairly obvious up-and-down and said, "Is it possible you got better looking since I saw you last?" He tossed an unreadable look at Emily, who said nothing, though Catherine could see the muscles in her jaw working.

"Well, that's very nice of you to say. I'm afraid I have to pass on lunch, though. Thanks anyway."

To his credit, Clark looked genuinely disappointed. "Next time then," he said. As if noticing Emily for the first time, he spoke directly to her. "You heading out? I'll walk you to your car." Catherine would've bet money Emily'd prefer anything else, but she gave him a curt nod, then turned to Catherine.

"Thanks for meeting with me. I'll be in touch." Then she lowered herself to Mo's level and spoke to him in a voice Catherine couldn't quite make out. She kissed the top of his head, then stood back up, smiled, and said good-bye.

Catherine watched them go, struck by the complete opposite bearings they each had. Clark moved fluidly, like he hadn't a care in the world, as if everybody was looking at him and he totally knew it. Emily's stride was stiff, angry, and at the door he held open for her she shot him a look could only be labeled a "death glare."

What's that about?

⊷

"What the hell was that about?" Emily hissed at her brother as soon as the doors to Junebug Farms clicked closed behind them.

"What? What was what about?" Clark asked, but his expression told Emily just what he was doing: faking his innocence.

"The asking Catherine to lunch? The *leering* at her?"

"Leering at her? Well, that's an ugly word. I didn't leer at her. And I asked her to lunch because I happen to like her." They reached their cars, parked side by side. Clark turned to her with a smirk and added, "Plus, the bet."

"There is no bet, Clark! God." Emily unlocked her car, got in, and keyed the engine, slamming the door shut on any response her brother might have. He often drove her crazy, but that was the job of big brothers, wasn't it? Sometimes, he was a great guy. But the way he'd looked at Catherine? Ugh. Emily wasn't sure that Catherine had seen it…or all of it, at least. God, he could be such a douche. She backed out of her spot and pulled away before he could catch up with her.

She needed to get as far away from him as she could as quickly as she could.

That's how it was with Clark sometimes.

In the back of her mind, Emily knew that if she was going to be honest with herself, she needed to understand exactly why it bothered her that Clark had been ogling Catherine. True, the ogling was rude. Sexist. Ungentlemanly. But those weren't the real reasons she was so angry with him. There was only one real reason.

It was Catherine.

Emily didn't want him looking at any woman that way, but most of all, she didn't want him looking at *Catherine* that way.

"Why?" she asked out loud as she sat in her car at a red light, rubbing her hands together to create warmth. Why did it matter if Clark—or anybody—eyed Catherine Gardner that way? She didn't belong to Emily. Hell, she didn't really even like Emily— although she'd started to second-guess that assumption today, as they'd worked so well together. Still, they were business acquaintances. Nothing more.

Weren't they?

Did Emily want something more with Catherine, as her mother feared?

There were so many reasons to say no to that question. So many. There was a huge conflict of interest. They had little in common. Their lives were different. Their views were different.

But there was a pull. A definite pull for Emily, something that tugged her toward Catherine. And she had to believe it was there for Catherine as well...otherwise, why offer to meet with her today? She could have very easily put Emily off, let her meet with the others, the ones who were in charge of marketing and advertising and fundraising...all those things that Catherine really had nothing to do with. But she hadn't. She'd offered to sit with Emily. So there was something there for her, too, right?

"I can't think about this. I can't." She shook her head, willing the train of thought to abandon her brain all together. Her brain, in a valiant attempt the thwart her, tossed her an image of Catherine's mouth in that split second Emily had been close enough to kiss her. The way her lips were slightly parted, the fullness of that bottom one... Emily recalled how her heart rate had kicked up what felt like a hundred notches and she'd had to squat down to play with the dog to keep herself from doing something very, very stupid.

Maybe she needed to stay away. That might be the best solution. Remove Catherine from the equation all together. That made sense. "I mean, I don't *have* to go there. I have lots of other places to deal with. Spending time at the shelter isn't a *necessity*." Emily had realized pretty quickly in this job that her way of doing things, of being good at what she did, was to be fairly hands-on. She liked knowing the ins and outs of the places her family money went. It was important to her to know they were not only in need, but used the funds in the best possible way. And she liked to help. Volunteering at the shelter's fashion show, helping hand out meals at the mission on Main Street, sorting through donated clothing with the women at the Volunteers of America. Emily was a hands-on kind of person.

But fantasizing about getting her hands on Catherine Gardner was a bad idea.

A very, *very* bad idea.

Which didn't stop Emily from fantasizing about it.

A lot.

CHAPTER TEN

THE SUNDAY NIGHT BEFORE Thanksgiving had given Catherine the nasty little gift of the inability to sleep. They'd been short-handed at Joplin's on Saturday, so that day was shot. She'd spent Sunday cleaning and catching up on laundry. Then she'd done a little online shopping, finally ordering herself a new pair of boots (brown leather ankle boots with knit trim and a two-inch heel she'd been eyeing for a while now). After that, she worked with Mo on his training and obedience (he was a stubborn little S.O.B.), and by the time she'd fallen into bed Sunday night, she'd been thoroughly exhausted. So what was with the cosmic joke of not being able to sleep when you're so tired you can barely move your limbs? What exactly was that about?

By Monday morning, she wanted to lay her head down on her desk and nap for three or four hours. If she closed the door, nobody would notice, right? Besides, it was Thanksgiving week. Things in the office would be quiet. She looked over in the corner at the round dog bed she'd picked up for Mo so he could come to work with her. Not only was he curled up in it, looking ridiculously comfortable, but he was snoring loudly, apparently to rub it in.

"That's just mean," Catherine said. Just as she decided maybe she'd lay her head back against her chair and close her eyes for a few minutes, then stood to close the office door, Anna appeared in the opening. The look on her face was pretty clear: she was pissed, as expected and predicted.

Terrific. Annoyed at herself for missing the chance to take the bull by the horns and address things before Anna had to come to her, Catherine sighed quietly before saying, "Hey. Come on in." She needn't have offered an invitation, as it was obvious Anna had no intention of *not* coming in. She stomped through the door and shut it loudly behind her. Mo jumped awake, a startled little woof escaping him.

"You want my job now?" Anna asked, her voice tight. She stood in front of Catherine's desk, braced with both hands on the surface. Catherine knew she was exercising the ability to be the person standing higher, but at barely five feet tall, it didn't have a lot of effect other than to cause Mo to growl low in his throat.

"Of course I don't want your job." Catherine glanced at the dog. "No, Mo. It's okay." He stayed on his bed, but seemed to watch Anna with very careful eyes.

"Then why are you meeting with people to go over marketing strategies? Last time I checked, that was my job." Her blue eyes flashed and her cheeks were flushed and Catherine would have been surprised if she hadn't seen Anna like this a million times before. Anger was her default, even when it was unnecessary. Still, Catherine had created this mess. She deserved Anna's ire and she knew it.

"Look," Catherine said, holding up a placating hand and scrambling through her brain to find a story that would work. "I wasn't trying to step on your toes. I promise I wasn't. It was sort of a fluke thing that just happened. Emily said she had some ideas. Jessica and David were both busy. And honestly? Her ideas might have been terrible. I didn't want you to waste your time if that was the case, so I thought I'd...sort of screen them for you." *Wow. That actually sounded believable.* She mentally high-fived herself.

"And were they?" Anna's voice had tempered slightly.

"Were they what?"

"Terrible. Were her ideas terrible?"

Catherine pursed her lips and glanced out the window before telling Anna the truth. "No. They weren't terrible. Some of them were really good."

"And you were going to share them with me...when?" The tight voice was back again. Catherine knew she'd had this coming, but Anna's condescending tone was starting to grind on her.

"I've been a little busy, Anna. Okay? I'm sorry. I don't know what more you want me to say."

Anna studied her for a moment, something Catherine had never liked. She felt like a specimen of some sort, like a cell under a microscope. Finally, Anna squinted at her and asked, "Why were you even at lunch with them?"

Jesus, did she know everything? Catherine made a mental note to kill Jessica later for spilling every last bean. "I was invited," she said truthfully.

"By who?"

Whom, Catherine corrected in her head. "By Emily Breckenridge. She asked me to come."

"Oh, really?" Anna cocked her head to the side and her expression went from righteous anger to smarmy sarcasm in the space of half a second. Another quality of hers Catherine was not fond of. The woman could turn on a dime. "You should probably be careful. Being a pushy pervert might run in the family. I've heard stories about her."

Oh, you have not, Catherine almost said. But she feared that even a whiff of what looked like her defending Emily would not go over well, so she simply nodded. "I'll keep that in mind."

That seemed to take the wind out of Anna's sails and she was silent for a blessed moment. If Catherine had learned one thing in her time with Anna, it was that not engaging with her was the best course of action. Nodding and pacifying worked wonders, as it did here, thank God. After a beat, Anna stood up straight. "Fine. Email me the ideas. I'll decide what to do about them. If anything." With a glance at Mo, who was still watching her with guarded eyes, she left the office.

Catherine blew out a breath. "Good Lord," she whispered. Mo must have sensed something because he padded over, put his front paws up on her chair, and laid his head on her thigh. She smiled and fingered his velvety ears. "I'm okay, pal. Thanks for looking out for me."

God, she hated that kind of meeting. While it was true that Catherine was fairly tough and rather no-nonsense, most people were shocked to realize that she did not handle confrontation well. It made her nervous and jerky and she didn't like feeling either. She avoided it when at all possible. With Anna, avoiding it was almost never possible. Now. Back when they'd been together, it was different. In that very short time, Anna never argued with her. Not only was there no conflict, there was barely any disagreement. At all. Ever. Anna seemed perfectly content to do whatever Catherine wanted whenever Catherine wanted to, barely expressing any opinion of her own.

That had gotten super old, super fast.

Once they'd broken up, however, Anna was suddenly full of opinions, most of which were the opposite of Catherine's. They butted heads often now, which Catherine's mother said was a good thing, as those true colors of Anna's would have come out sooner or later and how exhausting—not to mention frustratingly impossible—would it have been to try to build a life with somebody like that?

The adrenaline rush caused by Anna's appearance had overshadowed Catherine's fatigue for a bit, but now it came flooding back. With her feet, she rolled her chair back a bit and patted her lap, encouraging Geronimo to jump up. He did and settled himself warmly there. Catherine let her head fall back against her chair and let out a long, slow breath.

She was unsure how much time passed before the gentle rap on her door made Mo jerk in her lap, which startled her into sitting upright.

Regina stood in the doorway of the office holding a vase of brightly colored flowers. "These just arrived for you," the volunteer said, her smile wide with excitement.

Catherine furrowed her brow. Who the hell was sending her flowers and why? It only took a moment for her to surmise it was most likely Clark Breckenridge. *Ugh.* What was with him suddenly asking her out like he had last week? Now that he wasn't the shelter's liaison, did he think she was fair game?

She stood and took the flowers from Regina, who commented, "They're beautiful, huh?"

"They are." When it was clear she was hoping to learn who they were from, Catherine merely looked at her and arched one eyebrow.

"Oh. Right. Sorry." Regina took her leave, albeit reluctantly. Once the door closed behind her, Catherine plucked the card off its little plastic holder and slid a finger under the envelope's flap.

Apologies for my brother and his lack of tact. I promise it doesn't run in the family. ~Emily

Well. That was interesting. Catherine had wondered why Emily'd suddenly gotten so rigidly awkward that day. Now she knew. Clark had embarrassed her. It was that simple. And while Catherine hadn't really dwelled on his pass much at all, she found herself enjoying that it had bothered Emily...something she knew she shouldn't read too deeply into.

Still...

Catherine had received flowers many times in her life. And while she thought they were a nice gesture, she also tended to think of them as a waste of money. They were damned expensive and they only lasted a few days, if you were lucky. Generally, when she got flowers, she took them out to the front desk and let the volunteers and visitors enjoy them.

This time, she did not.

Clearing the corner of her desk nearest the window, she set the vase there and turned it half a rotation a couple times until the arrangement looked just right. White daisies, pink carnations, and a couple of purple lilies made for a bright and spring-like gathering, and Catherine was surprised to feel the smile on her face. Moving to the doorway, she surveyed the placement and decided she liked them there. The card, she put in the middle drawer of her desk as she sat back down.

Returning to her previous position, she let Mo hop back up to return to his and they sat together, enjoying the colors and lovely scents of the flowers. There was work to be done, Catherine knew. But that's not what was on her mind at that moment.

No. What was on her mind was curiosity about what Emily Breckenridge was doing right that minute.

About eight miles away, Emily Breckenridge sat in her office in the Breckenridge Building, gazing out the window at the light snow flurries. Noting the silence of the phones, she remembered that it was a holiday week. Three days of work, then a long weekend, which she was looking forward to. She could admit that, even though she was really, *really* enjoying this new job. Time off was important. To her sanity and to her sense of fun. Too much work and not enough play tended to make Emily a little bit cranky. In fact, with this early snow, it might be a good time to head up to the family's cabin and do a little skiing. *That* would be fun.

I wonder if Catherine skis.

The thought materialized in her consciousness with such immediacy, Emily literally put a steadying hand to her head, fearing it would spin clean off her neck if she didn't.

It wasn't new, really. Catherine had been on her mind fairly often since they'd first met. Emily was drawn to her, which sounded so lame when she said it out loud. Was that even possible? To simply be drawn to somebody? To be tugged in their general direction, regardless of anything else? Anything sort of important like, does that person even like you? Because she didn't really get the warm fuzzies from Catherine, but she was drawn to her anyway. She was drawn to her still. Regardless.

Nobody had ever confused the crap out of her the way Catherine Gardner seemed to, and Emily was not happy about this fact. The flowers were probably a dumb idea, though they seemed like a great one at the time. Clark was being his usual, idiot self, and his pass at Catherine was so unbelievably obvious and out of line, Emily wanted to crawl in a hole when he'd actually asked her out. She wanted to apologize up and down, but she couldn't really do that with Clark standing right there. Her brother was often a dumbass, but he was also her brother and she would never embarrass him in front of people like that. At the same time, she needed Catherine to know that his behavior was not okay with her, that she did not condone such unprofessional conduct.

Thus, the flowers.

Right?

That *was* why she sent the flowers, wasn't it?

Was she obsessed? Emily sat quietly, honestly analyzing the question. It was a part of her personality to go "all in," so to speak, when something intrigued her. She'd done it with skiing, taking lessons every chance she had for two winters straight, even though it was simply a way to make the winter go by faster. She'd done it with marketing, focusing as much of her attention as possible on her college classes and even taking more at night after she'd graduated, just to keep fresh and current with trends. Now she was doing it with her new job, reading everything she could get her hands on when it came to nonprofits and charity giving.

Was she about to do the same thing with Catherine Gardner?

Throw herself into learning everything she could about the woman? Having her brain occupied day and night by her? How freaking unhealthy would that be?

There were two very good reasons why she hoped this was not the case. First, though she threw herself into whatever she was obsessed with at the time, her awareness and intrigue inevitably waned until she lost interest almost completely. Just ask her bag of knitting needles stuffed in her closet or the dozen baking cookbooks that lined her shelf, collecting dust. And second, Emily's mother was right, much as she hated to admit it. Catherine was not only a work colleague, but the positions they were in—Catherine's organization depending on outside money and Emily's being a large source of it—did not bode well for them being anything beyond colleagues, no matter how "drawn to" Catherine she may have felt. Emily's mother would kill her and she doubted Jessica Barstow would be happy about it. No, there was way too much at stake.

A laugh burst forth from Emily's lips at that moment, so unexpected, it surprised even her. What was she doing? What was she even thinking? Sitting here going over reasons why she and Catherine shouldn't be together despite the fact that there had been no indications either of them were leaning that way, other than in Emily's own head.

"I *am* obsessed," she whispered aloud, then closed her eyes and shook her head.

Okay. Enough of this. No more.

She'd managed to immerse herself in learning about a local homeless shelter she was scheduled to visit next week for a solid half hour when her phone rang. Not taking her eyes from the web page she was reading, she snatched up the handset.

"Emily Breckenridge."

"Emily. It's Catherine Gardner over at Junebug Farms. How are you?"

The voice was so unexpected, the name was so unexpected, that Emily sat blinking for several beats.

"Emily?"

"Uh-huh. Um…" She stuttered like a nervous prom date, but finally managed to form words. "Yes. Catherine. I'm here. Hi."

"Hi," Catherine said on what sounded like a gentle chuckle.

Emily cleared her throat. "This is a nice surprise."

"No, a nice surprise would be the flowers you sent me."

Catherine's voice was uncharacteristically warm and that made Emily feel…weird inside. A good weird. "Ah. Yes. Well."

"You didn't have to do that."

"Apologize for my brother? Yes, I did."

"They're beautiful. Thank you."

"You're very welcome." This conversation was bizarre. They were acting like opposites of their true selves, and Emily was slightly freaked out by it. Catherine was being kind and inviting. Emily felt nervous and anticipatory, but in a good way, like having butterflies in your stomach just before doing something you've been waiting anxiously for all day.

"Is it a busy week for you?"

"Not really. You?"

"No. It'll be pretty quiet until after Thanksgiving. Then things will pick up with adoptions for Christmas."

"Oh, right. That makes sense. You get a lot of that?"

"Too much, really. There will be a percentage of the adoptees returned after the holidays because people didn't think it through first."

"People are dumb," Emily said and was rewarded with a rich, silky laugh, smooth as milk chocolate.

"They are."

There was a moment of quiet and then, before she could catch herself, Emily asked softly, "Hey, would you be at all interested in maybe grabbing a cup of coffee with me sometime?"

Catherine seemed to hesitate before answering.

"Or not," Emily hastily added with a chuckle that she hoped didn't sound as forced and uncomfortable as it felt. "It's okay if you'd rather not. I just—"

"No, no. I'd love to. I think that would be nice."

"Oh, good." Emily took a moment to absorb that Catherine had actually accepted. Then, she pushed forward. *No backing out now.* "How about Wednesday? Are you working?"

"I am, but there won't be a lot to do. What if I work a couple hours in the morning and then we meet up at Starbucks at, say, eleven?" Catherine's voice had slipped slightly back toward business mode, and for some reason, that made Emily feel a little less uncomfortable.

"That sounds great. Which Starbucks?"

They settled up the details and said their good-byes. Emily sat with her hand on the receiver for long moments, replaying the conversation in her head.

She had asked Catherine to coffee. Out of the blue. And just after committing to not being obsessed with her. Just after she mentally ran down all the ways getting involved with Catherine would be a capital-B Bad Idea. Worse, she didn't even know what she intended with the invitation. Was this a date? Or a business meeting? Emily honestly didn't know and didn't want to dwell on it.

Which was probably a good thing. Right? She was so confused.

What the hell had she just done?

More importantly, how long should she wait before she sent more flowers?

CHAPTER ELEVEN

"WHAT THE HELL IS going on with me?" Catherine asked the question aloud to her empty office, forgetting that she'd left Geronimo home that day.

It was ten o'clock in the morning on Wednesday, and Catherine wanted to knock herself in the head with a hammer. What the hell had she been thinking? What the *hell* had she been thinking? Accepting Emily's invitation to coffee. Which was essentially a date, right? *I mean, seriously, how else could she be looking at it? She sent me flowers. I called her to say thank you and she invited me to coffee. Date!* After all the ways in which she realized that the very woman she should never accept a date with, for so many important reasons, was Emily Breckenridge, she'd gone ahead and accepted a date with Emily Breckenridge.

Catherine's eyes were pulled to the glass vase of flowers that sat on her desk, still colorful and spring-like, still beautiful, still able to pull a tiny smile from Catherine every time.

Every time.

She wasn't acting like herself. At all.

A glance at the empty dog bed had her wishing Geronimo was here. At least that would keep her from talking to herself. But she knew she'd be stepping out for awhile, and to do that, she'd need to put him in one of the kennels in the dog wing. She worried that would upset him, that he'd think she was leaving him there, so she'd decided letting him stay home today was the better plan. She'd be home early anyway, as she had a shift at

Joplin's later, and she knew from experience that the night before Thanksgiving would be slammed.

Her attempts to occupy herself for another forty minutes were very nearly successful, as she was able to tamp down her nerves at least a little while she responded to several e-mails. But when her phone buzzed to remind her it was time to head out, the butterflies in her stomach morphed into fighter jets and churned up enough acid to remind her that she hadn't eaten anything yet today.

No new snow had fallen in a couple days, but it was crisply cold and Catherine pulled her long coat tightly around her as she headed to her car. The parking lot was dotted with only a few vehicles, most people choosing to stay home today in preparation for the holiday weekend. Once in her car, she started the engine and let it run for a few minutes to warm up, the muscles in her shoulders aching slightly as she hunched to keep from freezing. Luckily, hers was a little powerhouse of a car with all-wheel drive and was blasting heat on her in no time.

Driving in the winter always made Catherine a little nervous, but today, she was happy to focus on that rather than the other thoughts clouding up her head. Concentrating on the road allowed her to push Emily aside, at least for a short time. She'd been in an accident as a college kid driving home for Christmas break and ever since, she'd been a little fearful behind the wheel when it was slick. But the roads were clear and she arrived at Starbucks by 10:55. Once parked, she took a deep breath and blew it out slowly. In her purse, she located a tube of lip gloss, stroked it across her lips, then rolled her eyes at herself. *What am I doing?* Throwing it back into the bag with more force than necessary, she headed into the coffee shop.

Emily was already seated at a table near a back window. She smiled and waved, and Catherine felt herself smiling back. Widely. Without giving herself permission. Irritation crept in, but she did her best to keep it at bay as she headed toward the table, pulling her gloves off.

"Hi," Emily said, standing. Her smile was big, her cheeks flushed slightly. It was a good look on her, Catherine noticed, as was the off-white hooded sweater with the chunky buttons. Underneath was a chocolate brown tank top that left enough collarbone visible to pull Catherine's eyes there. Again, without her permission. The dark hair was loose and gentle waves curled near her shoulders. Brown eyes danced and Catherine understood that Emily was genuinely happy to see her.

That was the moment Catherine realized that the feeling was mutual.

Emily gestured to the chair across the small table from her. "Sit, sit. What can I get you?"

"I can get it," Catherine said automatically, not sitting.

"I can get it, too," Emily countered, amused.

Catherine stopped, looked at her, held her gaze. "I can pay for my own coffee."

Emily cocked her head, still amused, one corner of her mouth quirking up slightly. "I'm sure you can. But I'd like to. If that's okay with you."

They stood there for what seemed like a long time, but was certainly only a couple seconds. Emily held her gaze, but gently, if that made any sense. It was the only way Catherine could explain it. Emily held it until Catherine finally acquiesced. With a nod of acceptance, she said, "Okay. A mocha latte, please."

"You got it." Emily earned points then by not celebrating her victory in any way. "Anything to eat? I'm starving."

"A blueberry muffin would be wonderful, if they have one."

"One mocha latte and a blueberry muffin, coming right up." And she was off, taking her place in the line that was surprisingly short for Starbucks.

Catherine took off her coat and hung it on the back of her chair, then put her purse there, too, and sat. Looking around, she took in the various types of people in the small café. She knew many had a love/hate relationship with Starbucks, but hers was only love. She loved the coffee, despite its ridiculous price tag—it was one of the few splurges she allowed herself. The food was always passable. Most of all, though, she loved the atmosphere. It was quiet and casual, but not silent. More than once, she'd come here with her laptop or some printouts to go over, got herself a latte and a comfy chair, and had gotten a ton of work done simply by not being in the office. The change of scenery was good for her and she enjoyed mixing up her day every now and then.

Pulled from her reverie by the steaming cup set in front of her, Catherine focused once again on the woman across from her. A large muffin bursting with plump blueberries followed. The gentle scent of Emily's perfume tickled her nostrils and Catherine absently wondered what brand it was. Emily took her seat.

"What did you get?" Catherine asked, gesturing to Emily's cup with her chin.

"Peppermint Mocha. Holiday time calls for holiday coffee."

"I see."

"Busy at work today?"

Catherine scoffed. "No. Very quiet. As expected." She took a sip of her latte, savoring the creaminess of the coffee and milk, the touch of chocolate. "You?"

"Oh, God, no. Probably half the staff took the day off and the ones who are in are screwing off anyway. It's to be expected."

"I suppose it is."

"What do you do for Thanksgiving?" Emily leaned her forearms on the table as if trying to get closer to Catherine... which Catherine realized with a jolt that she didn't mind.

"We go to my grandparents'."

"You have a big family?"

Catherine shook her head. "Oh, no. Small. My mom is an only child and there's just me and my sister and my nephew."

"What about your dad?"

"He lives in Colorado. I don't see him much." Never comfortable talking about herself, Catherine turned the conversation around. "What about you? Is there a big Breckenridge Family Banquet? I picture a long table with about twenty guests, really good china, and a kitchen staff." She hadn't meant it to sound sarcastic, but she knew by the quick zip of discomfort that flashed across Emily's face that it had.

"Actually, that's pretty accurate." Emily sat back in her chair and sipped her coffee.

"It is?" Catherine was surprised.

"We can be pretty stereotypical sometimes." Emily chuckled, but it seemed forced.

"So, who all is there? I don't know much about your family." Maybe if she got Emily talking, she could erase that slightly pained expression from her face—which felt important, although she wasn't sure why.

"Well, there's me and Clark, as you know. I don't have any other siblings. My mom and dad. My dad has two brothers—all of whom are part of the family business—and they each have wives and kids and some of the kids have kids. My mom has a brother and a sister. My uncle has two kids and my aunt has three and two of those five have kids. Plus, my grandma on my mom's side and both grandparents on my dad's. So, yeah. It's a lot of people."

"Wow," Catherine breathed, unable to imagine how to begin to deal with such a large group of people.

"It can get loud. And a little chaotic."

"I bet." Catherine tore a piece off her muffin and popped it into her mouth. "Do they all come over for Christmas, too?"

Emily nodded, and the uncomfortable expression was replaced by a gentle smile. Thank God. "Usually, yes. We used to go to my grandma's, but it got hard for her to do everything she wanted to. She's big on the holidays and not-so-big on knowing her own limitations now that she's older. And my parents' house is bigger, so they just started having everybody over there. Plus, having a kitchen staff helps when there's that many mouths to feed." She sipped her coffee and watched Catherine for a moment. "To be honest, I always wondered what it would be like to have a small, cozy holiday, you know? Without all the extended family. I mean, don't get me wrong, I love my entire family. They're good people. But something smaller, more intimate? I bet that'd be nice." And when she met Catherine's eyes and their gazes held, it was suddenly clear to Catherine that Emily was a bit embarrassed to have revealed that. She wasn't sure how she knew it, but…she did. And she wanted to fix it.

Before she could stop herself, she blurted, "You should come by my grandma's for dessert tomorrow. Give yourself a break from the noise and chaos."

Emily studied her for a moment before one corner of her mouth quirked up. "I'd like that."

Catherine immediately wanted to kick herself, tossing out an invitation like that. Especially after her internal discussion about what a bad idea this coffee date was. *Hey, why don't you come over my place for a major holiday? That won't be weird or complicate anything. Geez, Catherine.*

With no other recourse, she decided she'd shake it off and just keep Emily talking. Something about the sound of her voice —soft, feminine, almost pretty—made Catherine want to hear it more, so she focused on that.

"Who are you closest to in your family?"

"My mom. Easy."

"Yeah? How come?"

"Because she's awesome." Emily's grin grew and Catherine followed suit.

"Tell me why she's awesome." She chewed more muffin and listened raptly, suddenly perfectly comfortable being exactly where she was.

Emily looked up at the ceiling while she gathered words. Her thinking face was adorable: half smile, half concentration. When she looked back at Catherine, her eyes were dancing again. "Well, let's see. She's super smart, first of all. You can't pull one over on my mom. She's really intelligent and she reads people with scary accuracy. She's a pro at separating work and home…which can be difficult when you work for her." Emily leaned in a little closer, lowered her voice, and said, "I am just finding this out and it's been…interesting to deal with, to say the least."

"Yeah? How so?"

Emily launched into a story about a screw-up at the company when she was still in marketing and how weird it was to have her mother go from Mom to Boss in a split second.

Catherine watched and listened, completely sucked in to the sound of Emily's voice, the shine on her lips, the expression in her eyes. She used her hands when she talked, waving them around like a matador. Catherine found herself, shockingly, completely entertained, even laughing out loud at the descriptions Emily gave of coworkers, conversations, and situations.

"You're funny," she said when the story had come to its end. Catherine finished her coffee, nearly cold now. Only crumbs were left of her muffin.

"One of my many talents." Emily's coffee had been gone for a while and she toyed with her empty cup.

The crowd had thickened and then thinned as they sat, and for the first time, Catherine wondered how much time had passed.

As if reading her mind, Emily picked up her phone and clicked it on. "Wow."

"What?"

"It's after two."

Catherine felt her eyes go wide. "Are you kidding me?"

"I am not kidding you." Emily turned her phone so Catherine could see the big 2:07 plastered over the face of a brindled pit bull. "Who's that?" she asked, pointing to the phone.

"That's Dave."

"Oh, right. Dave who loves stuffed animals."

Emily looked surprised. "You remembered." She turned the phone back so she could look at it. "He's my love."

"That is the best dog name ever."

"Thanks." For the first time since they'd sat, there was a lull in the conversation. But only a short one because Emily said, "Hey, text me your grandma's address and maybe I'll pop by."

With no way not to do that, Catherine complied. Emily probably wouldn't come anyway, given how many of her own family she'd be in the midst of. *I mean, really, what would she have in common with my family? Little to nothing, that's for sure.*

"This was a lot of fun," Emily said, pulling Catherine from her thoughts. "Thanks for suggesting it."

"Well. Thanks for the flowers. They're expensive and they don't last long…you didn't have to do that."

"Wait…are you saying you don't like flowers?"

"No, no. I just think they cost so much and…" Catherine's voice trailed off, no way to recover from the obvious direction her words were going.

"And you think they're a waste of money."

She couldn't tell if Emily was insulted, amused, or a little of both. She swallowed and looked away.

"Well, *I* am glad I sent them because we ended up here, so…" Emily let the sentence dangle for a beat before smiling and standing up. They gathered their things, bundled up, and walked together out the door into the parking lot where their cars were parked at opposite ends. "Maybe I'll see you tomorrow," Emily said, her expression soft, her eyes warm.

"Maybe." Catherine gave a slight nod. "If not, have a great Thanksgiving."

"You, too," Emily said, and before Catherine even saw it coming, Emily had wrapped her in a hug. It was firm and warm and for a split second, Catherine let herself sink into it, to fill her lungs with the citrusy scent of Emily's hair (lemons? oranges?). It really was only a second, though, and then she gently extricated herself, feeling a weird combination of uncomfortable, embarrassed, safe, and aroused. And suddenly, all the reasons why this was a bad idea came flooding back like high tide.

"Bye," she said quietly, not meeting Emily's eyes. She turned and headed for her car, hoping she didn't look like she was hurrying, because she most certainly was. She was sure she could feel Emily's eyes on her, but she didn't look back. Once closed safely in her car, she keyed the ignition, cranked the heat, and let out a long, slow breath. Running her gloved hands slowly along the steering wheel, she gave herself a moment to chill out and relax. So Emily hugged her. So what? People did that. *Friends* did that. It meant nothing more. She was worrying needlessly.

Anyway. She was being ridiculous. There were other things to deal with. She had to get home to Geronimo, who hadn't been left alone this long before.

Right. I'll focus on that.

Because if she focused on the rest of it, she might go insane.

Turned out, Geronimo had no problems amusing himself while he was alone. Apparently, he had decided he preferred not to be blocked into the kitchen. He must have jumped over the gate Catherine had put in the doorway because it was still there, just as she'd left it, but Mo was curled up comfortably on the couch, surrounded by bits and pieces of the HGTV magazine that must have bored him so much he shredded it. He lifted his head when Catherine entered the room. She stood with her hands on her hips and just looked at him. He gazed back at her, his innocent expression clearly saying, "What?"

"What are you doing in here? Hmm?"

He blinked his big brown eyes at her.

"Did you read something you didn't agree with?" she asked, indicating with her eyes the shreds of paper all over the room.

"Are we going to need to crate you? I have one. I can do that, you know."

His mouth opened in a huge yawn, his pink tongue unfurling like a New Year's Eve party horn.

"Oh, am I boring you? Forgive me, Your Highness." Catherine shed her coat and gloves, crossed the room, brushed aside the magazine detritus, and took a seat on the couch. Mo wasted no time moving to her and resituating himself across her lap. When he looked up at her, she couldn't help but grin. "You are a piece of work, pal. You know that?" Staying angry with him was going to be a difficult, if not impossible, task. She gave up this time and scratched behind his ears, then grabbed his face in her hands. "I love you," she said to him and kissed between his eyes. "But I'd love it if you wouldn't chew up my reading material. Okay?"

His response was to swipe his warm tongue across her chin.

"I'll take that as a, 'Yes, Mommy, I totally get what you're saying and will never do it again. I'm so very sorry.' Come on. Let's go out."

Mo didn't stay outside long, but did his business like a good dog and hurried back in. It was in the thirties—not terribly cold —but his hair was short and light and Catherine doubted it kept him very warm. She made a mental note to see what Maggie had in the gift shop for sweaters and coats.

"You would look super cute in plaid, you know. Maybe something green?" It didn't escape her notice that talking out loud to Mo was a way to keep her thoughts from dwelling on the situation with Emily, but she did it anyway. Mo stood at her feet, looking up at her with such rapt attention that she couldn't help but laugh. Scooping him into her arms, she kissed all over his face as she carried him upstairs. "Come on. I need to change into some cozies. You and I are gonna veg in front of the TV and not think about the lovely Miss Breckenridge and all the reason why we need to control ourselves. Okay? What do you think?"

It was nice to be in the quiet of the living room, just her and Mo, and it was also bittersweet. Catherine swallowed down the lump in her throat that developed when she thought about how many times she'd curled up on the couch with Pablo—even though he was slightly too big to be on the couch. Mo was about a third the size of Pablo and he seemed to want to be touching her in some way at all times, she'd noticed. Either leaning against her hip or with his chin resting on her thigh. That was, if he wasn't fully on her lap, which he was now. His warm body was curled into a ball, half on her lap, half on her stomach as she sat on the couch with her slippered feet on the coffee table. She did her best to derail the vision her brain tossed her of Emily sitting on the couch next to her, close to her, by pointing the remote at her television, she toggled between *Bar Rescue* and an old episode of *Criminal Minds*.

"Just wait until next week," she murmured to Mo. "Hallmark will start showing their holiday movies and I'll be lost. Lucky you, you get to watch them with me." She kissed the top of his head as an incompetent bartender was being chastised on the screen.

Catherine was well into her second hour of brain-melting television when her doorbell rang, startling both her and the dog. Mo jumped off her lap and sprinted toward the front of the house, barking his little doggie head off. At the front door, she held him back by his collar, which proved to be more difficult than expected. Grabbing up his wiggling body, she plopped him in the kitchen and put up the gate, pointing at him with a firm "Stay," as she walked down the hall to the door, hoping that his being able to see her would keep him from vaulting the gate (which she now knew he could) and zipping her way to attack the doorbell ringer.

He stayed put. He kept barking, but he stayed put.

Catherine pulled the door opened, surprised to see a gorgeous arrangement of flowers.

"Catherine Gardner?" the delivery man asked, face hidden by the bouquet.

"Yes."

"Here you go. Enjoy. Happy Thanksgiving."

She took the flowers from him and watched as he got into his little truck and backed down her driveway. Carrying them down the hall, she stepped over the gate into the kitchen, Mo watching her carefully, obviously curious.

The bouquet was large, but not obnoxiously so. Less spring-like and more full of autumn colors than the one in her office. Yellows and oranges and reds. Roses and daisies and irises. Plus some baby's breath and other filler that made it look full and lush. It really was beautiful and for a moment, Catherine actually reexamined her indifference to delivered flowers. She set the vase on the counter, sniffed deeply from a blood-red rose, and plucked the card from its little plastic fork-like holder. Mo sat patiently at her feet, as if waiting for her to read it aloud to him. Which she did.

"'Thank you for the coffee date and the conversation. I had a great time. Can we do it again? Happy Thanksgiving. Emily.'" She ran her thumb across the letters in Emily's name, then over the word "date."

Yes, she'd noticed that.

Intentional word choice or coincidental?

She had no way to be sure. "Other than the fact that she sent flowers," she said aloud. "What do I do about this, Mo? Anything?" Mo cocked his head to one side in that way dogs do when they're listening carefully. Catherine looked at him for a beat, then shrugged. "You're right. Nothing. I'm doing nothing."

She picked up the vase and found the perfect spot for it in the living room near a large window. The flowers would get plenty of sunlight there and their colors gave a nice pop to the room. She flopped back down onto the couch, put her feet up, and waited for Mo to settle himself half-on, half-off her lap. Remote in hand, she unpaused the TV show as her eyes were pulled to the left toward the bouquet.

Plus, I can see them from here.

Catching herself, she shook the thought from her head and forced herself to relax. Tomorrow was Thanksgiving and there would be a ton to do. She would have no time to dwell on anything in regard to Emily Breckenridge or the ridiculous splurge that those flowers must have been, thank God, because this was bad. Wasn't it? It was bad. There was a line. They both knew it. They both saw it, didn't they? But the brainstorming and the coffee date and the flowers—all the damn flowers—were pulling them dangerously close to that line. And while Catherine knew she needed to step back, step away from the line, move in the opposite direction…some part of her didn't want to.

She groaned, causing Mo to stop what he was doing and look up at her with concern in his doggie eyes. Even he seemed to know.

This was very, very bad.

CHAPTER TWELVE

THE THANKSGIVING CHAOS OF Emily's parents' house had died down to a more palatable level, but it had been pretty crazy for a while there. Having more than two toddlers running around was a fairly solid recipe for noise. Emily didn't enjoy sitting in the living room or the study chatting with the adults; she'd much rather roll around on the floor with the kids. So that's exactly what she'd done. And now, after stuffing herself full of turkey and dressing and cranberries, she was reasonably certain she was about to bust out of her pants. Not to mention, she felt a couple of welts and bruises that had appeared in moments when she'd forgotten how solidly a pudgy, three-year-old fist could land on the soft flesh of her arm or how interested toddlers with new teeth were in putting things into their mouths—things like the fingers of other people.

Emily had been comfortably recovering in an oversized leather chair for the past half hour. Football was on the enormous television mounted above the gas fireplace, which was kicking out just the right amount of heat to push the tryptophan-dosed members of the Breckenridge clan dangerously close to napping. Two identical easy chairs were at one end of the room. Emily's father dozed in one, Clark sprawled in the other. Three cousins sat on the couch while two younger ones sat on the floor scrolling on their phones. The rest of the family—mostly the women who had no interest in the game—was still in the dining room. Occasional bursts of laughter would emanate from that direction, causing Emily to smile when she picked out her mom's.

"Hey." Emily looked up into the smiling face of her cousin Melinda, mother to two of Emily's wrestling opponents from earlier. "Both my kids are conked right out in the guest room upstairs. Thank you so much for playing with them."

"You're welcome. I had a blast. And I am going to sleep good tonight." Emily grinned.

"Well, then, *you* are welcome." Melinda gently patted Emily's foot, then crossed the room to sit next to her husband on the couch.

As Emily watched them cuddle together, her mother's voice caught her attention from the doorway. "Who's ready for dessert?" She looked beautiful in a simple but elegant green dress and silver pumps. Cheryl Breckenridge rarely did not look beautiful. At the very least, she always had an air of refined sophistication about her. When she walked into a room, not only did everybody look, but she commanded instant respect. And she got it. Emily could only hope to be that admired one day.

"What are the options?" Clark asked from his chair, his socked feet up, a glass of wine in his hand. Something about the combination of his position and his tone made Emily roll her eyes and she suddenly wanted to be away from him. It was a feeling she was finding all too familiar lately.

"Actually," she said, rising from her seat. "I'm going to go visit a friend."

Her mother looked surprised. "You are?"

"Yeah, I was invited for dessert, so I thought I'd make an appearance. No big deal."

"Who are you visiting?" Clark asked, just as her mother asked the same question.

Forcing a nonchalant shrug, Emily told the truth. "Catherine Gardner from Junebug Farms."

Cheryl raised her eyebrows. "I didn't realize you were friends."

"Oh, Emily wants to be more than friends," Clark said waggling his eyebrows in the most suggestive way possible.

"Shut up, Clark. I do not."

"You want to win the bet, don't you?"

"Oh, my God," Emily said, suddenly exasperated. "There is no bet."

"What bet?" Cheryl asked.

"There's no bet," Emily said again, walking around her mother to the coat closet.

"I bet Em that I could land Catherine before she could." Clark had pushed the footrest of his chair down and he was sitting upright, his face suddenly animated and energetic. The others in the room looked on with rapt attention.

Emily's mother looked properly aghast as she glanced in her daughter's direction.

"There's no bet, Mom," Emily reassured her as she pushed an arm into her coat.

"There had better not be," Cheryl said, clear disapproval in her voice. She turned her gaze to her son, who visibly withered, if only a little bit. "First of all, we give money to that place and we have a reputation to uphold. Secondly, that's incredibly sexist, Clark, and I'll have no more of it."

From behind her mother, Emily stuck her tongue out at her brother. Melinda chuckled from her spot on the couch.

Cheryl turned back to her daughter. "And third, *there had better not be a bet.*" The emphasis this time was solid, urgent, and left no room for argument. "Is that understood?"

Emily swallowed hard and nodded. "Yes, ma'am."

Cheryl leaned in for a peck on the cheek, her demeanor back to normal. "Watch your driving."

"I will."

Emily managed to snag a bottle of Zinfandel from her mother's wine rack before scooting out the front door. Then she got into her car, plugged in her phone, and called up the address Catherine had given. When the navigation came up on the console screen, Emily looked at it and stared for a moment, her mother's voice echoing in her head.

And yet, she very consciously reached out and slid the gearshift into Reverse.

Fifteen minutes later, she was pushing the glowing doorbell button on a cute little bungalow just outside the city. The night air was brisk, but Emily liked it, inhaling, pulling the cold into her lungs. It energized her somehow, as did the thought of seeing Catherine—though she didn't dwell on that too much as her mother's voice rang sharply in her ears.

The door was opened by a woman who could only be Catherine's mother. She was tall and lean, with hair the same chestnut color as Catherine's and the same soft cheekbones. Only their eye color was different; this woman's were a gentle brown as opposed to Catherine's cool blue.

"Hi," Emily said. "Is Catherine here? I'm Emily Breckenridge. She invited me for dessert."

The woman's smile widened. "Yes, she's inside. Come in. Come in." She stepped back, and she seemed genuinely happy to invite Emily into the warmth of the house. It was small and the dining room table, occupied by a handful of people, was visible now that Emily was inside. She smiled and locked eyes with Catherine, whose face showed an odd mix of emotions. A lot of surprise. A little panic. A glimmer of happiness. Emily saw them all in quick succession. *Amusing*, she thought.

"Let me take your coat," the woman said, then laughed. "And where are my manners?" She held out a hand. "I'm Denise. Catherine's mother."

Emily shook the offered hand, took in how much Denise's smile mirrored Catherine's. Denise was definitely more…worn. It wasn't a flattering word, but it was an accurate one. The woman was attractive, certainly, but she also gave the impression that she had worked very hard her entire life and probably still did. Emily suspected Denise looked tired pretty much every day.

She was pulled from her musings by a wet nose pushing at her hand and she looked down to see Geronimo, tail wagging like crazy. Emily squatted down to give him attention. "Hey there, pal. How are you? Hmm?"

Following Denise into the small dining room, she took in the occupants. An older couple that could only be Catherine's grandparents, he sitting at the head of the table, she on his right. Catherine was on her grandfather's left. An empty chair sat next to her that must belong to Denise. Across the table was a woman with bleached-blond hair and the same worn look Denise had. Emily guessed this to be the sister. Next to her was a young man of maybe nineteen or twenty.

"Everybody, this is Catherine's friend, Emily, who is joining us for dessert. Jason, get another chair, honey."

Everybody stood and welcomed Emily with outstretched hands and smiles. She handed the Zinfandel to Emily's grandmother, who ooh'd and ahh'd like Emily had handed her gold jewelry. It was sweet and Emily liked her instantly.

Once settled in her chair next to Catherine, Emily turned and met her gaze.

"Hi."

Catherine grinned at her, her cheeks slightly flushed. "Hi."

"Pumpkin pie, Emily?" Catherine's grandmother, Bea, asked.

"I'd love some. Thank you." Within seconds, a pretty china plate with a large slice of homemade pie slid her way. A glass of wine was set next to her and soon everybody was eating dessert, sipping drinks, talking and laughing as if they did so every day and Emily was simply an accepted part of it all. The cherry on top was when Mo settled down under the table with his chin on Emily's foot.

Next to her sat Catherine, and Emily had never been so hyper-aware of anybody before in her life. It was a brand-new feeling for her and she wasn't quite sure what to do with it. While she didn't actually turn to look at her all that often, she was alert to everything Catherine said, to every move she made, to the very specific timbre of her voice when she spoke. She could smell her body wash, her shampoo, and her perfume, all separately, all intoxicating. The royal blue of the sweater she was wearing filled Emily's vision any time she turned her head, and it looked so soft she had trouble not reaching out to touch the sleeve of it.

Needing to shake herself free of this delicious prison she'd found herself in, she spoke. "This pie is delicious," she said, scooping another bite into her mouth.

"Thank you," Denise said, her face flushing a light pink, so much like her daughter's tended to.

"Did you make it?"

"I did." Denise gave a slight nod.

"Aunt Denise is always in charge of the pies," Jason, the teenager, told her. Emily again put him at maybe nineteen or twenty. College age. His sandy hair was a bit too long, and he tossed his head to get it out of his eyes. He wore black-rimmed glasses and seemed slightly awkward, but in that adorable way that made you want to protect him.

"Do you volunteer at the shelter?" Catherine's grandfather, John, asked.

"Sometimes. Yes." Emily nodded as she scooped another piece of pie.

"Grandpa. She's Emily Breckenridge." Catherine put emphasis on the last name.

"Oh," John said. Then his eyes opened wide. "Oh! Breckenridge." With a chuckle he said, "So, you keep the place running then, do you?"

"I don't get it," Catherine's sister, Vicky, said. She hadn't said much since Emily had sat down, but she'd felt the woman's eyes on her more than once.

"The Breckenridge Foundation, Mom," Jason said, leaning toward Vicky. "They donate a lot of money to a lot of causes, including Junebug Farms."

"Oh. So, you're rich. Is that what you're saying?"

"Geez, Vicky. Tactless much?" Catherine laid a warm hand on Emily's thigh and said quietly, "I'm sorry."

Surprised she was able to form coherent words with Catherine's hand on her (and did she leave it there longer than necessary? Emily was pretty sure she did…), she shrugged. "No, no, it's fine." Turning to meet Vicky's gaze, she said simply. "Yup. Filthy stinking."

Denise choked on a swallow of wine and Emily saw Bea cover her grin with her fingers while John chuckled openly. Vicky flushed red (must run in the family) and Emily felt Catherine squeeze her thigh before removing her hand.

Emily looked around the table at this small family, at their smiles, felt the warmth of the holiday in the happy voices. More than that, she felt the presence of Catherine right next to her, solid and sexy and gorgeous, and that overshadowed everything else because—damn it—she *liked* Catherine right next to her. Which was not good, her mother's voice was too quick to tell her.

Except that it *felt* good. It felt right.

When her mother's voice got louder, Emily did her best to tamp it down by focusing on the story Bea was telling about the bird-watching group she'd joined recently. Catherine's eyes were on her grandmother, but when she glanced at Emily and smiled, Emily's entire lower body tingled and she wanted to sit at that table forever.

And all she could think was, *Rules be damned. At least for tonight.*

⚶

Monday came too soon as far as Catherine was concerned. She'd had the day off from the shelter on Friday, it was true, but she'd waited tables at Joplin's Friday and Saturday. Both nights had been packed houses, which was awesome for her tips, but not so awesome for her aching feet. She spent Sunday taking Geronimo for a long walk (again, making her feet less than happy, though her dog was ecstatic) and cleaning her house. Monday morning's alarm had gone off way too early and she very nearly chucked her phone across the room when it had.

Now, Mo was curled up on his dog bed in the corner of her office as she answered e-mails and phone calls. The shelter was quiet so far, but the holidays were in full swing and Catherine knew from experience that things would be picking up very soon.

She'd closed her door to keep some of the residual, everyday noises out, hoping that would help her tired brain concentrate. Unfortunately, she found herself flashing back to Thanksgiving over and over again. Well, not Thanksgiving exactly.

Thanksgiving dessert. And Emily.

She blew out a long, slow breath. *Emily.*

What the hell was she supposed to do about Emily?

Catherine had been nothing less than shocked when Emily had shown up at her grandparents' door. Sure, she'd been invited, been given the address even, but Catherine never really thought she'd show. *Who does that?* Chuckling at her own question, she answered it aloud with, "Does what? Shows up someplace after they're invited? Yeah, pretty much everybody."

Mo lifted his head and looked at her, obviously wondering if she was talking to him. After a beat or two, he went back to napping while Catherine gazed out the window at the gently falling snow, her shoulders slightly hunched against the chill in her office. Emily had fit right in, had slid seamlessly into her family gathering…which she was still having trouble understanding. How had it been so easy? True, Catherine hadn't exactly been happy to see her at first. (Okay, that was a lie…she'd been a *little bit* happy to see her.) But from the moment she'd sat down at the table, it was like she belonged there, like she'd been sitting in that spot at the table, right next to Catherine, for years. She'd even handled Vicky's attempt to establish dominance with class and wit, facing her head-on instead of withering away or trying to deflect. Catherine was pretty sure she'd earned Vicky's grudging respect in that moment.

There had been no pressure for Catherine. That was the weirdest part for her. No pressure to be a buffer, to answer questions for her, to smooth the way. With Anna, that's all

Catherine had ever done. She'd been like Anna's interpreter, translating for her, leading her by the hand, asking the questions she was too shy to ask. Catherine couldn't count the number of times they'd left a family gathering of one sort or another and all she'd wanted to do was take a handful of Excedrin and a long nap.

Emily hadn't been exhausting. She'd been fun. And funny. And intelligent. And entertaining. The whole family had adored her and Catherine's grandmother had asked when she'd be back. Emily's response had left eyebrows raised and Catherine speechless. "That's totally up to your granddaughter." Catherine grinned now as she recalled her grandmother's answer as she dismissively waved a hand. "Pfft! She's not in charge. You can come by anytime you want. I'm an old woman with little to do. I'd love the company."

Before she'd left, Emily had hugged her. Again. And it had been just as disconcerting as the last time, in Starbucks. Emily's hair had smelled the same, like citrus, and her arms around Catherine had been firm and strong. Probably because she'd had a little wine that day, Catherine had let the hug go on a bit longer this time. She'd hugged back. And it had felt…perfect. And she'd wanted to hold on longer. And Goddamnit, that was unfair. She was supposed to be keeping Emily at arms' length, not pulling her closer.

A gentle tapping on her door pulled Catherine from her musings and she reluctantly called for the person to enter. Jessica came in, wearing her navy blue down coat with a white wool scarf and carrying two cups from Starbucks. Her auburn hair was pulled back into a ponytail and her ears and cheeks were rosy from being outside.

"Good morning. Man, it's cold." She handed Catherine a cup. "Latte for my favorite accountant."

"Oh, you're a lifesaver," Catherine said as she took the cup and held it with both hands, warming her fingers. "My radiator has been acting up again. And by 'acting up,' I mean refusing to do its job and keep me warm."

"Ugh. Our HVAC is older than me. I'm sorry. I'll send Bill in to take a look at it." Jessica paused for a minute, and her expressions was uncertain. "You got a minute?" she asked and indicated one of the empty chairs with her eyes.

"Of course."

"How was your Thanksgiving?" Jessica asked as she stripped off her coat. Underneath, she wore navy slacks and a navy and green argyle V-neck sweater. She settled herself into the chair as she waited for Catherine's reply.

"It was really nice." Catherine knew Jessica, had known her for years, which meant she knew her methods as well. When she had something serious to talk about, she prefaced it with small talk. Things like "How about this weather?" Or "Did you see the game yesterday?" Or "How was your Thanksgiving?" Catherine blew on the the very hot coffee, took a sip, then asked, "Yours?"

"Oh, it was fine. You know how it is. The whole family gets together and it's awesome...until it's not." She laughed and Catherine joined her, waiting for her to get to the real topic of discussion. "So," she said, her face becoming serious. "I saw Jason earlier. He's helping Jamie set up for the agility class tonight."

Catherine nodded and sipped again as Mo ventured over to Jessica and sniffed her knee. Then he sat and waited patiently for her to pet him, which she did. Hand on his square little head, she stroked him and kept her eyes on him as she said, "He told me Emily Breckenridge came by your grandparents' for dessert."

"She did." Catherine didn't offer more. She had an idea where this was going, had almost been expecting it.

Jessica looked up then, her blue eyes gentle and her expression hesitant as she asked, "Are you seeing her?"

Catherine shook her head and sipped her coffee while Jessica studied her.

"Do you want to see her?"

It took a moment, maybe two, for Catherine to think about that one. When she finally answered, it was honest. "I don't know. Maybe?"

Jessica pressed her lips together in a thin line as she seemed to think about her words before she spoke. "You know I love you, right?"

"Yes."

"I'm worried." Jessica let the words hang in the air. Catherine waited her out, something she did often. People tended to avoid silences, needed to fill them. Catherine did not. In fact, she enjoyed silence just fine. After a beat or two, Jessica said, "I like Emily. I like her a lot and I can see why you'd be attracted to her." She was obviously uncomfortable, judging from the flush in her neck and the way her eyes darted away from Catherine's. She didn't like this conversation. It was obvious. "It wouldn't look good, Cat. You know?"

Catherine nodded slowly, understanding exactly what Jessica was saying and trying to tell herself that it didn't really matter because nothing had happened anyway, and probably nothing would. "Look, I like Emily. I didn't at first, I can admit that, and there are still things about her that drive me a little crazy. But she's nice and genuine and...I like her." She cleared her throat and needlessly rearranged a few things on her desk. "And I think she likes me as well."

"You understand where I'm coming from, though, right?"

"I do."

"I just…we've got a reputation. Breckenridge donates a lot of money to us. A *lot* of money."

"I do the books, Jess. I'm aware."

"I know you are. I know. Sorry." Jessica rolled her lips in and bit down on them, then repeated herself. "I just worry."

"I know."

"Any appearance of…I hate the word impropriety, but…any appearance of something like that, something questionable, and people will talk. When people talk, the donations decrease. You know how social media can be. Nothing gets past anybody and even something tiny and insignificant can be blown out of proportion…" Jessica had started to ramble, which Catherine understood completely. They were friends and this was not a conversation Jessica wanted to be having, but Catherine had left her no choice. This was her own fault, Catherine knew, and she felt awful. When she couldn't take it anymore, she held up a hand.

"Jess. You're right. You're right. I know exactly what you're saying and I will make sure the shelter's reputation stays intact." She did her best to stay calm and reassuring, but inside, her stomach was churning sourly. The idea of the shelter's reputation coming under fire because of her literally made her feel ill.

"I'm sorry," Jessica said as she stood, her voice quiet now. "I don't mean to come across as a controlling bitch. I just—"

"You worry. I know. I've met you." Catherine went for a gentle smile, but was pretty sure she hit "I smell something foul" instead.

Jessica looked at her for a moment before gathering up her coat and coffee. "Okay, well." She was uncomfortable now and she felt bad. Catherine could tell both things easily as she'd known Jessica for years. The fact that she'd caused her to feel this way only made Catherine feel worse. Jessica was right. She was totally right. Maybe Catherine had just needed to hear it, uncomfortable and embarrassing as it had been.

"Okay," Jessica said again. "Thanks for hearing me out."

Catherine watched her go, called to Mo when he started to follow her. Much to her surprise and his credit, he came right back and sat next to her, and put his front paws on her thigh so she could reach him. Looking down at his gorgeous face, at his soulful brown eyes, she said simply, "Ugh."

—◇—

Catherine wasn't sure if the day had kept Jessica busy or if she'd just been avoiding her. Frankly, she was fine with either, as the more she thought about their earlier conversation, the more embarrassed she became about it. God, she should know better. She was a professional in a business environment, not some intern just learning the ropes. Jessica was right to be concerned. Junebug Farms might be a nonprofit, but that only made its reputation that much more valuable. Screwing with it would only bring trouble. Catherine should know that, damn it.

She'd taken advantage of the quiet day and gotten a ton of work done, which always made her feel better. Finishing up her response to an e-mail, she hit Send and then reached up over her head to stretch out her back. Rolling her head around on her shoulders caused some alarming cracking sounds to come from her vertebrae, but it felt good, so she let it go. Lowering her arms, her eyes fell on the vase of flowers from Emily, still colorful and lush even after a weekend in her chilly office and the fact that

Catherine had let the water evaporate almost completely before remembering to refill it. She'd been able to push Emily out of her head for the duration of the day, but now she came screeching back in, her face combining with Jessica's concerned words to make her mind one giant soup of confusion. She blew out a frustrated breath and shook her head.

"Well, that seems ominous." Emily's voice startled Catherine as she looked up and saw her standing in the doorway. *Did I just conjure her up?* Mo popped up from his bed with a happy yelp and ran to the door, wagging tail shaking his entire body in his excitement to see her. "That was quite a sigh," she said as she scratched Mo's ears. "Can I help?"

"What are you doing here?" Catherine asked, then realized how it sounded and added, "I didn't expect to see you today."

"I had some free time this afternoon, so I thought I'd come and walk a couple of dogs." She looked amazing today, and Catherine absently wondered if it was because she now had an invisible *Do Not Touch* sign hanging around her neck thanks to Jessica. Her jeans were faded, snug, and looked soft. Her shirt was a simple hooded top in gray and green slashed stripes, and the sleeves were long enough to cover the palms of her hands. Yet again, she looked both casual and elegant, and Catherine was envious even as she felt a flutter low in her stomach.

"That was nice of you. I know Lisa can always use help with that."

"I enjoy it." Emily gave a half-smile. "I also wanted to…talk to you. About something."

With a nod, Catherine gestured for her to sit. Emily surprised her by closing the door first, then moving to the chairs. Once she'd sat—and Mo had jumped up into her lap—Catherine asked, "What's up?"

Emily grimaced and moved her gaze to the window. "This is…um…" She scratched at her eyebrow, then shifted her eyes to rest on Catherine. "It's sensitive. Kind of."

Catherine furrowed her brow. "Okay."

"The other day, Thanksgiving, when I told my mother where I was going…"

"To my grandparents'?"

"Yes. To your grandparents'. But, to see you, really." Emily cleared her throat. She was clearly uncomfortable, and she shifted in her seat and dropped her gaze to Mo. Focusing on his face, his ears, his fur seemed to steady her. "My mom knows me pretty well."

Catherine nodded once and waited.

"The next day, she called me in to see her because she wanted to address the possibility that I might…"

Catherine cocked her head when Emily neglected to finish the sentence. "That you might—?"

"That I might be attracted to you." Emily looked up at her.

Their gazes held. Catherine felt her heart skip a beat and that fluttering in her abdomen kicked into high gear. "I see. And if you are?"

"That it's not a good idea to…" Emily cleared her throat again. "Pursue anything. Because of how it might look."

"I see," Catherine said again.

"Do you?" Emily sat forward in her chair, which Mo decided he was unhappy with and jumped down to return to his bed.

"I do because…" Catherine didn't realize she was going to say it until the words actually left her mouth. "I had a similar conversation with Jessica this morning."

That surprised Emily. Catherine could tell by the way she raised her eyebrows, sat back in her chair, and allowed a ghost of a satisfied smile cross her face. "You did?"

Catherine nodded, caught her bottom lip between her teeth, and arched one eyebrow, which caused what could only be called a soft whimper to come from Emily.

"Enough with the eyebrow thing. You're killing me over here."

Catherine swallowed hard. She could feel the heat start at her chest, rise up her throat and color her face.

Emily seemed amused by it and said quietly, "I love it when you blush, especially if I'm the cause."

"Stop it," Catherine said on a whisper.

Emily inhaled slowly, then exhaled. "Here's what I know: I *am* attracted to you. And I think you're attracted to me, too—even if you haven't admitted it."

If you only knew, Catherine thought, but managed to keep the words inside.

"So?" Emily asked. "What do we do?"

"I don't know that there's anything we *can* do. Your mother is right. My boss is right."

"I know."

"I think we need to...keep it professional." Catherine had to force the words out, but she knew it was for the best. There was the work issue and it was a big one. There was also the fact that they came from such radically different backgrounds. They were very different people without a ton in common. Yeah, this was definitely the best course of action. No doubt about it.

"I agree." Emily nodded, looking down at her hands. "It's for the best, really."

"It is. It's for the best."

They sat quietly for several moments. Catherine wasn't quite sure what to say at that point. She suspected Emily was in the same boat, and she allowed herself a small glimmer of mirth over Emily at a loss for words.

With another audible sigh, Emily slapped her hands on her thighs and pushed herself to a standing position. "Well. I guess I should go." Catherine stood as well. Emily stared at her shoes for a beat. When she looked up, her eyes were soft, tender. In a voice that was barely above a whisper, she asked, "Can I at least hug you? It feels kind of like good-bye and…I'd like to give you a hug. If that's okay."

She looked so sweet just then, Catherine couldn't have stopped herself if she'd tried…which she didn't. Emily stood looking at her, a gentle smile on her face, a tinge of hope in her voice, and Catherine was stepping toward her almost immediately, watching as Emily opened her arms and took her in, embracing her tightly. They were nearly the same height with Catherine in her heels, and their bodies fit together perfectly, like they were supposed to. Emily's arms were strong and tight around Catherine's torso, her body warm, and Catherine found herself feeling oddly protected, safe from the world around her. She inhaled quietly, took in the fresh, outdoorsy scent of Emily, of her hair, her clothes, her skin.

Knowing she could stand right there, wrapped up in Emily's embrace for hours, didn't help Catherine to keep a clear head, but she gently began to extricate herself, relieved to feel Emily doing the same. They parted slowly, but when they stood face-to-face, almost nose-to-nose, Catherine felt Emily's fingers tighten on her sides, preventing her from stepping away. She knew what was about to happen, but she couldn't stop it. She didn't want to stop it—a thought that both frightened her and turned her on in a way she hadn't felt since before Anna. Emily's brown eyes were locked on hers, the heat in them, the desire, plain to see.

And then Emily's mouth was on hers.

Emily's mouth was on hers and—oh, my God—all coherent thought was lost, sucked right out of her head and thrown into the atmosphere. Catherine's hands tightened on Emily's shoulders because she was sure if she let go, she'd fly off into oblivion. Emily's kiss was soft and hard, giving and demanding, shy and bold. She tasted like honey, sweet and clingy, and when she pushed her tongue into Catherine's mouth, Catherine whimpered. Actually whimpered.

The concept of time completely fled from Catherine's brain and when the kiss finally—slowly—ended, she had no idea how long they'd been fused together. Minutes? Hours? Days? She had no clue. Her head was fuzzy, her lips were swollen, her stomach was fluttering. Foreheads touching, she heard Emily whisper softly, "Oh, shit."

"Yeah."

Emily raised her hand, touched Catherine's bottom lip with her thumb, and said breathlessly, "God, you're a good kisser." And before Catherine could respond, Emily's hand slid around the back of her head and pulled her in for another soul-searing kiss that went on for days.

This time when they parted, Catherine put her palm flat against Emily's chest and gently pushed her to arm's length. Breathing raggedly, she said, "We have to stop."

Emily nodded, but words seemed to elude her and she looked so ridiculously sexy in that moment—her cheeks flushed hotly, her lips glistening, her pupils dilated—that Catherine had to grit her teeth and squeeze her eyes shut to keep from pulling her in for a third make-out round.

"Okay," she said, not happy with the tremor in her voice. "We…this…" She gave up for a moment, swallowed, gave herself time to catch her breath. Trying to focus more on keeping Emily away than on how close her hand was to Emily's breast, she wet her lips. "Okay," she tried again. "This doesn't change anything. At all. Everything we said earlier still applies."

"I know." Emily seemed to finally breathe at a normal rate. "I know. You're right."

"So. We have to…we just…" Catherine's knees felt weak and she felt too dangerously close to Emily at this point. Pushing away from her, she retreated to her chair and tried to sit like a normal person rather than drop into it, which was more what she did. "We're adults. We know this is a tricky situation. We're professionals. So…we act like it."

"Act like professionals," Emily said, nodding yet again.

"Yes."

"I can do that."

"Yes, you can. So can I."

Emily sucked in a deep breath. "Okay. Good. I'm glad we settled that."

"Me, too."

Jerking a thumb over her shoulder, Emily said, "I'll just go walk some dogs now."

It was Catherine's turn to nod like a bobblehead doll. "Okay. Good. You do that."

"I'm gonna go do that." Emily turned to the door, grasped the doorknob. As she pulled the door open, she looked back at Catherine and there was a mischievous glint in her eye. Then she winked and was gone.

Catherine gave it a beat. Two. Three. Then she dropped her head to her desk with a thump and groaned loudly enough that

Mo came over to her and tried to get to her face with his snout. She looked at him, suddenly thrilled to have his company. His head in her hands, she looked deep into his eyes and asked him, "What the hell do I do with that, Mo? Hmm? Tell me what to do now."

CHAPTER THIRTEEN

JESSICA WAS AN OBSERVER. She liked to sit back and take it all in, and she knew her people well. In fact, she would be willing to bet she knew them better than any of them realized. It wasn't because she was nosy, or because she was looking for anything to hold over them. It was because she cared. Plain and simple. She knew Maggie Simon had arthritis in her knees, so Jessica made sure to keep an eye on how much lifting and bending she did in the gift shop, popping in "unexpectedly" to help more often than not. She knew that Bill Tracey didn't have anybody at home to talk to or appreciate him, and that he would stay at the shelter twenty-four hours a day if he could, so she made sure to thank him for his hard work and let him know every day how valuable he was to Junebug Farms.

She pushed through the double doors to the dog wing and walked halfway down the row to Lisa's desk. She knew about Lisa, too. She knew Lisa'd had a decade-long rift with her mother, and she'd known when Lisa had been fighting her attraction to Ashley. Jessica had watched from the sidelines, stepping in once or twice just to place some perspective in front of Lisa before stepping back out again. Jessica considered herself a silent observer. It wasn't her place to meddle—though if she thought the shelter was being aversely affected, she'd stick her nose in. For the most part, though, she sat back and watched, amused by life in general.

As she stopped in front of Lisa's desk, she noticed Emily Breckenridge heading out the back door with a large Lab mix of some sort on a leash, and she was reminded of her discussion with Catherine that morning. To Lisa, she said, "You got yourself another dog walker, I see."

Lisa was poking at her keyboard, but turned to follow Jessica's gaze, then nodded and turned back to her computer. "Yup. I'll take as many as I can get."

Jessica half-sat on the corner of Lisa's desk.

Lisa glanced up at her, saw her stance, and stopped typing. "Oh. There's a discussion about to happen? Is that what's going on here?" She grinned.

Jessica was still looking after Emily, who was now outside, the door having closed behind her. Pointing in that direction, Jessica said, "I remember when you were first starting to look at Ashley." She turned back to Lisa. "I mean, *really* look at her. That way."

Lisa nodded, a half-grin pulling up one corner of her mouth.

Still pointing, Jessica asked, "Have you noticed…?" She let the sentence trail off, but didn't have to wait long.

"That Emily looks at Catherine that way? Yup."

Jessica groaned. "Yeah, I was afraid I wasn't the only one who saw that."

"Well," Lisa said, propping her chin in her hand. "She's been pretty subtle about it. You know? She's not obnoxious like her brother, that's for sure."

Jessica snorted. "Thank God. I talked to Catherine about it earlier."

"You did? What do you mean?"

"I was just trying to get a feel for whether the attraction was mutual."

"Ah," Lisa said, obviously catching the drift. "That could be…dicey."

"Exactly."

"I bet that wasn't an awkward conversation at all."

"Oh, no." Jessica chuckled, but it wasn't a happy sound. She didn't like being in this position. She and Catherine were friends, after all. Had been since school. And Jessica liked to think she ran the shelter with a very light hand. She didn't have lists upon lists of rules. She was laid back. Casual. She wanted everybody to be happy and comfortable and she didn't think getting involved in the dating lives of her employees was something she needed to be doing. As an example, Catherine and Anna had hooked up and, though they were civil, their tension was obvious to those around them. But Jessica left it alone mostly. They were grown women who could handle their own messes. Still, that didn't really affect the reputation of the shelter like Catherine and Emily had the potential to. No, this was a completely different situation.

As if reading her mind, Lisa asked, "Are you worried about what people might say?"

Jessica scoffed, no words necessary, and nodded even as potentially damaging Tweets and Facebook posts and Tumblr messages rocketed through her brain. The Internet was a blessing and a curse for a business—that was for certain. She turned her gaze to Lisa.

Lisa's and Ashley's situation was different. Ashley was a volunteer. She had her own job someplace else and if things had become disruptive, Jessica could've easily asked Ashley to stop volunteering. Of course, that hadn't happened, and she didn't expect it to, as Lisa and Ashley had "forever couple" written all over them, something that alternately made her smile with delight and grimace with sour envy. The Catherine and Emily situation, on the other hand, was a scandal bomb with a short

148

fuse. The woman in charge of finances at the shelter entangled with the shelter's biggest donor? Was no one else braced for the explosion?

"Want me to give her advice?" Lisa asked, waggling her eyebrows as she looked in the direction of the double doors. Sheath of papers in hand, Catherine was clicking down the hall, all business suit and serious glasses. Whispering, Lisa said, "She loves me, you know."

Jessica rolled her eyes and laughed, then turned to watch Catherine's approach. Though they'd known each other much too long for Jessica to feel any sexual attraction to Catherine, she could never deny the woman was gorgeous. Her brown hair was partially pulled back today and her suit was royal blue, which really made her eyes stand out. Emily Breckenridge could not be faulted for her taste—that was for sure.

As Catherine stopped at the desk and opened her mouth to speak, the back door opened.

Lisa and Jessica both glanced that way to see Emily coming back in with the Lab mix. She smiled and waved. "Hey, Jess," she said cheerfully. Jessica waved back at her and when she turned back, Catherine had a hand near her mouth, her fingertips touching her lips, her cheeks flushed pink.

Catherine quickly set the papers down on Lisa's desk, muttered, "Here are those reports I borrowed," and turned on her heel to click back the way she'd come. At the other end of the hall, Emily grinned in what was obviously amusement, leashed up a new dog, and headed back out the door.

Once each door had closed tightly, Jessica and Lisa looked at each other. Lisa's eyebrows were raised in what Jessica predicted was a duplicate of the expression on her own face. Blowing her hair off her forehead, Jessica slowly shook her head back and forth.

"Oh, shit," Lisa said.

"Exactly." Jessica rubbed at her forehead with her fingertips, feeling the oncoming headache like a Mack truck barreling down the highway.

Catherine couldn't focus.

Not only could she not focus, she was angry about it. She did not handle it well when her concentration was messed with. She didn't enjoy being distracted. She was a professional and she had things to do, damn it. Work to take care of. Calls to make and e-mails to answer and figures to go over. You know: work.

Instead, she sat at her desk during the last part of the afternoon, absently stroked her dog's head (he was on her lap because she was doing nothing at all, so why shouldn't he put that space to good use?), and gazing dreamily out the window. All she could think about was that kiss.

That kiss.

One of the very first thoughts that had entered her mind once Emily was blissfully gone from her office was that Anna had never kissed her like that. And Anna had been a decent kisser as far as Catherine was concerned. They'd had their issues, but sex hadn't been one of them. They'd been quite compatible. But Emily? God, the way Emily kissed her was...it was so many things. All at once. It was hot, it was demanding, it was promising, it was gentle, but not. It was like a preview of what was to come should they go further. And that's the part that scared Catherine because she, absolutely and without a shade of doubt, wanted to go further. She couldn't. She shouldn't. She wouldn't. She knew all of those things.

But she wanted to. Dear God, she wanted to.

And that was the problem. She was much too affected and that wasn't good. To be affected by somebody else meant she didn't have complete control over herself, and that was never okay with Catherine. Just as she was about to fall into a spiral of pros and cons and everything that was wrong with her life at the moment, her phone rang and she snatched it up.

Five minutes later, she felt better. Joplin's was short a waitress tonight and asked if she'd mind. It was a Monday, which meant it might be busy. Lots of restaurants were closed on Mondays, so Joplin's raked in the displaced diners and fed them well. Could be a chance to make some nice tips. Plus, it would take her mind off of the current subject dominating her brain. This was good. She felt better already.

She had one arm pushed into her coat and Mo on his leash when she turned to see Emily appear in her doorway. Catherine's stomach did an instant flip-flop.

"Hi," Emily said. Her dark hair glistened with melted snowflakes and her cheeks were rosy from having been outside with the dogs.

"Hey."

"Heading out?"

"I am."

Emily nodded. "Do you think..." She hesitated, wet her lips as she gazed out the window, seemingly collecting her thoughts. Catherine watched her throat move as she swallowed. "Do you think we could grab some coffee again? Or something? Drinks?"

No. We absolutely should not be grabbing anything of the sort, because all I'll want to do is kiss you some more, and that's not an option here. Catherine's thoughts were loud and clear and rational and logical. Apparently, her mouth disagreed. "Sure, I don't see why not."

"Great." Emily's smile was wide and radiant and Catherine's stomach poked at her again. Or maybe it wasn't her stomach, as it was a bit…lower… "How about tonight?"

"Oh, no, I can't. I just took a shift at Joplin's. They're shorthanded." It shocked Catherine how she could be so relieved and so disappointed at the same time.

"Oh. Bummer."

Catherine wondered if Emily could possibly be going through the same gymnastics in her own head, wanting but knowing she can't, understanding but angry about it. "Maybe another time?"

Emily nodded. "Sure. Be careful driving tonight. The roads might be slick."

Her concern warmed Catherine a bit. "I will."

With that, Emily was gone. Catherine watched her walk up the hall, her eyes drawn to the very pleasingly shaped ass those snug jeans were hugging. Catching herself, Catherine jerked her eyes down to Mo and shook her head. "Okay," she said to the dog that, as usual, was riveted by her words. "That was good. Right? Polite, but good. I can be polite and not say no, but then never be available, right? Is that mean? She'll eventually give up. Won't she?" *Ugh*. This felt awful and she knew immediately she wouldn't be able to play that game. Not with Emily.

Geronimo cocked his head in that adorable way dogs do, completely intent on her face.

"Come on. Let's go home." Tugging the leash and making a clicking sound with her tongue, she and Mo headed home so she could feed him and get ready for her shift at the restaurant. She felt better, like things had been nipped in the bud and it made her wonder if the Universe sent her the unexpected shift at Joplin's on purpose, the intention being to keep her from accepting Emily's invitation.

No matter. She felt relief and headed to the restaurant whistling a little tune and ready to make some money. She had her eye on another pair of boots; she was going to order them this week.

Joplin's was pretty busy, which was good. Not only did that mean more tips, but it also made the night go by faster. She'd been working steadily for two hours when something caught her eye and made her stutter to a stop, very nearly causing the two entrees she was carrying to slide right off their plates.

Emily sat at Joplin's small bar, sipping a drink and scrolling on her phone.

Catherine had trouble processing the emotions tossing around inside her like ships on rough waters. She was annoyed. How dare Emily come to her place of work and just…sit there? She was thrilled. Emily had taken it upon herself to come to Catherine's place of work and…what? Hang out? Worst of all, she was turned on. Completely. Emily had come to her place of work, took a seat, and…Catherine didn't know what. But it was something. It meant something. Didn't it? On top of the annoyance and the, yes, slight anger, there was exhilaration.

Which she immediately did her best to tamp down. This wasn't good.

Pasting on a smile, Catherine delivered the entrees to her customers and politely asked if there was anything else they needed. Once they had smiled and shaken their heads, she walked purposefully over to the bar, taking in the sight of Emily as she approached.

The jeans were the same as earlier—Catherine could tell by the spot near Emily's knee that was washed nearly white, but the rest of the outfit had been dressed up a bit. A black leather jacket hung off the back of the barstool and Catherine did her best not to think of Emily wearing it or how sexy it probably looked with the knee-high black boots she had on. On top, she wore a V-neck shirt, deep purple with subtle silver stripes running through it. Her dark hair was down, the ends curling in on themselves, and it was all Catherine could do not to reach out and twirl a chunk of it around her finger, give it a gentle tug.

"What are you doing here?" she asked quietly when she reached the bar.

Emily glanced up and the smile she gave Catherine was radiant. "You ask me that a lot."

"Because I never know."

"I thought I'd wait for you to finish your shift and make sure you got home okay. It's been snowing for the last hour." When Catherine eyed her drink, she added, "Club soda."

Catherine pinched the bridge of her nose. "I can get home on my own."

"I know that."

"We talked about this today, Emily. About how this is a bad idea."

"Yeah, I know that, too. But I asked if we could go for a drink, and you said yes."

"I was being polite!"

"I don't believe that for a second."

Their gazes held and the current that passed between them was palpable. Catherine tried to think of the right thing to say, but instead, she stood there looking. Just looking. Which seemed to amuse Emily, who leaned in close enough for Catherine to inhale her spicy perfume.

"I think that table needs you," Emily whispered and gestured with her eyes.

Catherine whipped her head around to find a fifty-something man making eye contact with her. When she looked back at Emily, she was still smiling.

"Go. Work. I'll be right here when you're done."

"You're infuriating."

"You're not the first person to tell me that." Emily grinned, picked up her phone, and went back to scrolling.

The rest of Catherine's shift was weird for her. She was hyperaware of Emily at the bar, and though she was far enough away not to cause a distraction, she still managed to be distracting. She wasn't always looking in Catherine's direction when she glanced her way, but there were occasions when she was. And Catherine's body reacted, much to her great annoyance and irritation. She flushed hotly. Her stomach fluttered. Her hands got shaky. It was not good. Not good at all. This needed to stop.

Finally, the last customers left and the waitstaff counted up their tips so they could tip out the bussers. Catherine was exhausted. *This is why I don't normally work here on weeknights*, she thought, trying not to think about her aching feet.

"Hey, who's the hottie at the bar and why is she still here?" Bradley stood next to her at a table as they tallied up cash and receipts.

Catherine glanced up. Emily still sat on her stool, but now she was chatting up Ken, the bartender, who busted out laughing at something she'd said. Catherine found herself smiling before she realized it. When she returned her attention to Bradley, he was scrutinizing her, his expression squinty.

"Is she here for you?"

Catherine sighed and lifted one shoulder in a half-shrug. "Sort of."

"Sort of? What's that mean? You need to give me more."

"I can't right now, Bradley. I'm so tired and…I'm not even sure about any of it. Just…give me some time and I'll tell you the whole story. Okay? Not right now. My brain is too fried."

It was obvious Bradley didn't like that answer, but he respected her enough to let it go. Which didn't mean he stopped looking in Emily's direction. "She's really attractive. She's got a slick sense of fashion. Not too dressy, but not too casual."

Catherine agreed wholeheartedly with him, but said nothing, letting him put color commentary to whatever Emily was doing.

"Oh, the black leather jacket is sexy. God. You need to snap her up, Cat. Seriously. Get on that."

Catherine grinned and shook her head. "So many complications, my friend. So very many. You have no idea." Before he could respond, she finished what she was doing and stepped away. "Goodnight. Get home safely."

Gathering her things together from the back room specified for the staff, Catherine thought about the day and how it had been all over the map. Her conversation with Jessica this morning had been sobering, but she'd accepted it. Also sobering and—if she was being honest—a little sad had been her conversation with Emily. People didn't want them together before they had even had a chance to discuss it themselves, just the two of them. So it had been a bummer of a day all around.

Except when Emily had kissed her.

God, how many times had she replayed that at this point? Twenty? Fifty? Three hundred? She was simultaneously impressed by Emily and angry with her. Impressed that, even after all their talk about why the two of them together was a bad idea, Emily had still kissed her, thrown caution to the wind and said, "Screw all those people. I'm doing this." Angry that she'd given Catherine even the smallest taste of what she'd be missing out on, as now it was all she could think about.

Oh, my God, that kiss.

She shook her head, trying her best to literally shake the thoughts away. Donning her coat, she headed back toward the dining room. Bradley stopped her.

"The hottie said she'd meet you outside." He waggled his eyebrows, causing Catherine to roll her eyes at him. "I expect details soon," he said, his tone a warning.

"I know, I know," she muttered, turning around to exit through the employee entrance in the back of the building.

Emily hadn't been kidding about the snow. It was early in the season, but was often par for the course in upstate New York. The flakes coming down were light and fluffy, more pretty than annoying, and several cars in the parking lot were running, warming up while their owners brushed them clean. Catherine's was not running, obviously. It was, however, clean. No snow on it at all.

Next to it, a shiny BMW in baby blue was idling quietly. Emily Breckenridge sat behind the wheel, and when she looked up to meet Catherine's eyes, she smiled and got out.

"Hey," she said as Catherine pushed the button on her key fob, releasing two beeps and two blinks of the lights from her car. "I would have had this running for you, but I don't have your keys. Obviously." She blew into her hands. "It's cold tonight."

Catherine opened the door, got in, and started the engine. "Did you clean off all the snow?"

"I did."

"Thank you."

"You're very welcome."

"I have all-wheel drive, you know. I'll be fine."

"Yup. You probably will."

They stood for a moment and Catherine marveled at the awkwardness, given she'd had her tongue in Emily's mouth earlier the same day. She pretended to fiddle with the heater, not sure what to say and not trusting any words that might spring forth from her lips.

Emily spoke first. "I was wondering if you wanted to have that quick drink. I know it's a weeknight and we both have to work tomorrow, but..." She looked off into the distance as other cars pulled away. Various people waved to Catherine and called goodnights as they exited the restaurant. "I wanted to see you."

"You saw me already today."

With a wan smile, Emily said, "I wanted to see you again."

Catherine debated. And she was angry that she was actually debating. "This is a bad idea, Emily."

"It is. I know." Emily still smiled at her.

"It's kind of late on a Monday to go out for a drink."

"Which is why I talked your bartender into selling me a bottle of wine. It's in my car. You guys don't mess around with the wine selection."

Catherine grinned, knowing it was true. Their wine list was impressive. And expensive.

"What do you say?" The wind kicked up some snow, swirling it around as Emily bounced on her boot-clad feet. She had to be cold, standing there. As if on cue, she balled her fists together and blew into them.

"I have Geronimo at home," Catherine said. "He's been alone for a while now."

"I know. Your place? I promise not to stay long. I just…" She gazed off again and Catherine realized she liked when that happened. It gave her a moment to study Emily's beautiful face without her seeing. Snow had melted in her hair and now sparkled among the strands of midnight. Her cheeks and the tip of her nose were red. Catherine skipped right over her mouth because concentrating on that would bring her nothing but flashbacks. She moved on to Emily's chin, which led down to an elegant throat…Catherine swallowed hard. "I just had this uncontrollable urge to spend another hour with you." Thank God she'd spoken and cut off Catherine's train of thought. Catherine blinked rapidly several times, trying to focus on the words. Emily was looking at her now. "Also, I'm freezing."

"Okay," Catherine heard herself say. She was surprised, but not, as she was beginning to understand that her defenses sucked when it came to Emily Breckenridge. She'd need to work on that. Resigned to this fate, she added, "But only for a quick drink. I'm exhausted."

"Deal," Emily said with a nod, and the way her face lit up was adorable even though Catherine tried to pretend not to see it. "I'll follow you. Be careful. It's slick. And watch for deer."

"Yes, Mom," Catherine said with a playful roll of her eyes.

Turning the music up very loud—too loud, really—was the only way Catherine could prevent herself from completely overthinking this. She drove carefully, keeping a close eye on the wooded sides of the road. Joplin's was located outside the city and next to a vineyard and winery, which made their outdoor seating area simply gorgeous in the summer. In the winter months, however, the three-mile stretch of country road leading from civilization to the restaurant could be slippery and dangerous. Add to that the possibility of deer crossing and it became like playing a video game, eyes straining to see obstacles that may or may not be there in the first place, hoping against hope that you can hit the brakes in time to prevent disaster. But she managed to stay alert, singing loudly along with Lady Gaga, the headlights in her rearview mirror offering a comfort she didn't expect. In twenty minutes, she pulled into her driveway, Emily sliding to a stop behind her.

"Maybe I should have been following you," Catherine commented with a glance at Emily's not-for-winter tires.

"I admit, my car's not the greatest in the snow." Emily grimaced.

With a shake of her head, Catherine slid her key into the lock and went inside, met instantly by twenty pounds of wiggling, licking, very excited dog. Catherine couldn't help but laugh. She set her purse and keys on the table inside the door and squatted down to love on Mo while Emily closed the door behind them.

"That is quite a greeting," Emily said.

"It's definitely something I missed," Catherine said, trying to talk without opening her mouth as Mo bathed her face in dog kisses. She'd learned the hard way—more than once—that he was super quick with the tongue.

"Where's your corkscrew?" Emily asked, toeing off her snowy boots as she held up the bottle. "And wineglasses."

Catherine stood. "Here, give me your coat. Let's do this like civilized people." She smiled at Emily as she took a hanger from the nearby closet. Mo turned his attention to the company, jumping at Emily's leg until she noticed him. "Yeah, the jumping is something we have to work on. Mo, off." He listened, but it was evidently torture for him, judging by the way his entire body thrummed with excitement. "Okay," she said to Emily. "Now you can love him."

"Oh, good boy!" Emily set the wine bottle on the table next to Catherine's keys and then padded into the living room in her sock feet, just far enough to sit on the floor with Mo and let him jump all over her lap. Catherine watched, amused and strangely warm inside. After a beat, she picked up the wine and took it into the kitchen.

She set it on the counter and pulled open the drawer that held the corkscrew. That's when she actually looked at the label. "Um...Emily?"

Emily appeared in the doorway, Mo sniffing at her feet. "Mmhmm?"

"This is a crazy expensive bottle of wine."

A shrug. "I guess."

"No, there's no guessing. It is. Like $250."

"Okay, well, open it. Let's see if it's worth it." She smiled and squatted back down to play with Mo.

Slicing the label with a knife, Catherine tried not to listen to the little voice in her head. The one that was saying, *That's a car payment. She just spent a car payment on a bottle of wine that will be gone in four glasses.* As she punctured the cork with the corkscrew and turned the handle, it continued. *How much dog food would that buy for Mo? How many of Mom's bills could I pay with that money?* The cork made that wonderful pop that corks do when they're pulled free of their bottle.

"I love that sound," Emily said as she stood. Catherine could feel eyes on her. "You okay?"

Catherine nodded as she pulled two glasses down from a cupboard. Still felt the eyes.

"Is it the wine?" When Catherine didn't make eye contact, she added, "The cost of the wine?"

"It's just a little hard for me to wrap my brain around." Catherine didn't enjoy the fact that Emily could read her so easily. She finally looked at Emily, who was wearing her usual smile of amusement. Turning away, she poured the wine. "And why do you always look at me like that?"

"Because I find you endlessly entertaining."

"I don't know how to take that." Handing a glass to Emily, she said, "This had better be fabulous wine."

Emily held up her glass. "To ridiculously expensive wine and the girl it makes uncomfortable." Emily touched her glass softly to Catherine's.

"It doesn't make me uncomfortable," Catherine said, trying unsuccessfully to keep the defensive tone from her voice as Emily sipped.

"Yes, it does. But that's okay because it will also shut you right up. It's that good."

Catherine pursed her lips as she gave Emily a little glare, but then she sipped. "Oh, my God."

"See?"

Catherine took another sip, let the flavors coat her tongue. "Oh, my God."

Emily laughed. "I know."

"It's so…complex."

Emily nodded her agreement as she sipped again.

"It's soft, but bold…a little bit of fruit, but just a touch." Catherine gazed up as she searched for the right descriptors. "Some pepper or…what is that? Leather, maybe?"

162

"I get the pepper, but not the leather. I get more…almost coffee or something."

"Yes! Coffee! Just a tiny touch, though, like it's barely there. On the back." They stood in the kitchen, sipping wine and just sharing space. "This is the most delicious wine I've ever had," Catherine said finally.

"Yeah? Worth the money?"

With a snort, Catherine said, "Worth *your* money, yes."

Emily burst into laughter. "I like you, Ms. Gardner. I like you a lot."

"Yeah? I'm glad," Catherine said quietly.

The room suddenly felt too warm. And full of words. So many words that Catherine should be saying. Words like, *this is a bad idea. Doesn't matter that we like each other, we can only be friends. That's what we decided, remember? I can't risk the shelter's reputation. I'm a professional and I'm respected. You're supposed to outshine your brother, not cause another problem for your family's company. See? Us together is dangerous. Also, I can't believe you spontaneously spent $250 on a bottle of wine to drink with me. And my God, you smell good.* Instead, she simply sipped her wine and watched over the rim of her glass as Emily did the same.

After what felt like hours of looking at each other (but was in reality probably only a few seconds), Emily spoke. "So, this is your place." She looked around the kitchen, made a show of studying the cabinets, the refrigerator, the stove.

Chatter about mundane, ordinary things. Oh, thank God. Catherine nodded. "It's not much, but it's home."

Emily turned and walked through the living room. Catherine followed, but stayed in the doorway, leaning one shoulder on the doorjamb and trying not to be self-conscious about her modest home.

"I like it." Emily wandered past the well-worn couch, the bold print chair that Catherine had vacillated about buying for over a month before finally parting with the money, the gas fireplace. She sipped her wine as she looked over the framed photographs, picked one up.

"That's Jason when he was little. You met him at Thanksgiving."

Emily nodded in recognition and replaced the frame. She looked at the fireplace for a long moment, and Catherine wondered if she was thinking about turning it on. The thought had occurred to her as well, but she'd waved it away, knowing it would make things far too cozy and warm. Seemingly coming to the same decision, Emily stepped away from the fireplace and moved to the coffee table. Picking up a magazine with half the cover torn off, she grinned and said, "*People* looks a little different than I remember it."

"Yeah, Mo decided he doesn't really care for Ben Affleck."

"I prefer Matt Damon myself." Emily set it back down and gave the room a once-over. "I like it," she said again, this time with a nod. "It's very you."

"It is? In what way?"

"Well, it's tidy. Orderly. Serious and sophisticated." Emily gave her a half-grin that made her stomach tighten. "But once you're in here and you look around, soak it all in, it's warmer than you initially thought. Comfortable. Inviting."

Even though Emily was across the room, their gazes held and Catherine was almost sure she could feel Emily's hands on her, roaming over her skin. It was the strangest sensation and it both aroused her and made her uncomfortable. Catherine spoke, her voice surprising her with its huskiness. "You should probably go," she said quietly, then cleared her throat.

Emily nodded. "I think you're right." She downed the last of her wine while still standing in the living room. Then she walked toward Catherine who, in a completely uncharacteristic attack of bravery, didn't move out of the way. She simply turned sideways in the doorway to allow Emily to pass, but in order to do so, she had to slide through while facing Catherine. She stopped and stood there, barely a breath of air between them, their noses almost touching. Catherine's lips were parted and her brain warred with itself in her head, voices contradicting each other. *Kiss me, don't kiss me, kiss me, don't kiss me, please kiss me, don't you dare kiss me...*

Emily's dark eyes were nearly black and later, Catherine would wonder how she managed it, but she pushed her way past Catherine and into the relative safety of the kitchen where she set her glass on the counter next to the sink.

Catherine couldn't decide if she was relieved or disappointed.

"Well," Emily said finally, and had to clear her throat and say it again. "Thank you so much for allowing me to crash your night." As she spoke, she seemed to relax, as if her comfort was directly proportional to the space between them. Gesturing to the wine, she said, "You keep that, but finish it within the next three days or so. Don't waste it."

Catherine wanted to tell her it was absurd for her to leave the wine after she paid so much for it, but she couldn't seem to find her voice. She watched as Emily went through the other doorway of the kitchen to the foyer, and she walked farther into the kitchen so she could see her putting on her boots. Mo approached, sniffing her jeans.

"You gonna help me put my boots on, buddy? Hmm? I bet you smell Dave." Emily talked softly to him and Catherine realized it was a coping mechanism. It was how she kept herself from looking at Catherine. Finding her own coat in the closet, she put it on hastily, pulled her keys out of the pocket, and gave a half-hearted wave in Catherine's direction. In any other case, Catherine might have found this all incredibly insulting, but the thing was, she got it. She totally understood Emily's need to get away immediately, so she gave a wave back.

"Thanks for the wine," she said quietly.

"You're welcome." Emily held her gaze again before it seemed that she forcefully pulled her eyes away, opened the door, and was gone.

Catherine didn't move a muscle until she heard Emily's car start and the crunch of snow under the tires as she backed out of the driveway. Only when the glare of her headlights through the kitchen window faded away did Catherine let out the breath she'd been holding. She set down her now-empty wine glass and covered her eyes with both hands. Mo poked at her with his nose and whined softly. Removing her hands, she looked down at him, then dropped to the floor and sat with her legs crossed. He wasted no time climbing into her lap and curling into a ball, reminding her that it was way past bedtime.

Words failed her. She couldn't latch onto a single one as they swirled through her head like dead leaves on a windy fall day. Not a single one.

Instead, she simply closed her eyes and shook her head slowly back and forth.

CHAPTER FOURTEEN

EMILY WENT TO BED furious with herself, and though she woke up feeling the tiniest bit better, she still felt a jumble of thoughts tossing around her head. As she lay there in her queen-sized bed, Dave stretched languidly, straightening all four legs and making himself as long as possible. He took up more of the mattress than she did.

"That probably wasn't smart of me, huh?" she asked her dog. "I mean, how hard is my head?" Glancing in his big brown eyes, she added, "Don't answer that."

The clock on the nightstand told her it was 6:27 a.m., which meant she had a little time before she needed to get into the shower. So she rubbed her hand along Dave's soft belly, snuggled into the thick down comforter, and her thoughts turned back to the night before.

Watching Catherine work had been…Emily didn't even have the words for it. Catherine hadn't noticed her right away, so for a while, it was almost as if Emily was spying on her. (She didn't like that descriptor, but had to admit to herself that it was somewhat accurate.) She'd spent time chatting with Ken, the middle-aged guy who'd been tending bar for nearly thirty years and really knew his stuff. He'd kept her mind from wandering into dangerous territory, though he didn't know it, and she'd tipped him generously. Catherine was excellent at her job. Emily wasn't sure why she'd been surprised given her own experience on her terrible blind date, but she had. The customers loved her. She laughed and joked with them—which was a side of her Emily hadn't seen at the shelter—and many seemed to be familiar with her, which told Emily that there were customers who came back here for her. Emily wasn't a girl who was affected one way or the other by any type of uniform, but Catherine wore her black pants, white oxford, and black waist apron with unexpected sophistication. It also didn't hurt that the pants were snug and that Catherine had a great ass.

Emily hadn't really thought it through as she'd driven to the restaurant. That wasn't the way she did things. She was a spontaneous person, one who tended to leap before looking, and she suspected Catherine was exactly the opposite. She'd wanted to see Catherine last night, Catherine had other plans, Emily jumped in so she could see her anyway. Solved. Simple. It wasn't until she'd pulled into the parking lot of Joplin's that she had stopped for a second and wondered what exactly she was doing. Her mother would be unimpressed, to say the least. She knew that without a doubt, but also had no plans to tell her. But what if Catherine had been equally unimpressed? What if she had seen Emily sitting at the bar, stormed over, and told her to get lost? Emily had forced herself to entertain that possible scenario. The only course of action then would've been to leave. She'd hoped that wouldn't happen.

It hadn't.

In fact, when Catherine first saw her, Emily was pretty sure she'd seen a ghost of a smile and a slight blush. Catherine wasn't free with the smiles, so even the shadow of one made Emily giddy and she let herself believe that Catherine might actually have been glad to see her, even though she may have also been a bit irritated.

The wine had been a last-minute idea, as had brushing off Catherine's car for her and following her home. It all seemed like a grand plan, but once they'd been in Catherine's house, alone together, drinking excellent wine in the subdued lighting of her cozy living room? Good God, Emily had had a very, *very* difficult time controlling herself. She'd never been around anybody— *anybody*—who turned her on the way Catherine did. Just being across the room from Catherine did things to her. She'd started to sweat and her underwear dampened and there was a ringing in her ears that almost drove her nuts. As she stood in Catherine's living room and sipped her wine, their eyes locked on each other, Emily knew one thing and one thing only: she had to get the hell out of there or she was going to tear Catherine's clothes off her and take her right there on the kitchen floor. She'd felt her left hand ball into a fist at her side and it was all she could do to keep from actually running.

It all seemed a little silly now. The intensity of nighttime tended to ease enormously in the light of day, and now she simply lay there in her bed with her dog and felt a little foolish, like she should apologize. Should she?

"What do you think, Dave?"

The dog opened his eyes, which had been closed in bliss at the belly rub he was getting. He shifted off his side and onto his stomach so he could look at Emily's face. She grinned as it occurred to her that he was actually listening, interested in her voice.

"Did I make a fool of myself? I might have." She caressed the side of his face, rubbed a velvety ear between her fingers. "Do I leave it alone? Apologize? Try to see her again?" With a groan of frustration she said, "God, she makes me crazy! Why does she make me so crazy? I should just stay far, far away from her. This will do nobody any good. Right?"

Dave still studied her, even cocked his head to the side as if analyzing her words.

"Seriously, Dave. Would I be any different than Clark if I went there? I mean, I would. Of course I would. I'm not a creep. But…it would still come down to how it makes the Foundation look, right? There'd be no way around that. People are horrible, and they'd immediately assume Junebug gets more money because I'm banging their accountant. Because people suck." She blew out a huge breath, then said quietly, "My mother would be so disappointed in me."

She stared at the ceiling for long moments, then—against her better judgment—voiced another thought. "There is one other thing to consider, though," she said to him, holding up a finger. "That kiss. Did I tell you about that?"

In response, Dave army-crawled farther up the bed so he could lavish his own kisses on her face, which made her laugh, she couldn't help it.

"Yes, you are a good kisser, Dave, I promise. But her?" Emily made what sounded like a growl as she shook her head back and forth on the pillow in wonder. "I have never been kissed like that in my life." She turned to her dog. "*In my life*, Dave. God." After a beat, she said, "I can't think about this anymore. I'm going to drive myself insane." Pulling her dog in close, she kissed his head several times in quick succession, causing his tail to beat loudly against the mattress. "Thanks for listening, pal. You're the best."

Their lovefest ended, Emily hauled herself out of bed, used both hands to scratch all over her scalp, then headed for the bathroom of her downtown loft. As she walked past the dresser where her cell sat charging, she raised her eyebrows at it, a notion tickling at the back of her brain. She shrugged it off and decided to revisit it after her shower.

━◆━

"Catherine?"

Regina's voice sounded over the intercom and made Catherine flinch guiltily in her chair, as if she'd actually been caught daydreaming. Clearing her throat, she responded. "Yes?"

"Can you come out here for a minute?" Regina's voice held a smile. She was endlessly cheerful. Some days, Catherine thought it was nice. Today, it just grated on her nerves like nails on a chalkboard or a fork scraping against a plate.

"Be right there." Generally when Regina called her to the front desk, it was for her to answer some inane question about the computers. Catherine was the most computer-savvy one in the building, and it was difficult to get their IT person on the line when there was an issue, so Catherine was the next best thing. "Stay," she said to Mo, curled up on his bed in the corner. His tail thumped the floor once, but he obeyed. With a sigh, she pushed herself up out of her chair and headed to the front desk, her legs feeling heavy. She'd gotten little sleep last night—not surprisingly. Her head wouldn't shut up. It insisted on analyzing and re-analyzing and overanalyzing every single thing that had happened last night. Everything that was said. She distinctly remembered, at one point, Mo was snoring comfortably at the foot of the bed and she had to consciously prevent herself from nudging him awake with her foot, so envious of his slumber she was.

Things were starting to pick up for the holidays, as was expected. There were several people wandering the lobby, a few in the gift shop, and the doors to the dog wing opened and closed regularly.

She saw the enormous bouquet of flowers before she even got close.

Oh, she did not...

"These are for you," Regina said, smiling like she knew something even though she didn't. "Who's the Romeo?" she asked, waggling her eyebrows.

"There is no Romeo," Catherine said, taking in the arrangement, which had to be nearly twice the size of the last one—which was still alive and flourishing colorfully on her desk.

Regina did a lousy job of hiding her disappointment and Catherine felt bad. Forcing a smile, she thanked Regina in as friendly a tone as she could muster, hefted the vase (no easy feat), and carried it back to her office where she set it on her desk and sat down in her chair. The flowers completely obscured her view of the door and they were beautiful—carnations and lilies and daisies and black-eyed Susans and white roses and snapdragons. A huge assortment, gorgeously full of color, enough to brighten the room and the five closest other rooms on this dismal and gray winter day. It must have cost an arm and a leg.

The white envelope containing the card seemed to taunt her as she tried to keep herself from grabbing it. She had a stare-down with it until it won, and she snatched it off its little plastic fork with a growl and tore it open.

I know I surprised you and probably shouldn't have.
I know we discussed it all and made a decision.
But I had a great time last night. I hope you did, too.
SorryNotSorry
Emily

God, she was frustrating! When Catherine realized she was smiling, she had to work hard to wipe it off. This was ridiculous. They *had* talked about it. They'd decided together to back off, to keep the relationship strictly business. They'd agreed.

They were failing miserably.

She made a sound that apparently caused Mo some concern, as he came over from his place in the corner of the office and put his front paws on her thigh. Catherine swiveled slightly so he could jump, and he did, curling himself into her lap. She stroked his fur, felt the warmth of his body heat as she continued to gaze at the flowers.

"Well, I have to say thank you, don't I?" When Mo lifted his head to look up at her, she shrugged. "It'd be rude not to, right? I'm not a rude person. I mean, look at these. They must have cost a fortune and a half." She gestured at the flowers, the arrangement bigger than the dog. He settled his head back down and sighed, evidently unimpressed with her line of reasoning. Stretching her arms over his body, she reached for her keyboard and typed up an e-mail.

━◇━

Emily unwrapped a block of extremely good cheddar—the kind with little crystals of joyous flavor in it—and set it on the cheese board alongside the smoked gouda and the baby Swiss (which she hated, but she knew Sandy loved more than life itself). Crackers went into a basket. The oven timer beeped as she was setting stuff on the four-seat high-top table near the windows in her loft, and she slipped her hand into an oven mitt and pulled out a tray of jalapeño poppers.

She loved Girls Night. Due to uncooperative schedules, they hadn't had one in over a month—and it was odd for them to meet mid-week, but it was time. She hadn't seen her girls since that lunch before Thanksgiving—and lunch didn't count as Girls Night since there was no alcohol. Now it was careening toward the middle of December faster than she could keep track of. The onslaught of the holidays took up everybody's time and Emily knew she probably wouldn't see them again until after the first of the year.

"Unacceptable," she said aloud to Dave as he followed her around the house, hoping with all his doggie heart that she'd drop something delicious. She rewarded his poor behavior by giving him a cracker. "Hi, I'm Emily and I'm an enabler," she said to him as he chewed happily, taking his time and apparently savoring, despite the fact that he could easily swallow it in one gulp—and often did. As he munched, she took a last look around the loft. She had tons of food, she had wine, she had water, she had Pandora playing the Katy Perry channel she'd created for Michelle. She had Christmas gifts for each of them. She was so ready to have a night with her friends.

An hour later, they were laughing around the table, wine glasses in hand.

"So," Michelle said to Sandy, gesturing to the colorful streak in her blond hair. "Green?"

"You don't think it's festive?" Sandy asked, self-consciously raising a hand to her head.

"I do," Emily said. "I love it."

"Thank you, Em." Sandy stuck her tongue out at Michelle.

"I didn't say I didn't like it," Michelle said, defensive. "I just wondered why green? I assume you had to color somebody's hair recently?" She and Emily were both familiar with Sandy's habits involving her work. She often tended to mimic what was hot in her salon at any given time.

"Exactly. We did a bunch of different people recently and Jonathan and I caught the color bug. He did his a really deep maroon color. But not a streak. All of it." She sipped her wine and shrugged as she spoke about her coworker. "It looks really cool on him. Actually, we should do yours with a streak, Em. A bright purple would look so cool in your dark hair."

Emily scoffed and popped a hunk of cheese into her mouth. "You want my mother to have a coronary?"

Michelle launched into her uncanny impression of Cheryl Breckenridge. "Now, Emily, see here, young lady. We have a reputation to uphold at The Breckenridge Foundation, and though I have no problems with your chosen sexuality, I'm afraid I cannot abide your lesbian hair."

They all laughed and Emily took no offense. She knew Michelle and Sandy both loved her mother—and she them—and this was just in good fun. It was true; Emily's mom didn't really understand the "choice of lifestyle" versus being born gay debate, but to her credit, she tried her best and always had.

"Speaking of the Foundation," Michelle said, biting into a crostini she'd slathered with spinach artichoke dip. "How are things going with work?"

"And more specifically," Sandy added, "with the hot accountant chick at the animal shelter. The one who hates you."

Emily knew by the twin expressions of curiosity staring back at her from across the table that they'd been talking about things to each other. She raised her eyebrows and called them on it.

"We may have had a…small discussion." Michelle shrugged and chewed, maintaining eye contact with Emily, a half-grin on her face. "You can't stare me down, Brecks. Stop trying."

Emily groaned and gave up, reaching for a popper. "Things are fine."

"Things are fine," Sandy echoed. Glancing at Michelle for support, she said, "I don't think that's an acceptable response. Do you?"

Michelle snorted. "Hardly." She sipped her wine and ordered, "More."

"More what?" Emily asked.

"Details. Give 'em up. Does she still 'hate you?'" Michelle made air quotes to show what she thought of Emily's earlier assessment of Catherine's opinion.

"I don't think so, no." Emily used a large hunk of cheese and a cracker to buy herself some time, as she knew she'd end up telling her friends the truth about all of it—including what she had begun to refer to as The Hottest Kiss in History. She just wanted to figure out the right approach.

"You don't think so." Sandy set her chin in her hand and studied Emily. "Interesting."

Michelle then mimicked the position so Emily had two weird versions of The Thinker staring at her. Intently.

"Fine!" she said after a moment. "Fine. You win. I kissed her."

Two sets of eyes widened in surprise. Two pairs of eyebrows rose up into hairlines. Two gasps sounded in the room. Emily said nothing more, sipped her wine, and waited. The silence must have bothered Dave, as he left his spot on the couch and wandered over to the table as if checking to make sure things were okay. He went from one woman to the next, sniffing and accepting pets on his head

Sandy spoke first. "Um…can we go back for a second? How did things go from 'she hates me' to 'I kissed her' in the space of about, what, a week? Two weeks? Not a lot of time, is my point."

Michelle simply nodded and Emily gave herself an imaginary point for rendering her loudly opinionated friend speechless. At least momentarily.

Looking down at her plate, Emily used her fork to push around the pile of hummus sitting next to the baby carrots and stalk of celery, trying to decide how best to approach the subject of Catherine with her friends. Hell, she barely knew how to approach the subject of Catherine with herself. Finally, she took a deep breath, said, "It's a situation that's completely new to me and...I think I'd really like your thoughts. You guys know me better than anybody and..." She stopped, looked from Michelle to Sandy and back, picked up her glass and took a sip of the peppery Cabernet. "I'm kind of at a loss here." She tried to smile at them but was pretty sure it came out as a weird grimace instead.

And she told them the whole story. From the beginning, through the kiss, including the talks with her mother and Catherine's boss, to Emily sitting at the bar of Joplin's for nearly four hours, and ending with the flowers she'd sent on Monday. When she finished, she picked up her wine, took a very healthy mouthful, and waited for her friends to comment, pass judgment, or have her committed. Whatever they decided.

"Wow," Michelle said, then reached across the table to snag a popper. She glanced in Sandy's direction. Sandy looked back at her. It was like they were communicating telepathically and Emily didn't like that she didn't know what they were saying to each other.

"You like to send the girl flowers," Sandy commented.

Emily grinned. "She thinks they're a waste of money, so yeah. I send them."

"I see."

"What does that tone mean?" Emily asked, furrowing her brow.

"You're sending flowers to somebody who doesn't like them."

Emily looked to Michelle, who shrugged and bit into a cracker. "I didn't say she doesn't like them. I said she thinks they're a waste of money. I'm pretty sure she likes them a lot. I mean, who doesn't like to get flowers?" She turned back to Sandy. "If you got flowers every day, would you hate that? When somebody sends you flowers, aren't you happy?"

Sandy nodded. "I love to get flowers."

"Exactly. I'm just trying to make her happy. That's all."

"Interesting," Michelle said, then chewed some more as she squinted at Emily.

"What's interesting?" Emily asked.

"The 'I'm just trying to make her happy' statement."

"Oh." Emily honestly hadn't realized she'd said it, but now could see why it might cause eyebrows to raise. "Well, I don't really mean it like *that*." It was lame. She knew it.

"Screw that," Sandy said, leaning farther across the table. "I want to know how the kiss was."

Emily felt her face heat up and was powerless to stop it.

"Wait." Sandy squinted at her, then her face lit up with glee. "Are you *blushing*? Actually blushing? Oh, my God, you are. You'd better spill all the details right now. And…go."

Emily was torn. Seriously torn. On the one hand, she wanted to tell them everything, every teeny tiny thought and feeling she'd had during that amazing make-out session with Catherine. After all, these were her very best friends in the world. They knew everything about each other and they were always there for one another. She could tell them anything. At the same time, she felt protective. Protective of what, she wasn't quite sure.

Protective of herself? Protective of Catherine? It was all so confusing and she knew she needed to find some middle ground, something that would satisfy Sandy's curiosity, but that wouldn't compromise the personal joy of the moment. It was then that she noticed Michelle was strangely quiet.

"Talk to me," Emily said to her friend.

Michelle shrugged and looked as though she was hesitant. After a beat, she pushed forward. "I just…I see where your mom and Catherine's boss are coming from."

"You do?" Sandy asked.

Michelle turned to her. "You don't own your own business, but I bet if you asked the owner of your salon if she was okay with you hooking up with her biggest client, she might have some…reservations. I do own my own business and I can tell you, *I'd* have an issue."

Sandy squinched up her face and looked like she was considering it seriously.

Michelle went on. "So, you have two sides here, neither of which is terribly positive. What if you hook up with Catherine and then things go public? And then other organizations that The Breckenridge Foundation gives money to start talking? 'Oh, sure, Junebug Farms gets all kinds of money because their accountant is fucking a Breckenridge.'" When Emily opened her mouth to protest, Michelle held up a hand. "I know, I know. That's harsh. It was meant to be because, let's face it: people suck. Especially in this age of Twitter and Tumblr and Facebook. Trolls. They exist, and they talk. A lot. Do you really think nobody would have an issue? That nobody would say anything?"

"But—"

"No buts. Sorry. The Internet gives people license to be assholes and believe me, they take it."

Emily took a slug of wine, not liking this conversation anymore.

"Now," Michelle went on. "Let's go the other way. You guys hook up and it falls apart. You crash and burn badly. It could happen. I know it probably wouldn't. You're not really a crash-and-burn kind of girl. You're more the 'crawl into a hole and whither away quietly' type. But it *could* crash and burn, and that's the point. You guys implode and it's horrible and you don't want to have anything to do with her or her shelter anymore. And now maybe the Foundation stops donating to the shelter altogether. Or they have to appoint a different liaison because you can't stand the sight of the accountant any longer, and that ends up awkward and uncomfortable for everybody. Not to mention unprofessional. *That's* the point Catherine's boss is making." She paused and looked intently at Emily, then softened her voice. "Do you see what I'm getting at?"

Sandy had been quiet this whole time, but now she spoke up before Emily could, which was good because Emily felt all kinds of miserable at that moment. "You forgot another possibility."

"What's that?" Michelle asked, reaching for the wine bottle to refill her glass.

"They hook up, it's awesome, and they live happily ever after." Sandy shrugged and smiled. "That could happen, too."

Michelle tipped her head from one side to the other, as if weighing the possibility. "I suppose it could."

Emily held her glass up to Sandy. "Thank you."

Sandy touched her glass to Emily's. "Welcome."

"Is that what you see happening?" Michelle asked, her expression completely serious. "Not that happily ever after would stop the trolls from talking anyway."

Emily ignored that last part and took a moment to honestly think about it, but she really had no answer. "I don't know. I mean, we don't know each other that well, if I'm being truthful. We haven't spent that much time together. We could be a hot mess. We're super different…" She let her voice trail off.

"But?" Sandy asked.

"But I have this irresistible urge to slow dance with her." Emily turned to her with a grin, felt her insides warm, then grow hot. "Just, hold her close and sway." She searched the air for words. "I have never, ever been that affected by a kiss before. I have never, ever been so physically drawn to somebody before." At Sandy's raised brow, Emily nodded vigorously. "Yeah. I mean it. When I'm around her…I can say this to you guys because you know me, but it's hard to articulate, and it makes me feel like I'm some teenage boy. When I'm around her, it's like…like I get tugged in her direction and…" She gave a low chuckle. "I'm sure it's because I've already gotten a taste. Figuratively and literally. My eyes get tugged. I am always looking at her and she's so freaking gorgeous I can't seem to stop. My nose, I want to inhale her scent all the time, which I know is kind of creepy, going around smelling somebody, but her perfume or soap or lotion or whatever it is…it's intoxicating. My hands, though I've managed to keep control of them so far because…" Emily swallowed hard, looked up at her friends with pleading in her eyes. "I want to touch her so badly," she whispered and was mortified to feel her eyes well up. Taking a moment, she pulled herself together, grabbed a chunk of cheese and chewed it slowly. "I don't know what to do," she finally admitted quietly.

It was then that she realized she probably wouldn't get instant answers tonight because, judging by the expressions on her friends' faces, they had no idea what she should do either.

"Well," Emily said, with a resigned sigh, "I'm scheduled to go there Friday and walk some dogs. I guess I have until then to figure out the mysteries of life, love, and sex, huh?" She looked from one bewildered face to the other and back again. "Yeah, you two have been tons of help. Thanks for exactly nothing."

Michelle grinned, as did Sandy. Raising her glass, she said, "To the mysteries of life, love, and sex being solved by Friday."

"And to slow dancing," Sandy added.

Emily simply shook her head and raised her glass to touch theirs.

Friday. Two days from today and she'd see Catherine again.

Then what?

CHAPTER FIFTEEN

FRIDAY WAS, TO PUT IT simply, chaos.

To start the day, Catherine had awakened with a splitting headache. She surmised that it came from—once again—not enough sleep. She couldn't seem to get her mind to shut off at night. It rolled around every possible problem or concern she had in life, and amplified it in the darkness of her bedroom. By the time her alarm went off in the morning, she felt like she'd garnered maybe three hours of total sleep, but in fifteen-minute increments throughout the night. It was beyond frustrating.

To add to her stress and crankiness, a knock sounded on her front door ten minutes before she was scheduled to leave. Her neighbor, Scott Turner, stood on her front stoop with Geronimo in his arms. Which was weird, considering Catherine had just let him into the backyard a few minutes ago.

"What in the world?" she asked with a gasp, reaching for her dog.

"He was wandering down the street," Scott said. "I was heading to work and I noticed him. Luckily, he came right to me." He was a handsome guy, short and stocky, but with a warm, friendly face recently covered over by his annual winter beard. He was a mechanic and wore his usual navy blue coverall.

Catherine cuddled Mo close to her chest and could tell by his slight squirming that she might have been squeezing a little tightly, but she couldn't help it. She kissed his head. "You could've been run over, buddy. You're kind of hard to see in the snow, you know." She looked up at Scott. "Thank you so much. I don't know what to say."

Scott smiled. "No problem. I'm glad I saw him. You might want to get the gate on your fence checked. I think it's open." He reached over and scratched Mo's head. "Stay with your Mama, little guy. Okay?" With a wave, he was gone.

Now, Catherine sat in her office trying to focus on work, but glancing every couple of minutes at Geronimo sleeping soundly on his bed in the corner. Once she'd closed the door behind Scott, her entire body had begun to tremble. Not a person who scared easily, she'd had to accept how much the thought of Mo being hurt frightened her. Her first cup of coffee that morning had felt like acid in her stomach and she hadn't been able to eat breakfast at all.

E-mails came fast and furious today, and she worked diligently on them. The phones rang like crazy and it was glaringly obvious by the overload of visitors—she could hear them in the lobby as she sat at her desk—that the holiday rush was definitely upon them. Christmas was next Thursday and people were beginning to lose their minds, the way they always did when the holidays got close. She went over figures, checked reports, dealt with incoming and outgoing checks and funds until her eyes burned. She had three meetings set up for today, one down, two to go, and she packed up her necessities for the next one.

"You stay here," she said to Mo and gave him a chew toy to keep him occupied. Then she closed the door behind her and headed out to the conference room to meet with Jessica and David.

As expected, the lobby was bustling, and four volunteers manned the front desk rather than the usual two. As Catherine's heels clicked across the faux-marble floor, she glanced up at the front doors and saw Emily pushing her way through. Once inside, she stomped her snow-covered feet on the mat and looked up to meet Catherine's eyes.

They locked.

For a split second, it felt as if all the air, all the sound, had simply been sucked right out of the room, like Catherine was under water, her ears registering only muffles, her lungs empty...

And then it was over. Air came rushing back. Sound barked back into being. Catherine blinked rapidly several times, raised a hand to wave at Emily, then forced her feet to continue taking her to the conference room. Once there, she dropped into a chair and worked quietly on breathing like a normal person.

If quizzed later on exactly what was said during the meeting, Catherine would fail miserably. She estimated that she caught maybe fifty percent of the things they discussed. And that was being generous. *God, I'm useless today*, she thought, annoyed with herself. She caught more than one look of concern tossed in her direction by Jessica, but she ignored them and pretended to focus on the pages in front of her. When the meeting wrapped up, Catherine was flooded with relief.

On her way out the door, Jessica stopped her with a gentle hand on her arm. "Hey, you okay?"

Catherine gave a nod. "Yup. I'm fine."

"You look tired." Jessica's face showed unease, worry, but Catherine found herself irritated instead.

"I'm good." She left Jessica standing in the doorway, knowing she'd been rude, but not caring at the moment. She wanted to get back to her office, pet her dog, and finish her work so she could get out of here and go home. What the hell was wrong with her?

After a number of years working at Junebug Farms, Catherine had grown used to the noise. Some days it was louder than others, that was the truth, but generally, her brain had learned to shut out any excess sound—barking, whining, howling, the constant hum of conversation, phones ringing, doors swinging open and closed. It was an endless symphony of commotion, but she no longer noticed.

Until today.

Today, it all seemed amplified. The barks were almost unbearable. The ringing phones seemed extra loud and extra frequent. Even the cats' meowing seemed to be at a higher decibel level than normal. Catherine looked around and for just a moment wondered if she was having a stroke or suffering from a brain aneurysm. She blinked hard, glanced at the double doors to the dog wing as they opened, saw Emily halfway down the aisle, dog leash in hand. Again, she glanced up as Catherine was looking and their gazes caught.

Why is today so weird?

Shaking herself loose from Emily's invisible tether, she headed down the hallway to her office. When she opened the door, Mo greeted her, put his front paws up on her leg, and she felt instant relief. She inhaled slowly, a big, full breath, and then gradually let it out, feeling every part of her relax. Finally. Mo was apparently good for that. His soft ears felt amazing between her fingers and she rubbed them gently, realizing that the act soothed her as much as it did him. She had a box of treats on a filing cabinet against the wall and reached to grab one. Mo—already no dummy—sat patiently at her feet waiting. As she turned to give it to him, she glanced up and out the door into the hall.

The offices of Junebug Farms each had an entrance from a single hallway off the lobby except for Jessica's. Hers was down a different hall. Catherine's office was situated at the very end of the main hallway of offices. When walking down the hall from the lobby, you'd pass David's office on the left, Anna's across from his on the right, then Donna Christenson's office—she was the event coordinator at the shelter—and a supply room across from hers, and at the very end was Catherine's office. So if you walked straight down the hallway without stopping, you'd end up standing in front of Catherine's desk.

Which was exactly what Emily Breckenridge appeared about to do.

Catherine saw her coming, had an array of emotions run through her body like a small child hopped up on sugar—fear, excitement, worry, arousal, fear, arousal, fear, arousal—but was unable to move her feet. Or her hands. Or anything at all. All she could do was stand there, watch Emily's approach, observe as Emily closed the office door behind her, her eyes never leaving Catherine's, and wonder at the dark, heavy look of desire she wore as she crossed the room, took Catherine's face in both hands, and kissed her on the mouth.

Hard.

There was nothing Catherine could do except kiss her back. Nothing at all. She had no choice.

Maybe she should have been angry. Insulted. Appalled. Furious.

She was none of those things.

What she was? Turned on. Completely, utterly, undoubtedly turned on. Her heart was racing. Her stomach tightened. Her underpants were wet (already?). God, Catherine didn't know what the hell kind of power Emily had, but she had it in spades and Catherine couldn't seem to break free of its spell no matter how hard she tried. Which wasn't hard at all, really, because this was the best kiss she'd ever had. Even better than the last one… and that was one for the books. But this one? Surpassed it. By far. Emily's lips were soft and warm and pliant and her tongue was both gentle and demanding and it gave Catherine a very R-rated preview of what could maybe come down the road, no pun intended. She tasted like strawberries—how was that possible? Strawberry season couldn't be farther away than it was now in December, in upstate New York. Emily's hands were tender but firm, holding onto Catherine's face, making her feel safe, sexy, and wanted all at the same time, and all Catherine could do was hold on. And kiss back.

As if giving in, deciding not to analyze or resist what was happening here, Catherine gave as good as she got—and then some. The dog treat fell from her hand—she was vaguely aware of Mo crunching on it near her feet—and she slid both hands up Emily's sides and around her back, up to her shoulders where she pulled her in tighter, pushed her mouth more firmly into Emily's, and was rewarded with a soft moan. It was delicious and Catherine wanted to hear it again, so she thrust her tongue into Emily's mouth, opened her own mouth wider to take more of her in. She felt Emily's body shudder under her hands. That was accompanied by something that could only be classified as a growl and then Emily wrenched their mouths apart.

They stood there, in the middle of Catherine's office, chests heaving, lips red and swollen, breathing ragged.

"Oh, my God," Emily whispered as Catherine touched her own mouth with her fingers.

Catherine tried to speak, but no sound would come, so she just stood there, blinking.

"I have been wanting to do that all day," Emily said softly, smiling, still only inches from Catherine. She held up a finger. "No. Wait. That's a lie. I have wanted to do that since the last time I did that."

Still unable to find her voice, Catherine just looked at her, took her in, the beauty, the softness, the smooth skin and silky hair and smiling eyes. Catherine was not a person who was overwhelmed easily, but in that moment, overwhelmed was exactly how she felt.

"Listen," Emily said, still standing distractingly close, toying with the ends of Catherine's hair, wrapping it around her fingers. "What are you doing this weekend? Are you working at Joplin's?"

"Tomorrow night, yes."

"What about during the day?"

Catherine mentally went through the schedule she'd made for herself. She was going to get up, take Mo for a walk, maybe play a little ball with him in the backyard, do the remainder of her online Christmas shopping (she was way behind), mop the kitchen floor. Nobody was more shocked than she was when the words left her mouth. "Nothing. Why?"

"I will pick you up at eleven then."

"And take me where?" Catherine squinted at her.

"It's a surprise. Dress warm. Okay?"

Catherine wasn't spontaneous. She wasn't a last-minute kind of girl. She didn't like surprises; she liked schedules. Doing something unplanned was hard for her. But there was something in Emily's eyes that she couldn't discount. It would be irritating, making unexpected changes to her Saturday, but it could be done. She could shop later. She would still have time to get a good walk in with Mo. It wasn't that hard to give Emily what she wanted. And the weird thing was that's exactly what Catherine wanted to do: give Emily what she wanted. Anything and everything she wanted.

With a nod, she said simply, "Okay."

Emily blinked at her, clearly surprised. "Okay?"

"Okay."

"Wow. I had a whole other speech prepared. I was sure I'd need to do more convincing, but…this is awesome." The way her face lit up was more than enough to tell Catherine she'd made the right decision, and before she could say anything further Emily was kissing her again. Softer, this time. Gently. Tenderly. But Catherine knew if she didn't break it up soon, they'd end up in the same heated, breathless state they were in earlier and quite honestly, she wasn't sure she'd survive it a second time. She pulled away, her entire body screaming in protest as she did so.

"You should probably go," she said, her voice quiet, husky.

Emily nodded. "I probably should." Yet she made no move, which brought a small grin to Catherine's face.

She pushed gently at Emily's chest and ordered, "Go."

"Yes, ma'am," Emily whispered. She took a step back, but grasped Catherine's chin in her hand and gave her one last kiss. "See you tomorrow," she said as they parted.

And she was gone.

Catherine wasn't sure how long she stood rooted in the same spot after Emily's departure, but she was pretty sure if she tried to move her legs, she'd collapse in a boneless heap onto the floor. That's what Emily did to her: turned her to jelly. Liquified her insides. Scrambled all coherent, rational thought.

When she finally felt like maybe she could take a step, or two, she moved slowly back to her desk and literally dropped herself into her chair, the breath forced from her lungs as she landed. Mo took the opportunity to leave his bed—where he'd retreated after realizing he wasn't getting another treat—and hop up into her lap, his warm body comforting her. She swiveled the chair slightly so she could gaze out the window at the gorgeous winter landscape. It really was beautiful, the fresh blanket of snow making everything seem clean. New. A blank slate.

Before she could wax poetic any further, a knock sounded on her doorjamb. She was about to mentally thank God for giving her something new to focus on until she saw that it was Anna who stood in the doorway looking at her with suspicion, and the gratitude died away.

"Hey," Catherine said, hoping she hadn't actually sighed the word (she was pretty sure she had). "What's up?"

"Was that Emily Breckenridge?" Anna asked, jerking a thumb over her shoulder.

Catherine nodded. "It was."

"Were you two having another brainstorming session about marketing? Without me?" There was a slight sneer in her voice, because of course there was.

"No, Anna. We were not brainstorming." *What we were doing was so much more fun that that.*

Anna folded her arms across her small chest and leaned against the doorframe. "Then why was she in here?"

Catherine shrugged, feeling uncharacteristically flustered at the accusation in Anna's tone. Or was it actually guilt she was feeling…? "She's walking some dogs today. She stopped in to say hi." Catherine looked back out the window, not enjoying the sensation of having not only to explain herself to her ex, but having to lie. When she turned back, Anna had narrowed her eyes, scrutinizing her as she leaned slightly forward. "What?" Catherine asked, annoyed now.

Anna straightened and her eyes widened for a second, as if she'd just had a light-bulb moment. Then a satisfied look crossed her face. "Nothing. She still hasn't come to see me, you know. Emily. Isn't she supposed to come to me with her ideas?"

Catherine closed her eyes and scratched at her neck. "I'll be sure to remind her. All right?"

"You do that." Anna held her gaze for another moment, then turned to leave. Stopping, she looked over her shoulder at Catherine. "I'd be careful if I were you. Those Breckenridges may have money, but they don't have much in the way of class. From what I hear." She shrugged and left, walking down the hall and turning into her own office.

"Nice," Catherine muttered. She didn't like what Anna had said about Emily. She liked even less that Anna now thought she knew something. But she also knew if she started to dwell on it —on Anna talking to Jessica, on Jessica realizing that what she told Catherine should not happen might actually be happening, on what would occur after that—she'd be lost for doing anything useful for the remainder of the day. Which, luckily, wasn't much. Another hour or two and she'd be free.

Free to wonder where on earth Emily was taking her tomorrow.

The smile appeared on her face all on its own.

⋙◆⋘

Saturday dawned with a clear sky and sunshine. A quick check of the weather told Catherine the high temperature was going to be in the low-thirties, but no snow was predicted. Also unpredicted was where on earth Emily was taking her today, and she had to admit, the idea had her a little bit excited. Which freaked her out just a tad.

What was she doing?

It was the question she'd ignored whenever possible, and when she couldn't, it had kept her up, kept her overthinking, kept her shaking her head. What. Was. She. Doing? There were so many reasons this was a bad idea. Jessica had a list of them. Catherine was sure Anna could come up with a few more. Throw Emily's mother in there with her reasons and the idea of Catherine seeing Emily in any way, shape, or form other than in a business capacity, looked like the stupidest thing either of them could possibly do.

So then, why was she looking forward to today?

Up by eight, after having actually gotten a fairly good night's sleep, she took Mo for a long walk, which also helped her decide what she should wear today. Emily had said to dress warm, so Catherine could only assume they'd be outside. Were they hiking? Going for a walk in a park someplace? Ice skating (which she hoped against, as she was a menace on skates of any kind)? The air was brisk, but the sun helped it to feel warmer and the wind had, thankfully, chosen to blow someplace else today. Mo was being his usual terrier self, stopping to sniff, pee, or both, about every six feet.

"You know, this pace doesn't really get me much exercise, pal," she said, as she stood near a leafless tree in front of a house about three blocks from hers. Geronimo ignored her and sniffed the same two-inch section of bark for another four minutes before they moved on.

Back home and showered, Catherine stood in front of her closet and perused her options. Layers were probably the smartest choice, and if she overdid it, she hoped she'd be able to remove a few in the car. She donned a pair of silk long johns for under her jeans. A white turtleneck under a zip-up fleece hoodie in electric blue went on top. She pulled her hair into a ponytail so she could wear the blue and pink fleece headband to keep her ears warm, opting to forego a hat. (Subconsciously, she knew she was worried about her hair ending up a disaster, but she chose not to dwell on the reasons why it mattered.) Soft socks and her cute, brown boots with the fold-down knit sides finished up the outfit and she took a look in the full-length mirror. Turning first one way, then the other, she turned to Mo, who lounged on the bed gnawing on a Nylabone.

"What do you think?"

He stopped chewing and looked at her, head cocked to one side as if actually contemplating her outfit. After a beat, he went back to his bone.

"I'm going to take that as approval," she said, turning back at the mirror. Adding a spritz of perfume, she glanced at the clock —10:45—and realized she had butterflies in her stomach, which was not typical behavior for her, and she was honestly unsure what to do with it.

Choosing the option of "ignore," she headed downstairs and was rinsing out her morning coffee cup when the doorbell rang. Mo barked and Catherine went to the door. One hand on the knob, she smoothed the other over her hair, took a deep breath, and pulled the door open.

Emily stood there, looking radiantly gorgeous in her winter garb, her smile wide, her cheeks slightly flushed. "Hi," she said.

"Hi," Catherine said back and tried not to notice how much better she felt when she was standing within three feet of Emily. She stepped back and allowed Emily to enter the foyer.

Emily made a show of scrutinizing Catherine's clothes. "Perfect. It's gorgeous out, so I'm not worried about us getting cold. And how is it that you can wear things to keep you warm and not look like Randy from *A Christmas Story* like I do? Unfair."

Catherine laughed. "You do not look like Randy from *A Christmas Story*. Trust me." Emily wore jeans as well and had an expensive looking pair of winter hiking shoes on her feet. Her down jacket was black and sleek, and Catherine could see the peek of a red sweater underneath. The cream-colored wool hat that just covered her ears but let her hair shine was adorable, and Catherine immediately wondered why she never looked that cute in a hat.

"Well, that's a relief. Still." Emily used a finger and moved it up then down to indicate Catherine's outfit. "You look amazing. And I'm glad to see you're not wearing heels. I half-expected you to be."

Catherine gave a mock gasp of indignation. "I have several other pairs of boots—including a new pair I just bought—but I also have a brain. Most of those with heels don't tend to be terribly warm, nor do they have much room for thicker socks. These do."

"I think you have a shoe fetish," Emily said with a grin as she squatted down to give Mo some love.

"I will not argue that point." Catherine grinned back and grabbed her coat, gloves, and headband from the closet.

Once settled into Emily's BMW, Catherine asked, "Where are we off to?" Then she tried to be nonchalant about rubbing her hand against the leather seat and managed to keep from giggling in delight at the warm sensation she felt through her jeans from the obviously heated seats.

"You'll see when we get there." Emily put the car in gear and backed down the driveway.

"Have me back here by four?"

Emily slid her Ray-Bans on and said, "Your wish is my command."

Donning her own sunglasses ($10.99 at Target), Catherine snuggled into her seat and looked out onto the beautiful Saturday morning. It was sunny, the sky was a stunning ceramic blue, and she was sitting next to one of the most gorgeous women she'd ever had the pleasure of knowing (or kissing). It was going to be a good day. She just had a feeling.

The drive was short and when she realized they were headed in the direction of the lake, Catherine suspected their destination. "Are you taking me to Cold Rush?" she asked, referring to the local winter carnival.

Emily glanced over with a hesitant expression. "That depends. Would you want to go to Cold Rush?"

"I would love it."

"Excellent. Then that's where we're going." Emily grinned and directed the car into the parking lot.

It was busy, and Catherine chalked it up to the gorgeous day. There were booths and games and food and a huge toboggan run that shot sleds across the shore near the not-quite-frozen water. Some years, the lake did freeze, but mostly it did not. Catherine could smell a combination of hot dogs, cotton candy, and funnel cakes wafting through the air.

"I will need to get some fried dough," she said as she smoothed back her hair and pulled her headband on to cover her ears.

"You'll *need* to?" Emily asked, amused as she pushed a hand into a glove.

"Yes. Need. You obviously don't understand the importance of fried dough in the grand scheme of life."

Emily laughed. "I await enlightenment." She held out an elbow to Catherine. "Shall we?"

Catherine happily tucked her hand into the crook of Emily's elbow and they headed toward the entrance.

The crowd was a huge melting pot of people: toddlers, kids, parents, couples, teens. The weather and the upcoming holiday had not only brought people out from where they tended to hibernate in winter, but it seemed to put smiles on their faces. Everybody looked so happy that it might seem weird if you didn't actually live here. But Catherine had been born and raised in upstate New York, so she got it. She got the depression and laziness that was often caused by stark, cold weather, and she got how freeing and wonderful it was to see some sunshine in the middle of December, to be able to be out in the fresh air and not worry that your fingers and toes might fall off. The snow crunched under their feet and reflected the sun back so brightly that not wearing sunglasses wasn't an option.

"Should we get fried dough now?" Emily asked, interrupting her thoughts.

"What? No, that's for the end of the visit. We get that last."

"Oh, I see. I didn't know that."

"Stick with me, kid. I know a lot of stuff."

"I think I will." Emily held her gaze for a beat, then asked, "Hot chocolate then?"

"That sounds perfect."

Catherine stood by the merry-go-round while Emily got in line at the hot chocolate vendor's booth. It was a small ride designed for toddlers, and they were so cute Catherine found herself smiling openly. One little gondola contained a boy of about five holding tightly to what Catherine could only assume was a little sister of about three. She sat between his little legs and he had his tiny arms wrapped protectively around her. Catherine had no trouble picking the parents out of the crowd, a smiling couple in their late twenties, both holding up their phones and snapping photos, calling out instructions, reminding their children to hold on to each other.

"You want one of those?" Emily asked, suddenly close. She handed a steaming Styrofoam cup to Catherine.

Catherine took the cup and blew on the contents before taking a sip of the rich chocolatey goodness. "What, a merry-go-round?"

Emily laughed. "Funny. No. A kid."

Catherine gazed at the ride as it began to slowly spin. "I honestly don't know. Some days, I think I do, that it'd be great. Other days, I can barely handle my laundry. How could I raise a child?" She sipped again. "What about you?"

"I guess I'm sort of in the same boat." Catherine studied Emily's face as she looked off into the distance. The clean line of her jaw, the strong outline of her nose. "I'm not really sure yet." She looked back at Catherine. "Is that bad, do you think? For us to be in our thirties and still be undecided?"

Catherine shrugged. "I think we're smart for not jumping into something we're unsure of."

"I guess. But don't you usually just *know* if you want to be a mother? I feel like we would, like we'd feel it. In our bones or something silly like that."

"Maybe."

"Your sister has a kid, right? Did she know right away?"

Catherine's chuckle held a note of sarcasm. "My sister had unprotected sex at seventeen and ended up with my nephew.

Who is a great kid, don't get me wrong. But Vicky isn't the person to be asking about a desire to be a parent. She didn't give herself the choice."

"Ah." There was a beat of silence before Emily said, "Want to walk?"

They finished their drinks and tossed the cups away, then sauntered along the perimeter of the carnival, watching the different game booths. At the dart shoot, Emily stopped and watched. A wall containing rows of small blue and white inflated balloons stood about ten feet away from the counter. Above the booth hung a wide variety of stuffed animals and Catherine pointed to a white and brown dog off to the left.

"That one looks a little like Geronimo, doesn't it?" she asked, amused.

Emily's brown eyes glittered as she said, "It does. You should have that."

Catherine scoffed. "Please. These games are rigged. And expensive to play. I wouldn't waste my money." She started to wander to the next booth before she realized Emily was not with her. Turning back, she saw her handing over cash to the barker. She took off her gloves, put them in her pocket, and accepted five darts.

"Three out of five gets you a prize!" the man said loudly and in rhythm. "Four gets you more."

Catherine shook her head as she backtracked. "Seriously," she said to Emily, who was taking aim with her first dart. "You're doing this?"

"I am," Emily said. She made a fist and blew into it, presumably to warm up her hand, then took aim again and let the dart fly. Its path ended with a loud pop as she burst a balloon.

Catherine blinked in surprise. "Nice shot."

"Thanks." Emily repeated the movement and it ended the same way.

"That's two for the little lady here!" the barker cried, hoping to draw in more players.

Emily took aim, holding her third dart directly in front of her eye. She took two tiny practice tosses before letting it go. *Pop!*

"Oh, my God," Catherine muttered.

"Three in a row!" the barker cried, and now a small crowd did start to form.

Emily never moved her feet. She stood rooted to the same spot, two darts left, and blew in her hand again. Going through the same process, she threw the fourth dart and it hit its mark. The gathering crowd applauded and Catherine couldn't help but smile.

"One more, ladies and gentlemen. She's got one more." The barker seemed as riveted as the rest of the crowd. He'd even quieted his voice a bit. "Can she do five for five? Let's see."

Emily squinted as she aimed her last dart. Her brow furrowed in concentration and Catherine felt that tightening in her stomach, that feeling that had been so absent for so long, but since meeting Emily, had reappeared with a vengeance. Catherine swallowed hard.

The dart flew.

The balloon popped.

The crowd went wild.

Emily turned and looked at Catherine for the first time since she started the game, and her face was radiant, smiling and gorgeous and it was only by supreme force of will that Catherine kept herself from scooping Emily up, swinging her around, and kissing her right on the mouth.

"We'd like that dog," Emily said to the barker, who happily unhooked it for her. Emily took it and thanked him, then handed it to Catherine. "There you go."

Catherine hugged the toy to her chest, momentarily speechless. Nobody had ever done something like this for her. And she realized it was a bit silly, childish even, but she didn't care. She was thrilled, and she couldn't keep the smile from her face. "Thank you," she said softly.

"You're welcome."

They began to stroll again. "How did you learn to throw darts like that?" Catherine asked.

"My parents have a dartboard in the downstairs rec room. I've been playing since I was about twelve. It's one of the few things I could beat Clark at, so I've kept up my mad skills."

"Well, I imagine being able to beat the big brother at something is a necessity. It's like that with big sisters, too."

"Yeah? What can you beat yours at?"

"You can't laugh."

"I won't," Emily said with a chuckle.

"See? You already are."

Emily forced herself to model a straight face. "No. No, I'm not. Promise."

Catherine made a show of squinting at her, studying her expression, before finally giving a nod of approval. "Okay." She took a deep breath. "Word searches."

Emily furrowed her brow. "Word searches? Like the puzzles in books?"

"Yes. My grandmother always got us each a big book of them for Christmas and Vicky and I would race to see who could finish finding all the words in a puzzle first. I always won."

Emily grinned. "That's pretty impressive. Those suckers can be hard."

"They can. For the longest time, Vicky thought I was cheating."

"How can you cheat on one of those? I mean, the answers are in the back, right? Flipping the pages back and forth would be kind of obvious, I'd think."

"Exactly. We sat right next to each other when we did them. She finally had to accept that I have a special talent she doesn't." Catherine shrugged.

"You can see a word before anybody else. That *is* a talent. You need a superhero name," Emily said. "And maybe a cape."

"I would rock a cape," Catherine said with a nod.

"Totally."

They stopped walking at the base of the toboggan run and watched as another sled came whipping down the chute, four friends sitting in a row, arms up, shrieking at the top of their lungs. Catherine watched with a combination of amusement, excitement, and crap-your-pants fear. When she glanced in Emily's direction, Emily was smiling at her.

"What do you think? Wanna give it a try?"

Catherine looked back up, listened to the next round of screams, and wasn't sure if they were joyous or horrified. This wasn't something she took part in. Heights and speed combined? No, thank you. It was fast and crazy and maybe even a little dangerous. Not her cup of tea at all. She should say no.

"Absolutely. Let's do it." Catherine grabbed Emily's hand and they got in line.

Things moved much more quickly than Catherine had expected and before she knew it, they were next. Her heart hammered in her chest and she tried not to look around, because that would remind her just how high up they were. The toboggan the guy set in front of them looked like it had come out of a cartoon, all flat surface and curled front. Emily wasted no time straddling the sled, then indicated the space in front of her.

"You're smaller. You sit here. I'll sit behind you."

Catherine nodded, her voice apparently having fled like any sane person should have, and did as she was told. She sat and straightened her legs so her boots were tucked under that front curve of the sled. The stuffed dog went between her feet so she'd be sure not to lose him, and she was embarrassed to feel her muscles start to tremble with a combination of cold and fear.

Until Emily sat down behind her.

Suddenly, it was as if the temperature had inexplicably risen. Emily's jean-clad legs came up alongside of Catherine's. Her arms wrapped around Catherine's torso and tugged until Emily's front was snugly up against Catherine's back. She tried not to dwell on the fact that Emily's center was pressed firmly against the small of her back. And then Emily's voice in her ear sent a different kind of tremor through her body.

"You okay?" she whispered, lips close—too close—to Catherine's ear.

All Catherine could do was nod and grip the sled.

"Hang on, ladies," the guy manning the run said, then gave them a shove, and the next thing Catherine knew, she was falling.

Falling hard.

And fast! The sled went even faster than she'd expected, but instead of feeling terrified, she was suddenly exhilarated. Emily was a sure and solid presence behind her. The air whipped her face as the white of the run whizzed by and Catherine actually remembered to look to her right and admire the huge expanse of Lake Ontario, spread out before her and glittering with sunshine.

She was shocked to hear a delighted whoop burst up from her own chest and she pushed one arm straight up into the air as if she were on a roller coaster. Their toboggan shot like a bullet along the steep and icy run, down to the bottom, where it was spit out of the track and continued to whiz along the shore of the lake for quite a span. A ride that probably only took about thirty seconds seemed to imprint itself onto Catherine's brain forever. She knew the moment their sled skidded to a stop that she'd never forget this moment.

"That was awesome!" Emily's grin was wide, her face was flushed with excitement as she stood up and held out a hand to help Catherine to her feet.

Tucking the stuffed dog under her arm, Catherine nodded her agreement even as she glanced at her watch.

"It's not time to go yet, is it?" Emily's tone held an adorably childlike quality that made Catherine smile.

"Not quite yet. Know what it is time for, though?"

Emily's eyes widened. "Fried dough?"

"Fried dough."

The carnival had grown crowded, but Catherine didn't mind. Somehow, being close to Emily was all that mattered in the moment. They followed their noses to the fried dough trailer and stood in a line that was longer than either of them had expected. Luckily, it moved quickly and within fifteen minutes, they each had a paper plate that held a slab of golden fried dough sprinkled with powdered sugar.

"Is there a trick to eating this without making a mess?" Emily asked, turning her plate, obviously looking for the best place to grab.

"Nope. Not possible." Catherine kept the stuffed dog tucked under her arm so she could use both hands. One held the plate, her thumb keeping the dough in place while the other hand ripped a hunk from the main slab, steam wafting up into the air. Catherine stuffed it into her mouth and when she looked up, Emily's eyes had gone a little dark. "What?"

Emily cleared her throat. "Nothing. Nothing. You just...have a little..." She reached out with one finger and swiped at the corner of Catherine's mouth. "Sugar."

"Thanks," Catherine said, her mouth full and her heart skipping a beat.

Emily mimicked Catherine's movements and took a bite. "Oh, my God," she said, mouth full. "Oh, my God, that's good."

"Right?"

"Oh, my God." Emily put another hunk in her mouth and Catherine watched her until she realized she was staring.

"Have you never had fried dough before?" Catherine asked, amazed and saddened at such a thought.

"Not like this," Emily said, using her tongue to get some sugar from her upper lip.

Refocusing her gaze to anything else but Emily's beautiful face, she noticed the snow sculptures in the distance. "Let's wander that way."

Emily followed her eyes, then nodded. "Okay."

Movement was good, Catherine decided. It helped her focus on other things beside the fact that she was ridiculously attracted to Emily and how bad that was in regard to their jobs. Not even just their jobs. Their lives. Their families. They were so completely different. It would never work anyway, so it shouldn't matter that Catherine was imagining Emily's body under all her winter garb.

"Don't you think?"

Catherine blinked rapidly, pulling herself back to the present. "I'm sorry?"

Emily studied her with a knowing expression on her face, and Catherine couldn't decide if that irritated her or turned her on more. "I said I think these people are such amazing artists, not to mention the science they have to factor in."

"Oh, absolutely," Catherine agreed—probably too vehemently—and did her best to concentrate on the works of art before her. The most impressive had to be the wild horses. She and Emily walked slowly around the sculpture, being careful to stay behind the ropes, and chewed their dough in silence as they took in the beauty of what seemed to be three enormous equines bursting out of the snow with great strength and speed. The details of their manes—individual hairs visible—was astounding. The hard lines of muscle and sinew were so smooth and perfect, Catherine wanted to reach out, run her hands across it, expected she'd be able to feel the heat and strength under the ice and snow. They strolled to observe from all angles, and the silence between Catherine and Emily was a testament to how breathtaking the work was. Four people were still working on it, some with trowels and sculpting tools, others with spray bottles of water. It was fascinating to watch.

"Have you ever seen sand sculptures?" Emily whispered.

Catherine shook her head, whispering back, "No, but I imagine it takes a similar combination of artistry and science."

"It does, though I think sand is harder to keep from falling apart." Emily looked at her and a wide smile split her face. "Why are we whispering?" she whispered.

"I have no idea," Catherine whispered back, grinning. "It feels like we should."

"I know. How come?"

Catherine shrugged. "No clue."

Their gazes held as they quietly giggled together and Catherine felt it again, that combination of fear, excitement, dread, and arousal that Emily seemed to cultivate within her. Then, in unspoken agreement, they continued to wander.

"You know what I would love to do with you?" Emily asked.

"Tell me."

"Slow dance." Emily met her gaze. "I'd really love to slow dance with you."

"Oh, I don't dance," Catherine said quickly, the image of being wrapped up in the warmth of Emily's arms, their bodies touching from hips up to shoulders, their mouths scant millimeters apart. The sheer intimacy was too much to think about.

"You don't even slow dance?" Emily's eyes were wide with disbelief.

Catherine shook her head and pointed to the next sculpture, hoping to effectively change the subject. It worked, as Emily followed her and they quietly discussed the next work of art they came upon.

The next half hour went by way too quickly for Catherine's liking, but it was probably better that she get home. She was having much too good a time, which would not help her keep her distance from Emily. As it was, she found herself walking much closer to her than she would anybody else she'd been at the carnival with. She could see Jessica's face in her mind, unimpressed and etched with disapproval, but she did her best to shake it away. She looked at Emily, who frowned.

"It's time, huh?"

"I'm afraid so. Can't be late for my shift."

Emily nodded, took Catherine's empty plate and stacked it with her own, then found a trash can to discard them. "Okay. Your chariot awaits." As they walked toward the parking lot— rather slowly, Catherine noted with warmth—Emily asked, "How come you work a second job? If you don't mind my asking."

Catherine lifted one shoulder in a half-shrug. "I've always had at least two jobs," she said. "In high school, all through college, after I graduated. I've had the job at Joplin's longer than I've been at Junebug."

"Really? How come you didn't quit when you were hired full-time?"

"We didn't have a lot when I was growing up. My mom worked her ass off to keep us fed and clothed, but we never had brand-name stuff. Always sale items, generic things. Her work ethic was all I knew, so...I guess I mimicked it. As I got older, I found I like having the extra money." She looked at Emily and one corner of her mouth quirked up. "Shoe fetish, remember?"

"Ah," Emily said with a laugh. "It all makes sense now. Do you have a favorite brand of shoes?"

Catherine gazed up into the clear sky, contemplating the question. "Not really, though I do have a fondness for boots." She gazed down at her feet. "I could use a few more pairs."

Emily laughed again and Catherine decided right then that she loved the sound of it, an odd combination of husky and feminine, slightly exotic, very contagious.

They reached the car, and Emily opened the door for Catherine, then got inside and started the engine.

"Listen, I wanted to ask you something," Emily said once they were out of the busy lot and onto the road home.

"Okay."

"Are you busy next weekend? It'll be the Saturday after Christmas and I assume most of the holiday chaos will have died down a bit…"

Catherine nodded. "What did you have in mind?"

Emily took a deep breath and Catherine got the impression she was hesitant to continue. Nervous maybe. She wet her lips and finally said, "I'd like to take you to my family's cabin for the weekend. It's about an hour and a half from here, and we'd have it to ourselves. It's gorgeous and cozy and we could hike or we could ski or snowshoe. We could hang out by the fire…" She let her voice trail off, eyes glued to the road as if afraid to look at Catherine.

We could hang out by the fire… Catherine let Emily's words replay in her head even as she studied her, her profile, the gentle slope of her nose, the delicate whorls in her ear as she tucked her hair behind it, her long, feminine fingers. *We so would not be hanging out by the fire. Or if we were, we'd be naked. You know this. I know this. I'm not stupid. This is a bad idea. Your mother thinks so. Jessica thinks so. Even you and I think so. A weekend away together in an isolated cabin in the woods? That is a terrible idea. Of course I will not go with you…*

"That sounds great. I'd love to go."

Emily's head whipped around and her expression was one of excited disbelief. "You would?"

"I would."

Braking for a red light, Emily took in a slow, deep breath and nodded subtly. "Okay. That's great." She turned her sparkling brown eyes to Catherine. "I'll pick you up Saturday morning. Around nine?"

"Make it ten. I'll need to drop Mo off at my mother's."

"Ten it is."

"And I will pick *you* up so we're not driving this expensive deathtrap of yours in a blizzard."

Emily grinned and nodded again. "Fair enough, Ms. Bossypants. I'll text you my address."

Catherine smiled as she looked out the window and wondered what she'd just gotten herself into. Why couldn't she resist Emily? Especially when every thought in her head was a reason why she should? It was like her brain and her mouth had no connection whatsoever. Her brain was logic. Her mouth was impulse. Maybe Geronimo actually was rubbing off on her, creating in her a propensity to leap before she looked, which was something so against her nature that a part of her worried there was something wrong. Could a brain tumor be doing this? Messing with her impulse control? It was silly, she knew, but she had no other explanation except for...

She turned to look at Emily and was yet again struck by the beauty sitting in the driver's seat. Emily Breckenridge was stunning. Gorgeous. Ridiculously so. Catherine had never been so physically affected by a woman before. Ever.

She wasn't quite sure what to do with that.

"You're staring at me." Emily's voice pulled Catherine out of her own head.

"I am. Sorry."

"Don't be." Emily glanced at her with a sexy smile that made Catherine glad she was seated, as she was reasonably sure her legs had turned to jelly.

After what seemed like an eternity, but wasn't even close, Emily pulled the car into Catherine's driveway and shifted into Park. Catherine's heart rate kicked up a notch and she had the sudden urge to get out of the car immediately. Which she tried to do, only to find her door locked. She looked back at Emily, who was giving her a rakish grin.

"I have to let you out," she said, her voice low. "Automatic locks."

"Oh."

And then Emily was leaning toward her, and it was like she was a magnet and Catherine was made of metal; she leaned in, too. She couldn't help herself. Their lips met softly at first, tentatively, as if they needed a moment to reacquaint themselves with one another. Catherine felt Emily's hand on her knee, the warmth, the weight of it only serving to make her lean in closer, to push her mouth more firmly against Emily's. They kissed slowly, deliciously, but then Emily's other hand slid around Catherine's neck and tightened its grip. With her hair in a ponytail, there was nothing between Emily's fingers and Catherine's skin and the contact was exquisite. Emily pulled Catherine in tighter and Catherine didn't resist. Instead, she pushed her tongue into Emily's mouth, pulling a moan from deep in her throat that sent wet heat directly to Catherine's center.

They kissed a bit longer, Catherine allowing herself another minute or so of ridiculous pleasure before gently pulling back, breathless.

Emily looked as though all words had left her. She simply shook her head slowly, back and forth, back and forth. Her face was flushed pink, her lips were glossy and a little swollen, and her eyes had gone dark. Catherine had never seen a sexier sight.

"I had a great time today," she said quietly.

"Yeah? Good. Me, too." Her eyes never leaving Catherine's, she reached behind her and the door locks popped. "I'm really looking forward to next weekend."

"So am I." Catherine smiled at her and pulled the door handle. As she turned to get out, she felt Emily's hand on her arm.

"Wait."

Catherine turned back to her and was unsurprised by one more kiss. This one was gentle, soft, just a brushing of lips on lips, which somehow made it almost more erotic than the make-out session they'd just had. Catherine swallowed hard, whispered, "Bye," and managed to haul herself out of the car. Emily waited until, on shaky legs, Catherine made it to her front door and slid her key home. She waved at the car, then went inside. She shut the door behind her and very nearly fell against it, weak-kneed and completely turned on.

Geronimo came running to her, jumping at her legs and wagging his tail, but Catherine couldn't even move. She brought her fingers to her lips and simply stood there, absently wondering if her legs would ever work again.

CHAPTER SIXTEEN

THE NEXT ENORMOUS BOUQUET of flowers arrived at the shelter late on Monday afternoon, and this time, Catherine wasn't at all surprised. A smile stayed plastered on her face as she carried them down the hall and set them on her desk. In fact, she'd almost expected them, and they were no less gorgeous than the past arrangements, all full of huge blooms and bright colors. Her office had never looked so cheerful before, nor had it ever smelled so sweet. Plucking the card from its little plastic fork, she read.

> *There's nobody I'd rather shoot down an ice slide at a thousand miles per hour with than you. Thanks for indulging me. Can't wait for next weekend.*
> *Emily*

Before she could get all dreamy and/or worried about the impending cabin-in-the-woods weekend, her phone rang and saved her. She set the card on the desk next to the flowers and went around to the other side to answer. Dropping into her chair, she listened to the donor and answered his questions, even as she recognized her new heels were killing her feet. Knowing she couldn't just take them off or she'd never get them back on again, she bent forward in her seat to rub the back of her heel while she absently mhmm'd and uh-huh'd the man on the phone. Saying good-bye, finally, she sat up to place the handset back in the cradle and was surprised to see Jessica standing in front of her desk.

In her hand was the card from Emily.

Catherine swallowed, but said nothing, wanting to see how Jessica was going to play this. She rolled her lips in, bit down on them, and waited.

"I was wondering where the flowers had been coming from. You're the talk of the shelter, you know." Jessica said, holding up the card.

Catherine said nothing.

"Anna suspected something was going on."

Catherine cleared her throat, but forced herself to keep quiet about what Anna could do with her big mouth and her gossip.

"She said that Emily left your office the other day and when Anna came in to see you, you looked 'flushed and satisfied.'" She made air quotes around the last three words and tinted them with sarcasm. Jessica glanced at the flowers. Her expression wasn't angry, which surprised Catherine, but she couldn't put her finger on exactly what was going on inside her friend's head. "What's next weekend?"

Catherine swallowed. "Um...Emily invited me to her family's cabin."

"I see." Jessica seemed to search for words. Catherine had known her for a long time, but she was still hard to read. Uncertain whether she was angry, confused, fine, or some combination of all of those emotions, Catherine chose—again—to wait her out. It took several long beats before Jessica spoke again. "Didn't we talk about this?" Her tone was surprisingly calm.

Catherine nodded slowly. "Yes."

"Did I misunderstand?"

"No."

"Did you?"

"No."

"Then maybe you can help me here."

Catherine turned her gaze to the window as she tried to think of something to say that made sense. It got dark so early this time of year, and dusk was already closing in. Finally settling on being as honest as she could, considering she was in uncharted waters, Catherine looked into Jessica's blue eyes and said, "I don't know what to tell you because I'm not really sure what to tell myself."

Jessica squinted at her.

"Nothing has happened," Catherine said, then added, "Not really."

"And you think that will still hold true after a weekend away in a cabin?"

Catherine looked down at her hands.

Jessica sighed. "Cat...I just..." She shook her head. "It worries me," she said finally. "That's all. I have concerns."

Catherine scoffed quietly. Who didn't have concerns around this situation?

Jessica leaned forward, bracing her hands on the desk. "Look. This isn't just about the shelter, okay? I don't want you to think it's all that. It's about you as well. I care about you and... I don't want my shelter to get hurt. But I don't want my friend to get hurt either. Okay?"

Catherine nodded. "I know."

"Do you?"

"I do."

"Okay." Jessica stood back up. "Good. Just...be careful. All right? Please be careful." There was so much packed into those few words. Jessica was saying to be careful. She was also saying *I really hate that you're doing this* and *why her?* and *I know your love life is none of my business* and *if you jeopardize my shelter, I may have to kill you* and *I love you, please don't let her hurt you.* So, so much in those few words; it was all in Jessica's emotional blue eyes.

Their gazes held as Catherine read all those things and then Jessica gave a small, sad smile and left without another word. As Catherine watched her friend retreat down the hall, she saw Anna peek her head out of her office. She looked at Jessica's passing form, then turned her gaze to Catherine, a half-grin pulling up one corner of her mouth.

Catherine looked away first.

━◇━

Things were quiet in Emily's office on December 23. It was a Tuesday, and she wished they'd been busier. Maybe that would keep her mind from focusing on things other than Catherine. Catherine's eyes. Catherine's smile. Catherine's mouth…

She didn't have a window in her office, which was a bummer, as people who walked by would see she was gazing out the window rather than staring off into space like she'd been doing for over an hour now.

They'd texted several times since the winter carnival on Saturday, but either Catherine was super busy (which is what Emily suspected) or she just wasn't a person who was playful in texts (also a possibility). The messages were friendly enough. Light. But a bit serious. Maybe Catherine was just one of those people who needed facial expressions and tone of voice before she understood what was being said, whether it was joking,

216

playful, or serious. And while Emily's office was as quiet as a library, Catherine's was maniacal, as she'd predicted it would be days before Christmas. Because of that, Emily didn't feel as neglected as she might have if she knew Catherine wasn't busy. Instead, she did her best to find things to occupy her mind. Tomorrow was Christmas Eve and there were lots of things she could help her mother with. Christmas was Thursday and though the office was closed on Friday, Emily would most likely come in and try to get some work done in order to keep herself from going out of her mind anticipating Saturday morning. She could hardly wait to swoop Catherine off to the cabin and have two full days of her all to herself.

It was going to be amazing.

Before her brain could go off on that fantasy tangent it was so fond of—the one that tossed her all kinds of things she and Catherine might do together...most involving little to no clothing—her phone rang, startling her.

"Emily Breckenridge."

"Hey, Brecks. Merry Christmas." Sandy's voice was cheerful and Emily smiled in response, always happy to hear from her.

"Hi there. What's new?"

"I forgot when we were together last time to remind you about my New Year's Eve party."

"It's back on? That's fantastic!" Emily was excited, as Sandy had always hosted New Year's Eve for her friends, but had to cancel it last year.

"It is. I missed it too much."

"This is good news. What can I bring?"

She could hear the smile in Sandy's voice as she said, "A date. You could bring one of those."

Emily was pretty sure she surprised her by replying, "I just might do that."

Sandy's gasp was audible. "Seriously?"

"It's possible."

"The sexy numbers girl from the shelter?"

"Mmhmm. Do not tell Michelle yet. Please? I don't want another lecture. We're getting enough of that from everybody else."

"Still, huh?" Sandy's voice held sympathy, and Emily loved her for that.

"Yeah, but…we haven't really been listening…" She let her voice trail off.

"What?" Sandy laughed. "You'd better give me details *right now*, young lady!"

Emily smiled widely as she launched into the story of how she waited for three hours at Joplin's, how they'd had the wine at Catherine's house, and how the sexual tension hung in the air like fog. She told Sandy all about the winter carnival, what an amazing time she'd had, and how shocked she'd been to have Catherine accept her invitation to the cabin this weekend.

"Oh, my God. Em…" Sandy took a beat and her voice got quiet. "You really like this girl."

Emily sighed. "I do."

"Does she feel the same way?"

"Well, that's the complicated part. I'm not sure."

She could almost see Sandy's face, her eyes squinting as she ordered, "Explain."

Emily leaned her head back against her chair and stared at the tiled ceiling of her office as she tried to think of the best words with which to describe Catherine. "She can be hard to read. She doesn't say a lot, but she sees everything, takes in everything. She doesn't miss a trick, even if she doesn't talk about it. And you know me, I talk about *everything*." Sandy's laughed only served to confirm what she said. "So, while she hasn't come right out and said anything to make me think she feels the same things I do, she hasn't told me to get lost either. She has accepted every invitation I've extended. And she hasn't returned any of my flowers."

"Any? How many bouquets have you sent?"

"Three? Four, maybe?"

"Wow." Sandy chuckled. "You do enjoy that. So. The cabin, huh?"

"Yeah."

"Just the two of you, I assume?"

"Yup."

"Are you excited? Nervous?"

"Terrified? All of the above? Yes."

"Well, I've been to that cabin before. It's crazy romantic."

"It is." Emily replayed all the things she'd just said about Catherine. They were all true. Catherine had never come right out and said she liked Emily. That she wanted to date her. That they might have something. Not in those words anyway. But Emily didn't care, because she'd kissed Catherine and Catherine had kissed her back. On more than one occasion. And you couldn't fake that kind of passion. There was no way. Emily would know. If Catherine wasn't into her, it would be obvious in her kiss. Emily was sure of it. The thought of kissing Catherine again in a few days set her stomach to flip-flopping and her blood warmed. The thought of doing more than kissing made her fully expect to spontaneously combust right there in her desk chair.

"All right, sweetie, I've got to run. I've got some last-minute gifts to grab at the mall." Sandy said the last two words with frightened horror.

"Have you never heard of online shopping? What's the matter with you?"

"I know. I know. Next year."

"That's what you said last year."

"Stop harassing me, Brecks!" Sandy laughed. "Have a very merry Christmas, honey, and let me know how the weekend goes. I'll see you on New Year's Eve if not sooner, yes?"

"Definitely. Back atcha on the Christmas wishes. Tell your parents I said hi. Love you."

"Love you back."

Emily set the phone down in its cradle and just stared at it for long moments. This weekend was either going to be the best of her life or one of the worst. She was pretty sure she knew which, but was afraid of being too cocky. Afraid the Universe would decide such overconfidence should be balanced with a good dose of bad Karma. So instead of focusing on the upcoming joy of the weekend, she returned to staring off into space.

The day dragged on like a reluctant child heading to naptime.

CHAPTER SEVENTEEN

CHRISTMAS WAS ITS USUAL wonderful, chaotic, stressful, and tiring undertaking. Denise loved Christmas. Absolutely adored it. She was also completely thrilled when it was over. There was such a build-up, such a lead-in. Prepping. Shopping. Cooking. Wrapping. She didn't mind any of it. In fact, she would almost say she enjoyed the weeks that led up to Christmas Eve and Christmas Day. Her family was small, but tight-knit, and Denise was happy for any excuse to spend time with her parents and her children. Not to mention her only grandchild.

Despite the fact that her parents were both in good health and active, they were also in their eighties and Denise was becoming more and more aware that she wouldn't have them forever. And Jason would get married and maybe move off to start his own life. Her family would slowly splinter, dissolve, and these holidays together meant the world to her.

Christmas Eve was traditionally held at her parents' house. Then they came to Denise's small bungalow for Christmas morning, where they opened presents and had an early dinner together. The day after Christmas was a traditional day out for Denise and Catherine. They always went to a matinee at one of the local movie theaters, then out to dinner, just the two of them. It had started innocently enough one year when they'd decided they were bored sitting home and went to see a show. After that, boom, instant tradition.

Which is why they sat in The Railhouse now, enjoying the remainder of the bottle of Pinot Grigio they'd split and

Catherine spooned a hunk of Bananas Foster into her mouth. Ordered by Denise, of course.

"Are you scheduled at Joplin's this weekend?" she asked her daughter, then sipped her wine.

"No, I actually took the weekend off." Catherine's blue eyes —so much like her father's—darted around the restaurant, looking at anything but her mother. "And I wanted to ask you if you could watch Geronimo for me."

"Tomorrow?"

"Yes. And overnight."

Denise's eyebrows rose in mild surprise. "Of course. Where are you off to?" It wasn't like Catherine to be at all cagey or mysterious, so this was interesting. As was the obvious uncertainty on her face. Denise sipped her wine again and waited.

"Emily Breckenridge invited me to her family's cabin for the weekend." Catherine said it matter-of-factly and if Denise didn't know her daughter so well, she might not have noticed the speed with which she blurted the explanation. It was the only sign that Catherine wasn't entirely comfortable with this conversation.

"I see." Denise studied Catherine for a beat before stating, "You're nervous."

Catherine gave a sigh and picked up her own wine glass. "A little. Yes."

"How come?"

"I'm not sure." The expression on her face told Denise she was being honest and that explained a lot. Catherine was not the kind of woman who enjoyed flying by the seat of her pants. She liked to know the reasons for things and not understanding why she was nervous about the upcoming weekend obviously didn't sit well with her. Denise had to make a conscious effort not to grin, because it was clear to her why Catherine was nervous. Seriously, for a woman as highly intelligent as her youngest daughter, Denise was often amazed by how oblivious she could be.

"You seem to like Emily." Baby-stepping it.

Catherine gazed off into the restaurant. "Yeah."

"She obviously likes you, inviting you to her cabin for the weekend. That's pretty sweet."

Catherine nodded slowly.

"I kind of love that she sends flowers so often." Denise had happily shown Catherine the Christmas bouquet that had arrived at her house from Emily the day before Christmas. Catherine had stood there, taking in the enormous arrangement, simultaneously annoyed and thrilled.

"They're so expensive," Catherine said quietly. "And they're dead in two weeks. It seems like such a waste of money."

"Well, they make me happy. And I'd bet you whatever's in my wallet right now that it makes Emily happy to send them." She smiled at her daughter to take the sting out when she said, "So how about you smile and say thank you and enjoy them when they arrive?"

A small grin tugged up one corner of Catherine's mouth. "I can do that."

"Good." Denise sipped her wine. "Now, tell me what's going on in that head of yours."

"I wish I knew," Catherine said.

"Are you making more out of it than you need to?" Denise raised her eyebrows, gave Catherine a knowing look.

Catherine caught it, and her quiet laugh lacked humor. "Possibly. Probably."

"You're such a worrier, sweetheart. You always were. You overanalyze *everything*. It's exhausting to watch." Again, Denise smiled so Catherine wouldn't think she was being insulted. "Why don't you try relaxing and just, I don't know, going with the flow?"

"When have you ever gone with the flow, Mom?"

"Not often at all. And you know what? I wish I had. Worrying is so needless. There's hardly ever anything you can do about the things that worry you, so just…" Denise held her arms up and opened her hands as if releasing something into the air. "Give it up. To God. To the Universe. To whom or whatever. Just let it go, baby." She leaned forward and smiled at Catherine as she whispered, "Let it go." When Catherine tried to smile, but ended up grimacing instead, Denise couldn't help but laugh. "Oh, my sweetheart. I know you so well. Right now, you're thinking that letting it go is easier said than done."

Catherine did laugh then. "That's exactly what I'm thinking."

"Will you at least try?"

After a moment, Catherine nodded. "I will."

"Good. Life is too short, honey. Too short to not grab on with both hands. Maybe this weekend will be nothing. Maybe you'll come home on Sunday night and you'll roll your eyes at me as you pick up your dog and you'll say, 'See, Mom? Told you. Nothing. Boring. Moving on.'" Denise leaned in again, her smile widening. "But maybe—*just maybe*—it'll be the best weekend you've ever had in your life. Maybe it'll be the start of something new and wonderful. Maybe it'll be the start of the next big chapter for you. Anything is possible. Right?"

What Denise could only label as relief seemed to pass across her daughter's face. Even if it was just momentary, Denise decided she'd take it. Anything to replace the constant expression of concern that Catherine sported more often than anything else.

"Right." Catherine picked up her glass and held it toward Denise. "To anything being possible."

"I will so drink to that."

The glasses made a sweet, musical ping as they touched, and Denise watched Catherine as they sipped. Unsurprisingly, the look of slight concern was already back.

Denise could only smile and subtly shake her head.

My girl, she thought, *carrying the weight of the world on her shoulders.* And her heart swelled with a mother's love and the understanding that there was nothing at all she could do but watch.

The next morning saw Catherine packing and unpacking, packing and repacking, utterly lost over what she should be bringing. The reality of the situation was that she was going to be alone with Emily for two days and one night. Alone. With Emily. Catherine was no fool and had become painfully aware of how weak she was around the sexy Ms. Breckenridge. She knew if Emily made any moves that led them in the direction of sex, Catherine would most likely be powerless to stop herself...nor did she want to. She was painfully aware of *that* as well.

Dwelling didn't help a damn thing, and she finally muttered, "Screw it," and threw some clothes into her bag. Grabbing some toiletries from the bathroom, she packed those as well, nodded once, and declared herself done.

Mo had watched her intently throughout this whole process and it occurred to Catherine—belatedly—that he actually understood what it meant that she was packing a bag. His normally joyful-looking ears lay flat against his head, his tail was wagless, and when she looked into his weirdly light brown eyes, she actually thought he looked sad.

"It's okay, buddy." She laid her hand on his head and stroked him lovingly. "You're going to stay with Grandma and I'm pretty sure she'll spoil you rotten. No worries." Then she bent close to him so they were nose to nose. Giving him her most sincere expression, she told him, "I promise I'm coming back. Okay? I promise. I will never leave you."

She wasn't sure if it made the dog feel any better, but it helped Catherine.

Dropping him off at her mother's wasn't nearly the ordeal Catherine worried it might be. Geronimo wandered the house, sniffing and sniffing and sniffing, before jumping up onto the couch and settling in.

"Nice. So glad you're going to miss me," Catherine said, with a relieved chuckle. Then she kissed him on the head and moved toward the door. To her mother, she said, "Make sure everything is latched on the fence, okay? He will bolt if there's an opening. We're working on it, but I have yet to meet a person who is as interesting to him as a squirrel, so…"

"Don't worry." Her mother squeezed her shoulder. "You go, have a good time, and relax. My granddoggie and I will be just fine."

"Okay. Thanks, Mom."

As Catherine turned to open the door, her mother said, "I mean it, honey. Relax. Enjoy yourself." As Catherine met her gaze, they said together, "Let it go."

"I know. I know. I promise to do my best." Catherine kissed her mother's cheek and was off to her next stop.

Light, fluffy snowflakes began to fall as Catherine followed Siri's directions to Emily's downtown address. The temperature hovered right around thirty, but the forecast called for a sharp drop later in the day and the light, fluffy stuff would become heavy and slick. She wanted to be safely tucked away in Emily's cabin with plenty of time to spare.

When she pulled into the parking spot marked with Emily's apartment number, Catherine shifted her car into Park and just stared. The six-story building was new and modern, and she remembered reading about it in the news when it was first erected four or five years ago. The Downtown Lofts, they were called. Simple and sophisticated. They were spacious, elegant, and very expensive. Catherine knew this because she'd gone online for giggles and looked at all the photos, envisioned herself living in one of them, cooking in the gourmet kitchen, pouring wine and mixing fun cocktails in the bar area for all the friends she'd invite over, stretching out in front of the huge stone fireplace, feet crossed at the ankle on her steel-and-glass coffee table as she gazed into the flames. Of course, she'd have to work seven extra jobs, not one, to ever be able to afford such luxury, but it was nice to fantasize about it for a while.

Inside the first set of heavy glass doors was a foyer, nicely appointed in bright, modern colors of aqua and cream, all the glass and metal polished so perfectly that Catherine could see her own reflection everywhere. On the wall was a block of mailboxes and buzzer buttons. Emily was—unsurprisingly—on the sixth floor, and Catherine pushed the corresponding doorbell. An intercom she hadn't noticed made no sound as it came to life. It was as if Emily's voice was suddenly just *there*.

"Hey, I saw you pull in. Come on up."

And then, rather than buzz, the second set of heavy glass doors simply clicked and Catherine pulled one open.

The inner lobby was enormous and airy, with a large staircase in the very center and elevators on either end. Apparently, no apartments were on the first floor, as Catherine's curiosity had her wandering the space. Doors for laundry, a fitness center, a storage area, and underground garage access circled the open space. That must be why she didn't see Emily's car in the lot. It had its own weather-free underground garage.

Returning to where she'd begun, she decided on the elevator rather than climbing six flights of stairs. As everything else in the building was so far, the car was clean, spacious, and modernly silent. Catherine barely felt like she'd moved before the doors opened to the sixth floor. To her left, a door was open and Emily's face peered out, adorned with a huge smile that made Catherine feel warm inside almost instantly.

"You found me," Emily said.

"Wasn't that hard."

"Come in. Meet Dave."

Catherine crossed down the hall and followed Emily inside to the nicest apartment she'd ever seen in her entire life. Everything about it was inviting—which surprised Catherine. She'd expected modern and sleek to equal cold, and Emily's place was anything but. It was warm, both in temperature and in décor, all deep purples and light beiges, very earthy and comfortable. Her furniture was big, bulky and overstuffed, the kind that made you want to kick off your shoes and flop onto it with a good book, and it would suck you in, cradle you like a lover. One side of the living room was covered by floor-to-ceiling windows that looked out over the city and framed the falling snow—a Christmas card view. It was stunning.

Before she could take in any more, Catherine's attention was pulled by a stocky, barrel-chested dog with a square head and soft, gentle eyes. He nuzzled her hand and waited patiently for her to notice him, though his entire hindquarters vibrated with the effort to control himself.

"You must be Dave," she said and squatted to look him in the eye. "You are just as handsome as your mom says you are, you know that?" She took his huge block head in both hands and let him swipe his tongue across her cheek, just once, very gently. "Oh, you are such a sweet boy."

"He's a ladies' man," Emily said, pride evident in her voice.

After another moment of dog love, Catherine stood back up. "Your place is beautiful."

"Thanks. I like it."

"That view is amazing." Catherine pointed at the windows.

"That's why I bought this one. I had to haggle and it took a long time, but this apartment has the best view in the building. Sometimes, I turn the lights off, click the fireplace on, and just sit there watching the city go by. It's super relaxing."

"I bet."

"So." Emily clapped her hands once and rubbed the palms together, and for the first time since she'd arrived, it occurred to Catherine that Emily was nervous. Somehow, that made her feel better. "Let me grab my bag and we can get going, okay?"

"What about Dave?" The dog sat next to Catherine, who'd been absently petting his head nonstop.

"My friend Sandy's going to pick him up later this afternoon and take him for the weekend." Looking down at her dog, she said to him, "You're gonna go have a sleepover with Spike, huh?"

Dave's ears pricked up and in her head, Catherine heard a Scooby-Doo sounding "huh?" that made her grin.

"Sandy's dog Spike is a Yorkie who thinks he weighs eighty pounds. He'll spend all weekend reminding Dave that he is the boss. And Dave will let him, which is why they get along so well." Emily held up a finger. "Be right back."

Ten minutes later, they were on the road, Emily gently giving directions as she sat in Catherine's passenger seat like she was always meant to be there. It was a strange feeling and Catherine did her best to ignore it.

"So, tell me about this cabin of yours," she said, needing a distraction.

"Well, we have two. This is the smaller one."

"You have two?"

"In the same vicinity, yes. The bigger one belongs to my grandparents and we used to all go up there together during the holidays and winter breaks, back when me and my brother and cousins were all kids. We'd sled and build snowmen and go snowshoeing and cross-country skiing. Stuff like that. As we got older, my parents decided they needed a smaller getaway for themselves, so they bought the little cabin. It's just a one-bedroom with a kitchen and fireplace that allowed them to escape the madness of young, loud teenagers." Emily chuckled at that and the sound made Catherine smile. "The entire family still uses the big cabin. My cousins have kids. They bring their in-laws. We actually had to make an online schedule and sign up, like we're customers. But, it works."

"And the smaller cabin?"

"That's just for us. My parents and me and Clark. My parents will let others use it if they ask, but it's mostly just ours." Emily turned to her and her soft brown eyes sparkled. "I think you'll really like it."

"I think you're right."

A few beats of silence went by before Emily gestured to the radio. "Do you mind?"

"Knock yourself out."

Emily fiddled with the buttons for a few moments before settling on a country music station.

"Country? Really? I would not have pegged you for a country music fan."

Emily subtly bobbed her head to the beat of the Luke Bryan song as she gazed out the window. "I like all music, really. Country, pop, rap, R & B, jazz, classical. Just depends on my mood."

"Well, you are full of surprises, aren't you?"

Emily turned to look at her, eyes suddenly heavy with—Catherine refused to analyze it—as she said, "Oh, you have no idea."

Catherine squeezed her thighs together as her entire lower body tightened with arousal. She looked back at Emily and purposely arched one eyebrow. "Oh, I think I do."

Emily dropped her head back against the seat with a defeated groan. "The damn eyebrow. Such an unfair tactic," she said as she laughed. "I probably shouldn't have told you how that affects me."

"Probably not."

The remainder of the ride went quickly as they talked about everything from the mundane to the somewhat serious, as if they were on a first date and collecting all the data about one another that they possibly could. City became suburbs, which blended out into country as the snow continued to fall gently. Before Catherine knew it, Emily was directing her to turn into a driveway that was camouflaged by the trees; she'd never have seen it without instruction.

"The driveway's plowed," Catherine said, surprised.

"Yeah, I called ahead."

They drove slowly up a winding path that spit them out onto an open lot where an adorable log cabin sat, something out of an architectural magazine. Or more accurately, an HGTV show. The light-colored logs looked striped with white as the snowflakes blanketed the tops of each row. A charming front porch covered the entryway where a red door beckoned to visitors like an aproned grandmother. *Come in, come in! Cookies are just out of the oven...*

Emily's slamming door jarred Catherine from her reverie and she followed, popping the trunk and pulling her overnight bag out. Reaching for a second bag, she said to Emily, "I brought some wine. For having me." At Emily's smothered grin and raised eyebrows, she blushed and amended, "For *inviting* me." She couldn't help but smile and shake her head.

"That was very sweet of you." Emily swung her arm out in a huge sweep. "Follow me, young lady."

The porch was cleared of snow. "Your plow guy shovels as well?" Catherine asked.

"No, I did that." Emily slid her key in and pushed the door open.

Inside, Catherine simply stopped and stared.

The cabin was something out of a movie. The cathedral ceiling made it feel huge. The walls were log beams and held ski lodge décor: old-timey snowshoes made of wood, a pair of crossed skis from decades ago, a sled that Catherine thought was something her grandfather might have used as a kid. A huge fireplace took up an entire wall, and much to Catherine's surprise, a wood fire burned in it, warming the living space and giving off just enough scent of wood smoke to make her want to sit down and relax. In one corner, a Christmas tree that had to be nine feet tall stood, completely lit and decorated. Small, twinkling lights reflected off the two gifts wrapped in silver paper sparkling beneath it. The furniture was chocolate brown leather; a large couch and two oversized chairs with matching ottomans. Beneath it was a thick, soft-looking beige area rug, presumably to keep bare feet from being too cold on the gorgeous hardwood floor that matched the walls. In front of the fireplace was a second rug, similar in color scheme, but it looked even thicker and softer. To the right was one door—the bedroom and bath, Catherine guessed. To the left, entry to the kitchen. Catherine stayed where she was for a moment, knowing if the kitchen was half as beautiful as the rest of the cabin, she'd get light-headed and possibly faint from pleasure.

"What do you think?" Emily asked from beside her. When Catherine looked at her uncertain expression, she was shocked to realize that Emily was worried.

"What do I think? I think I'm in a dream. This is…it's just so beautiful, Emily. Why aren't you here every single day?"

Emily chuckled and Catherine could hear a note of relief. "It's a hell of a commute to work."

"True, but possibly worth it." Catherine winked and toed off her boots. "Um…crazy question for you: how is there a fire going? And a lit tree?"

"Oh." Emily took her own boots off, then took Catherine's coat from her and hung it in the closet next to the boot tray. "I was here yesterday." Catherine was sure she saw Emily's skin tint pink. "I wanted it to be pretty for your visit, so I got the tree and decorated it, brought in wood, changed the linens, stocked the fridge, stuff like that. We have a caretaker who lives down the road. He got the fire going for me—" she glanced at her watch "—about an hour ago."

"Wow. You thought of everything."

"I tried to."

They stood face-to-face for a long beat before Emily leaned forward and kissed Catherine on the mouth. It was soft, almost chaste, but not quite, and she pulled back before Catherine had any time to sink into it.

"I'll show you around." Emily slid her hand down Catherine's arm and grasped her hand in a move so natural, Catherine simply went with it, following her around the cabin as she pointed out rooms and artwork and told stories of her times there. "This is the bedroom," Emily said, her voice growing husky at the same time Catherine registered the one king-sized bed. "There's a bathroom off in the corner there." Emily quickly tugged Catherine out of the doorway and toward the kitchen.

"Wow," Catherine breathed as she entered the modestly sized but richly appointed room. Granite countertops in black topped light oak cabinets and brushed iron handles and knobs tied the two together. All the appliances were stainless steel and top-of-the-line, including the double convection oven and the Sub-Zero refrigerator. A large window over the sink gave a stunning view of the woods out back, the trees reaching their bare branches toward the misty gray sky like mothers' arms stretching for their children. "This is...it's breathtaking."

Emily looked absurdly pleased by the comment, her smile widening radiantly. "I'm glad you like it. I've got stew in the fridge for later, if that sounds good. I wanted something hearty, but simple. I'm hoping we'll work up an appetite." At Catherine's arched eyebrow, Emily laughed and added, "Hiking. We'll work up an appetite *hiking* and being out in the fresh air. Get your mind out of the gutter."

The rest of the afternoon went just like that. Catherine couldn't remember the last time she'd enjoyed spending time with somebody so much. It wasn't the best of days for snowshoeing—the sky remained gray and got grayer as the day went on. Just as the meteorologists had predicted, the snow turned from happy, fluffy flakes to near-sleet, and the wind kicked up a bit, pelting them in the face with tiny frozen ice balls. But the woods were gorgeously serene and Catherine happily pushed through the snow behind her hostess, who seemed to know the land like the back of her hand.

"I used to build forts here with Clark," Emily said, gesturing to a small, cleared space. "In the summer, we'd each build our own 'camp.'" Her mittened hands made her air quotes less distinguishable, but Catherine got the gist. "I'd find two tall sticks that had a Y-shape on one end and I'd stick them into the dirt. Then I'd find another stick to lay across the top in the Y's and boom. Instant doorway."

Catherine smiled as she watched the memories play across Emily's face.

"And then I'd lay sticks all around the area I wanted to be mine." As she tromped in a circle in the snow, the small clearing became more delineated. "And lastly, I'd gather stones and put them in the center of the room and lay small twigs side by side across them to make a sort of grill for my 'stove.'" More mittened air quotes. She looked up at Catherine then, her cheeks red with cold, but her eyes sparkling with the recollection of a happy childhood. "I had the best camp around. Way better than Clark's. And he wasn't allowed in mine. He always tried to make his like mine and never could, so he always wanted to come in."

"No boys allowed?"

"No boys, no brothers, and no jerks. He hit all three sometimes." Emily smiled and after a pause, she added, *"You* could have come in. I'd have let you."

"Yeah?"

"Yeah. But just you. Nobody else."

"Well. I'd have been honored to be a guest in your stick camp." When eye contact threatened to become too intimate, Catherine looked around the woods. It was so peaceful, with the wind singing a soft, mournful song through the bare branches of the trees. "It's so quiet out here," she said on a whisper, simply because it felt like she should.

"Isn't it?" Emily asked, just as quietly. "I used to love to come out here and just...be." She turned to her right and pointed. "There was an old tree stand in that direction. The hunter my parents bought the land from must have put it up. I used to swipe my mom's romance novels and climb up into the tree stand and just sit there and read for hours." Her expression became wistful. "Sometimes, I still want to do that."

"You read romance novels?" Catherine asked, her mouth quirked up in a half-grin. "Like, Harlequins? Danielle Steel? Like that?"

Emily squinted at her. "Oh, sweetheart, you had best not be mocking the romance novel. Them's fightin' words."

Catherine couldn't help but laugh at Emily's statement as they turned to head back toward the cabin. "I guess I just never would have pegged you for a romance reader. Sci-fi maybe. Or mystery. Something with a puzzle to figure out. But romance? You already know how they end."

Emily shrugged. "What's wrong with that?"

"Don't you find that boring? Knowing the ending before you even start?"

Emily scrunched up her face in an adorable display of thinking and Catherine, walking next to her, had to bite back a grin. "But, it's not about the ending. It's about the *ride*. Yes, they're going to end up together. That's the whole point. But I read the book because I want to take part in the ride. I want to tag along, sit in the back seat and watch, see how they get there. Haven't you ever heard the saying 'life is about the journey, not the destination?' I'm all about the journey. That's the meat and potatoes of life. It's what makes it all worth living, that journey."

Catherine looked at her then, tromping through the snow in her snowshoes, red ski cap covering her head, her dark hair dangling from beneath it. Her cheeks no longer looked cold to Catherine; rather, they looked healthy. Full of life. That sparkle in her rich brown eyes was suddenly not just cheerful, it was gorgeous, one of the most beautiful things Catherine had ever seen. The corners of Emily's mouth were always quirked up just a touch, but Catherine now understood how rare that was, for somebody to be so perpetually pleased with life. Watching all of this, taking it all in at that moment, Catherine was envious, but for once, it wasn't of Emily's money or status. She was envious of her view of life. And more than that, Catherine wanted to *emulate* Emily. She wanted to be that content with life all the time. She wanted people to be around her and feel like smiling, they way she felt any time she was next to Emily. Catherine's own smile slowly stretched itself across her face and she let herself feel it even as she concentrated on her footing in the deep snow.

"What are you smiling at?" Emily asked, her gentle voice still surprising Catherine in the quiet of the trees.

After a beat, Catherine answered honestly. "I'm just having a really good time."

Emily beamed at her and they continued walking back to the cabin.

By the time they'd made their way onto the front porch, the wind was steady and the snow was wet and heavy. They removed the snowshoes, leaving them on the porch, then stomped any remaining snow from their feet before pushing through the front door to the warmth inside.

It was nearing dusk—alarmingly early, it seemed to Catherine, but such was winter in the northeast. As she toed off her boots and glanced up, it occurred to her, not for the first time, that there was something serenely beautiful about a room lit up by only the lights on the Christmas tree. The fire had died down considerably while they were out, so it was now softly glowing embers of red and orange. Next to it, the tree stood tall, twinkling joyfully. Despite Christmas being over, Catherine took a moment to stand there and simply look at it, take it in.

"I love Christmas," Emily said softly beside her.

"Me, too."

They stood in silence for a long moment before Emily asked, "You hungry yet?"

"Starving."

"Hiking through the snow will do that to you. Let me stoke up the fire and then I'll get dinner going." Emily started across the room.

"I can do it," Catherine said, following.

"Yeah?" Emily raised her eyebrows.

"Yeah. Go get the food started before I eat my own arm."

"Yes, ma'am." Emily chuckled, then surprised her by giving her a quick peck on the cheek before disappearing into the kitchen. "Build me a fire, woman."

Catherine shook her head with a grin as she grabbed a couple of nearby logs and the poker from the stand and went to work. She had things just on the verge of roaring again when a glass of red wine appeared before her. She looked up into Emily's smiling eyes.

"The first reward for a hard day's hiking," Emily told her.

"The *first* reward?"

"Oh, yes. There are many, many more."

"I'm intrigued."

"You should be." Their gazes held electrically until Emily held out her own glass. "To you being here with me."

Their glasses touched and they sipped.

"Oh, this is good," Emily said.

"You think? It wasn't $250, but it's a decent wine." Catherine winked.

"Delicious. Stew's on. It just needs to heat up." Emily sat down next to Catherine on the thick, soft rug, and together they gazed silently into the flames.

Catherine absorbed the warmth of both the fire and Emily's solid presence next to her. She felt completely, utterly comfortable. Content and warm, relaxed. So relaxed that she didn't think twice about leaning toward Emily and covering her mouth in a sweet, gentle kiss. Slowly, she tasted Emily's lips, savored the wine on them along with Emily's own unique flavor. It was unhurried and wonderful, and Catherine was shocked by the realization that, though she had every intention of going further with Emily, she could easily kiss her like this for a long, long time.

After a few sensuous moments, two things became apparent: the stew needed stirring and the danger of spilling wine onto the light, expensive carpet was real, so they parted by mutual understanding, breathless.

"Damn, you are an amazing kisser," Emily breathed out as she swiped a thumb across Catherine's bottom lip, then pushed herself to standing.

"Thanks." Catherine felt herself blush and sipped her wine as Emily headed back to the kitchen, watching her go, taking in the fabulous view of Emily's ass.

Her cheeks puffed as she blew out a breath and willed her heart rate to slow back to normal.

In the kitchen, Emily braced both hands on the counter and let her head drop between her shoulders. "Oh, my God," she whispered over and over as she rocked forward and back, waiting for her breathing to even out. Kissing Catherine was…magical. Which was a totally corny thing to say, she knew, but it was true. It set fireworks off in her head, colors exploding behind her eyelids. It was invigorating and relaxing at once. It was all those things and more, and Emily had to consciously hold herself back, force herself not to run back into the living room and strip Catherine of her clothing right there in front of the fire, bury her hands in Catherine's hair, her head between Catherine's thighs.

It's so much. So much… Emily clenched her teeth so hard she expected to crack one. But gradually, her blood stopped racing, returned to a normal speed of flow through her veins. She wished Catherine would say more, talk to her instead of sitting quietly as she tended to do, in her own head the majority of the time. It was hard to know what she was thinking, where Emily stood with her.

Taking a large spoon from a drawer, Emily lifted the lid from the stockpot on the stove and stirred the beef stew as her brain kept on running along its path. Catherine had said she was having a great time today. That may seem like not much, but Emily was learning that even such a simple statement was unusual for Catherine, so Emily was taking it as an enormously good sign. She smiled as she thought about it. She was so used to Michelle and Sandy and, hell, even Clark. The people around her said what was on their minds, sometimes to their own detriment (Clark). Emily herself was the same way. If she thought something, she said it—unless it was tactless or hurtful, of course, which was where she and her brother veered off in different directions. Somebody who kept her cards close to the vest was new to Emily, and navigating these unfamiliar waters with Catherine wasn't easy.

Emily was pretty sure it was worth it, though.

She tasted the stew, added some salt as the timer went off, letting her know the rolls needed to come out of the oven.

"Can I help?" Catherine's voice was soft, but still startled Emily, so lost in her own thoughts was she. Standing in the doorway, shoulder leaning against the doorjamb, Catherine looked simply delectable as she sipped from her wine glass. There was no other word. Her jeans were dark, but soft-looking, nicely broken in, and hugged her curves as if they were tailored especially for her body. Her socks must have been wet because they were now gone and Catherine stood there barefoot, her toenails polished a festive blue. The long-sleeve white thermal T-shirt was snug, giving Emily no choice at all but to skim her eyes over Catherine's breasts. The flannel shirt was unbuttoned, the plaid of pinks and purples and the cut-in at the waist making it very clear this was a *woman* underneath. Catherine had cuffed the sleeves a couple of times so her smooth forearms showed.

Did something happen to the oxygen in here? Am I the only one who can't breathe?

She needed a beat to collect herself, but Emily finally smiled. Gesturing to a cupboard with her eyes, she said, "Grab me two bowls?"

Catherine pushed off the doorjamb, set her wine on the counter, and reached for the dishes, then handed them to Emily. "Smells amazing."

"Yeah? Well, hopefully, it tastes as good." Emily pulled the rolls from the oven.

"I'm optimistic." Catherine smiled at her. "More wine?"

"Please."

Catherine topped off their glasses and Emily scooped steaming stew into each bowl, added a roll, and reached for spoons.

"Dinner is served. Table or in front of the fire?"

Catherine scoffed as she took her bowl. "That question doesn't even deserve an answer." She turned and headed back into the living room.

"In front of the fire, it is," Emily said, grabbing her own bowl and wine and following Catherine. Once there, she hit some buttons on her phone and soon soft, instrumental Christmas music emanated from the small speaker on a side table.

"That's nice," Catherine said with approval.

"Glad you like it."

They sat on the rug, cross-legged, wine glasses on the hearth, bowls of stew in their laps. Emily was pretty sure this would be what Heaven was like.

Catherine took her first bite and her eyes closed as she hummed. Emily had to look away. "This is delicious," Catherine said after swallowing. She scooped up another spoonful. "Did your mom make it?"

"Nope. I did."

Try as she might have, Catherine couldn't keep the surprise from zipping across her face. "You did?"

"Mmhmm." Emily watched her, amused, then asked, "You thought my parents' cook made it, didn't you?" It was difficult to see it in the dim lighting, but Emily was pretty sure Catherine had turned a lovely shade of pink. "I happen to enjoy cooking. So there."

"Emily, I…" Catherine swallowed and looked embarrassed. "I'm really sorry. I didn't mean to offend you."

Emily shrugged. "You didn't. I'm just finding that I enjoy surprising you. It's fun."

Catherine shifted, obviously uncomfortable. "For you, maybe."

Emily set her spoon in her bowl and closed her hand over Catherine's bare forearm, using all her willpower to ignore the feel of the warm, bare skin under her palm. "Catherine. Relax." She smiled softly. "It's no big deal. You just need to skew the way you think a bit." With a shrug, she let go and picked up her spoon again. "There's a lot more to me than my bank account, you know?"

Catherine nodded, clearly chastised and still embarrassed. "I do know that. I'm sorry."

"Good. Done. Moving on." Emily widened her smile to help alleviate the tension. When that didn't seem to work, she set her spoon down again, grasped Catherine's chin in her hand, pulled her closer, and kissed her on the mouth. She pulled back, whispered, "Let it go," and went back to her stew. The expression that crossed Catherine's face was odd, but Emily didn't ask about it. She simply chewed.

Catherine might not say words often, but in this particular instance, her face was a pretty easy read. Emily watched as she remained embarrassed, quietly ate her stew while gazing into the fire. And just like the first time they'd hit this issue, Emily let her sit with her embarrassment, feeling a little bad that she'd caused it, but also thinking Catherine needed to feel it in order to learn. It only took a few moments, but the clouded look on her face gradually cleared and she seemed to relax.

Emily took the cue.

"So," she said, putting her empty bowl on the hearth and reaching under the tree behind her. "It seems Santa may have stopped by here." She pulled two packages out.

Catherine's eyes widened. "For me?" Her voice held a bit of incredulity, which made Emily grin and mentally give herself a point for yet again surprising Catherine.

"Yes, ma'am." She handed the smaller of the packages over. "This one is for you, but it's sort of to share." At Catherine's furrowed brow, she shrugged and said, "Open it. You'll see."

Catherine paused for a quick second before a huge grin broke out on her face and she tore through the wrapping paper like a small child. When she'd dropped the paper to the floor and sat with two identical word search books in one hand and a pack of fine-tip Sharpies in the other, the grin got even wider.

"You didn't," she said.

"Oh, I did," Emily replied, thrilled by the joy she saw so clearly on Catherine's beautiful face. "I plan to see this incredible talent of yours firsthand. I challenge you, Ms. Gardner, to a word search duel."

Catherine leaned in close and whispered, "You're going down, Breckenridge."

"We'll see. I wonder if your word search prowess has been overstated."

Catherine gave a mock gasp and pressed a hand to her chest. Then she narrowed her eyes and said, "Challenge accepted."

Emily burst out laughing, loving every moment of this exchange, feeling like she had just seen the real Catherine Gardner, the one with no guards up, no walls erected, no filter for her words or facial expression. Just Catherine. Simply Catherine. Emily vowed to get a look at that woman every chance she could.

"Okay, but before that battle begins, you have to open this one." Emily slid the larger of the two presents toward Catherine.

"Another one?" Catherine's voice was much softer this time. "But...I didn't..." She swallowed and this time, Emily felt bad about her embarrassment.

"Hey, no, stop that." She reached across the short space between them and laid her palm against Catherine's cheek. "I didn't get you a gift because I expected one from you. I actually really enjoy giving people stuff." With a cock of her head she added, "Haven't the twenty-seven bouquets of flowers I've sent you sort of clued you in on that?"

The blush was back, and Catherine muttered, "Waste of money."

Emily laughed. "I knew you'd say that. Predictable."

As their gazes held, a sizzle passed between them, so hot and strong, Emily wondered if another person might have actually seen it. One thought shot through Emily's head so loudly she was sure Catherine must have heard it.

I cannot wait to get my hands on this woman.

Emily swallowed down the arousal that threatened to erupt from her body like lava from a volcano and watched as Catherine opened her gift, taking her time with this one, gently untaping each end with painstaking care. When all the paper was unfastened, she uncovered the box, looked at it, and her head snapped up. Her blue eyes snagged Emily's as she said, "You did not."

Emily just smiled.

"You did *not*," Catherine said again as she left all gentleness aside and pulled the box open. Inside sat a pair of sexy black boots, all supple leather, two-inch heels, and silver accents.

"I did." She watched as Catherine took one out of the box, holding it as gently as she would a baby. These were knee-high and Emily had easily pictured Catherine wearing them with a skirt or even jeans. Or nothing else at all. "Do you like them?" she asked, trying not to sound uncertain.

"Do I like them?" Catherine dropped the boot down into her lap and met Emily's gaze. "Do I *like* them? I love them. *I love them!*" And then she did the most uncharacteristic thing she could have done. She leaned forward and grabbed Emily in a sloppy, awesome hug, all long arms and hair in each other's faces. "Thank you," she whispered in Emily's ear, sending a pleasant chill down the middle of her back. "Thank you so much."

"You're very welcome," Emily said, returning the hug tightly. They parted slowly and when they were face-to-face, Catherine pressed her lips to Emily's. Softly. Tenderly.

"Thank you," she said a third time as she pulled back.

Emily cleared her throat. "I think, before we begin the word search battle of the century, you should go try them on. For me."

"For you?" Catherine arched that one sexy eyebrow and everything south of Emily's rib cage tightened in response.

"Yes, please," she whispered.

Obviously pretending to contemplate the request, Catherine laid a finger along her own jawline. "Hmm. Well. Okay. I guess you deserve that." She stood up, boots in hand. "Refill my wine while I'm gone?"

Emily was on her feet in an instant, grabbed up both glasses, and skedaddled into the kitchen where she, once again, paused to catch her breath and allow her heart rate to slow a bit. Was there a sexier woman in life than Catherine Gardner?

"I don't think so," she said aloud, quietly. She refilled each wine glass, emptying the bottle, and tried not to dwell on how the hell she was going to manage to keep control of herself for a little while longer. *I can do this. I can do this.*

Picking up both glasses, she headed back into the living room…and stopped dead.

Catherine stood there in dim light tossed from the tree and the fireplace, and she was wearing the boots. She hadn't changed any of her clothes, but she still looked insanely sexy to Emily, who could do nothing but mutter, "Oh, good God," and stand there with her mouth hanging open.

"They don't really work with this outfit, but they do fit. Perfectly. And they're really comfortable, which I didn't expect." As she looked down at the boots and continued to talk about the fit, her voice faded out and Emily could only hear her own blood rushing in her ears.

She crossed the room, a glass of wine still in each hand, walked right into Catherine's space (while taking delighted note of the fact that she was now an inch taller than Emily), and pressed her mouth to Catherine's. There was no hesitation at all on Catherine's part as she grasped Emily's head in both hands and gave as good as she got, pushing her tongue into Emily's mouth without preamble of any kind. Long, sensuous moments went by before Catherine pulled back just enough to be able to talk and whispered to Emily, "Don't you drop that wine."

Emily blew out a shaky breath and grinned. "I am using every fiber of my being to keep from doing so, but it is *not* easy."

Catherine took a step back and relieved Emily of one glass. She took a sip, eyes never leaving Emily's. "Do you think I'd have an unfair advantage in the word search challenge if I left these on?"

"Um, yes. I'd be all, 'Words? What words? All I see are boots.'"

With a put-upon sigh, Catherine said, "Fine. I'll take them off."

"For now," Emily amended.

Catherine shot a wink over her shoulder before disappearing into the bedroom. Emily took the opportunity to stoke the fire, add a log. Catherine was back quickly, grabbed the word search books, and tossed one to Emily before sliding her glasses on. "It's time." She ripped into the pack of Sharpies and tossed Emily one of those as well. "You choose the puzzle."

"Me?"

"Yep. This way, there can't be any complaining about me rigging things."

Emily squinted at her. "You can't rig a word search."

"My sister says differently."

With a chuckle, Emily moved to the couch. Catherine followed and they each sat against an arm, their legs tangled together as they faced one another. Emily flipped through the pages before a title caught her eye.

"Oh, this one. *Wines and Vines*. Page 119."

"That's the one?" Catherine adjusted her position, seemed to wiggle her butt more comfortably into the cushions, and pushed her glasses up her nose with a finger.

"That's the one. Are there rules?"

"Not really. It's a word search. Find all the words. First one done wins. Pretty basic."

"Okay. Ready?"

"Ready."

Their gazes held and that sizzle zipped between them again, causing Emily to break out in a grin. "Go."

There was little sound in the cabin. The soft Christmas music played a piano version of *Silent Night* and the fire crackled cheerfully. Every so often, the sound of a pen circling a word could be heard, but with the exception of the wind that had begun to pick up, the cabin was quiet. At one point, Emily looked up and caught Catherine gazing at her with such a weighted look on her face, it was all she could do to keep from diving across the couch to touch her.

"Stop that," Emily said quietly.

"Stop what?"

"Looking at me like that. I think you're trying to read my mind to help you find words because you're worried I'm kicking your shapely ass." Catherine grinned at her as Emily continued. "So just stop. My brain is like a steel trap and you cannot pry your way in with your Jedi mind tricks." She pointed her pen at Catherine. "I see what you're doing. Not happening."

"You see what I'm doing?" Catherine asked.

"Yep."

"Huh. That's weird then."

Emily narrowed her eyes. "What's weird?"

Catherine gave a nonchalant shrug. "It's weird that you don't know I'm done. Or that I've been done for the last three minutes and have just sat here looking at you."

Emily paused her pen in mid-circle. "You are not done."

Catherine turned the book around so Emily could see a black line drawn through every word listed at the bottom, and a mess of circled words crisscrossing all over the puzzle.

"Give me that," Emily gasped. She grabbed the book out of Catherine's hand while Catherine sat there looking far too self-satisfied. Emily matched each crossed-off word to each circled word before looking up in disbelief. "You finished."

"I did."

"I'm not even halfway done."

Catherine made a face that said, "Sorry, Charlie," and shrugged again. "Told you I was good."

"This is impossible."

"The evidence says otherwise."

"I may have to side with your sister on this."

Catherine tried to feign being insulted but ended up laughing instead.

"Although she didn't really seem to like me," Emily amended, recalling Thanksgiving. "She might not want me on her team. Hmm." She pursed her lips, pretending to be deep in thought.

"Well," Catherine said as her book hit the floor, followed by her pen, then her glasses. She changed her position so she was on her knees and crawled her way to Emily where she grabbed Emily's book, then her pen, and sent them both the same way her own had gone. "Luckily, *I* like you." She brought her face close, so close to Emily's, until they were breathing the same air.

"You do?" Emily whispered.

Catherine nodded and whispered back, "A little bit, yeah," just before crushing her mouth to Emily's.

That was pretty much the end of any slice of self-control Emily had managed to hold on to. And God, it was such a relief to let it go. Wrapping her arms around Catherine's body, she pulled her down, wanting nothing more than to be completely covered by her, to feel her heat, her weight, her want. They kissed like there was no tomorrow, like this was it, their very last night on earth and they wanted everything from each other. Everything. Emily had never felt such a drive to strip somebody naked and she had to consciously tangle her fingers in Catherine's hair, in her shirt, to force herself to slow the pace. Catherine's tongue was doing unspeakably wonderful things in her mouth, and if Emily had burst into flames right then and there on the couch, she wouldn't have been at all surprised.

Her earlier thought came back to her then, echoing through her head. *I cannot wait to get my hands on this woman.* She knew then that it was okay to follow through, and she found the hem of Catherine's shirt with her fingers. The skin of Catherine's back and sides was warm and smooth and soft and Emily let her palms just wander all over it for long moments, nearly bursting with aroused desire. Her hands seem to move of their own accord as they stopped at Catherine's bra, flipped the clasp open, and circled around, palming both breasts at once and tugging a moan from deep in Catherine's throat that had Emily's bikinis instantly wet.

Zeroing in on Catherine's nipples, Emily lavished attention on each, pumping them with her fingers and thumbs, causing Catherine to push her knee hard against Emily's center, a gasp ripping from her own lungs. Unable to maintain the slowly torturous pace any longer, Emily pushed up, taking Catherine with her until Emily was in a sitting position, Catherine straddling her lap.

"I need to see you," Emily whispered, surprising herself by gently and calmly undressing Catherine from the waist up, pulling off her two shirts and then her bra, rather than simply ripping them from her body—which was what she really wanted to do. Once Catherine sat there, her upper body completely bare, Emily took a moment to just look, to simply gaze upon this gorgeous woman, to remind herself how lucky she was to be able to touch, to hold, to kiss her. But only a moment; she wasn't made of stone after all. Wrapping her arms around Catherine's torso, she pulled her close and took one breast into her mouth, sucking greedily, hungrily, using her teeth on the erect nipple until Catherine gasped and her fingers tightened in Emily's hair as Emily moved on to the other breast.

And then Catherine pushed and Emily found herself on her back again, all control effectively torn from her hands as Catherine's tongue reclaimed its rightful place in her mouth and her hand slid up under the front of Emily's sweater, kneaded her breasts through the fabric of her bra, first one, then the other, back and forth until Emily felt as if she was wearing no bra at all, as if there was no barrier between Catherine's hand and her own sensitive skin. She wrenched her mouth from Catherine's when she thought her lungs might explode from lack of oxygen, but that only forced her to look into Catherine's blue eyes, dark and clouded with desire. They held hers as Catherine toyed with Emily's nipple, stared as Catherine's fingers forced reactions from Emily, made her breath hitch, made her swallow hard, none of it within her control. Catherine had all of it, every last molecule. If she'd told her to, Emily would have gladly quacked like a duck if it meant Catherine would keep touching her.

Emily's breast still in her hand, Catherine whispered, "Can we move this over there?" She shot a look over her shoulder.

"To the fireplace?" Emily asked. At Catherine's nod, she grinned and said, "I thought you'd never ask."

They moved quickly, Emily grabbing the blanket from the back of the couch just in case. Once on the rug, she didn't allow Catherine any time to react before she recaptured the reins, crushing their mouths together and pushing Catherine onto her back.

There was something sensual and indescribably sexy about the way the firelight played over Catherine's bare skin. Shadows combined with a soft orange glow to highlight the peaks and valleys of her body. Emily pushed up to her knees and gazed down on this gorgeous woman as she slowly unfastened her jeans, slid the zipper down, grasped the waistband. She tugged them off, taking her time, letting her fingers linger on the skin of Catherine's legs as she freed each foot and tossed the pants at the couch. Catherine lay there now in only a pair of simple hot pink bikini bottoms and Emily was certain she'd never seen a more beautiful sight. She drank it in, let her eyes roam, committing every inch of Catherine's body to memory.

She reached a hand out, stroked her fingertips over Catherine's stomach, which made her flinch and chuckle. "Ticklish," she said as explanation.

Emily smiled at her. "So noted." Her eyes never leaving Catherine's, she hooked a finger over the elastic of the bikinis on one side, then used the other hand to do the same thing on the other side. Catherine propped herself on her elbows and held her gaze as she lifted her own hips slightly and Emily slid the underwear off, sent it to be with the discarded jeans.

And now Emily had all of her. All of Catherine. Laid out before her, naked and aroused, flushed and wanting. Her full lips were parted and glossy, and her chest rose and fell more rapidly than normal. Their eyes stayed locked for a long moment before Catherine reached up with both hands and whispered, "Come here."

Emily obeyed, wanted to cry with joy as Catherine's legs parted to allow room for Emily's hips to settle there. Unable to wait one second longer, Emily devoured Catherine's mouth with her own, taking and giving, pushing and pulling, wishing and expecting. So lost in the kiss did Emily become that it took her a long moment to recognize that Catherine had unfastened her jeans and was pushing at them, her angle making it impossible for her to get them past Emily's hips.

Pulling back, Emily grinned at her. "Did you want something?"

"Yes. I want these off."

"Demanding."

"You ain't seen nothing yet."

Emily swallowed back the desire that surged up into her throat, then kicked off her pants more quickly than she ever had in her life. When she looked back at Catherine, she was smiling widely.

"That was impressive," she said.

"You ain't seen nothing yet," Emily whispered back to her before silencing her with her mouth.

Emily had never experienced anything so sexy, so sensual, so arousing in her entire life as lying in front of the fire, naked, with Catherine Gardner. Catherine's knees pressed against her hips, her hand was in Emily's hair, her other hand sliding up and down Emily's back, a finger dipping lower every so often.

Catherine's full breast in Emily's hand was mind-blowing—how was that even possible?—and Emily couldn't get enough. She wanted to speed up and slow down. She wanted to have Catherine—to taste her, to push her higher, to send her over the edge—and she wanted to savor her, take her time, take forever, just touch her skin, kiss her mouth, push against her wet heat.

But waiting was no longer an option. Emily could feel the urgency now, tried to fight it, but was powerless. She wanted Catherine. She *wanted* her. *Now.* Unable to stop herself, she lifted her weight up onto her knees a bit so she could slide her hand between their bodies. With no warning or preamble, with no exploration or preparation, she pushed her fingers directly into Catherine's center and two things happened at once. Catherine gasped and then whimpered, and the hot, slickness of her closed around Emily's fingers instantly. The combination sent Emily's own arousal through the roof and she surprised herself by making her own sounds of joy and desire. She braced herself on her free hand, above Catherine, looking down on her gorgeously flushed face, on her heavy, darkened eyes, and held her gaze as she moved inside her, slowly out, slowly back in, shocked by how wet Catherine was for her, by how desperately she grasped at Emily with both hands.

They moved that way for long moments before Emily kissed Catherine slowly, drawing out every moment of arousal she could, then ran the very tip of her tongue down along Catherine's throat, between her breasts, over her stomach and around her belly button, down to her very center. One hand on Catherine's thigh, Emily pushed it, opening her as far as possible, before she buried her face, her mouth, and made love to Catherine slowly, precisely, erotically. She tasted every inch of her, salty and sweet, swiped her tongue through the folds, drank from Catherine's body until she was writhing beneath Emily, soft pleas tickling Emily's ears, fingers flexing and opening in Emily's hair. Catherine picked up Emily's rhythm and soon they were rocking together, gently, but in perfect sync, Emily's fingers still inside, her other arm stretched up so she could toy with a nipple, which seemed to send Catherine impossibly higher.

And just when Emily was sure things couldn't get any sexier, Catherine sucked in a huge breath and let out a low, steady moan, one hand closing on a handful of Emily's hair and pulling her face in tightly against her center, the other, clamping around a chunk of the blanket from the couch, hips lifting off the rug as Emily fought to stay with her. She stopped stroking, but kept her tongue firmly pressed against Catherine for long moments, feeling her heartbeat, feeling the muscles contract rhythmically, until Catherine slowly lowered herself back down to the rug and her fingers began to relax.

Gently, Emily took her mouth away. When she began to withdraw her fingers, Catherine clamped her hand over Emily's. "No. Stay. Just a little longer?"

Emily smiled. "As long as you want." Catherine's legs dropped down straight, as if she had no control over the muscles any longer and the bones had simply flopped to the floor. Emily laid her head on Catherine's thigh and just looked at her, her vantage point allowing her to see the smooth stomach, the gorgeous breasts, nipples still very erect, the chest rising and falling at an almost normal rate now, and that face. That beautiful, hard-to-read face.

"Do you realize you have perfect breasts?" Emily asked quietly.

Catherine's body moved as she chuckled. "They're just regular."

Emily lifted her head. "Um, no. I beg to differ. They're perfect. Not too big, not too small. Nipples of exactly the right sensitivity. Smooth skin all around. They don't get much more perfect than yours."

Catherine reached for her, ran her fingers through Emily's hair. "If you say so."

"Oh, I do. And I know these things."

"You're an expert, are you?"

"More like a connoisseur."

"I see."

Emily pushed herself up—careful to keep her fingers deep inside Catherine's warm body, absently thinking she may never want to leave there—and braced herself so she was above Catherine, looking down at her face. "Know what else is perfect?"

"What?" Catherine asked quietly, blue eyes darkening again already.

"Your mouth." Emily brought hers down onto Catherine's in what was intended as a soft and gentle kiss, but which rapidly turned hot, and within minutes, Emily's fingers were moving inside Catherine again, a new surge of wetness coating them.

"God," Catherine moaned, breath ragged. "How did you do that?" Breath in, breath out. "Again?" Breath in, breath out. "Already?"

"You fit me," Emily said by way of explanation. And it was true. Their bodies fit alarmingly well together, like they were supposed to be this way.

Catherine was rapidly approaching climax again, Emily could tell by her breathing, by the way she moved, by the sounds she made, and it thrilled her that she knew this information, that she was privy to something so few people on earth got to witness. "But...it's your turn now," Catherine managed even as she gripped Emily tightly, squeezed her eyes shut, and rocked with her.

"We'll get there," Emily assured her, pushing deeper, using her thumb to stroke the warm, wet flesh. "I'm not worried. I'll have my turn."

And she did.

Twice.

It was almost five hours later—nearly two in the morning—before they finally called it a night. Emily managed to summon enough energy to stoke the embers in the fireplace and add a couple logs before she fell down next to an already crashed-out Catherine because her rubbery legs wouldn't hold her up any longer. She pulled the blanket up around them, put her head on Catherine's shoulder, and threw a leg over Catherine's thigh.

With a long, deep, very contented sigh, Emily happily relaxed and followed Catherine into slumber.

CHAPTER EIGHTEEN

CLARK BRECKENRIDGE WAS IRRITATED.

And he was irritated about being irritated because it was so rare that he was irritated. But today? He was irritated.

This hadn't been a great year for him. He was starting to wonder if people just didn't get him. His mother seemed to have less and less patience with him lately, and that was new. He'd always been her golden boy, the child who could do no wrong. He'd always been the favorite. No offense to his little sister, but it was the truth. Parents never admitted to having a favorite among their children, but they absolutely did. It was just something that wasn't talked about in the open. Clark knew.

But over the past six or eight months, his mother had begun looking at him differently. Literally differently. He could see it in her eyes when she turned to him. That glow she used to get when she gazed his way had dimmed considerably, and he wasn't sure why or how to get it back. All he was sure of was that things were different now and he didn't like it.

Sliding his Ray-Bans on even though there was no sun, he squinted a bit until his darkened view cleared. It was snowing gently, but he knew it was going to pick up again. His head pounded lightly now, thank God. It had been bad when he'd opened his eyes two hours ago. He'd tied one on last night (but man, that blonde was so worth it), so much so that he wondered if he was still a little bit drunk. He felt fine behind the wheel and just vowed to pay close attention to the speed limit and stuff. As long as he didn't get pulled over, he'd be fine in an hour or so.

Grabbing the handful of Motrin he'd tossed into the cup holder of his Benz, he tossed them into his mouth and chased them with a huge swallow of lukewarm coffee.

Thoughts drifting back to his mother, he replayed the conversation he'd overheard her having with one of the VPs of the company, John Callen, the other day.

"Looks like Emily's doing a terrific job with the Foundation." *John's voice held a smile. He'd always had a thing for Clark's mother and Clark was pretty sure she knew it.*

"She is. Lots of kudos from clients. I honestly didn't expect that."

"No? Why not? You had to know she'd do a better job than Clark." *His voice dropped then and Clark had had to strain to hear it without making it known he was hovering in the hallway. "If that boy spent as much time on business as he does on honing his sex appeal and flirting with everything in a skirt, he'd be a force to be reckoned with."*

There was a beat and Clark stood there wearing a half-grin, fully expecting his mother to leap to his defense, as she always did. What she actually said pulled the corner of his mouth right back down again.

"While it's okay for me to say such things about my son, John, I do not appreciate them coming from you."

"Yes, ma'am," Callen had stuttered. "I apologize."

"That being said," his mother went on, "you're absolutely right. He was becoming an embarrassment to the company. A horny teenage boy who refuses to grow up. Probably my fault for coddling him. Emily was a smart choice. She's really cleaned up a lot of his mess..."

Callen said something else, but Clark couldn't listen to any more. He hurried back the way he'd come, wondering if he'd make it to the men's room before he got sick.

Now, he drove. The sky was gray, like dull steel, and he scoffed as he decided he needed to take off the Ray-Bans. They looked damn good on him and he knew it, wore them for that reason. Since nobody was in the car to see him—and he couldn't see much of the road with them on—he opted to look not quite as awesome.

The intensity of the snow picked up as he glanced at the clock on the dash. Almost ten. He'd kept careful track of the few cars he'd passed on the slick road and none of them had been his sister's baby blue Beemer. He hoped Emily was still there. He was surprised when his father mentioned she'd gone to the cabin for the weekend. Seemed unlike her, but maybe the job was getting to her. Maybe she was stressed out and needed some space and he could say, "See? I told you so," even as he asked her what he could do to make things better in his own new position. And better in the eyes of their mother. Emily was logical like that. She'd have some suggestions.

It bugged him that his mother's disappointment stung him so much. He'd like to not care. Who gives a crap what your mommy thinks? But the sad truth of it was that he'd always cared what his mother thought. Always. Everything he'd ever done was to please her. He couldn't care less what his father thought. Didn't matter. His mother was his light and his world when he was a boy, and it hadn't changed all that much as he'd grown. But to be in his thirties and have her be disappointed in him? That was a pain he never expected to feel.

He had to fix it. Emily would know how.

Trying to shake the fog out of his head, he drummed on the steering wheel and attempted to rap along to Jay-Z as he approached the driveway of the cabin and turned in. Emily's tire tracks had been covered overnight and apparently, the plow guy hadn't shown up yet this morning. His Benz slid several times and it was slow-going, but he finally made it to the end, where the driveway spit him into a clearing and he saw a car he didn't recognize, but no sign of Emily's.

"Huh," he said aloud, as he turned down the music. "That's weird."

><

Catherine knew she was being a bit...ginger...when she walked, but it made her grin regardless. Honest to God, she'd never been so deliciously sore in her entire life. Between bracing herself above Emily's gorgeously naked body and keeping her own legs spread wide for longer periods of time than ever before, her quads were screaming this morning, as were her biceps. In fact, her entire body was sore and she could do nothing but smile about it.

Sex with Emily.

Catherine stood still in the living room, gazing down at the rumpled blanket and the pillows from the bedroom that Emily had commandeered in the middle of the night when they'd woken up with stiff necks and had each other yet again. It was obvious what had happened in front of the fire. One look painted a very clear picture and Catherine knew she should clean it up, but instead, she simply stood there and stared. And remembered. And smiled.

Sex with Emily had been...what was the right word? Mind-blowing? Limb-melting? Insanely wonderful? Intensely erotic? All of those things and more? Catherine had no idea what would happen next, where they'd go from here, and at this moment it didn't matter. She refused to allow herself to panic and try to plan out the future (which would be her normal course of action). No, she'd decided to do the very best she could, to make the most distinct effort possible, to follow her mother's advice. To let all her worries go and just live in this moment.

She touched her fingertips to her lips as she recalled all the things her mouth had done last night, everything it had tasted, sucked on, bitten, and she felt a surge of dampness between her legs. *So much for my clean change of clothes,* she thought with a grin. She'd showered, had refused to let Emily in with her, knowing there would be little to no actual washing being done. Her hair was still damp, but she was in her clean clothes and all packed up, just waiting for Emily to finish her own shower and come join her. She'd promised she'd clean up the living room, but if she left it all where it was, maybe she could convince Emily to go one more round with her...

Her thoughts were interrupted by the sound of the front door opening, which startled her so much she let out a tiny gasp.

Clark Breckenridge stood in the foyer, looking just as surprised as Catherine judging by his wide eyes and the way he'd pretty much screeched to a halt. He was dressed impeccably, as always, and Catherine was suddenly reminded of how much he and Emily looked alike. Hair color, the shape of their eyes— though his were underscored by dark circles today. His jeans were expensive, as were his boots and winter coat. He hadn't shaved, and the shadow on his face gave him an air of mysterious sex appeal.

His eyes left Catherine's as they scanned the room, stopping briefly on the Christmas tree, Catherine's overnight bag she'd set on the couch, and the makeshift bed in front of the fire. Catherine practically watched as the pieces clicked into place for him and his expression went from wide-eyed surprise to understanding to...something else. Something unpleasant.

"Well, well, well," he said, as he kicked off his snow-covered shoes and slid out of his coat, and his tone started a slow churning in Catherine's gut. "If it isn't the lovely Miss Gardner. Right here in my family's vacation cabin. An unexpected surprise, to say the least."

Catherine cleared her throat. "Hi, Clark. Did Emily know you were coming? She didn't say anything. She's, um..." She glanced toward the bedroom. "She's in the shower." She felt suddenly, weirdly uncomfortable, like she was scantily dressed in front of him, even though she wore jeans and a sweater.

"Oh, no. No. She had no idea I was dropping in. I called but..." He cocked his head and gave her a conspiratorial look as he lowered his voice to a near-whisper. "I bet she turned her phone off."

His implication made Catherine blush, and she couldn't help it. She couldn't help it, and that pissed her off. She didn't like Clark Breckenridge knowing what she and his sister had been doing. It was none of his business and, judging by the wicked smile on his face, he didn't plan to let it go.

He sauntered into the room and flopped himself back onto the couch, propped his ankle on the opposite knee, and spread his arms out that way that guys do, so he claimed ownership of the entire piece of furniture. Catherine remained standing and fought the inexplicable urge to cross her arms over her chest.

"Well, damn," he said and his eyes indicated the makeshift bed in front of the fireplace. "Looks like Emily won."

"Won what?" The churning intensified.

"Our bet."

Catherine narrowed her eyes at him.

"Oh, she didn't tell you?" He sat forward, forearms on his knees. His creepy smile widened, and for a split second,

Catherine wondered if he'd been drinking. "We had a bet, me and Em. We made it that first day when I brought her to the shelter to meet you guys."

Catherine swallowed hard.

"It's a thing we've been doing for a long time. At least since she told me she liked girls. So…high school?" He chuckled and it was like needles scraping at Catherine's skin. With a shrug, he went on. "I usually win. News flash: Emily's not terribly competitive. But it looks like you were all the incentive she needed."

Their gazes held as the sound of the shower continued in the next room, both of them knowing that Catherine would ask. She couldn't not, but she fought it as long as she could until it tore its way out of her. "What was the bet?" she whispered.

Clark grinned triumphantly. "Why, to see which of us could bed you first, of course."

Catherine's eyes immediately filled with tears and that made her angry. "I don't believe you," she said, but her voice cracked with its lack of conviction and *that* made her angry.

"Aw, that's cute." Clark tilted his head slightly as if he was talking to a small child. "And you were obviously quite a challenge. What's it been? Almost two months now? But let's be honest. You don't *really* know my sister very well, do you? Think about it. You have no idea what she might actually be like." He leaned toward her and she took a step back, even though he was far enough away not to be able to reach her. He spoke quietly and his voice was like a razor blade, slicing through her feelings, peeling them away to reveal the uncertainty underneath. "And so somewhere in the back of your mind right now, you're replaying the night, aren't you? 'What did she say? Was she lying to me?

Was her goal to get into my pants? Did I resist enough, or was I just an easy lay?'"

Catherine flinched at his words, hating that he was actually reading her thoughts even as she fought them.

"I can see it on your face, Catherine," he said, cruelly. "You *do* believe me. You don't want to. But you do." He sat back again, spread his arms out once more along the back of the couch, glanced at his expensive watch. "How long does it take a woman to shower, anyway?" he asked, his voice back to normal volume. "Come out here, little sister. You need to collect your winnings."

He winked at Catherine and that was it. She couldn't stay any longer. She needed to get out, to get away from him, away from Emily, away from her stupidly naïve decisions. With a small cry of anguish, she grabbed her bag from the couch next to him and crossed to the foyer, shoved her feet into her boots, grabbed her coat and her keys and was out the door before the tears spilled over. The cold air hit her like another punch to the gut and she wondered for a moment if she might be sick right there in the snow. Somehow, she choked it down and managed to get into her car. It took three tries, but she got the key into the ignition despite her shaking hands and turned it. Giving the engine no time at all to warm up, she yanked the gearshift and spun her tires in the snow before rocketing down the driveway, heading for home as a sob ripped up and out from her lungs, the tears blinding her to anything but the rapidly falling snow. She didn't want to believe it, didn't want to believe that Emily was the kind of woman who would do this to somebody, but...what evidence did she have that she wasn't? She'd mentioned no exes. She didn't seem to be dating actively. And the biggest question of all, the one Catherine had tucked away in a box on a shelf so she wouldn't have to answer it: what would somebody like Emily, with her family status and more money than she knew what to do with, want with somebody like Catherine, a modest, job-driven middle-class woman who didn't even come close to being in Emily's league?

"I was a bet," she said out loud, and the idea was so horrifically embarrassing, so unthinkably humiliating, she didn't know if she could bear it. "Oh, God, I was a bet." Was she in an honest-to-God romantic comedy—as the butt of the joke? "I should have known better."

Too good to be true.

The thought blasted through her brain on an endless loop as she covered her mouth with a hand and let herself cry.

She was too good to be true.

⊷

Emily had stayed in the shower until the water ran tepid, and she knew that she'd smiled like an idiot the entire time. What a night. What. A. Night. She still couldn't believe it had actually happened. Sure, she'd hoped it would, but she wouldn't have pushed if Catherine had seemed at all hesitant or unsure. That hadn't been the case. Instead, Catherine had been right there with her, every step of the way, giving and taking in equal measure, and so, *so* hot...

My God, that was the best night of my life.

That thought had played through her head all morning long, from the moment she'd opened her eyes, her body curled up around Catherine's still sleeping one, warm from the dying fire, pleasantly sore from the lovemaking gymnastics they'd performed together...

She took a deep breath and covered her face with the thick, red towel and just reveled in memory, just let herself flash back for one more moment before drying off and grabbing the soft robe off the back of the door. She ran a comb through her hair as she wondered how she could stretch the day. Catherine needed to get home, to pick up her dog, and had some errands she wanted to run, but Emily was fairly certain she could convince her to stay just a little longer.

The smell of coffee brewing caught her nose and tugged her out into the living room while she silently hoped maybe Catherine hadn't cleaned up their little fireplace bed quite yet.

The sight of her brother sitting on the couch sipping from her mug brought Emily up short and she practically skid to a stop like a cartoon character.

"Clark. What the hell are you doing here?" She glanced toward the kitchen as she quietly hissed the question.

Clark shrugged, looking far too comfortable. "I came looking for you. Dad said you were here."

"You came all the way out here? Why didn't you just call?" Emily tightened the belt of the robe around her waist, suddenly remembering that she was naked underneath.

"I did." He looked pointedly at her and she could feel her face heat up.

"My phone died and I forgot to charge it." She looked around now, wondering where she'd left it. It hadn't been a concern last night; she hadn't wanted anything to distract her from the beautiful woman who'd graced Emily with her company.

"Not smart, Em. What if there's an emergency?"

"Judging by the way you're nonchalantly lounging on the couch and drinking my coffee, I'm gonna go out on a limb and guess this is *not* one."

"Yeah, but you wouldn't have known that."

Glancing at the kitchen again, Emily'd had enough. "What do you want?"

"Oh, she's not in there." He sipped his coffee, and Emily noticed his eyes, slightly red.

"Have you been drinking, Clark? Jesus, it's not even ten in the morning." His words registered belatedly in her brain. "What do you mean she's not in there?" Emily pushed into the kitchen, but Catherine was nowhere in sight. The cabin wasn't large and there really was no place else she could be. Picking up the pace, she went back into the living room. "Where is she?" she demanded of her brother, who was now looking so smug she had the nearly irresistible urge to slap the expression right off his face.

"She left."

Emily blinked at him, not sure she'd heard him right. "What?"

"Yeah. She left." He glanced at his watch. "About fifteen minutes ago. Man, you take long showers."

"Clark."

He sat forward and set his mug down. "So, I need to talk to you about Mom."

"Clark." She said his name through gritted teeth as she glanced around the room, noticing for the first time that Catherine's bag, coat, and boots were all gone, as were her keys off the table. "Oh, God. Oh, God. Oh, God." She raced to the front door and yanked it open. Catherine's car was gone.

"I told you. She left." Clark patted the couch cushion next to her. "Come sit so I can get your take on this situation with Mom."

Emily slowly closed the door, then stood with her forehead against it for long moments. "What did you do?" she asked quietly.

"Nothing. We just had a conversation. Now come sit down with me for a minute. I need you."

She turned slowly to look at her brother, this man she'd alternately admired and been embarrassed by her entire life, and her heart began to pound. Her voice still low and even, she asked him again. "What did you do?"

For the first time, a flash of hesitation crossed his cocky expression, like the shadow of a bird flying between the sun and his face as it passed overhead. "Come on, Em." He chuckled, obviously forcing it. "Your big brother needs your help. I was at the office yesterday and—"

"What did you do?!" She screamed it at him, shocking herself almost as much as she shocked her brother, judging by his rapid blinking and the way all the color drained from his face.

"I told her you'd won the bet," he said so quietly, she almost didn't hear him. And then she wished she hadn't.

"Oh, my God, Clark, please tell me you're lying. Please tell me you didn't say that to her. Please."

"I was just kidding around," he said, but his lame tone combined with the sheepish expression on his face told her the truth and her anger bubbled up like hot lava ready to erupt.

"You just couldn't take it, could you?" she said crossing the room toward him. "You just couldn't take me having something you couldn't. Our entire lives, it's been like that." She looked at him then, saw a spoiled, self-centered man who thought of nobody but himself and her heart broke. For the brother she thought she had that she obviously didn't. For Catherine, and how horrible it must have been to hear what he said. And for herself. Mostly for herself. Her eyes welled up, much to her horror—she'd spent her entire childhood conditioning herself never to cry in front of her big brother—and she said quietly, "You bastard. I love her." Wiping angrily at her face, she shook her head, unsure if she could ever look at Clark the same way again. "What have you done?" she asked softly. "What have you done to me?"

She stared at him, at the horrible expression of realization on his face, realization that he couldn't take back what he'd said, what he'd caused, and then she moved. It was as if her body had snapped into motion, leaving her brain a step or two behind. She ran into the bedroom, ripping off the robe and dressing faster than she ever had before. Jeans, a hooded sweatshirt, socks. Her hair was still wet, but she didn't care. She ran back out into the living room to the foyer and stomped her feet into her boots.

"Give me your keys," she said to Clark, not looking at him as she grabbed her coat.

"What? But that's the only car—"

"*Give me your keys.*" She held out her hand and knew her face brooked no argument. Clark stood, reached into his pocket, and pulled out his keys. She snatched them from his hand and was out the door like a shot. She yanked open the door of the Benz and was skidding out the unplowed driveway within seconds.

There was only one thought on her mind. She had to fix this. She had to make it right, because what she'd said to Clark was suddenly crystal clear to her. Honest and solid and true. It had surprised her, but it hadn't.

She loved Catherine, which made everything much worse. Everything. All of it. So very much worse.

But…she had to tell her.

CHAPTER NINETEEN

THE DRIVE WAS DICEY, but that ended up being a good thing for Catherine. It forced her to focus on the road and on her driving rather than dwelling upon an incredible night that had morphed into the most horrific of mornings. Now as she pulled into her mother's driveway, though, it all came flooding back.

She didn't want to believe it. In fact, it was almost physically impossible. For Emily to be so callous? Catherine couldn't see it. She hadn't really shown signs of that, had she? Narcissism? Deception? She'd been nothing but charming, and as far as Catherine could tell, honest. But then she heard Clark's words—*You don't really know my sister very well, do you? Think about it. You have no idea what she might actually be like*—and the doubt came rushing in like a flood. Because he was right. She didn't know Emily that well. It was entirely possible that Clark was telling the truth.

Wasn't it?

Unbidden, her mind threw her a memory from the night before, of Emily above her, inside her, their eyes locked, their bodies moving together as if nobody else in the world existed but the two of them. Emily had been focused, completely with her. Hadn't she? Had Catherine misread that?

Running had been a dumb idea. She'd figured that out when she'd passed from hazardous, mostly unplowed country roads to the black pavement of city streets, but at that point, she was nearly to her mother's and turning back wasn't an option. And she also felt silly and childish. Emily at least deserved a chance to defend herself, didn't she?

Catherine dropped her head against the steering wheel and groaned. "God, I'm a mess," she said to the emptiness of the car. Giving herself a moment to decompress, she then took a deep breath and got out of her car, steeling herself for the barrage of questions sure to come from her mother and sifting through her brain for answers that wouldn't make her burst into tears.

At the door, she knocked, then stepped inside. The sharp bark that came from the kitchen made her smile, she couldn't help herself, and Mo came skidding out to see her. Squatting to pet him, she wrapped him in her arms and held on, mortified to feel her eyes well up. "It's so good to see you, pal," she whispered even as he squirmed to free himself from her too-tight grasp.

"So? How was it?" Catherine's mother's smile was evident in her voice, though Catherine kept her eyes on her dog, not yet trusting herself to look her mom in the face and not lose it. "You're earlier than I expected."

"Yeah, well." Catherine let that sit as she continued to kiss all over a wiggling Mo, and her mother's silence told her that she was simply waiting until Catherine was ready to address the subject. Knowing she had to stand up eventually, she decided it was better to simply get it over with. Sighing as she rose, she met her mother's smiling, expectant face, and watched as her expression changed to one of worried concern.

Laying a warm hand gently against Catherine's face, Denise said, "Oh, baby, what happened?"

This was not the gesture that was going to keep Catherine from crumbling into a blubbering mess, and she felt her eyes well up again immediately, much to her dismay. What was it about the gentle, loving touch of your mother that could so instantly pull all your emotions out into the open, leave them crying on the floor?

"I'm not sure," Catherine answered honestly, as one tear spilled over and coursed slowly down her cheek.

Her mother wiped it away with her thumb. "Do you want to talk about it?" she asked softly.

Catherine shook her head. "Not yet."

"You're sure?"

A nod was all Catherine could muster. She didn't trust her voice any longer.

"Okay. I'll be right here when you're ready." Her mother pulled Catherine into a hug that Catherine simultaneously wanted, needed, and wished to avoid at all costs. It was only by clenching her jaw so tightly she expected a bone to crack that she was able to keep from openly sobbing in her mother's embrace.

Gently extricating herself, Catherine wiped her face and wordlessly took the leash her mother handed her, bent to clip it to Mo's collar.

"He was an angel," her mother said, the cheerful tone of voice telling Catherine she was doing her best to lighten the mood. "Well, except for when he found the bathroom wastebasket."

Catherine gave her dog a look. "Mr. Geronimo." He cocked his head at her. "It's a damn good thing you're so cute. Thanks, Mom." She avoided making eye contact, knowing it was the best way to maintain control, and took her dog home.

The remainder of the morning and into the afternoon was spent cleaning her house. She dusted. She vacuumed. She mopped the kitchen floor—her least favorite job on the planet. She did laundry. Anything to keep her hands and mind occupied.

Mo followed her around the house in curiosity for a while before giving up and retreating to the couch to nap.

She should call Emily. She knew she should. Also, though, she was kind of surprised Emily hadn't called her. Unless she was embarrassed that her secret had been revealed. Catherine swallowed hard as she sprayed Windex on the window of her front door. If Clark had been telling the truth, it made perfect sense that Emily wouldn't call, didn't it? But still. She should call Emily, if not to give her a chance to explain, if not to apologize for running away like a child, then at least to let Emily know how much she'd hurt her.

This is how her thoughts went for the better part of four hours. Around and around and around. And just when she was about to go mad, ready to scream in frustrated anger, her cell phone rang. She stopped cleaning the stove, her hand stilling in mid-scrub, and she stood perfectly still.

Pulling the phone slowly from her back pocket, she saw a name that surprised her. She let it ring one more time before thinking, *This oughta be good*, and answered.

"Hello."

"Catherine? It's Clark Breckenridge. Look, I'm really sorry about earlier. I was out of line. I shouldn't have said what I said and I'm so, so sorry." He was talking quickly and his voice held a strange tone she couldn't identify, but seemed a lot like worry.

"Mmhmm."

"Listen, I'm calling because, um…" He cleared his throat. "There was an accident."

Catherine's heart began to pound in her chest. "Emily?"

"Yeah. She…she left the cabin and went after you in my car, and I never put my snow tires on, so—"

"The roads were bad. It was so slippery. Oh, my God." Catherine turned in a circle in her kitchen, looking for...she didn't know what. Her brain raced, her breathing came in shallow gasps. "Is she all right?"

"I think so. I'm not sure. I had to get someone to come and get me. They took her to the hospital, then called me after the police found my registration. She didn't have any ID with her. She was unconscious. They didn't know who to call." His voice cracked, something so utterly unexpected from the likes of Clark Breckenridge that it made Catherine stop and consciously process the sound.

"Which hospital?" she asked quietly.

"General."

Catherine hung up the phone and ran to her coat closet.

Emily had been in an accident.

She grabbed her coat, stomped into her shoes, yanked her purse from its hook, grabbed her keys, and was out the door in five seconds flat.

Emily had been in an accident.

In that moment, any anger, any hurt, any confusion left Catherine, at least for the time being. All that mattered was that she get to Emily, touch her, make sure she was all right. She started her car, jammed it into gear, and drove toward the hospital like a lunatic.

When she pulled into the hospital's parking garage twenty minutes later, she was kind of shocked she hadn't been pulled over. She'd pushed her speedometer to numbers that were much too high and now that she'd arrived at her destination, she felt the guilt settle over her. Two car accidents in one day would just be stupid.

She found a spot, race-walked/jogged to the entrance, and stopped at the Information Desk to get a room number.

Sixth floor.

Not the ICU.

Thank God.

With a deep breath in and a slow breath out, Catherine stepped into the elevator and willed her heart to ease up, to relax a bit. She stood next to a handsome young man in blue scrubs as he scrolled on his phone. He'd gone a little heavy on the aftershave that day, and she watched the numbers above the door, willing them to hurry so she could have some fresher air. At six, the doors slid open and Catherine stepped out, looking left and right until she figured out where room 612 was.

As quickly as she'd moved since Clark's phone call, she now walked very slowly. A sense of trepidation fell over her for two reasons. First, what kind of shape would Emily be in? That worried her. Seeing her banged up, hurt, struggling in any way would be hard. Second, Catherine needed to talk to her, needed to talk about this morning. Clark had apologized. Did that mean he'd been lying? While she hoped so, she also knew that wouldn't shine the best light on her.

She stood outside room 612 for a long moment, eyes on the 'E. Breckenridge' lettered in black marker on the small whiteboard next to the door. Another deep breath in, steeling herself. She knocked gently and pushed the door open.

Emily lay in the bed, eyes closed and underscored by dusky bruising. Dark hair down and disheveled, her left hand in a green cast, and Catherine was so relieved to see her looking only slightly injured that a small cry of relief escaped from her lips before she could stop it.

Emily's eyes opened and she turned them on Catherine. A very clear succession of emotions ran across her face: happiness, then hurt, then anger. Catherine saw them so plainly, they almost frightened her, almost kept her from approaching, but she pushed forward as she stepped toward the bed.

"Thank God you're okay." Catherine moved to the bed, stood there.

Emily studied her, her brown eyes burrowing into Catherine's, making her squirm. Catherine had to make a conscious effort not to look away, but she couldn't last long. She lay her fingers on Emily's bare forearm where it rested on the sheets. With her eyes, she indicated the cast on her other arm. "Broken, huh?"

Emily lifted it, looked at it as if for the first time, then dropped it back down. "Yep. Here's a tip: you shouldn't brace yourself with your wrist when you're about to skid into a tree trunk."

Catherine reached for Emily's face, but Emily's good arm came up to block it. Gently, but it was still a rebuff. "Your face..."

"Bloody nose. Airbag. No big deal." Emily brought her own fingers to her nose. "Black and blue for a while."

Catherine swallowed. "Emily..."

"You believed him."

Catherine chewed on her bottom lip and was silent for a moment before responding. "I know. It was knee-jerk, just a reflex, but..."

Emily's eyes filled with tears, which obviously irritated her because she shook her head and turned toward the window, as if she no longer wanted to look at Catherine.

"I shouldn't have. I know. I just…he was so smarmy and cocky, and the way he sat and the things he said…" Catherine looked away. "I panicked."

"After the night we had?" Emily's voice was low, but sharp, and she was clearly angry now. Catherine flinched at her words. "Seriously?"

"It was an amazing night," Catherine said softly. "It was. I… being with you is so new and different than anything I've ever experienced before. I—"

"How am I supposed to know that?" Emily's eyes flashed. "From all the times you've told me? From all the times you've mentioned how you feel? From how open you are when you talk to me? Oh, wait…"

Catherine bit down hard on her lips. "I know," she said softly. "I don't often say what I'm thinking."

"No, Catherine, you don't *ever* say what you're thinking. You let me flounder. You let me wonder. You let me figure it out. You're like a goddamn endless puzzle. And I have worked so hard these past two months—*so hard*—to understand you, to learn you, to not try to change you because I happen to like you just the way you are and I think you're worth the effort. And yet, the first time you hear something unflattering about me, do you stop to ask me? Do you give me a chance to respond? Are you at all interested in what I might have to say about it? No. What do you do? You run. You make a judgment and you run. Because apparently, I'm not worth the effort to you."

"Emily…"

"No, it's okay. I get it now. I understand. It's crystal clear. No worries. You can go."

Catherine didn't know what to do, what to say. She'd never seen Emily angry—and this was more than anger. It was hurt. It was pained anger and Catherine had put it there. She searched for words, was almost glad she couldn't find them, as she wasn't sure she could push them past the lump in her throat. Emily was right. Her anger was warranted and everything she'd said had been correct...except the part about Emily not being worth it.

"Go." Emily turned her gaze back toward the window, effectively dismissing Catherine.

"Emily, please. I just want to say—"

Emily's head snapped back in her direction, which must have caused her some pain judging from the wince that crossed her face. "Oh, *now* you want to talk?" Her dark eyes, normally so soft and full of joy and love, flashed with anger and hurt, the bruising under them only serving to accentuate it, her brows meeting above her nose. "Well, guess what. I don't feel like it. We should have just listened to everybody who told us what a bad idea this was. You know? I had to listen to it from my mother for over an hour when she got here. With a possible concussion, so you can probably imagine the raging headache I have right now." She waved her hand toward the door, and when she saw the unshed tears glimmering in her eyes, Catherine knew that Emily wasn't angry at her. She was devastated by her. Which was so much worse.

"Emily." Catherine tried unsuccessfully to swallow down the anguish she felt.

"Don't you see it, Catherine?" Emily's voice was barely a whisper. "They were right. They were all right. You and me? We're a terrible idea." She turned away. "Just go. Please." Her voice cracked on the last word.

Catherine's breath hitched and she couldn't stop the one tear that spilled out of her eye and rolled down her cheek.

Emily didn't look at her again.

At the door, Catherine turned back and almost ran into the woman who, up to this point, she'd only seen in photographs and on the news. Cheryl Breckenridge was even more regal, commanded even more attention and respect in person. Catherine was no shrinking violet, but the glare she received from Emily's mother was enough to make her skin flush hotly and sever eye contact.

"What are you doing here?" she asked coldly.

"I'm sorry. I—" Catherine flinched as she was interrupted.

"I don't want to hear your apologies or your sorry excuses. Haven't you caused enough trouble?"

It was a line straight out of a nighttime soap opera, and yet it still had the intended effect. Catherine's eyes welled up and her throat clogged, preventing her from speaking.

"Mom." Emily's voice was quiet but firm. "Leave her alone. She's leaving."

"I should hope so." Cheryl looked her up and down, and Catherine could tell by her expression that she'd been found to be lacking.

Catherine turned to look over her shoulder and when she met Emily's gaze, she saw what she could only believe was a mirror image of her own emotions: anger, yes. Hurt, definitely. Sadness, of course. But there was something else there as well, something Catherine hadn't seen because she hadn't allowed herself to see it.

Love.

She was sure of it. She was sure of it because she knew what it felt like. What it looked like. And she knew.

"Are you waiting for me to hold the door?" Cheryl's voice snapped her back to the room, back to reality.

"No," Catherine said softly. She looked at Emily once more, but she'd turned away again. "I'm sorry, Emily. I hope you know that."

Emily didn't look at her. Catherine avoided the searing eyes of Cheryl Breckenridge, swallowed down the lump in her throat, and turned to go, pretty sure she could feel her own heart cracking in her chest.

⋙⊷⋘

Emily had to give her mother some credit; she waited a good three minutes after Catherine's departure before she started in on her.

"That girl," she said while shaking her head in disapproval. "I told you to stay away from her."

"I know," Emily said quietly.

"You don't think we've had enough of this type of thing from your brother?"

Emily turned to face her mother, saw the flash of anger in her eyes, but rather than make her feel ashamed, it only served to stoke Emily's own anger. "It's hardly the same thing. I didn't sexually harass Catherine, you know."

"Well, you certainly did something." Cheryl huffed out a breath and sat in the chair next to Emily.

Yes, I did, Emily thought. *I fell in love.*

She should have been surprised. It was the first time she'd admitted it to herself. It had been in the back of her brain since the winter carnival, but she'd refused to acknowledge it, knowing it would make everything that much more complicated. But now, lying in her hospital bed, head pounding like a freight train was rushing through it, she couldn't get Catherine's face out of her head.

"That girl," Cheryl muttered again, and Emily held up her good hand.

"Mom. Stop."

Her tone must have caught Cheryl's attention because she looked at her daughter, her expression a mix of surprise and confusion, and she waited.

"It wasn't all Catherine, you know. Clark was the instigator here. You should be at least as angry at him, if not more so."

That seemed to take some of the wind out of her mother's sails. She took a deep breath and fingered the hem of the thin sheet that covered Emily. "I will deal with your brother. I've had enough of his antics."

Silence blanketed the room for several long moments.

"Mom, I need…" Emily swallowed, took a moment to collect her thoughts, find the right words. "I need to talk to you about something. And I need you to listen."

Cheryl opened her mouth to speak, but something on Emily's face must have made her think twice. The shadow of dread in her eyes told Emily she probably had an inkling, but it didn't matter. Emily needed to talk this out.

Ready to spill her guts, she stopped, gave her mother a small, sad smile, and said simply, "I love you."

Cheryl's entire demeanor visibly softened. "I love you, too." She took a deep breath and settled into her chair. "Now, talk to me."

And Emily did.

Catherine was not a crier. Oh, sure, she'd shed a tear here and there. A sad movie or something touching might mist her up, but she rarely openly cried. It was interesting to her then that, since she'd met Emily only a couple months ago, she'd teared up on a somewhat regular basis. And after today, she'd sobbed like a baby during her entire drive home. At one point, the man in the car next to her at a red light had rolled down his window and handed her a tissue, asking if she was all right.

By the time she opened her front door and got inside, her head was pounding like she'd been severely over-served the night before and Geronimo's happy barks over seeing her felt like stabs from an icepick hacking into her brain. She let him out the back door and went off to see if she had anything stronger than Motrin. Back in the kitchen, she poured herself a glass of water, downed three Excedrin Migraine tablets and wondered how the hell she was supposed to get through the rest of her day.

When she heard the car horn and the screech of tires outside, it didn't really register immediately. She stood with her elbows on the counter, her head cradled in her hands for several beats before something—like some awareness knocking on her aching skull—made her snap her head up and look toward the back door.

"Oh, no," she whispered. "No, no, no, no..." She ran to the front door and yanked it open just as Scott Turner was sprinting up her walk. The look on his face confirmed her worst fears and she blew past him in her slippers, fell to her knees in the road where she slid to a stop next to Geronimo's little white body lying on his side in the street. He whimpered and his breathing was labored, but didn't move, the one eye Catherine could see wide with fear.

"Okay, buddy," she whispered. "It's okay." She very gently pet him as a woman came up behind her, clearly distraught.

"I'm so sorry," she said, wringing her hands. "I didn't see him. He just darted out in front of me and I didn't have time to stop."

Catherine shook her head, the tears back again. "It's not your fault, she said. It's mine. It's my fault. It's all my fault. Everything is my fault."

Scott knelt next to her. "What can I do?" he asked.

Catherine turned anguished eyes to him. "Can you drive us to Junebug? There's a volunteer vet there today."

"You got it." He was up and off running to his truck.

"Hang in there, Mo. Mommy's here. Okay?" She stroked his fur and felt him calming a bit, his breathing—alarmingly ragged a moment ago—evening out some. There was no visible blood, but she wondered about the possibility of broken bones. She was hesitant to move him, but he tried more than once to get up, so her concern about any kind of spinal injury was lessened.

Scott's truck skidded to a halt and he got out and helped Catherine lift the dog, who whimpered slightly. Catherine kept up a steady stream of words, reassuring him, telling him he was loved.

The ride was a blur, though it seemed to take forever to get to the shelter. She did her best to act as a human shock absorber, trying to protect Mo from any excess bumps that might cause him more pain. Once they finally arrived at Junebug, she directed Scott to drive around back; she didn't want to parade an injured animal through the main lobby.

Around the back of the building, Ashley was walking a Lab mix back toward the door. Her eyes widened when she saw Catherine get out of the truck, cradling her dog.

"Oh, my God, what happened?"

"He got hit," Catherine said, and her voice cracked and she started to wonder how the hell she was going to make it through this day without simply crumbling to the ground in a pile of emotion. "I can't take anymore," she whispered to herself. She was pretty sure Ashley heard her, as the woman sprang into action.

"Okay, come on," she said. "And watch your step. It's slippery." Her eyes indicated Catherine's feet and only then did she realize she was still wearing her slippers.

Catherine held Mo gently, high against her body, close to her chest so he could hear her. "It's okay, baby. It's okay. I've got you. We're gonna get you all fixed up."

Ashley held the door open for them, handed the lead to a bewildered Scott, and ran down the hall. In minutes, she was back with Jessica in tow, as well as the on-call vet for the day, a thirty-something plump woman named Dr. Stein that Catherine liked very much. One of the vet techs came up behind them as well.

"What happened?" Jessica asked.

"He was hit by a car in front of Catherine's house," Scott informed them, as Catherine's voice seemed to have left her.

One look at Catherine's face must have told Jessica all she needed to know. She said gently, "Okay. Let's let Dr. Stein have him, okay, Cat?" She wrapped her arm around Catherine's shoulders as the vet took Mo from Catherine's arms.

"I've got him," Dr. Stein said with a soft smile. "Don't worry. We'll take good care of him."

She and the vet tech hurried away with Mo, even as Catherine was saying quietly, "I'm right here, buddy. I'm right here. Oh, God, this is my fault. It's all my fault. All of it."

Jessica's office was much larger than anybody else's and had its own private bathroom. As the story went, when her grandmother had first opened the shelter, she didn't have enough volunteers to run everything and she often ended up falling asleep at her desk or on the couch in her office, spending the night there. After this happened several times, Jessica's grandfather decided that, if he couldn't get his wife to leave the animals overnight, he at least wanted her to be as comfortable as she could while she was here. So he built her a bathroom, complete with a large vanity and a big tub with a shower. Each board member had a key and was welcome to use it any time.

Catherine never had.

"Sit." Jessica led Catherine to the sofa, helped her take a seat. She'd sent Scott home, promising to deliver Catherine there when she was ready. Moving around her desk to one of the cabinets in the credenza, she pulled out a bottle and a glass. Pouring two fingers of whatever amber liquid it was—Catherine couldn't see the label—into the glass, she handed it to Catherine. "Drink."

Catherine did as she was told, felt the alcohol burn as it coursed down her throat, made a face. Jessica refilled the glass and Catherine downed another shot with the same effect.

Setting the bottle and glass on her desk, Jessica pulled a chair up so she sat facing Catherine, their knees touching. "Talk."

Catherine finally looked at her. "You are very wordy today." She was going for light, for joking, but her eyes filled with tears, which upset her. Again. She shook her head and let them fall.

Jessica closed warm hands over Catherine's. "Cat. Honey. Talk to me. Tell me what's going on?"

"My dog got hit by a car."

Jessica? cocked her head and made a face that told Catherine she knew there was more. "And what else?" When Catherine said nothing, Jessica reached out her hand, wiped away a tear with her thumb. "You kept saying everything is your fault. What does that mean?"

Catherine rubbed at her eye, looked over Jessica's shoulder, swallowed hard, but couldn't stop the tears, which just kept coming as if on a faucet of some kind in her head.

"Catherine," Jessica said softly. "Talk to me. Is it Emily?"

The faucet turned on higher as Catherine nodded, but couldn't push any words past the lump that now nearly closed up her throat.

"Tell me what happened." Jessica's voice was soft and gentle, the tender sound of somebody who cared about Catherine, and that almost made it worse. She'd gone against Jessica's wishes, had completely disregarded them, and now Jessica wanted to help her feel better. A small cry of anguish escaped her chest as a sob broke through. Jessica laid a hand against her cheek. "Tell me."

It all came spilling out then. Every last detail. The cabin. The hike. The word searches. The expensive boots. The sex. (*The sex! God!*). Clark and the bet. The hospital. Cheryl Breckenridge. Geronimo. Catherine told her every single thing that had happened to lead her to where she sat now. "I was such a coward," she whispered. "She's right. I just ran. She deserved better than that, but...I panicked."

"Why?" Jessica asked her. "What made you panic?"

"I'm not exactly sure," Catherine said. "I've been trying to figure it out since my visit to the hospital. There was so much working against us anyway. We knew it was a bad idea. You told us. Her mother told us. Our friends told us. God, I'm such an idiot. Plus…" She let her voice trail off, but Jessica simply waited her out. "I thought she was too good to be true."

Jessica furrowed her brow. "How so?"

Catherine shook her head as she looked off into the middle distance. "She's beautiful and smart and really nice. And also incredibly wealthy."

"And?"

"And I'm out of her league. So the bet…didn't seem too far-fetched to me. In that moment, with Clark being…*Clark*, showing up at the right moment, in the right place, after everything that had happened the night before, it just didn't seem too far-fetched either."

Jessica sighed. "Oh, Cat." She shook her head. "You're such an idiot."

"I know. I just said that."

"To make matters worse, you have trouble seeing past her money."

"God, that makes me sound like such an asshole," Catherine said, knowing Jessica was right.

"Well, you come by it honestly, so there's that. You grew up fairly poor. You've worked two, sometimes three, jobs your entire life. It makes sense that you'd be leery of somebody who never had to deal with that."

"Right?"

"However," Jessica said, holding up a finger. "Let me ask you this: what has Emily done to make you think her money defines her?"

Catherine swallowed. She didn't like this question.

"Here, let me help." Jessica sat back in her chair and ticked off her fingers as she went. "Let's see. She not only donates a lot of money to homeless animals, but she also volunteers her time. So there's that."

Catherine nodded.

"She likes to send flowers."

Catherine scoffed. "She *loves* to send flowers."

"Horrible woman," Jessica said, shaking her head. "Horrible." Catherine glared at her, but Jessica had known her for too long for it to have any effect. She simply continued with her list. "She whisks you away to her cabin in the woods for what I think sounds like a lovely weekend. And also hot and steamy."

Catherine made no comment, but felt her cheeks flush.

"She not only buys you Christmas gifts, but one of them— the word search books—is proof that she listens to you when you talk. That's *huge* in my world."

"It is." Catherine had to agree.

"And don't get me started on the other gift." Jessica shook her head. "Boots? Really? The woman knows you, Cat. She pays attention."

"She does."

"And finally, when you run away in a huff without allowing her to explain, what does she do? Does she let you go? Does she shrug and think what a jerk you are?" Jessica made a face. "Well, she might have, but she didn't sit by, did she?"

"No," Catherine said quietly.

"No. She smashed up her brother's fancy car trying to catch you so she *could* explain. It was obviously important to her that you hear her side."

They sat in silence for a long moment, Jessica evidently letting her words sink into Catherine's brain while Catherine chewed on her bottom lip.

"Does that sound like a woman who would use you to win a bet?"

Catherine shook her head and they sat quietly again.

Finally, Jessica broke the silence. "This is a mess."

"I know. I'm sorry."

"You should be." Anger flashed in Jessica's eyes. "Why are you so stubborn?" Her tone broadcast her frustration. "Damn it, Cat."

"I'm sorry," she said again, for lack of anything else to say.

They sat quietly for long moments. Catherine's tears finally dried. She took a tissue from the box on Jessica's desk, wiped her nose, did her best to clean up her smeared eye makeup.

Finally, Jessica cleared her throat. She pushed the fingers of both hands through her hair and spoke. "Well, I can see two things very clearly. One: Emily cares about you. That would be obvious to a blind person. And two: you care about her. That one's a little harder to see, but it's there. You can fight it all you want, deny it all you want, but you and I have been friends for a long time and I know you."

Catherine nodded. That was something she couldn't deny.

"And I am so mad at you right now because you are so obviously in love with this woman and that makes it a big fucking mess for me." Her voice got louder as she spoke. Conversely, Catherine's got quieter.

"I know. I'm sorry." Catherine sniffled, but held herself together. "For what it's worth, I'm pretty sure it's over. I did a good job of killing anything we might have had by not believing in her, by not trusting her, so there's that. You're welcome." And then the tears were back. "Damn it," she muttered, grabbing another tissue.

Jessica dropped her head back and stared at the ceiling. Catherine looked down at her feet.

They sat.

CHAPTER TWENTY

By WEDNESDAY MORNING, EMILY was feeling a little stir-crazy. They'd kept her in the hospital overnight on Sunday, just to make sure she didn't have a concussion or anything more serious than a broken wrist, but sent her home the next day. Speaking of her wrist, it was aching and a glance at the clock told her it was time for another pain pill if she wanted it. She scooped up the bottle, held it in her hand for a moment, then put it back down. While they certainly alleviated the pain, the pills also made her feel a bit loopy—not a feeling she enjoyed.

"I'll tough it out. Right, Dave?"

The dog was right at her feet, where he'd been for the past forty-eight hours. It was as if he knew something bad had happened to her and wanted to protect her from this point on. She loved him for that.

"I should probably eat something," she said to him, wandering into the kitchen. "What do you think? Grilled cheese and tomato?" When Dave sat down and blinked at her, she nodded. "You got it."

She had sliced a tomato and was buttering the bread—more difficult than she'd expected with a cast on her wrist—when there was a knock on her door. Odd, as visitors had to be buzzed in the downstairs lobby doors before they could make their way to the individual apartments. Must be a neighbor.

Dave close on her heels, she pulled the door open without checking the peephole and then stood still in surprise.

"Hi." Catherine stood in the doorway, Geronimo in her arms. His back leg was covered in a green cast and he wore a soft fabric cone around his neck.

"Oh, my God, what happened?" Emily let any other feelings go for the moment and reached out for Geronimo, whose entire body vibrated with excitement to see her. Catherine smiled and let go of him, let him shift into Emily's hands so he could bathe her face in kisses like he hadn't seen her in years. She kept her hands out, ready to catch the extra weight if Emily's bad hand couldn't handle it. Dave put his paws up on Emily's hip, wanting very much to sniff this new creature in his house. Emily squatted.

"Dave, this is Mo. Mo, meet Dave." They sniffed gently but exuberantly. Emily glanced up. "All right if I set him down?"

Catherine nodded and they watched as the dogs—one twice the size of the other—got to know one another.

"Be gentle, Dave," Emily said quietly. "Gentle." Dave seemed to listen and watched carefully as Mo maneuvered himself in a three-legged hop around the living room, sniffing furniture and the occasional dog toy he came across. Dave followed him as if acting as guardian angel.

The two women stood watching for as long as they could without actually conversing at all. Finally, Emily turned to look at Catherine. God, it was good to see her. And she looked beautiful, as usual. Her jeans were tucked into brown leather boots, and a green turtleneck sweater was visible beneath the collar of her coat. Her hair was down and glistened with the remnants of the falling snow outside. Her skin looked as porcelain-smooth as it always did, but there were dark circles under her gorgeous blue eyes, and Emily had to make a conscious effort not to be concerned whether she was getting enough sleep or coming down with something.

"What happened to Mo?" she asked quietly.

Catherine cleared her throat. "I forgot to fix the latch on my gate. He got out and was hit by a car in front of my house on Sunday."

Emily's heart began to pound. "Oh, my God." Catherine seemed very careful about not looking at her. "But he's okay?"

"Broken leg. Some bumps and bruises."

"We have matching casts."

A ghost of a smile. "I know."

They watched as Mo apparently grew tired of exploring already and settled in front of the fireplace, curling up on the rug. Dave sat next to him and looked to Emily, who smiled at him. "I was making some lunch," Emily said quietly after a beat. "You hungry?"

Catherine nodded, still not looking at her, expression a bit uncertain, but she bent to remove her boots. Emily went into the open kitchen without waiting, pulled out two more slices of bread.

"Can I help?" Catherine asked.

Emily pointed her knife at one of the stools on the other side of the counter. "You can sit." Catherine obeyed orders, keeping an eye on the dogs, who seemed perfectly content to doze by the fire. Taking a deep breath, Emily added, "And you can tell me why you're here."

Her blue-eyed gaze darted around the loft and Emily had to admit to herself that seeing Catherine so uncertain and out-of-sorts was a hard thing to watch. Her first instinct was to do what she could to make Catherine feel better—and that ticked her off. Biting the inside of her cheek, she turned her attention to the food in front of her and left Catherine to fend for herself.

It didn't make Emily feel good.

"I wanted...I needed to talk to you," Catherine said, and the tremor in her voice again had Emily wanting to embrace her, keep her safe. That also made her mad and she embraced that anger instead.

"So talk."

There was a long beat of silence while Catherine seemed to struggle with words. With one hand, she pushed her hair off her face and gave a sarcastic chuckle. "You're not going to make this easy for me, are you?"

"Nope." Emily put a frying pan on the stove, banging it down a bit louder than necessary. "Oh, I'm using this." She held up a brick of cheddar cheese from which she'd sliced pieces for the sandwiches. "Is it too expensive for you? Because I have regular cheap American in the fridge. I can just use that for yours if it makes you feel better." She raised her eyebrows in question, feeling awful but unable to stop herself. The look of pain that zipped across Catherine's face, that seemed to bruise her eyes, made it worse.

Catherine looked down at her hands and said softly. "Okay. I deserved that."

Emily went back to making lunch, sure she'd made her point, but not feeling any better about it.

"Look, Emily." Catherine stared at the countertop and spoke quietly. "I'm not proud of my...fear, my lack of trust. It was unfair to you and...I was a jerk. Unintentionally, but a jerk just the same. I jumped to conclusions and believed Clark rather than you, which seems crazy to me now. I never even gave you a chance to tell me the truth. I was stupid. And shortsighted..." Her voice trailed off and when Emily looked up from her pan, Catherine's eyes had filled with tears and she looked away, which squeezed Emily's heart, releasing all the anger in a matter of mere seconds even as the first drop spilled over and down Catherine's smooth cheek.

"Catherine." Emily said her name quietly. When Catherine looked at her, she set down her spatula and her voice cracked as she asked pleadingly, "Please tell me you know there was never any bet. Please."

Catherine nodded. "I do. Obviously. I don't know why I ever believed—"

"Because my brother is a sexist asshole." Emily thumped herself in the chest as her own tears threatened. "I am not."

Catherine nodded again. "I know."

"Do you?"

"Yes."

Their gazes held and long moments went by.

Finally, Emily gave a nod. "Okay. Good." She let Catherine's gaze go and turned to her task, flipping a sandwich expertly.

"Emily?" Catherine's voice was so soft, so tender, Emily felt it very low in her body. Too low.

"Yeah?"

"Look at me?"

Emily did as she was asked.

Catherine waited a beat, maybe making sure she had Emily's full attention. When she seemed satisfied, she said in an intense whisper, "I am *so* sorry." The expression on her face was pained and loving and beautiful all at once, and Emily suddenly couldn't breathe. In that moment, she realized those were the words she'd been waiting for, the ones she needed.

"I forgive you," she said softly. "And I'm sorry, too. For Clark. For what he did and said. That had to be…horrifying."

A sob pushed its way from between Catherine's lips, and she covered her mouth with one hand as she obviously tried to stem the tide of emotion about to flow out of her. She was unsuccessful and Emily had no choice but to round the counter and wrap her in a tight embrace.

"Shh," she said against Catherine's hair. "It's okay. Shh." Holding her tightly and doing a bit of subtle rocking, she let Catherine cry, Emily's own tears spilling silently down her cheeks. She soothed Catherine with her voice, continued to press gentle kisses against her hair, against her temple, until the sobs began to subside into hiccups and eventually stopped all together.

"Um, Emily?" Catherine said softly, finally.

"Hmm?"

"Your sandwich is burning."

Emily's head snapped around and her eyes landed on the smoking frying pan on the stove. "Shit." She ran around the counter and pulled the pan from the burner. With the spatula, she pulled the black square that was once a grilled cheese sandwich from the pan and slid it onto a plate. Pushing it toward Catherine, she said, "Yeah, that one was yours."

A laugh burst from Catherine's throat and Emily had never heard anything more beautiful. She just looked at her and when Catherine met her gaze and her laughter died down, Emily smiled widely and said simply, "Hi, you."

"Hi back," Catherine said.

They were quiet then and Emily was hyper-focused on the sandwiches. Catherine looked like she wondered if she should say anything more. Finally, she did.

"So...your mom. I should apologize to her." Catherine wet her lips and looked away, her expression anxious. Emily read it easily; her mother had that effect on people. While Emily knew Catherine wasn't easily intimidated, she'd bet her favorite leather jacket that Cheryl Breckenridge intimidated the hell out of her.

Emily set her hand on the counter and stared at the new sandwich in the frying pan, felt Catherine's eyes on her. "Yeah, maybe you should wait on that."

Catherine scoffed. "She must hate me."

"Well, she's not happy with either of us. But I explained Clark's role in all of this, so she doesn't want to kill you anymore."

"Can't say that I blame her for when she did want to kill me. She and Jessica should call each other."

Emily nodded and they were quiet. She made a second sandwich, plated both, then came around and took the stool next to Catherine. They ate in silence.

When they had both finished, Emily wiped her face, set her napkin on her empty plate, and turned to Catherine. Catherine met her gaze and they stayed like that for a beat.

"What?" Catherine finally asked.

"I have a question for you."

"Okay." There was more silence. Catherine narrowed her eyes at Emily. "Am I supposed to be trying to get the question by reading your mind? Because I should probably tell you I'm not good at that. At all."

Emily smiled. "No. I'm just...working up my courage."

Catherine laid her hand on Emily's thigh and Emily instantly felt better, more relaxed. Safe. "Just ask me."

Emily looked up, looked right into Catherine's stunning blue eyes, held her gaze. This was it. This was for the final rose. She wet her lips and asked softly, "How do you feel about me?"

Catherine furrowed her brow, obviously confused. "What do you mean?"

"It's a pretty simple question. How do you feel about me?"

Catherine swallowed audibly and Emily watched a succession of worries and concerns track across her face.

She laid her hand on Catherine's forearm, waited until she made eye contact, then smiled as tenderly as she could. "Wait. Let me clarify. If there were none of our current obstacles…if Jessica didn't care who you were with and my family's business was totally unaffected by who I'm with…if that was the case, if our jobs, friends, and families had no bearing on any of it, tell me honestly. How do you feel about me?"

"I love you." The words popped out so quickly and easily, Catherine just blinked.

A laugh burst from Emily's mouth. "Oh, my God, you should see your face right now. You look so shocked. It's kind of hilariously adorable." Then she softened her tone as she said, "That's exactly what I'd hoped you'd say. You know why?"

"Why?" Catherine whispered.

"Because I love you, too."

There. It was out. She'd said it to the person who mattered most.

Catherine looked down at Emily's hand, still resting on her forearm and Emily wondered what she was thinking, what was going through her mind at that moment. Finally, she seemed to shake herself and cleared her throat loudly, but her voice stayed quiet. "Not to spoil the mood, but…our situations haven't changed. We're in exactly the same boat, whether we love each other or not. Our jobs *do* have a bearing on things."

"That may not be true."

Catherine's head snapped up, and Emily could see her fighting not to let any excitement or anticipation in. "What does that mean?"

"It means that two guys in the marketing department at my family's company are retiring this summer."

"And? What does *that* mean?"

"I have already asked my mother about returning to marketing and helping to modernize some of our methods. Brainstorming with you really made me miss my marketing days, the creativity of it. Plus, I'd be the head of the department."

Catherine was trying to keep her excitement smothered; Emily could read it on her face. "You've already talked to your mother?"

"Right after you left my hospital room."

Catherine's eyebrows shot up.

"I was waiting to see what your next move would be."

"And I came here. And I told you I love you."

"And you came here. And told me you love me. Thank God."

"But, Em." Catherine looked down at her hands, seemed to struggle to find the right words. "You love the work you're doing for the Foundation. You can't just…change your whole life."

"Really? Which part of my life is more important to change?"

Catherine narrowed her eyes, confused. "I don't understand."

"I'm saying, I won't stop seeing you to maintain my job— which, yes, I do love. But I *will* switch jobs to keep seeing you. That is one aspect of my life I'm willing to change, because I happen to think you're worth it. That *we're* worth it."

"That's…huge."

"It's huge," Emily agreed. She gestured between them. "This. This is huge. For me, this is IT huge." Emily slid her hand from Catherine's forearm down to her hand, entwined their fingers. Then she picked it up, brought it to her mouth, and kissed a knuckle. "Does Jessica have a problem if you're sleeping with a volunteer?"

Catherine shook her head with a grin. "You've met Lisa and Ashley. She does not."

"Good. Because I'd like to keep doing that. I really like volunteering. I like that more than the rest of it. Coincidentally, I also really like sleeping with you."

Catherine's grin grew wider as she tightened her grip on Emily's hand. "Well, you've only done that once. Hopefully, after many, many, *many* more times, you won't like it. You'll *love* it."

"I have no doubt," Emily said, and then she leaned in and her mouth was on Catherine's. She kept the kiss gentle and tender. Loving. Reverent. God, the things she felt for this woman. They could scare her if she let them.

When they parted, Catherine ran a finger along Emily's jawline. "Listen, before you show me your bedroom, I have a favor to ask."

"Presumptuous," Emily said with a wink. "But okay. Shoot."

Catherine gazed around the loft until her eyes landed on the music dock for Emily's phone. Sliding her own phone out of her pocket, Catherine snapped it on, pushed a few buttons, and a ballad by John Legend began. Meeting Emily's eyes, Catherine walked back to the kitchen and held out her hand to Emily.

"Dance with me?"

Stunned, thrilled, and touched all at once, Emily swallowed the sudden emotion in her throat and put her hand in Catherine's. "Any time. Anywhere."

And suddenly, it was as if the past four days had never happened. Catherine pulled Emily in close with a hand around her waist, her other hand holding Emily's. Emily was careful not to knock Catherine senseless with her cast as she draped her arm over Catherine's shoulder and they began to sway gently. Emily looked into her eyes for a beat before turning her face so she could rest her head on Catherine's shoulder. They moved slowly, fitting together on the dance floor just as perfectly as they did in the bedroom.

"See?" Emily whispered. "It's not so bad."

"It's not."

"It's not too intimate."

"Oh, I beg to differ." Catherine pulled her closer, so their stomachs touched, their breasts. Emily lifted her head so they were nose to nose.

"Yeah, I guess it is kind of intimate," she whispered, and then pressed her lips to Catherine's. They kissed slowly and tenderly for a while, but Emily couldn't quite relax, her mind whirring her into distraction. She wanted nothing more than to settle herself against Catherine's form, to continue swaying with her, maybe sway her right into the bedroom, but she couldn't. She needed to clear something up, so before she could change her mind or lose the moment, she pulled back and furrowed her brow at Catherine. "We're not magically all better you know." She said it gently, but still saw a zap of embarrassment flash across Catherine's beautiful face.

Catherine nodded and looked a bit chastened. "I know that."

"You have to talk to me, Catherine." Emily didn't step away from the warmth of Catherine's body—in fact, they kept right on swaying to the music—but she did poke her in the chest with a finger, wanting—*no, needing*—badly to make her point. "When you freak out. When something's bugging you. When you're concerned or worried. I need you to tell me. Not shut down. Not run away. You have to talk to me or this will never work. Sadly, I can't read your mind." Her voice softened as she added, "Okay?"

Catherine took a deep breath. "It's hard for me."

"I know it is. I'm not sure why, but I intend to dig in and find out." Emily smiled. "You can always talk to me."

"I know."

"Well, knowing and doing are two different things."

"I'll try."

Emily stopped swaying and looked Catherine in the eye before adopting the voice of a fictional life guru. "Do or do not. There is no try."

Catherine chuckled. "Okay, Yoda."

Back to her regular voice, Emily said, "I'm serious."

Catherine's expression sobered. "I know you are. I'll do my best. How's that?"

"That's all I ask." Emily studied her face for a beat before saying, "You really are a lot of work, you know that?" She punctuated the statement with a quick peck on the lips.

Catherine responded by yanking Emily back up against her. "Shut up and dance with me."

❧

Intense.

That's a good word. That word works really well.

Passionate.

Oh, that's another good one. That one might be better for this particular description…

And then the words stopped. Emily had been trying to think of the best word to encompass her current situation, but her head was suddenly blank, now completely devoid of any and all words except for one.

"Catherine…" she whispered as a head bobbed between her open legs, a hand on each thigh gently spreading them farther. The mouth and tongue on her did unspeakably pleasurable things, making her muscles tighten and her breath hitch, as she reached down and dug her fingers into the soft, chestnut brown hair fanned out over her thighs. She tried to recall the last woman who'd filled her with such glory that Emily had called out her name, but she couldn't. She couldn't because it had never happened. Until now.

"Catherine…" She said it again, louder this time, unable to stop herself, and she could feel how it spurred Catherine on. She picked up the pace, and her tongue pushed directly into Emily, inside her for a beat before sliding back out and around her hot, wet flesh. Then, without warning, Emily's lungs sucked in a huge breath—as if she had no control over them—and what felt like every muscle in her body spasmed. Her back arched and her hips came up off the bed as the orgasm tore through her, ripping a moan from her throat, Catherine tightening her grip on Emily's waist in an attempt to stay with her, pressing her tongue to exactly the right spot—*oh, yes, right there!*—drawing it out as long as she could.

When Emily's body finally relaxed, her hips settled back on the mattress, her fingers still in Catherine's hair, but no longer clutching a handful of it, she became aware of Catherine's ragged breathing. It made her grin. She opened her eyes and looked at the gorgeous woman who owned her, body and soul.

"You worked hard," she said.

Catherine smiled at her so radiantly it stuck a lump right in Emily's throat. "I did. Totally worth it. Rest up because I'm going to do it again in a bit."

Emily's eyes widened. "What? Oh, no. No, no. Two is my limit."

"Psshh." Catherine waved a dismissive hand as she crawled up Emily's body. "I plan on shattering that record. I'm going for four."

Emily barked a laugh as she wrapped her arms around Catherine's naked body. "Yeah, I don't think so."

"You don't think I could?" Catherine snuggled up against Emily's side, tucked her head into a shoulder.

"Oh, I'm sure you could. I'm just not sure I'd survive it." Emily tilted Catherine's face up by her chin and kissed her tenderly. "I am not Supergirl," she whispered.

"You are to me."

"Sweet talker. You're just trying to get into my pants."

"Been there, done that."

They kissed again and then burrowed down into the bed together, watching the falling snow out the bedroom window. Dave and Mo were both sound asleep (not surprising, given it was after midnight) on the same dog bed, as if they, too, understood that these two lives were slowly merging into one. Emily marveled over the past weeks.

It hadn't been an easy transition. Not for anybody. Jessica had hated losing Emily as a contact at Junebug and made it clear to Catherine. Things were still a bit tense between them, but they'd been friends for a long time, and Catherine was doing everything she could to get herself back into Jessica's good graces.

"Hey," she whispered in Catherine's ear. "How's Mark doing?" She was referring to the new liaison for The Breckenridge Foundation, the man who'd taken her place.

"Good," Catherine muttered. "He's really nice and loves the animals."

"Think he'll win Jessica over?"

"Eventually."

That last word was barely mumbled, and Emily smiled as she pressed a kiss to Catherine's forehead.

Despite being physically exhausted thanks to the two-hour lovemaking session they'd just had, Emily wasn't ready to sleep. Her brain wouldn't let her. It swirled with ideas for the company, ways to bring the Breckenridge name further into the technological age. They were on social media, but not using it to its full potential, and Emily had spent much of the day brainstorming with her staff about ways to increase visibility. Much as she missed her job as liaison to the nonprofits to which her family donated money, she knew that marketing was where she belonged. And she was pretty sure her mother knew it, too. With Emily at the helm of the department, she'd brought in a couple younger employees and made sure to listen openly to those who'd been there longer than she had. It had only been a month now, but she could already see progress. And though she was reluctant to admit it, her mother was ecstatic over the changes.

Looking now at the object of her affection, Emily smiled. Catherine had fallen asleep. It wouldn't last, Emily knew, as Catherine hated to sleep naked. She claimed she "needed" to have clothes on and she waved Emily off if she tried to disagree. Of course, this was the third time she'd fallen asleep pajama-less and Emily planned to use that to her advantage, much preferring the smooth skin against her own over the fabric of her sleeping attire. Didn't matter how cute it was.

Emily pressed another gentle kiss to Catherine's forehead and tried to remember when she'd been so utterly content.

Sleep claimed her before she could come up with an answer.

EPILOGUE

SPRING WAS TRYING HARD to show up early to its own party. It was late February, less than a week to March, but the snow was virtually gone and the temperatures had been shockingly warm. Catherine did not complain. While she didn't mind winter (you couldn't be a resident of upstate New York and hate winter…that just made you silly for staying), she was always happy to wave good-bye to it and help usher in some sunshine and warmth.

Her morning had been chaotic and the din of barking dogs seemed louder today than usual for some reason. She'd had two meetings and a conference call already this morning, which had left her woefully behind on e-mail.

"Ready?"

Emily's voice startled Catherine. She looked up and her girlfriend stood in the doorway looking casually sexy in jeans, a green waffle-weave Henley, and a white down vest.

Her girlfriend. She loved that phrase, but had yet to get used to it.

"God, is it lunch time already?" Catherine glanced at the clock to see that yes, Emily was right on time for their date. She held up a finger to ask Emily to wait, finished typing up the e-mail she'd been working on, clicked Send, then stood. Emily snagged her jacket from the hook on the back of the door and crossed the room.

"You might not need this," she said as she placed a kiss on Catherine's lips. "It's really nice out."

Catherine grabbed it and tossed it over her arm, grabbing her purse and leading Emily out of her office. "Get me out of here before Jessica grabs me again."

They hurried out to the busy lobby where Anna stood talking to Regina. She glanced their way, then pointedly looked away and increased the volume of her voice. Catherine could only shake her head. If Anna wanted to act like a teenager, there wasn't much she could do about it but let her. She grabbed Emily's hand and they made it to the parking lot without incident.

Emily sighed and shook her head. "It's a good thing you can't actually be hurt when people give you dagger eyes. I'd be dead about ten times over by now."

"I know. I'm sorry. She's just…Anna."

"Nothing I can't handle, babe." They got in the car and, thankfully, Emily changed the subject. "What's going on with Jessica? Why is she keeping you so busy?" Emily asked, keying the ignition.

Catherine sighed, sliding on her sunglasses. "She's getting ready for the telethon, which is always stressful for her. But you know how Janet Dobson retired last year?" She referred to that anchor of the local TV news who'd hosted the Junebug Farms Telethon every year since before Jessica had begun running things. When Emily nodded, Catherine went on. "Well, the new anchor is young and green and doesn't know what she's doing." Catherine held up a hand. "This is according to Jessica, mind you. She's freaking out."

"Is the new anchor young and green?"

Catherine shrugged. "I have no idea. All I can tell you is that she's hot."

Emily gasped in mock-insult. "You've been looking at other girls?!"

"Please," Catherine laughed. "Turn on the news tonight. You'll be looking, too."

"Hey, Siri," Emily called out to her iPhone. "Remind me to watch the hot chick on the news tonight."

"Okay," said Siri. "I'll remind you."

Catherine shook her head with a grin.

The spring was especially busy at the shelter and Catherine didn't have a ton of time for lunch, so that little café around the corner had become a go-to place for the two of them. Even if she couldn't get away at all, Emily would stop and grab lunch, bring it to the shelter, and they'd eat together in Catherine's office. It occurred at least three times a week, and Catherine loved that it was a regular date for them.

"I saw your Twitter contest," Catherine said. "Looks like it's getting lots of play."

She was referring to Emily's newest attempt to bring her family's company into the twenty-first century. "We got a ton of hits this week." Emily's eyes lit up and she spent the next ten minutes regaling Catherine with examples of some of the responses they'd gotten. Catherine watched the animation on her face, the way she waved her hands around and her eyes got big when she described something that excited her.

God, I love this woman. It was the biggest thought in Catherine's world and it made her heart fill with warmth.

The changes to their lives had been hard, had seemed almost insurmountable at the time, but two months later, the wrinkles were finally starting to straighten out.

"So listen," Emily said a little while later as she took a bite of her turkey BLT.

Catherine set down her spoon and folded her hands on the table in front of her.

Emily narrowed her eyes. "What are you doing?"

"Well, I can tell by the look on your face, by the way your eyes are focused on mine, that you're about to tell me something important. I want to be sure I'm paying attention." She smothered a grin, but she was only half-kidding. Emily had a very clear "serious talk" face and Catherine had learned it well.

"You're making fun of me."

"Never."

Emily looked at her and grinned. "Fine. What I was going to say was that Easter is early this year and my mother wanted me to ask you if you thought your mom would like to come to our place for Easter dinner."

Catherine blinked at her for a moment before finally asking, "I'm sorry. What?"

Emily nodded as she chewed and watched Catherine's face. "You heard me."

"Your mother hates me."

"She's..." Emily gazed up at the ceiling as she apparently searched for the right words. "...coming around."

"Wow. That's...unexpected." It had been the hardest factor in the entire hot mess they'd created, and Catherine had a difficult time with the cool, reserved, unemotional side of herself that Cheryl Breckenridge showed whenever Catherine was around. Catherine did her best to not be intimidated (never worked), and she went to the Breckenridge house with Emily any time she was asked. But it was really hard for her to be so openly disliked by the mother of somebody who'd quickly become the most important person in her life. If this was a step toward a more pleasant coexistence, Catherine was all for it. "Me and my mom, huh?"

"Well…" Emily took another bite of her sandwich and gave Catherine a mischievous grin.

Catherine arched an eyebrow. "What does that mean?"

Holding a hand in front of her mouth, Emily said around her food, "It means you and your mom. And also your sister, nephew and grandparents."

Catherine's jaw dropped. Literally dropped; she actually felt it go, as did any and all words in her head.

"Yeah," Emily said with a laugh and her face looked so radiantly happy then that Catherine knew this was a huge step for them. "She wants to have Easter dinner with your whole family." After a beat went by and Catherine still hadn't spoken, she added, "I told you she'd get there. She just needed time. Plus, I think since she banished Clark to Florida, she's worried about losing me, too."

"Poor Clark," Catherine said, her tone broadcasting that she felt no sympathy whatsoever for him whatsoever. Apparently, there was an uncle who ran a branch of the family business out of Tallahassee and he was a real tough guy. He'd been tasked with whipping Clark into shape. Emily had received more than one whining text telling her how badly Uncle Keith was "busting his balls." As far as Catherine was concerned, if anybody needed his balls busted, it was Clark Breckenridge. "Couldn't happen to a nicer guy."

Emily smiled, but it was obvious her focus was not on her brother. "What do you think?" she asked. "About Easter."

Catherine scratched her temple. She looked around the café at the other patrons. She glanced down at her nearly untouched lunch, then back up at her girlfriend. "I think…I think…I think I wonder what you said to her to warrant such an invitation."

Emily swallowed, then took a sip of her soda, and Catherine could actually see her consider and disregard several responses before settling on one. "I told her I love you. That you're The One. Capital T, capital O."

"You told her that?" Catherine let that sink in while she looked deeply into the dark eyes staring back at her. "You told her I'm The One?" she asked quietly.

Emily gave a slow nod. "I did."

"Which one am I exactly?" Catherine asked, the happiness she felt suddenly making her pick on her girlfriend. "The tall one? The smart one? The sexy one?" She pointed her spoon at Emily. "I'd *better* be that one, that's for sure."

But Emily wasn't playing. Not this time. Her face remained serious even as Catherine teased. Looking at her, Catherine's voice trailed off until she grew quiet.

"*My* one," Emily said and smiled with such tenderness that Catherine could feel herself warm from the inside. Reaching across the table, Emily closed her hand over Catherine's. "The one for me. My one and only. The one that I want. All those ones. You're *my* one. I love you, Catherine. You know that, right?"

Catherine couldn't keep the smile from her face and she turned her hand over so she could grip Emily's. It wasn't news, that declaration of love, but she was pretty sure she'd never tire of hearing it. "Yeah, I know that."

"Do you?"

Catherine nodded. "I do. Promise."

"Good."

Catherine watched as Emily popped the last bite of her sandwich into her mouth, and she marveled at how skilled Emily had become at not pressuring her, not expecting her to say something back just because it was said to her. Emily chewed and looked around the café and didn't seem at all uneasy. That was all the reassurance Catherine needed.

"Hey, Em?"

Emily turned back to her. "Hmm?"

"You're my one, too."

THE END

By Georgia Beers

Novels
Finding Home
Mine
Fresh Tracks
Too Close to Touch
Thy Neighbor's Wife
Turning the Page
Starting From Scratch
96 Hours
Slices of Life
Snow Globe
Olive Oil and White Bread
Zero Visibility
A Little Bit of Spice
Rescued Heart
Run to You

Anthologies
Outsiders

www.georgiabeers.com